A RAINBOW LIKE YOU

ANDRÉA FEHSENFELD

free form Productions Inc.

A RAINBOW LIKE YOU

Cover and Jacket Design: Rafael Andres

Size of a Scandal Band Cards: Stu Mackay-Smith

Size of a Scandal Album Covers: Andréa Fehsenfeld

Back Cover Author Photo: Samantha Gill

ALSO BY ANDRÉA FEHSENFELD

COMPLETION

To all the musicians who have rocked my world.
And for my father.

CHAPTER ONE

A WISE MAN ONCE CAUTIONED ME: BE CAREFUL WHAT YOU wish for. When I woke up in the darkness of a tour bus and my only companions were a raging headache and the grind of a generator, I'd be lying if I said that warning didn't come to mind. After a yearlong hiatus my band was back on tour, and to say I'd been dreading this was a massive understatement. It didn't help that today was only day six of two hundred and ninety-three, a number I couldn't even think about without hyperventilating. Some guys live for the road. For me, touring was its own special kind of hell. A disease I couldn't shake.

That being said, the show last night in Phoenix felt good, and I should've been in a much better mood, but the reality was my heart ached more than my head. Last night, or early this morning, I drunk-dialed Suze, my ex-wife, ex-high school sweetheart, and we had it out, like we usually do. It always started out okay: I'd ask how she was doing, she'd say fine, then somewhere the conversation tipped. Before we knew it, she'd blame me for screwing up our marriage, which was only partially true. For years we both thought she was the reason why we were never able to have a kid, but the night I found out otherwise officially kiboshed our relationship.

I missed her though. Like a phantom limb, her absence was a

throbbing reminder that a vital piece of me had disappeared. Aspirin could never dull that pain, but I forced myself out of bed, stumbled into the bathroom and downed three for good measure. After a long shower, I toweled off and tried to focus on the positives. My eyes weren't bloodshot...yet. Recently trimmed, my hair was still long enough I could respect myself. Still carried a little jiggle in the gut from my year off but overall, on the outside, I was doing okay.

Today was a down day, however, and on the inside, they were the days I feared the most. With no performance to gear up for, all of a sudden there was so much time—the exact thing I didn't need. I'd been trying hard to ignore my current dilemma, becoming something of an expert in the fine art of avoidance. But after sifting through emails on my laptop, there was nothing else to put a dent in the morning other than finding my phone. I wandered out of the bedroom in search of it, feeling shitty all over again. After Suze hung up on me last night, I'd chucked it, frustrated with her, me, the whole world. I scooped the iPhone off the kitchen floor and was about to send her an apology text when an incoming call lit up the screen. It was Exile—my best friend, my drummer and, yes, that's his real name. I grabbed a can of Red Bull from the fridge, flopped onto one of the couches in the lounge and put him on speaker.

"Yo."

"My man," he replied. "How goes it?"

"Just woke up."

Ex stifled a yawn. "Jealous. Norm was moaning in his bunk all morning, hungover as shit. We dragged him to breakfast to sober up. You should've seen him, falling into his eggs." He chuckled. "Brother's gotta learn to pace himself."

"You guys go out last night?"

"Diego slept. I kept it reasonable. Norm...you know."

I did know. Norman Hunger was our bass player and the nerdiest of us all when we started out. Since then, he's embraced the rock-and-roll lifestyle in all the ways I've tried to avoid. I'm talking glitter boots, more tattoos than I can count, and an intimate knowledge of every STD in the book.

"Give him another week," I said. "It'll catch up to him."

"A week? You wanna put money on that?"

We both laughed: a losing bet if there ever was one. It was good to hear Ex laugh, though. In the weeks prepping for the tour, our communication had sputtered in fits and spurts. He'd warmed up recently, and it gave me hope that whatever had frayed between us had mended.

"What's going on up there?" he asked.

I cracked the Red Bull open and took a long swig. "Same shit, different day. What else is new?"

"Caleb treating you all right?"

Caleb Geary had been a major fan of ours since day one, tracking our rise with an obsession only a stalker could truly appreciate. He managed a fan website and a slew of social media handles devoted to us, although his regular job was sales manager of the Westin Kierland Resort, in Scottsdale. He finagled us a complimentary suite and parking, which was why my bus was here, at the far end of the hotel parking lot. My band mates, the boys, traveled on their own bus and opted to stay in Phoenix, closer to the action. I preferred the solitude and besides, fans like Caleb made us who we were today. I never forgot that.

"So far, so good. But it's tough to screw up a parking lot," I joked.

It felt like an eternity before Ex replied. "Always giving credit where credit is due, huh?"

Ex's Rwandan parents had built into him unflappable African pride and at 6'5, lean and built from years of capoeira, you'd be a fool to take him on in any physical sense. But I knew his inner core as soulful and sensitive. The bite in his voice was uncharacteristically off-key. The first sign.

"What did you think of last night?" I asked, switching gears. "The show went down pretty good, I thought."

"Yeah," he said, kind of flat. "For sure."

"That's it?"

"The crowd was digging it."

I took a long hit of the Red Bull. His comment was a weak offering and we both knew it.

"How's the writing going?" he asked.

"Good," I said and sat up. "Why?"

"We were just talking at breakfast and you know, after our Detroit run, we get that two-day break. Be cool to hit a studio and jam on a couple of the new tunes."

I stole a glance toward my office area, at the ream of blank paper that sat broodingly on the desk. Therein lay the problem. My song-writing ability had always been my Midas Touch but for the first time in my career, the songs weren't flowing. Any creative person will tell you there's nothing more soul deadening than staring at a blank page or screen, and I had squat so far. Not even a dribble of inspiration.

"We can do that," I said.

"Any hints?"

"On what?"

"The new songs. Are they badass? Ballads?"

This was starting to feel a little weird. "Why are you so interested?"

After a sticky silence he said, "Because I'm part of the band, brother."

He sounded bruised, which gave me pause. Of course he'd be keen to know. We had a deadline. But I also knew Ex's penchant for beating around the bush rivaled my legendary directness. Something else was going on.

"Have you been reading shit online again?" I asked.

Exile googled us way too much and took what every airheaded critic had to say to heart.

Sure enough, he came back with, "After the Portland show, some guy wrote we were phoning it in."

"Yeah, well, one guy. What does he know? Critics are frustrated musicians, happy to take down everyone else," I argued. "They have no skin in the game. Our dates are all sold out. *That's* what matters."

I tried to downplay it because I could hear it in his voice: this would eat him alive for days. Ex was the equivalent of eight elephants when it came to not forgetting.

"San Fran and Vegas said the same thing," he added, a little too quickly. "We haven't really mixed it up in a while."

"The set list?"

"That and you know..." He cleared his throat. "We're not really taking any risks."

"Risks?" The hair on my arms bristled to attention. "What does that even mean?"

"I'm just saying what I read," he said, all defensive.

"For Christ's sake." I drained the Red Bull, crumpled the can, and arced it high. A three pointer right into the kitchen sink. "Read it to me."

On the other end, sound distorted as he put down the phone. I gnawed on my thumb, waiting. When Ex came back on the line I sat up taller, a queer rush of trepidation in my belly.

"The headline," he started, "is 'Size of a Scandal: Does size equal stagnation?'"

"Dear god," I muttered. "Short-list him for the Pulitzer."

Ex continued in his rich baritone. "When Size of a Scandal first exploded onto the music scene and *My Fantasy Life* was on every station in America, I drank the Kool-Aid like everybody else. It's not every day the stars align and give birth to an addictively timeless talent. Make no mistake: front man Adrian 'Jazzer' Johnson *was* lightning in a bottle. Magnetic and mercurial, famously private and infamously driven, Johnson channeled Kurt Cobain by way of Jim Morrison. He was an incandescent troubadour whose immortal princeling looks..."

"Immortal?" I interrupted. "Is this a review or a eulogy?"

"...and devotion to his wife, Suzanne Ripley, set every woman's heart aflutter, while his staunch refusal to buy into any form of celebrity posturing endeared him to every guy. Johnson and SOS—a fan created moniker for the band—were exactly what we needed: an out-of-nowhere, uppercut of brilliance whose songs left us punch-drunk and delirious. But after five albums, has the band known for its catchy compositions and anthemic lyrics plateaued? After last year's cash-grab release of mostly garbage songs…"

"Garbage? It went platinum."

"…and the Molotov cocktail that was Johnson's personal affairs, it's safe to question if his mid-life crisis…"

"I'm thirty!"

"…is the beginning of the end. With no new material to support this tour and the band's inner circle notoriously tight-lipped on the next release, will subsequent shows go down like last night's performance? A greatest hits phone-in of the worst kind, Johnson's legendary showmanship was MIA, leaving bassist/hot mess Norman Hunger to rouse the crowd. It begs the burning question: is SOS's brand of magic officially dead? Time will tell. For devotees of the band, myself included, just showing up doesn't cut it. Not ten years in. And encoring with Jimi Hendrix tunes was at one point cool but now feels like a lame gimmick…"

"Dude, he's slagging *Hendrix*. You can't take this guy seriously."

"…Johnson, et al., need to come to the table with something fresh. Size of a Scandal is a band in desperate need of reinvention."

"*Desperate?*" I talk-shouted. "It's worked so far."

Another silence. Finally, Ex's voice quiet but very clear, "We kind of think he's right."

I digested that like a cup of rancid oil. "*We?*"

"Well, you know…"

"And right about what part?" I pressed.

"Uh, we were talking, and you know…" He took a deep, controlled breath. "This time around, we have some ideas in the song department."

Through the walls I felt the heat seeping in from outside, into the hollow of my bones. It was another eight-hundred-degree day, way too hot for this time of year. I tried, and failed, to sound level and calm. "So, what, you guys have a bunch of songs ready to go?"

"Hey man," he said, trying his best to soothe the situation. "It's not like none of your songs won't be good."

I stood up and started to pace. When it came to songs and our band, there was no 'we'. Exile could out-drum anyone on the planet, but he'd sooner crack the code for hieroglyphics than write a decent lyric; he just wasn't a wordsmith. Diego Guerrero, the sweetest thing on rhythm guitar and keyboards, was, at heart, a session man, content to be playing music for a living without the pressure to create it. This must have been coming from Norman. I had noticed him scribbling in a notebook and when I asked what he was writing, he snapped it shut and said poetry.

"How many does Norm have?" I asked, just to let him know I knew.

"Three or four. And they're decent." He let that hang, possibly waiting for my laughter. Maybe I should've laughed, because he started up again with vigor. "It's time to mix things up. Next phase, brother. Let's test them all out in the studio and see what's going down, all right?"

I stopped pacing. The silence on my end expanded to fill the bus.

"You still there?" Ex asked.

"Yeah, I'm here."

"Why don't we kick it old school today?" he suggested. "I could join you poolside. Rack up a nasty booze bill."

I really wanted to see him. We needed more hang time. But my brain was spinning. I knew myself well enough to know I'd never be able to relax.

"Probably not. With this new deadline, I better get cracking."

"All right," he said, without pushing back on my brush-off. "Guess we'll see you in LA."

"Yeah. Later, bro."

After we hung up, something fired in my gut. For the most part, we were a democratic band; or should I say, they all fell in line with whatever decisions I made. It wasn't that I couldn't welcome their input...it's just that the songwriting had always been my domain.

But I didn't have any songs.

Not even one.

Exhausted before the day even started, I slumped onto one of the banquettes flanking the kitchen table. My mind churned as I stared into space. A decade ago our debut album, *My Fantasy Life*, went multi-platinum and an 'inspired' reporter wrote: *Size of a Scandal is the band everyone loves and if you don't, then there must be something wrong with you.* After that article dropped, I couldn't escape my own face. Magazine covers. TV appearances. I drove down Sunset Boulevard and there was my mug, twenty feet high on a billboard, staring back at me. Trust me, it was weird.

Fame was never on my agenda. I was just a guy who loved music and could write songs. Good songs with good lyrics. Writing had always come easy for me, almost like having a superpower. When Mom bought me my first Gibson Flying V guitar, I knew right away what chords worked together, where a bridge went, how long and complicated a guitar solo needed to be. Songs were like puzzles and I knew how the pieces fit together; I understood the structure of a hit. Call it formulaic, but that understanding has served me well. At the same time, it created a hamster wheel of endless pressure.

As much as I hated to admit it, some truth lingered in that review. I'd struggled in Portland, as you do on some nights, trying to find the groove. But...

Huh?

My eyes focused on the far wall. Blinked. Refocused. At the front of the bus, next to the second bathroom, were several cupboards. One of the doors wasn't closed properly, and I never left any door ajar. I shook off a ripple of unease. On bare feet, I padded toward the cupboard, careful to avoid the squeaky section near the front entrance. Just as I raised my foot to push the door back into place, the faintest, most delicate *achoo!* drifted out.

The film of sweat on my body pricked like I'd been flash frozen.

Forget Exile and the boys.

The morning was about to blow up in my face.

CHAPTER TWO

"Who the hell are you?"

With the door peeled open, she cowered deeper into the closet, like a vampire avoiding the sun...if vampires were black girls...who wore headbands and jeans.

"Hi," she said, as if this were somehow normal. "I'm Hastings."

"Hastings," I repeated.

"Uh-huh. H, A—"

"I know how to spell, thank you very much. How did you get in here?"

Behind glasses as thick as my thumb, her eyes were huge and hesitant. "I snuck in."

My stomach plummeted. Sweet Jesus. The bus was spacious, but how the hell could I have missed another human? I mentally sifted through days I'd already tried to forget and came up with nada. "When?"

She twirled her lower lip between thumb and forefinger, a *should I answer?* gesture. In the silence, I quietly died. How long had she been in here?

"Let's go," I said, thumbing her out. "Party's over."

She'd created a right little nest amongst the Lysol Wipes and paper towels and struggled to unfold herself with a modicum of grace. When her foot snagged on the handle of the Swiffer, she tumbled out, arms flailing in an awkward swan dive. I caught her just in time. For two frozen seconds we were nose to nose.

"Don't even think about it," I said, pushing her away. "We're not going there."

After righting herself, she smoothed the front of her jeans primly. "I'm not worried about that."

"Yeah? Maybe you should be."

Her eyes, unafraid and pretty damn frank for an intruder, fixed on mine. It might've made me uncomfortable if any hint of sexuality sparked between us. The truth was, she looked severely young...and a little on the homely side. The real estate of her features reminded me of Nina Simone: the nose of a boxer, swollen from one too many hits; a generous mouth better suited to a larger face. Too many creeps in this industry would overlook all that and joke there's a right and wrong time to ask for ID. Lucky for her, I wasn't one of them.

"You're not my type," she finally said.

"Haven't you heard?" I joked. "I'm everyone's type."

A thin line creased her forehead. "You can't be everyone's type."

Of course she hadn't read *that* particular headline; it had to be older than her. But her immediate reaction to it—calling bullshit—oddly buoyed me. I never signed up to be a heartthrob. Call it luck of the draw I wasn't born entirely unfortunate looking. Mom used to call me her beautiful mutt because I inherited the best of her Romani genes: restless energy, a dancer's physique and dark brown hair that shined no matter how much I neglected it. But it was the hard symmetry in Pops' German DNA that forged my features; that made every girl look twice.

"That was a joke by the way," I clarified.

Her eyes flickered over me again. "You're too hairy. Even if I was old enough."

My smiley face boxers clearly didn't amuse her, and I probably should've put some pants on before investigating. I reached behind her to grab a clean bath towel from the cupboard and wrapped it around my waist. "Yeah, well, sorry I'm not your boy band fantasy. News flash: real men are hairy."

"I know," she said. "My dad was hairy."

The carriage of her chin lifted defiantly. She was a fighter, this one. Only I wasn't in the sparring mood.

"Listen, sweetheart," I said. "I'd love to hear about your dad and your mom and your stuffed animal collection, but you need to get outta here. I've got work to do."

"What kind of work?"

I cocked my head. "You do know who I am, right?"

She looked past me, at the Gibson ES 335 guitar cradled in its stand. A gift from Suze on my 21st birthday, it was a sweet custom with a sparkle finish. Intertwined on the fret board were our names, an intricate masterpiece created with mother of pearl inlay. That guitar meant more to me than anything, and I'd brought it back from the show last night to help with the writing...or at least that's what I told myself.

"You're a musician," she said.

"And what do musicians do?"

"Make music."

"Exactly. I need to write songs and I'm on a deadline, so—"

"How many songs have you written?" she interrupted.

I tightened the towel around me. Why the hell was she asking that? "I'm working on several."

"You mean you don't have any."

"I can't just pull them out of my arse," I said with a prickle of irritation. "Songs take time."

"Maybe you need help."

She watched me, gauging my reaction. Seriously? Of all the suggestions thrown at me over the years, none of them were as ballsy or downright ludicrous as that.

"I'm the guy who writes the songs, in case you didn't know."

"What about the rest of your band?"

"It's up to me," I said. "Always has been."

"It sounded like they had some ideas."

A muscle in my neck pulsed. This is not how I envisioned the morning. "So you've been eavesdropping on all my shit, too?" I asked. Did she hear the entire conversation with Suze the other night? What had I said? What *hadn't* I said? A burst of anger fizzed in my belly. "What is with you people these days? Haven't you ever heard of trespassing? Privacy?" I waved her toward the door. "Grab all your stuff because it's time to head home. Where do you live anyway?"

She inched back to the closet and snagged her knapsack, slinging it over a shoulder. "Close by."

With her sudden caginess, I feared the worst. "Are you a mole?" I asked. "Did the lovely Ms. Wylie put you up to this?" I wiggled my fingers in a *show me* gesture. "Give me your bag. I need to take a look."

"It's just my stuff," she said, handing it to me with a confused look. "And I don't know who Ms. Wylie is."

Jillian Wylie was the founder of Hot Shot News, a cretin-filled operation of celebrity stalkers masquerading as news crusaders. She and I had locked horns more than once, the last time resulting in a lawsuit, the outcome still pending and leaning in my favor. I wouldn't put it past her to deploy a plant. But a search of Hastings' pack for incriminating evidence only turned up clothes, a bag of trail mix and a lone toothbrush.

"Where's your phone?" I asked. "I wanna see what's on it."

"I don't have one."

She pulled out the inside flaps of her pockets as proof. Nowhere else on her slight frame could hide a phone. Still, damage control never hurt.

"Listen," I said. "I don't know what your deal is, but if I see any leaks online about anything you might've heard, *illegally* I might add, my lawyers will come after you. Hard." I tossed her the pack. "Understood?"

"I won't," she said, sounding wounded that I'd paint her with a brush of impropriety. "I promise."

"All right then, time's up. You've had your little joyride, met the Jazzer." From the wall outlet, I unplugged my burner phone, the one I used exclusively for interviews. "And because I'm a decent guy, you can borrow my phone to call your parents."

"Um..." She shuffled back a step. "Thanks, but I can get home by myself."

I shot her a long look. The silence grew thick.

"Hastings," I said, and I had to admit it was a cool fucking name. "It's not that I don't believe you, but I don't believe you. And a ten-year-old shouldn't be—"

"I'm thirteen," she interrupted.

If that were true, someone needed to be taken to task for not feeding her enough. The top of her Afro wouldn't touch my chin.

"Thirteen, ten, whatever," I said. "You're a kid. It's a Wednesday in March. You should be in school. And your parents are probably losing their shit wondering where you are."

She squared off her shoulders, suddenly going rigid. I interpreted it as steeling herself for a counterpunch, and cut that move short by striding over to the door and throwing it open. Did a quick up and down of the lot to make sure no one was around. "Out," I told her.

"But..."

My arm shot forward. "OUT."

After a sullen beat, her head dropped in defeat. To her credit, she didn't offer any lip as she slunk out the door. Outside, it was Dante's bloody Inferno. A hot wind blasted, the kind of breeze that offered no relief, just swirled the heat around, making you more aware of it. Hastings visored her hand against the gust and scanned left to right.

"Don't tell me you've got a posse waiting to ambush," I grumbled.

"No."

She glanced around the parking lot again, this time her look uncertain. Despite her initial bravado, fragility radiated off her, mirroring the heat rising from the asphalt. Even though she'd wedged herself in the closet for god knows how long, she didn't strike me as a wacko. (I'd been around seriously crazed fans and it was unsettling.) And for sure she wasn't a groupie. Those women prowled like rabid wolves, a calculating gleam in their eyes.

"Talk to me," I said. "How are you getting home? I need to hear it."

"I'll figure it out."

For the first time, a drawl slipped into her voice. Southern for sure.

"You always this friendly when someone's trying to help?" I asked.

"Look who's talking!"

"For the record, *my* help is realistic. I offered you the chance to call your parents and you turned me down, so now you're on your own," I said, feeling compelled to remind her of the circumstances.

"I know," she said.

Her gaze flittered up to mine, unreadable as she shifted her knapsack from one shoulder to another. In retrospect, this was where I should've ended it. Closed the door and walked away, like any sane person would. But at that precise door-closing moment, a random thought kicked in. I hadn't seen a wallet or any money in her pack. Her clothes were of the Walmart chic variety. Maybe her parents couldn't afford a car and she was too embarrassed to admit it? I knew that feeling all too well. How could I forget my fifth-grade buddy Alan Porteous innocently remarking at the dinner table how our cutlery looked just like Applebee's? How Pops scooped more Chef Boyardee ravioli onto his plate and only grunted. Mom's horrified expression.

No. Don't. Just...

Christ.

"Hold on, okay?" I said.

I snuck back inside to my bedroom. Under the mattress were stacks of twenties, an old habit. The world ran on algorithms, all our information jammed into the cloud. Anything could go wrong. If it did, I was going down prepared. And speaking of prepared, I swapped out the towel for a pair of shorts and a T-shirt, but not before taking a quick glance in the mirror. I don't know what she was going off about. My chest hair wasn't *that* out of control.

At the doorway, I stepped to the lowest stair and discreetly palmed her the cash. "Go up to the hotel. They can flag you a taxi or Uber. And if you're lying about living close, there's enough money here to take you across the state."

She inched forward, then hesitated, her eyes ballooning at the wad in her hand. "That's way too much."

"Please. Take it. And buy some lunch. You look half-starved."

"Thank you," she mumbled, and tucked the bills into her knapsack.

"Don't mention you got it from me," I warned. "And if you do, I'll deny everything."

She nodded, and for a few awkward seconds we stared at each other.

"You *will* go home, right?" I asked.

"Uh-huh."

"Then I'm going to watch you walk up there. No tricks."

As she turned and walked away, there was a vibration in the air I couldn't describe. When she became a dark shape in the distance, the temptation to call her back danced on my tongue, except what else was there to say? Instead, I closed the door and convinced myself I dodged a major bullet. Embrace the Hail Mary moment. But when I sat down at my desk, my mind wouldn't stop bouncing.

Reinvention.

On any other day, that review would've rolled off my back. But with Ex and then Hastings questioning me, it lingered like a bad smell. I tore open the ream of paper, the brilliant blankness intimidating. I didn't write music longhand very often these days, although something about seeing the notes, the structure, always comforted me. Pen in hand, I tried to summon the usual process: push my churning emotions into chords, a melody. Into *something*. I closed my eyes, twirled in the office chair. In the stillness, everything felt like before, yet different. The bus seemed bigger. Emptier. The morning felt impossible to fill.

But I would fill it.

I'd been here a hundred times before.

A song would come.

All I needed was some goddamned inspiration.

CHAPTER THREE

AN HOUR LATER I WAS STILL IN THE CHAIR, SONGLESS AND demoralized, when Sven, our tour manager, arrived with breakfast. Imagine a Swedish version of The Rock, minus any charisma, and that's our Svennie. Most managers prided themselves on looking like band members: jeans, T-shirts, maybe a button-down if they wanted to spiff up. Sven, on the other hand, could be mistaken for an off-duty Navy SEAL. Underneath his collared golf shirts and ironed slacks, coiled aggression simmered. 'Uptight' would be a generous term.

"Morning," he said.

I chin-nodded in his direction. "Hey."

With wide, flamingo steps, he sidestepped the crumpled balls of paper on the floor, moving with surprising grace for a man his size.

"How's the writing going?" he asked.

"Great," I said, eyeing the takeout box he placed on the kitchen table. "Better, if there's a shit ton of bacon in that."

He shook his head. "Egg white omelet with steamed kale."

"Thanks," I said. "I think."

Before the tour started, I mentioned once, offhandedly, about wanting to stay healthy. Sven, with his soldier efficiency, took command. The contents of my cupboards now resembled a health food store and Sven had retooled my breakfasts, hand-delivering them whenever possible. I didn't complain; it felt like it was his roundabout way of clearing the air. There'd been a hiccup at the end of our last tour, and keen to put it behind us, I'd called him personally to hire him this time around. The way I saw it, an occasional dustup between two A-types could be overlooked. In the end, Sven was loyal and damn good at his job. Besides, I didn't entirely mind being doted on.

Sven tucked his aviators into the V of his shirt. He was careful to look past me and seemed stiffer than usual. I'd stripped back down to my underwear and wondered if my smiley face boxers proved too much for him this early in the day.

"There's a girl sitting outside," he said. "She approach you?"

"Really?" My pulse quickened. I peeked out the blinds closest to me and saw nothing. "Where?"

He tipped his head left. "Other side."

I rolled in the chair to the other window and slivered the blinds open. Five yards away, Hastings sat cross-legged on a cement divider, the wilted sapling behind her offering zero shade.

"Jesus," I mumbled. In my boxers and full AC, I was barely surviving. It was hot enough out there to be naked and still be uncomfortable, and her skin glistened like it was glazed. What the hell was she still doing here? "Maybe she's just a guest at the hotel," I said, trying to sound casual. "Waiting for someone."

Sven joined me at the window. "Doesn't feel that way to me." He popped his knuckles, one vicious tug at a time. "Caleb told me twenty times he had security covered. This is why we don't veer off course."

"Don't take it out on him," I said. "It was my decision. As far as the girl goes, she's likely harmless. I mean, look at her."

"They're never harmless," he grumbled. "Someone always wants something. She's probably texted all her friends. Time to intervene."

A tour manager wasn't the glamorous gig some might think it was. It was long, hellish days of travel plus the grind of keeping the tour organized—all the thankless administration. On top of that, they got to babysit us. This involved keeping hangers-on in line. Sven lived for that part of the job. He was part Terminator, all papa grizzly when it came to intervention. Most fans knew when to call it a day, but those who didn't had seen a side of Sven not even his mother could explain away.

"Don't make a scene, okay?" I handed him an unopened bottle of water. "Give her this and ask her to politely move on."

Sven took the water with a quizzical expression. Cavalier wasn't my MO when it came to privacy.

"You don't think it's odd," he ventured. "Her just...sitting there."

On one hand, I could grudgingly appreciate his sixth sense. On the other, I wasn't in the mood for an interrogation. "It's not my job to think," I said. "It's yours."

Sven frowned. That was definitely a tad blunt, a tendency I'd been trying to rein in. So far, things were back on track between us, and I wanted to keep it that way. But Sven had managed our last three tours and there was something to be said for familiarity. In other words, he knew when to let things slide.

"On that note, this is for your hotel suite. Room 1105." He handed me a hotel key card. "And Ex wanted me to tell you they're all doing steak tonight if you want to join in. The Arrowhead Grill. Eight o'clock. Let me know and I can arrange a driver to pick you up."

I tossed the key card onto my desk, irked. Ex hadn't mentioned dinner and he knew I loved steak.

"Thanks," I said, "but I'll probably eat in the hotel."

"I could meet you back here, so you don't have to eat alone," he offered, and then quickly added, "if you want."

In the pause that followed, his eyes, typically blank as a canvas, hiding ruthlessness only a mobster could love, flickered with something that resembled sentiment. But I had to be mistaken.

"Nah. Party with the boys tonight," I said. "You and I can catch up another night."

With a curt nod, he left to deal with the situation. Through the blinds, I watched him approach Hastings. She accepted the water and squinted up at his mass. Their conversation started benignly, but as the seconds dragged on, she dug in her heels. I could tell from Sven's body language he wasn't amused. He had this funny way of twitching the more amped he got. Finally, he yanked her up by her arm.

"Whoa," I muttered and rapped my knuckles on the glass. "Settle down."

Hastings pulled out of his grip, eyes skipping back to the bus. "Don't touch me."

Sven threatened, "You want me to call the police?"

"Call them," Hastings countered. "I'm not doing anything wrong."

I cracked a grin. "Attagirl," I whispered.

But any pride was short-lived. We paid Sven well for a reason. He scooped her up like she was a sack of flour, threw her over his shoulder, and marched away. Her stunned look, head bobbing, was almost laughable, if the situation were funny. Sven wouldn't hurt her (I was 97% sure) but as the blinds fell shut, it struck me how his size and never-ending coolness were deceiving. Sven's nickname was The Iceman, and similar to a glacier, I could never pinpoint what lurked beneath his surface. Or how much damage he could really inflict.

The afternoon plan was to nap and start writing again with a refreshed mind, but so much for that. I woke up at 6:00 p.m., sweaty and grumpy, used Ms. February to relieve some frustration and followed up with an ice-cold shower for punishment. (Month fourteen of celibacy, and I wasn't wearing it well.) After shaving, I forced myself to sit at the desk. Before my snooze, I'd left one sheet of paper out to make it feel less intimidating. Staring at it now, the alternatives spooled into a tangled mess.

We only had one more album committed to our label, Six Devil Sounds, before our contract was up. The infamous Mackenzie Rosenthal—our longtime manager—insisted we entertain other offers and in theory, shopping around made sense. Realistically, the number of viable options could be counted on one hand. Our current deal with Six Devil was rarer than an honest politician, owing to the massive following, and leverage, we had before signing with them. As a result, we weren't tied in to 360 deals. I owned the master recordings of all my songs, and the chances of negotiating similar terms with any of the remaining labels were slim. And with a pending executive shift at Six Devil, things were in flux. Of course, we would deliver our final album (a shattered reputation *wasn't* an option), but even the thought of making just one record felt insurmountable, let alone committing to another four.

Because every album meant another tour...and our last tour almost killed me. After thirteen brutal months on the road, I needed a break —from everything. Six Devil agreed to defer the delivery of our final album, but with a catch: if we took the year off, they would release an in-betweener of B-sides and remixes, but we were to be back on the road after the break and delivering an album at tour's end. It was a dicey trade-off, although the decision was unanimous in that I said yes on behalf of the band. We took the year off and maybe I spent too much time in the Mexican sun. I hardly played, hardly talked to anyone. I got into the booze more than I should have.

It became a vicious cycle.

The longer I stayed away, the more I didn't want to come back.

I wadded the paper into a dense baseball and knuckle-balled it down the length of the bus. Nothing else would flow tonight, that much was certain. I gathered my necessaries and psyched myself up for dinner. Or quarantine, as I liked to call it, because there was something darkly isolating about eating alone in a hotel room. But it was better, barely, than sitting in a restaurant by myself, enduring whispers, stares and not-so-subtle phones filming me.

With a sigh, I pushed open the bus door and paused, momentarily disoriented. The screaming brightness of the day had disappeared.

She hadn't.

"Hi," Hastings said.

"You're back."

"Your friend dropped me off across the street at the mall," she said, making air quotes around friend. "I guess he figured all I needed was some retail therapy."

"Did he treat you okay?"

It was my moral duty to ask. Whatever gene they handed out that provided men with patience and understanding for females, Sven had somehow missed.

"Who is he? A guy that runs your errands?"

"Sort of. He's our tour manager," I explained. "You gunning for his job? Is that why you're still here?"

"No." She reconsidered. Tilted her head. "Maybe."

I should've known better. She was too spunky to just give up. I locked the bus door and walked toward the concrete divider she sat on.

"Kiddo," I said. "What are you trying to prove? Sitting in a parking lot all day in the heat. This isn't fun and games. Have you at least eaten?"

She dug around in her knapsack and, with an outstretched arm, offered back the stack of bills. "Thank you, but it didn't feel right spending your money."

"Jesus," I said, waving her arm back with alarm. "Don't flash that around."

"I won't tell anyone you gave it to me."

"I'm not worried about that. I'm worried about *you.*"

The words tumbled out, honest and unfiltered. She couldn't be more than a hundred pounds soaking wet. Not someone who should be missing meals, or missing in general. I edged closer and crouched down. In the fading light, she looked very young.

"It isn't easy being a teenager; trust me, I've been there. But whatever your problems are, they'll get fixed one way or the other."

Her brow knotted. "What if they can't be fixed?"

"Everything can be fixed."

Her slight frown let me know exactly what she thought of my bold-faced lie. What else was I supposed to say though? The situation demanded something appropriate and uplifting.

"Did you write a song today?" she asked.

I sat down on my heels. "Back to that, are we?"

"Did you?"

Indignation thrummed through me. She had this way of putting me on my back foot I wasn't used to. "I might've. Not that it's any of your business."

She studied me for a good three seconds. "Why are you so stubborn?"

"Me?" I asked, unable to hold back a laugh. "You're the one sitting here all day." Not to mention, I'd given her five hundred dollars she'd refused to spend—not even five dollars at McDonald's. Without asking, I knew she hadn't made any inroads on finding a way home. She'd made no effort to keep up her end of the deal. I stood up and called it a day. "As much as I'd love to continue this scintillating conversation, it's dinner time. I, unlike you, understand I need to eat."

"Then go have dinner."

She shrugged and I *almost* bought the cool indifference she tried to sell...right up until her jaw, proud and strong this whole time, wobbled. She noticed me notice and raised her chin even higher.

"Fine," I said. "Have it your way. Keep the cash and sit here all night. I'm out."

I didn't expect her to chase me, or suddenly change her mind. That would involve admitting I'd called her bluff. Women didn't cop to anything that weakened their bargaining positions unless they had to. So I walked on, my flush of righteousness waning with the evening light. Stars speckled in the darkening sky and a familiar outline shone brightly, high above the hotel roofline. When I realized what it was, my steps slowed and then stopped altogether. The space around my heart cramped. Words I'd never forgotten rang loud and clear in my ears.

"He is coming back for you, right?"

And just like that, all the memories came flooding back.

It would be easy to blame that long-ago April afternoon for setting the course of my relationship with my father. The truth was, we'd been at each other's throats long before that. He'd been pushing me to learn jazz ever since I could hold a guitar, but I didn't want to be the next Jarred 'Jazzer' Johnson, playing jazz in half-empty, backwater SoCal clubs, never making a dime, while slogging the day shift as deli manager at Von's. I loved rock and roll.

And so, in an ill-lit pawnshop that reeked of thrift store clothes and rat poison, the beginning of the end started when a salesclerk slung a Flying V around my shoulders. The finish was scuffed and dull and one of the tuning pegs was broken, but the guitar felt like silk in my arms, and the sound that came from it was symphonic and huge. The clerk flashed a grin at Pops—he'd been around long enough to know a slam-dunk sale—but he didn't know my father. Pops pointed to a beat-up Telecaster on the wall (the guitar he and his jazz buddies preferred) and said no way was he buying me a guitar designed for lowly headbangers. I dug in my heels in vain. I still remember the clerk tugging nervously on his goatee as we watched my father's '95 Dodge Caravan peel away, leaving a trail of blue smoke behind.

"He *is* coming back for you, right?" he'd asked.

He didn't.

To stay calm on the nine-mile walk back home, to remind myself something was stable, even though everything around me felt like it wasn't, I'd kept watch on the Big Dipper, high in the Long Beach sky. When I'd arrived home, Mom, already hysterical, went ballistic on Pops. "What kind of a father abandons his eleven-year-old son over a guitar?" she'd yelled, her arms tight around me. "You're a child, Jarred. Self-centered. The world doesn't revolve around you and your goddamned jazz."

Three days later, Mom bought me the V with her own money. The rest, as they say, was history.

But in the Westin parking lot, the hot hum of crickets loud in my ears, a drift of chlorine wafting in the air from the nearby pool, I couldn't shake a different history.

I looked up at the stars, the sky now thick with them.

You don't owe her anything, I warned myself. *Don't go there. Keep moving…*

When I turned around, Hastings' head perked up right away.

"If you want some dinner, I'm buying. But then you go home. Deal?"

Finally, a screwy little smile.

"Sure," she said and scrambled to her feet.

CHAPTER FOUR

BY THE TIME WE FINISHED THE TREK FROM THE FAR END OF the parking lot, the quiet transition from dusk to nightfall had finished. A hint of cool finally cut the heat and it was a gorgeous night, the kind that made you wish for a chilled bottle of wine and good friends to share it with. Yet here I was, skulking in the shadows of a hotel entrance with a stranger nowhere close to legal drinking age and absolutely no idea how I planned to pull this stunt off. The outdoor bell desk area was crammed with smartly dressed couples liquored up and ready for a night out. Bellhops juggled valeted cars and a stream of taxis. Not exactly a covert situation.

"I'll do some recon first and make sure the coast is clear," I said. "When I come back, you go up solo."

Hastings glanced at the whirlwind of activity, uneasy. "By myself?"

"We can't go in together," I whispered back. "I'll follow you after. Lay low here until I get back."

I ducked through the crowd, avoiding all eye contact. A blast of air conditioning assaulted me in the lobby and if my mind wasn't revving out of control, it might've been refreshing. All I could think about was how Adrian from a year ago would never have found himself in this situation. The current Adrian, however, had committed and my word was my word. If we ate fast, it would all be over in less than an hour. With that as inspiration, I did the lockdown loop as quickly as possible and handed her the room key upon my return.

"It's the top floor—room 1105. Through the doors turn left, go past the front desk and the elevators will be on your right. Give me ten minutes."

With a deep breath she squared her shoulders. "1105. Okay."

She threaded her way past the throng with ease, similar to girls on the floor at concerts who bust a move and shimmy their way to the front of the stage. I waited, pacing by the cactuses before booking it to the elevator. The eleventh floor, silent in an unnatural way, didn't stop me from looking over my shoulder as I walked down the hall. At the suite entrance, I knocked and identified myself. Hastings opened up and I locked the door behind me in every way possible. Time stood still as we stared at each other in the foyer, both of us a little uncertain. Yep, this was happening.

"Let's get dinner on the road," I said.

She followed me inside and took a seat at the dining room table, drinking in the surroundings with big eyes. Not to sound jaded, but after a decade on tour every hotel looked the same. Granted, this suite was bigger than most people's apartments and could easily host fifty people. Sixty, if you jammed a few on both balconies. It also had a kitchen and that's where I found the room service menu. I scanned it, decided on the rib eye, and handed it off to her.

"Order whatever you'd like," I told her. "Money's not a problem."

While I fixed myself a stiff drink at the minibar, she perused the offerings. "I'll have the quesadilla and an iced tea, please."

"That's it? What about dessert?" I wrapped my T-shirt around the hotel phone receiver and buffed it clean. "Ice cream?"

She set the menu aside and folded her hands neatly in front of her. "I don't eat ice cream."

"I thought all kids like ice cream."

"I'm allergic to dairy. And I'm not a kid," she reminded me.

I raised an eyebrow but said nothing. After placing our order, I excused myself and returned from the bathroom with two towels.

Laying both on the couch, I settled on top of them with my drink. Hastings watched with a mix of curiosity and confusion. I could sense she was waiting for an explanation. The irony wasn't lost on me, considering she needed to fess up to a few things herself.

I kicked both feet onto the coffee table and swirled vodka in my glass. "So, Miss Hastings. Talk to me."

"About?"

"I'll admit I'm curious. How did you poach my bus?"

If my question caught her off guard, she didn't show it, like she knew it was the price of admission. "I overheard some boys at my school talk about you. How you travelled in your own bus. I didn't break in though," she was quick to add. "The door was unlocked."

I mulled that over, knowing it *was* feasible. Since venues had security and crew were always coming and going, I left the door unlocked most of the time. And I couldn't blame Big Daddy, my driver, for being lax. Unlike most tour buses, mine was a semi rig, with a separate entrance and sleeping quarters for the driver, everything sound-proofed. Inside, I could scream until I was hoarse, and no one would hear a thing. Plus, it was an unwritten rule no one came into my space unannounced. She'd definitely picked the right bus. The question was why?

"Listen," I said, in good cop mode. "I'm not going to get all in your face about it. I'm not going to call the police, even though I could. But I can tell you're not a fan. Was this a dare? Your friends put you up to this?"

We tracked eyes, careful. In all honesty, she didn't strike me as one of *those* girls. The kind that pile into a bedroom and talk trash all afternoon, eating candy and listening to boy bands. The kind that get cajoled into stupid things. She was a lone wolf. And not used to another Alpha. In fact, my long look of waiting might've hung there forever if my cell phone didn't interrupt it. I slid the phone out of my pocket, enough to see the top of the screen. *AbNORMal,* my pet name for Norm, scrolled along the top. All my muscles tensed.

"Shit," I muttered. "Give me a sec." I got up, cranked open one of the balcony doors and stepped outside. A jumble of emotions seesawed in my chest before I answered. "What's up?" I asked. "I'm kind of in the middle of something."

"I bet you are. Since when is having your hand down your pants more important than dinner with us?"

Right away, with his belligerence, I rued picking up. "Let me guess," I shot back. "You want to talk poetry?"

"Jesus," he groused. "Now I can't even write down my thoughts without you spazzing? Don't be a douche. I mean, *try* at least."

Welcome to Norm. The best way to describe him was the runt of the litter. Scrawny to the point of malnourished, he had a chip on his shoulder from growing up poor and wore a permanent strung-out look that triggered strangers to ask about his health. He never met a fistfight he didn't like and would go down bleeding if need be. It was a personality that didn't mesh well with authority, including mine.

"Classy, getting Ex to do your dirty work," I said.

In the tight silence, he cleared his throat. "Since we're on the song front, Ex said you weren't entirely thrilled with our proposal."

Front—typical of Norm to use war terminology. And proposal wasn't exactly how Ex couched it. A dull throb started at the base of my neck. "Can we talk about this tomorrow?"

"Oh, *sooo* sorry to bother you," he needled. "It's not like songs are important for a band."

"Dude—"

"Forget it," he said. "Enjoy your filet mignon and Dom Perignon in your ivory tower."

The throb spread up my neck to the tips of my ears. That was his dig? "Me being isolated seemed to suit you just fine before."

The quiet right after that bomb felt ominous. Norm, voice leaden, finally broke the gloom. "One day you'll realize it wasn't all my fault. But I'm not holding my breath."

And with that, he hung up before I could, leaving me with nothing but a bad taste in my mouth.

"Who was that?"

Startled, I spun around to find Hastings standing right behind me, inside the suite. I'd left the patio door open, which was clearly a mistake.

"Do you always listen in on other people's phone calls?" I grumbled.

"It's hard not to hear when you have them on speaker phone."

She had a point, irritatingly enough. With a monitor jammed in my ear during every concert, off-duty I avoided headphones and did all my calls on speaker.

"That was my bass player, if you really need to know," I said.

"*My* bass player?"

"That's what I said."

"Is it your band?"

"Always has been."

"Is that why you treat them like that?"

An edge cut into my voice. "Like how?"

"Mean."

I turned away, uncomfortable with her stare. Norm and I were the rocky road duo and over the years, we'd clunked along, a wagon wheel stuck in a muddy rut. He'd tried off and on to hate me, but like his attempts at relationships, couldn't quite pull it off. In the name of survival he'd tolerated my leadership, although that never stopped him from resenting it.

The evening tarnished, I tried to shake off the lingering anger. In the distance, landscape lights twinkled in the dark caw of space that was the golf course. Soft piano drifted up from the outdoor restaurant below and I recognized the tune. A Sinatra number, one of mom's favorites. An ocean of memories, all my regrettable behavior, washed over me.

"It's not like you don't already know," I said. "They want to contribute songs to the next album." I turned around, crossing my arms. "I'm not sure it's going to work out."

"Do you want it to?"

She searched my face, all the uncertainty in it. Simply, she'd asked the least simple question of all.

"I don't know," I finally said.

"Maybe I can help," she offered. "With your songs."

A shimmer ghosted up my spine. I was acutely aware that somehow, I'd been waiting for this. "For the record, I don't need any help. But let's pretend I'm biting." I circled my finger in the air. "Explain."

"Have you ever heard of synesthesia?"

"Is that the sensory thing with colors?"

"That's one of the ways people experience it. The sound and color association is called chromesthesia," she explained. "That's what I have. Some people hear single notes as colors, but for me an entire song is always one color. It tells me things about the song."

"Like what? Death metal is black, the blues are blue, and your shirt is pink?" I bit back a smirk. "I could tell you that."

She looked down at her shirt and back at me, brows knitted. "My shirt is yellow."

"Whatever. Yellow then."

Her head tilted in some sort of reassessment of me. "Are you colorblind?"

"That's irrelevant. Color doesn't matter in music. Songs aren't paintings."

"But colors do matter," she countered. "Your songs are an expression of you—your moods, emotions, who you are. Those all factor into the colors I see."

I'd first heard of synesthesia years ago. Hendrix supposedly had some form of it, but he died before it became a thing, so there wasn't any info on how he used it, if at all. As much as I loved his music, he was also a fan of psychedelics. I was sure he saw a whole lot of things, including colors. Not exactly a bulletproof system.

"Moods and emotions, sure, I get that," I said, "but how does it work?"

"It's not so much how it works," she stressed. "For me, all songs are a certain color and each color means something different."

"Is one color better than the other?"

"No, but..."

"Do the colors *guarantee* anything?"

"No, but..."

"So there is no formula," I interrupted, again.

"I never said there was one." Off my now dubious expression, she continued. "I could listen to some of your songs and tell you what I see. Or why don't you sing me something you're working on?"

Even if I had a hundred new song options to pull from, what did it matter? She just admitted there was no rhyme or reason to this. I stepped back inside and took a seat on the couch. Hastings sat on the easy chair directly across from me.

"Listen, kiddo. I appreciate your offer, but what do you even know about music?"

"I took piano lessons," she said, with the boldness of someone whose closet contained a hundred Grammys. "And I love to sing."

I slung my arm over the back of the couch and laughed. "Oh, well, there you go. You're one step away from writing a hit song."

Call me traditional, but part of me blamed all the music reality TV shows for giving her, and everyone, a false sense of hope. The blueprint for success wasn't just a karaoke song away. It wasn't that easy. I mean, sure, some of those contestants had talent and could belt it out. But were they prepared to spend every waking minute pushing, asking, creating, dealing and hustling? I dropped out of school at fourteen and even with 24/7 commitment, the odds of being spat out of the biz disillusioned, broke and bleeding were stacked higher than the heavens. Except for me, failure was never an option.

"Are you scared to try something different?" she asked, the weight of her gaze a little too probing.

"I'm not scared of anything," I scoffed. "I'm a realist. If some color wheel solution to songwriting existed, someone would've been all over it by now." At this point, common sense said to drop the topic altogether, but the flame of indignation still burnt in my gut. Time to turn the tables. "All that aside, how 'bout I throw you a bone? Show me what you've got. Sing for me."

Her assuredness took a half-step backward. "Now?"

"Yup."

"What do you want me to sing?"

I picked up my drink and tipped the glass in her direction. "You're the musician, right? Pull one from your repertoire."

She straightened, eyes darting. Maybe it was the realization we'd reached the endgame. She'd sing and nothing would come of it other than a free dinner and a one-way Uber ride home. But like me, she was a fighter and wouldn't let a challenge go unanswered. After a deep breath, she closed her eyes and laid both hands on her thighs, like she was harnessing energy. Then, quietly, of all the songs in the world, she started to sing "We Belong" by Pat Benatar.

The smell of my parent's living room flooded my nostrils. Febreze, the old corduroy couch, Pops' rye whiskey sloshed and stale in the shag carpet. My heart seized with an ungodly pain. Mom was the original Benatar fan. When I started playing the guitar, she'd haul me into the living room on Sundays, her one day off, and crank Pat. While I fumbled, learning the chords, she'd sing along. Hastings' voice was incredible, way better than mom's, but I couldn't even appreciate it because everything started to shrink and go black. I stood up abruptly, staggering sideways. My drink tumbled out of my hand in slow motion. Across the coffee table, Hastings stopped singing and jumped to her feet.

"What's wrong? Are you okay?"

Her alarmed features started to blur, and the last thing I remembered was reaching for something...and finding nothing.

CHAPTER FIVE

I JERKED BACK TO LIFE, SPUTTERING OUT FRIGID WATER like a broken sprinkler head.

"Oh my god. Are you okay?"

My eyes zoomed in and out on Hastings, trying to focus. Crouched beside me, she clutched an empty glass.

"Yeah, I'm fine," I said, ridiculously. Flat on my back, skin clammy with sweat, all my limbs felt like hot jelly. "Aside from being wet."

"Sorry. I didn't know what to do." She set down the offending glass. "Should I call a doctor?"

"No. No. No," I said. "We're not calling anyone. I just fainted. Just...give me a minute."

I took several deep breaths until the room settled, or at least stopped spinning. The ringing in my ears wouldn't stop. I tried not to think about lying directly on the carpet.

"Have you fainted before?" she asked.

"No," I said. "I mean, yes. But not for a while."

There wasn't a lot about my year in Mexico I cared to remember. But it was hard to forget coming to, facedown on the floor, head cracked open and blood smeared across the tiles. Hard to forget your neighbor screaming when you knock on her door looking like a

Walking Dead victim. Hard to forget a doctor in the Puerto Escondido ER with dark rings under his eyes and a kind smile telling me it was a miracle I didn't die, and that perhaps I should take it easy with the booze.

Hastings leaned into my space, snapping me back to the here and now. She pointed at my fist, wrapped tight around a loop of rawhide that hung from my neck.

"Your fingers," she said. "They're turning white."

Inside my fist, the silver box pendant with mom's ashes inside had pierced skin. I could feel the warm blood. A wave of fresh nausea coursed through me.

"You don't look so good," Hastings said, her voice jittery. "Maybe we should call someone."

"No," I said, more forcefully. "We're not calling anyone. Just help me up. Please."

Being horizontal felt safer, but I needed to stand and reclaim the dynamic that had shifted between us. I grasped her outstretched hand, but she wasn't prepared for my weight. She pitched forward and we stumbled toward the dining room table where I collapsed onto one of the chairs. While I re-established my bearings, Hastings slipped into the kitchen and came back with a fresh glass of water. She set it in front of me and took a seat at the head of the table. Gravitas swirled around her like smoke. For a long time neither one of us spoke.

"Um…" I cleared away the huskiness in my throat. "Thanks. For helping."

"You scared me," she said. "I thought you were having a heart attack."

Real concern shone in her eyes; scrutiny too, as if she'd been in this type of situation before. Moreover, her look held no judgment for me being Adrian—not the smoke and mirrors media persona, just the regular, screwed up dude I was. But being so exposed in front of her unnerved me. It was hard enough pushing back all the memories trying to claw their way out.

"You have an amazing voice," I said, my way of admitting I'd been quick to judge.

A tiny smile crept across her face. "You think so?"

"How do you know that song? Pat's not exactly your generation."

"We sang it in our church choir. Our pastor, Dr. Cornell, he loved all kinds of music." She gestured at the image on my T-shirt. "He liked that guy too."

"Your pastor played Hendrix?"

"Was he the guy that lit his guitar on fire?"

I said yes, and I'll admit, was secretly impressed she knew. It was some of the most epic rock footage ever: Jimi at the Monterey Pop Festival coaxing flames out of his Stratocaster. A voodoo priest becoming one with the two most powerful elements on earth: fire and music. Some called him out for being too over the top, but I always dreamed of ending a show that way. (Nowadays, I'd probably get arrested for breaking some fire code.)

"I think Dr. Cornell was a little obsessed with him," she added. "He even bought a house close to the graveyard where he's buried."

And there it was. The slip.

All the blood drained out of my face.

Hendrix was buried in Renton...in Washington state.

I gaped at her in utter disbelief. "You got on my bus in *Seattle?*"

Her mouth formed into an "O" of *oh, shit,* and my mind skidded backward, thinking of the Seattle show. Rain had lashed like hellfire, the city under siege from a particularly wicked squall. Our buses were shrouded in mist, the crew hunched under rain gear, grumpy in the cold. Sound check went longer than usual, being the first show and all. It was the perfect storm, so to speak, for her to slip into the bus undetected.

"Sweet Jesus, girl." My temples started to pulse out of control. I'd operated on the assumption tonight would end with her in an Uber heading home somewhere close to Phoenix. The Pacific Northwest meant a flight. It also meant she'd been on the bus for five days. "Do your parents know where you are?"

"Uh...no," she replied, giving me the impression she had to think about it. "They're out of town. They don't know I'm gone."

"And they left you *alone?*"

"I'm thirteen," she said, with a lift of her chin. "I can be alone."

"Alone at home, maybe. Not in some stranger's bus. You need to call them."

"I don't want to," she said, and for the first time, sounded a little nervous.

I felt it then, like the prick of a needle: complications. More than I'd ever imagined. As the seconds piled up, a thought kept poking at my brain. If she was being abused, would she even cop to it? I doubt she'd be here with me if that were the situation, but in any event, some due diligence was in order. I slid out my phone and thumbed my password, *Suzanne.*

"Just so we're on the same page, what's your full name? And don't even think about lying."

With my fingers poised, ready to type, the wind appeared to come out of her sails. "You're going to google me?"

"Damn straight."

She grudgingly fessed up. "Hastings Fayola Sinclair. F, A, Y, O, L, A."

Surfing, I braced myself for the worst—a missing child or runaway alert— but to my great relief found nothing of any consequence other than an unflattering school photo we all hoped would never surface later in life.

Issaquah Middle School, Washington.

How was she going to get back there without me being involved?

In the throes of wondering what the hell to do next, the dinner I'd completely forgotten about showed up. We both jumped when room service knocked on the door. I thumbed Hastings into the kitchen to lay low and no one was more shocked than me to find Caleb standing in the hall, smiling his keener grin.

He waved both hands over the trolley with a magician's flourish. "Compliments of the house. Thought I'd bring it up personally."

It was startling how even a uniform refused to add years to our number one fan boy. At twenty-seven, Caleb was still a gangly mess of arms and legs, with an electric shock of hair and skin smeared with freckles. The hapless kid that got beat up on the playground solely on principle.

"Uh, thanks, man," I said. "Totally not necessary."

"Totally necessary," he corrected, with a wink. "I got lucky last night, if you know what I mean."

We'd comped him floor tickets to last night's show and from what I'd heard, he went home with a couple groupies, everyone flying high on tequila. I barely recalled seeing him backstage. I had slunk out, in a mood after Suze texted me saying she wasn't going to come to either of the LA shows. In fifteen years, she'd never missed a local gig. That thought alone was enough to make me ill. When warm food smells leaked out from the covered meals, my stomach pitched. I leaned against the doorjamb to steady myself.

"You okay, man?" Caleb moved forward, full of concern. "You look a little pale."

"I think it's just a bug. I'll be fine. I'm going to chill tonight on my own."

He said to call the front desk if I needed any medication, and we shot the shit for another minute or so until I begged off. After he left, I rolled the trolley inside and Hastings asked if she could help with anything. I told her to give me a minute. Lightheaded, everything started to swirl. I took a seat on one of the chairs and fatigue sunk around me like a fog. When my phone started to jig on the table, I barely summoned the motor skills to tilt it upwards.

I skimmed the one liner from Ex, a knot tightening in my throat.

E: We all need to talk.

"I can go into the bathroom if you need to make a call," Hastings offered, misreading my silence.

Right then, my vision started to swim, and Hastings flickered like a projection, a girl starring in the bad B movie spooling across my brain: a shot of a young girl calling her parents from a mystery hotel room a thousand miles from home, telling them she'd be home soon. There'd be questions. Hundreds, I imagined. Hysteria, possibly. A clusterfuck waiting to happen. More things to think about and coordinate and explain. I didn't want to think. I needed to lie down and sleep.

I forced myself to stand. "Let's get out of here."

Her head twitched back and forth like a bird. "Where are we going?"

"To the bus. Just for tonight," I said, surprised how weary I sounded. "I'll figure out a flight for you in the morning."

"A flight from where?" she asked.

"LA. That's our next stop."

She slid off the chair, utterly confused. I'd shooed her off the bus earlier and now she was back on? "What about dinner?"

"If you want to pack yours up, go for it. I'm not hungry."

She wrapped the quesadilla in a napkin, sneaking a look my way. Something had shifted and she couldn't figure out what. What I hadn't told anyone was that in the days and months following my fainting spell in Mexico, there were some iffy moments. My health was a definite concern, and if Sven, the boys, the label, anyone got wind of it, there'd be more scrutiny, more pressure I didn't need. The battle with the boys over songwriting had landed at the exact wrong time. I felt weird and disconnected. Vulnerable. And I didn't want to be alone.

We moved silently to the foyer where Hastings pulled on her sneakers. After shrugging on her backpack, her eyes skipped behind me.

"Um...I was going to ask after dinner." She looked back at me, sheepish. "Would it be okay if I took a shower in here?"

Her stowaway situation, the one I hadn't given any thought to, suddenly smacked me in the face. A flurry of bizarre questions rained down. Did she survive on trail mix the entire time? When did she use the bathroom? Five days without a shower? Just thinking about it gave me the creeps. It didn't feel right leaving her alone in the room—anything could go wrong and would circle back to me if it did—but I couldn't deny her the basic right of cleanliness. And despite the murkiness of her situation, that she wasn't being upfront with everything, the distinction remained clear in my mind: she was troubled, not trouble. We agreed to meet at the bus in half an hour.

I made my way outside where the night had a strange, dreamy

quality. A low quarter moon hung like a painting in the sky. The air buzzed, felt super charged, but as soon as I stepped inside the confines of the bus, the fairylike energy evaporated. I watched a future version of me move about in the space; getting frustrated with the lack of it. A vile taste filled my mouth and even a healthy pour of Grey Goose couldn't get rid of it. So I poured another and sat outside in the dark waiting for her. I told myself not to worry. Tomorrow she'd be back home. I'd figure a way to muddle through. I always did.

But that night, with the hum of the rig's tires underneath my bed, Hastings asleep on one of the couches, a recurring nightmare returned. In Mexico, I'd watched a bullfight on TV, repelled, yet unable to look away. I didn't understand why the bull kept chasing the flag. What hardwired instinct kept fueling it to the point of demise? The event traumatized me enough it infected my dreams every other week. This time, there was a twist. I was the bull and Hastings the matador, flapping her cape. She kept me running, egging me into a place I wasn't sure I wanted to go. I tossed and turned all night, more so than usual. As always, the dream never completed, which was probably a good thing.

Bullfights never ended well.

Not for the bull.

CHAPTER SIX

"Adrian?"

At the sound of her voice, my eyes snapped open. The abrupt yank into wakefulness was disorienting and my heart *boom-boomed* in the darkness.

"Yeah?" I called back.

Through the door, a little louder this time, "There's a phone out here that keeps beeping."

It was morning, or to clarify, it felt like morning. With blackout curtains on every window in my bedroom, it could be midnight or two in the afternoon. I groped around for my iPhone and found it under a pillow, battery drained. What the—? She must be referencing the burner. I flipped around and yanked up a corner of curtain, squinting into the searing bright. Instead of a blurred Interstate, our crew and various roadies hustled back and forth loading in gear at the Staples Center. That's what felt different. We weren't moving. I'd slept through the entire trip. And the interview at nine with The Winnipeg Press. God damn.

"Thanks," I said. "I'll be out in a minute."

I kicked off the covers, so not ready to face the day. It was the busiest day of the tour so far, with an exec meet and greet and photo shoot crammed on top of everything else. And somehow, I would sneak her away at the Staples Center in a zoo of activity.

Right.

Not much I could do about it now, I told myself. As Norm liked to say, I was balls deep. I peeled out of bed and quickly made myself presentable. Hastings looked up as soon I stepped through the door.

"Morning," she said.

"Hey."

It was strange seeing someone in my space again. Hastings sat on the couch all straight-backed, keenly observant and, thankfully, quiet. It would be a dramatic understatement to say I wasn't a morning person. I beelined for the kitchen, unplugging the burner phone from the charger to check the damage. Eight missed calls. Six from Sven. I quickly texted back, asking him to let the journalist know I'd call her back in twenty. A thumbs-up emoji flashed seconds later. I stretched and yawned, still a bit dopey, and plunked a Nespresso pod into the machine.

"You want a coffee?" I asked, holding up a mug.

"No, thank you," she said.

"Tea? Water?"

"A water, please."

I positioned my mug, pushed the BREW button, and dug out a water from the fridge. Handing it to her, our eyes met properly, and when our hands touched, I froze.

"Why are you looking at me like that?" Hastings asked, warily.

In the light of day, the intimacy that had cropped up between us last night suddenly felt...weird. The context was entirely wrong, but I imagined this was exactly what the morning after a one-night stand would feel like. Navigating too much that had been shared too quickly. What made it weirder was how the muted light created a halo glow around Hastings' Afro. A mirror image of Suze, sitting in the same place, on our second tour, when I'd encouraged her to keep her Afro natural instead of straightening it. She'd refused on the basis of me trying to control everything, including her.

"It's nothing," I said. "I just have a lot on my mind."

Hastings cracked the water open and took a small sip, watchful. "Are you feeling better?"

The double whammy of malaise and anxiety that freaked me out post-faint in Mexico hadn't reared its ugly head—yet. Part of why I felt off kilter stemmed from wondering when the other shoe would drop. Not a great way to go about the day.

"A little," I said. "What about you?"

"I'm okay."

My coffee finished brewing and I doctored it with cream from the fridge. Took a slurp. She didn't look okay. Seemed rather disquieted. Join the club. There were things to be said and I made my way to the opposite couch from hers and sat down. She crossed both legs, pulling them closer. Something in the way she kept a small footprint in here and in the hotel, made me wonder if she felt self-conscious about taking up space that wasn't hers.

"You seem like a good kid, Hastings. A good teenager," I was quick to correct. "And I hope you sort your troubles out. I know what it's like when your parents drive you crazy." She stole a cautious, sideways glance. I understood it to be a small confirmation on her part; that I'd touched on the right arena. "I feel like I'm doing the right thing here, getting you on a plane, but please tell me you understand this situation would be bad for both of us if you talked about it?"

She shook her head in a staunch manner. "I won't say anything about you, to anyone. I promise."

"Not even your friends."

After a small hesitation, her gaze dropped. "I don't have a lot of friends," she said, quietly. "Not the close kind."

For someone who hadn't revealed much on a personal level, that felt pretty raw. And judging from how studiously she picked at a hole in her jeans, not entirely comfortable for her to admit. I offered up some solidarity.

"That makes two of us."

"Really?" Her eyes lifted to meet mine. "I thought famous people had lots of friends."

"If I didn't spend so much time in here, maybe I would."

That seemed to trigger something for her, and she did a once over, up and down the bus. "How come you weren't staying in the hotel yesterday? It's so much bigger."

I cracked a cryptic smile. "It's a long story, but the short version is hotels are dirty. I only use them for meals."

"You don't get bored being in here all alone?"

Custom-built in Nashville and tricked out with every perk, there were, admittedly, worse places to wake up in than my bus. But in just five days, she'd experienced the reality: the mind-numbing solitary confinement of bus life. Last night she looked relieved to be sleeping on the couch, freed from the cupboard.

"I'm not going to lie; sometimes it does feel like jail," I said. "You should be happy to go home."

Her arms crisscrossed, tightening around her. "Where's home for you?"

"Here," I said. "For now. Maybe forever." Off her quizzical look, a tad blunter: "It's called divorce. I don't recommend it."

"Oh," she said, embarrassed, looking away. "I'm sorry."

With near-impeccable timing, my burner phone beeped. It was Sven, keeping me on my toes, confirming t-minus ten for the interview. The dog and pony show was off to the races. I shot gunned the rest of my coffee, dumped the mug in the sink and pulled on my Converse at the door.

"Give me an hour or so," I said. "We'll get you to the airport when I come back." I handily didn't mention there was no plane ticket. The thought of leaving a paper trail with my credit card had stopped me from pulling the pin last night. Loading her up with a bunch of cash kept me in the clear, but it was risky in other ways. I'd decide on the best course of action later, when my mind wasn't tripping with twenty other things. I slipped on my sunglasses and reminded her of the most critical thing. "This goes without saying, but I'll say it anyway. Do not leave the bus. For anything. Understood?"

If it wasn't for last night, how she'd handled everything, including coming back after her shower with time to spare, I wouldn't be so quick to leave her alone. The grinding in my jaw, however, made me fully aware I was going out on a serious limb, trusting her.

Hearing the tension in my voice, she nodded obediently. "If you're going to be an hour, maybe I could listen to some of your songs while I wait?"

Somewhere under my ribs, beyond bone, it touched me. In the midst of all this, she still wanted to help. Only later would I come to realize how similar we were. But this was only day two.

"It's been fun, kiddo," I said, "but I got this. You keep working on your singing. Maybe one day our paths will cross again."

With disappointment rising on her face, I stepped outside into a blast of sunshine and seventy-three degrees.

Welcome to LA.

CHAPTER SEVEN

IT TOOK THREE LAPS OF THE ARENA CONCOURSE BEFORE I could get the journalist off the phone. New and young, she clearly felt her questions were *searing* and *insightful* when in fact, the guy from the *LA Times* had asked me the same ones a few days ago. After, I made my way down to the stage to check in with our awesome crew. Most of them were regulars, part of the close-knit SOS family. This tour we'd pared down to basics and everyone was happier for it: fewer trucks, people, and headaches. No complicated special effects. As load-in wound down, I took a moment at the front of the stage. An empty stadium reflected back a sense of responsibility. Our ability to fill seats was never guaranteed, and reviews be damned, so far we'd packed out every venue. In a few hours the arena would be muggy, thick with fans and expectation. The two hours while we were on stage and gave 110 percent was the only thing that made all of this mayhem worthwhile.

I did a silent prayer to Hendrix, my pre-show ritual, and headed back outside just as the boys' bus pulled in. It barely came to a stop before the door flew open and Norm staggered down the stairs, gagging. He bent over and coughed up a loogie with all the grace of a gorilla.

"Awww," I said, walking over. "Princess hung over again?"

He cuffed his mouth and flipped me the bird. "Rule number one: no dumps on the bus. Do I need to make a sign?"

"Ouch. Diego still not feeling well?'

"I thought Mexicans were exempt from Montezuma's revenge," he grumbled.

"He was born in New Mexico," I reminded him. "You know...America."

"His parents are Mexican, dude. DNA knows no borders. Besides, what's the dif?" he asked in all seriousness. "Mexico, New Mexico. It's all one giant dustbowl."

I shook my head. Forget politically correct. Forget social graces. Norm's status was permanent foot in mouth.

"Remember the other day when we talked about the word filter?" I asked.

His phone started to chime, and he pulled it out of the lace-up crotch of his jumpsuit. "Speaking of no filter, fucking hell this one's a live wire," he muttered. "Hold on." He typed furiously, yabbering out loud at his phone. "Why don't you understand? No, I'm not your boyfriend. No, I don't want to be."

"You give them your real number?"

Ex made that mistake years ago and in the space of four days had over two hundred texts from a deluded groupie. He eventually needed a restraining order.

Norm jammed the phone back into his pubes and scowled. "Not anymore."

"Seattle or Portland?" I asked, partly as a test. After a long pause, he said Portland and I laughed in disbelief. "You actually had to think about it."

"At least I'm not resorting to a bunk sock, buddy."

"I don't sleep in a bunk."

"Oh, that's right," he said, waving his hand dramatically. "Lest we forget. Only the best for King Adrian."

My private bus irked Norm. He believed a band should be in the trenches together, but it boiled down to sanity for me. It's impossible to explain how close quarters on the road can crack you. After a month, the sound of someone's laugh could incite a riot. It was a miracle we survived our first tour intact.

"You can pay for your own bus too, you know," I said.

"Maybe if we all made the same money, I could."

Ah, so this is where we are heading.

"Are we really going to have this conversation?" I asked. "Now?"

"Remember last night when you said we'd talk about it tomorrow?"

The business of songwriting, publishing, licensing, and royalties was complex and layered. Tedious was an understatement. But I knew everything about it. When I first started out, my mission to understand the music industry bordered on fanatical. It's why I stalked Mackenzie, aka Mac, until he agreed to meet with me. Mac's clients were the crème da la crème of the industry and as a brash sixteen-year-old with big dreams, he was the only manager I wanted.

Mac made it sound like he was doing me a favor, but five minutes into our meeting it became obvious. He'd listened to my demo and knew gold when he heard it. Music aside, I also had another factor Mac considered equally important in "the success equation" for musicians. As we sat in a back booth at Izzy's Deli on Wilshire, Mac told me point-blank I was a stunner and with my talent, I had the goods to go all the way...if I worked my ass off. Our relationship flourished with a shared love of hard work and hard liquor. He was one of the few people I trusted. He could've taken advantage of me and instead, advised me to control all the publishing rights to my songs. Since I wrote all our songs, music and lyrics, technically, all the rights revenue should be mine. But band dynamics tend to turn janky when money's involved. I didn't want to alienate the boys, and Mac agreed. The deal was I got fifty percent; the boys split the other half three ways.

It wasn't enough for Norm.

Sensing a longer, more drawn out argument I didn't have the energy for, I threw up my hands. "What do you want from me that you haven't already taken?"

"How about you appreciate something beyond your own nose for a change?" Norm challenged right back.

"You think this is all about *my* glory?" I punted a small rock and it sailed in the air. "Look around you. We're a travelling circus. I don't take it lightly. I never have. It's employees, mouths to feed."

"That's what we are to you, isn't it? Employees."

"That's not what—"

"Spare me the lecture," he scoffed. "It's always the same with you."

He yanked a cigarette out from behind his ear, and with a lighter that barely worked, attempted to light it. When he finally got it going, he took a deep drag, his hand shaking. There was something else chewing at him, something bigger, but Norm would gladly splash around in the shallow end of jabs and back-handed comments, backing off whenever it came time to dive into anything deeper. After a lengthy, tense silence he scratched at his spiked, still glittered hair.

"I know you're not thrilled about the songs," he conceded, the cigarette bobbing in the corner of his mouth. "But can we put that aside and just enjoy the next two days?"

"You mean pretend to?"

He took another drag and blew out three perfect smoke rings. "Whatever it takes. Look at the bright side—only nine and a half more months 'til freedom. Be great to actually come out on the other side in one piece this time." He held out the cigarette, his version of a warped peace offering. "C'mon," he said, pushing it closer. "Don't make me beg."

Suze made me stop smoking when I was nineteen, two months before our wedding. There were times I missed it dearly. I took a deep hit and savored the chemical heat in my throat, the head rush. Then I started to cough uncontrollably. Norm grinned. He would always be an ugly duckling but his smile—loopy and unguarded—transformed him.

"Aren't you glad I talked you out of getting that stupid diamond inserted into your tooth?" I asked in between coughs.

"Talked?" Norm took a last drag of the smoke before dropping it and smothering the ember with his bejeweled flip flop. "You threatened to kick me out of the band."

"Did I?"

"Just remember this, dude," he said, pointing to the Size of a Scandal tattoo sprawled across his torso. "It means I'm balls deep. Committed. Think of that once in a while."

A wolf whistle cut across the parking lot and we looked over to see Sven marching toward us, a phone glued to his ear. His other hand signaled us to gather up the troops.

"Uh-oh," Norm said. "Here comes trouble."

Joining us, Sven radiated tenseness. "Yes," he said, to whomever he was speaking to. "They're all here." He glanced over our heads, and we turned around to see a limousine pulling in. "Copy that. It just arrived." After a series of clipped nods and uh-huhs, I knew something unexpected had cropped up.

"Who was that?" I asked when he'd hung up.

Sven slipped the phone back into his belt holster. "Bryce. Change of plans."

A knot twisted in my chest. In five years, Bryce Bentley had wormed his way up from intern to head of A&R at Six Devil Sounds. Although the artist and repertoire department had junior people to run interference with bands when a new album was in the works, he was personally overseeing our next album, although 'looming' was more like it. I could only stomach him in short bursts. He was the kind of guy that walked into a room, figured out who had the most power, and proceeded to brownnose non-stop. Lately, he'd been so far up my ass about the upcoming songs, the rest of him was turning brown.

"The KROQ interview got pulled to this morning," Sven continued. "Some scheduling screwup. They sent that limo. You go straight from KROQ to the Chateau for the executive meet and greet, then the photo shoot, then dinner."

"What?" My heart hopped with all the changes. I glanced back at the bus. "Who set up the dinner?"

"Bryce did. Ziegler, the new Canadian guy, is in town. Attendance mandatory."

Last year, Six Devil formed a loose alliance with Canadian billionaire beer mogul Harvey Ziegler. He'd snatched up interest in a pile of venues, determined to give rival Live Nation a run for their money. Rumor had it he was angling to take over the Six Devil empire from Jordy Schrager, the long-in-the-tooth CEO who'd helped Mac become the player he was. Jordy had built Six Devil from the ground up, however, and the counter-rumor was he wouldn't let his baby be sucked into someone else's vision.

Exile and Diego, sunglasses on and coffees in hand, filed off their bus to join us. Non-fans often confused Ex for Andre 3000 from Outkast. With similar affable smiles and natural magnetism, when either walked into a room, you noticed. Diego was all chill vibe, beard and bifocals, and he loved interacting with fans. Although we tipped Diego to be the cuddly mascot of our group, Ex's gentle giant gregariousness was the glue that held us all together.

Sven quickly filled them in.

"Oh man," Ex groaned. "I just *stopped* being in motion."

"How you doing?" I asked Diego, who looked a little run down.

He cracked a tired smile. "Still a bit verde."

"Just like the toilet bowl," Norm grumbled.

"I'm sick, dude," he snapped. "Vete a la chingada!"

Backtalk from Diego was rare, indeed. With two high-maintenance kids and a controlling wife, he actually enjoyed being on tour. Never complained, stayed out of the squabbles. At thirty-eight, he was the elder statesman of our group, a mantle he rallied hard against...as much as a guy who wore dad jeans could.

"Lucky for you I don't speak Mexican, but c'mon man, what is *this*?" Norm pointed at Diego's Tevas. "Socks and sandals? Is this how you want to be remembered?" He turned to Ex for help. "Could you talk some sense into him? We have an image to uphold."

"I got overalls on," Ex said wryly, acknowledging his faded Osh Koshes.

"But you're naked underneath," Norm argued. "And your nails..." He gestured approvingly at Ex's flip flops, at his fresh pedicure, a skull and crossbones adorning each big toenail. "All I'm asking for is some effort."

The limo horn tooted, and Sven waved back to the driver in acknowledgment. "Time to head out, guys."

Still hoping to buy some time, I suggested, "Why don't you guys get a head start and I'll join in in a bit."

"What?" Diego whipped his head around. "You're not coming?"

Exile gave me a surprisingly cool stare. Right then I remembered I hadn't replied to his text last night. "Since when do we do anything without you?"

"Nope," Sven interjected. "You're performing after the interview. All hands on deck."

Svennie gave me a wide berth on most things, but when it came to keeping the tour and our commitments on track, he was unmovable. Any more pushback would look fishy, although I couldn't help one last over-the-shoulder at my bus. Norm, who'd clocked my earlier look, leered with a devilish grin.

"Yeah, okay. Now I get it. The monk finally breaks down. You got some five-star pussy in there that needs servicing?"

My cheeks flushed with their collective scrutiny. "Shut up."

"You're divorced," he continued. "It's okay to dip your—"

"He said, *shut up*."

Diego looked at Sven with surprise. Ex, too. The bustle of activity around us melted into slow motion, our circle of silence becoming louder. Sven, who gripped his clipboard like a man overboard might clutch a life preserver, offered a terse good luck and hustled away.

Norm raised his star-shaped sunglasses with a *what's-that-all-about* look. "Is it me, or are Stockholm's Swedish knickers in a tighter knot than usual?"

"Chill, dude," I said. "Maybe he's having a bad day. It does happen."

"Of course you'd defend him," Norm flipped back. "He's your personal slave."

Ex shot me a look I couldn't quite figure out and said to Norm, "Maybe if you didn't rail against his home country at every opportunity, Svennie might bring *you* breakfast."

"Why you got such a hate on for Sweden?" Diego asked, genuinely intrigued. "They're the definition of neutral."

Norm considered this. "I don't know," he finally admitted. "What exactly are the Swedes? What do they stand for? No one knows. Its unsettling."

Diego barked a laugh. "Seriously? That's all you got?"

"Hey," Norm said defensively, as Ex and I joined in with disbelieving sniggers. "You know the drill. We've played all those countries up there—Sweden, Finland, Norway. They might as well combine them into one because I can't even tell them apart."

"Oh boy," Ex said, shaking his head. "And that is why we will never let you do an interview on your own."

"Whatever," Norm said with a *suit-yourself* shrug. "This is our town and we are going to *destroy* it." He unleashed an arch smile and corralled us all toward the limo. "Let's go have some fun."

CHAPTER EIGHT

NOT ONLY DID WE HAVE FUN, WE ABSOLUTELY SLAYED THE KROQ gig. On the limo ride over, we drained two bottles of champagne, arrived in high spirits, and cranked out a version of *Starlit Superstar* (one of our biggest hits) so smoking, their phone lines crashed with callers frantic to win tickets. While inching back to the Chateau Marmont through a snarl of traffic, we polished off a third bottle. Lightheaded and loose, we joked, farted, and took the piss out of each other. For a glorious few hours it was like old times. But my mood fizzled when we unloaded into the gothic, shabby-chic lounge of the Chateau and Bryce Bentley—French-cuffed, hair-plugged, body by Krispy Kreme—strode toward us with his shit-eating grin.

"Fellas!"

Fellas. His midwestern roots combined with indefatigable enthusiasm!

Ex slid past me to give him a high five. "Whassup, BB?"

"How'd the interview go?" Bryce asked.

"We killed it," Norm gloated, kicking a friendly leg in my direction. "And you were in fine form, weren't you, buddy?"

Diego, looped from the champs and whatever medication he'd

gobbled, was in a much better mood. "And for once you didn't have to correct anyone."

Ex laughed. "Or walk out."

Bryce narrowed his eyes in my direction. "Subtle as a sledgehammer, right?"

The Bentley made a big to-do about being chummy-chummy with artists, playing the good guy, and for the most part, he got away with it. But his snakebite smile didn't fool me. Few knew he was a failed musician, because he kept that buried deep. But it explained a lot. It had to fester, catering to rock stars he'd once dreamt of being. And since I was the pinnacle of a mountain he'd never ascend, he took every opportunity to slag me.

So I threw it right back at him. "Me or you?"

"Duh. You, obvs," Norm said, oblivious as always to Bryce's smarm and insincerity. "Eventually everyone learns not to piss you off." He tossed his fringed scarf over a shoulder with an impish grin. "Except me, of course."

A ripple of excited murmurs erupted behind us and, recognizing the sound, I immediately looked for an escape route. The Chateau prided itself on being egalitarian: it catered to everyone from superstars to no stars and thus was a celebrity-hunting favorite; the reason I avoided it. A group of Jersey Shore types had recognized us and were yanking out their phones. This kind of situation could escalate to a fever pitch and sure enough, as the dreadful snapping filled the air, the buzz in the lounge reached the patio outside and everyone started to rubberneck. I shouldered my way past Bryce to the elevators as a roided-out dude in a wife beater yelled, "Yo, Adrian! Give me a smile!"

"Hey," Bryce snarled, grabbing onto him. "Beat it. No photos." He staved off the encroaching wall of fans with surprising authority, allowing us safe passage into the elevator.

When were all safely crammed inside, I said to Bryce, "Sven been teaching you crowd control?"

"I only took half the course. That's why no one's bleeding."

The elevator creaked upwards and we digested Bryce's comment with somber nods, all of us privy at one point to Sven's carnage.

"So what's the 911 on this Ziegler guy?" I prompted. "Any insider intel?"

Harvey Ziegler sounded slimy on the conference call last week—Adrian this, Adrian that. (There was a direct correlation to the number of times someone said my name in a conversation and how much I disliked him or her. It wasn't surprising he and Bryce bonded like thieves.)

"Deep pockets. He's willing to spend," Bryce said, vaguely.

"And?"

"And try to play nice. For once."

That he was forced to look up at me explained the nip in his voice: the tragedy of short man syndrome.

"I'm always nice," I said angelically. "Until you piss me off."

Norm snickered in the corner.

"What?" I asked.

"Yo, Adrian!"

"Yo, shut your face."

Ex fired a grim look at Norm's crotch. "Y'all gonna make me heave, falling outta that jumpsuit."

"Scored this beaut at a vintage store." Norm preened, holding both arms out for us to admire the stripes. "Designer section."

"You sure it wasn't the Christmas section?" I asked.

Even Diego had to laugh at that. "You do look like a candy cane."

Norm turned to Bryce and sniffed. "You see what I have to put up with? Commoners. All of them."

On the penthouse level, a security guard with wraparound shades nodded as we all shuffled past him and inside. Cleared out for the reception, the main living area smelled of citrus and sunshine, everything bright and breezy. Scattered around the room and on the deck outside, suit-clad men clutched drinks and plates of appetizers. I recognized a few of the Six Devil executives but not the strange looking man who glided over, a shark dressed in Armani.

"Adrian," he said. "Finally, we meet. Harvey."

On the phone his soft, halting voice brought to mind an octogenarian. In person, I couldn't tell if he was fifty or eighty. Trim, with a sweep of dark hair, he glowed preternaturally and there were almost no lines on his face. Without even touching him, I felt like I'd been slimed.

"Hi," I said. "Thanks for the spread. It wasn't necessary."

All manners of seafood, meat, and vegetables were artfully arranged on buffet tables camped along the far wall. A chocolate fountain gurgled near the bar. Nothing at the Chateau was cheap, but for a billionaire this was a drop in the bucket. With a casual hand gesture, Harvey waved my comment away with that exact confidence.

"It's the least I could do. For someone who has the platinum touch." He raised his glass and gestured toward the boys, who were busy inspecting the sea of premium liquor at the bar. "And please, introduce me to your crew."

As Ziegler regaled the boys with news of events he had set up for us in Canada, I scuttled into the corner with a vodka soda and checked my phone for an update on Mac's arrival. As if the universe read my mind, a voice boomed from down the hall.

"You need to see my ID? Are you fucking serious? How about you step aside and be thankful I don't get your ass fired."

The quiet titter of cocktail party conversation screeched to a halt.

In no uncertain terms, Mac had arrived.

There were guys like me who got stares based solely on genetics. Mac inspired slack-jawed awe the way Ayers Rock or the Pyramids did —and not just because he was similar in size. In Gucci sunglasses, a black velvet three-piece suit, and vintage high tops, if there was such a thing as a musical gangster, Mac was it. A rough-and-tumble Israeli, rumor had it he was once tied to the Mossad. Let's just say he didn't ascend to the top of the industry by being polite.

Ziegler nervously straightened his tie as Mac strutted his way over to us. "Mr. Rosenthal," he said, "I've heard so much—"

"Fuck what you've heard," Mac growled, taking my face in both hands to lay a wet kiss on each cheek—a tradition I was forced to endure. He stepped back and assessed me. "How are you? You look thin. You eating enough? Or drinking too much, like me?"

"I'm good," I said. "Better."

Mac whipped off his shades and gave Norm, Ex and Diego each a hard, but endearing look. "You mofos doing okay? I know it's only week one."

Norm stuck out a cheek and tapped his finger against it. "C'mon. Who's your daddy?"

"You're sick, Norm," Mac laughed, "but that's why I love you."

He proceeded to lick Norm's face and when he was done, Ex held up his hands to speak for both himself and Diego. Ziegler, his expression still one of stunned dismissal, paled. He downed the rest of his drink and looked like he wanted to say something, but Mac grabbed my hand and pushed past him.

"Pardon us ladies while we catch up on some quick gossip."

He dragged me outside onto the far end of the deck. It was a beautiful LA day—clear, not too hot. We both slipped our sunglasses on and Mac spread his arms on the balustrade, taking in the view. He was a man in his element: at the top of his field, at the literal top of a city where pecking order was everything.

"The kids miss you," he finally said. "They keep asking where Uncle Adrian is."

"I miss them too. They're really sweet."

"They're sure as hell not getting that from me," he chuckled. "I was never cut out to be a father. You, on the other hand. If you need to crash at my place—anytime."

When I came back from Mexico, Mac insisted I stay at his Malibu compound, away from prying eyes. He had a young son and daughter from two of his three previous wives, and I'd wake up in the morning with them standing like soldiers beside my bed, all rubbery smiles and eager energy. "Time to get up, Uncle Adrian!"

Mac's Peruvian nanny was happy to let me take over. We built sandcastles on the beach. I tickled them until they screamed. Most nights I put them to bed. Mac left the house at 6 a.m. and when his Lamborghini roared back into the driveway, it was often midnight.

"When the tour's done, I'm buying another place out here," I said.

Mac nodded with approval. "I don't know how you lasted so long in Mexico. One week in the tropics and I'm out."

I stared out at the horizon, eyes not charting anything. "It was far away."

He glanced over. "Tell me the truth. Is this too close for comfort?"

Mac indicated the Chateau as "this," and his ability to zone in on my thoughts was part of his forensic charm. My old Hollywood Hills house was a couple miles away from here, only it was Suze's house now.

"A little," I admitted. "But whatever."

"Don't whatever me. But don't blame me, either. Ziegler insisted on this place. Fucking tourist." Mac's office resided on a quiet street in Santa Monica, a location chosen not only because of its proximity to Malibu. With a kind of sociopathic glee, Mac relished making the Hollywood or Burbank-based label execs suffer in traffic because he could. Dragging Mac into Hollywood, the Chateau no less, was unprecedented and Ziegler would one day experience severe repercussions.

"How's Suze doing, anyway?" he asked in a gentler tone.

I leaned onto the balustrade. "She hung up on me the other night. And she's not coming to either show."

"Look at me," Mac ordered, and when I did, he waved two fingers back and forth between our eyes. "You doing okay? For real?"

"How many times are you going to ask?"

"As many as I want."

"I'll let you know if anything changes."

"No, you won't and we both know it. Give me some fucking credit."

I broke off his gaze. "Like you said, it's only week one."

"Exactly," he stressed. "You need a lifeline, you call me. 24/7. Got it?"

"Got it."

I could tell he wasn't entirely convinced—and with good reason. Aside from Suze, the unfinished business with Hastings weighed on my mind. I'd managed to wrangle two short minutes with her before we took off for KROQ. With Norm yelling "Hurry up!" from the idling limo, I'd rattled off the change in plans, promising to bring her some food, telling her to stay inside with the door locked. She'd taken the news with surprising calmness.

"FYI," Mac continued, keeping it conversational, "there's something about Ziegler's Canadian ass that rubs me the wrong way."

I looked over. "Really? I don't think he could tell."

Mac smiled back, a flash of brilliant implants in his black beard. "These are the moments I wish you *were* my son so I could smack you, but seriously. I'm keeping my eye on him. You should too."

"What's your radar telling you?" I asked. After thirty-five years in the biz, Mac could sniff out talent, or a rat, in a heartbeat.

"Between us girls, ole Jordy's retirement date will be sooner than later, but you know what it's like when there's an empire to be had. The swords and the egos come out. Shit gets ugly. Ziegler's positioned himself just in time for the blood bath. And a new general always wants to leave his mark."

At the sound of Bryce's honking laugh, I spun around. Back in the suite, Bryce and Ziegler were cozied up to the boys. "You think Bentley's making a play? He's been extra irritating lately."

"Once a schmendrik, always a schmendrik. He'd suck Jordy's dick if he thought it would help." He lowered his sunglasses to give them a desultory once over. "Look at him. Lapping up whatever Maple Syrup says. Pathetic. You know they'll both be at the Toronto shows?"

"Great."

"I need you to be ears to the ground up in Canada. Don't trust anyone, especially Ziegler. I won't be up there for any of those dates, as you know."

"How long are you banned for?"

"Who knows, who cares," he scoffed, like it was badge of honor to have an entire country slam its doors in his face. "Everything Canada has, we have better. The point is, with your contract up after this album, it's shifty times. I know it. They know it." He lowered his voice. "I've already gotten some offers. Not saying who or how much. Gotta play everybody off each other to maximize."

"You don't think Six Devil would match any offer?"

He took his time positioning the delicate answer. "You pushed them with your disappearing act," he finally said. "Should it matter? On paper, no. The B-sides worked out, now the tour. The thing is, no one likes to be left holding dicks in the wind. Best behavior makes us all look good and keeps the money flowing, all right?"

Subtle when he needed to be, the small warning was there and duly noted. But one of his best qualities was not lingering once he'd made a point, and he transitioned from business chitchat with a stretch, both arms skyward.

"Is it just me, or does Ziegler remind you of Dracula with that freaking windswept hair?" he asked, shooting another dubious look in his direction.

"A Just for Men dye job gone horribly wrong."

Mac snickered. "Whaddya say we go party away some of his billions?"

I kicked off the balustrade with a smile. "Now you're talking."

And party we did.

We were all flying high when we stumbled down to the bungalow for our photo shoot. A buxom photo assistant with a stud in her tongue was enough to distract Norm, who usually groused about me being positioned slightly ahead of everyone else. Dinner followed—fresh crab and lobster, wine flown in from France—and was enjoyed in a private room where we could let our hair down. Stuffed to the point of comatose, we unloaded back at the Staples Center just as the backup band took to the stage.

Before joining the chaos of our dressing room, I snuck back to the bus. During dinner, I'd toyed with the idea of sending Hastings off tonight. Less eyeballs. Less hassle. But she was out cold on the couch. I didn't have it in me to wake her up. Besides, one more night wouldn't make a difference. I draped a blanket over her, changed, and left a doggie bag of rice and vegetables on the kitchen table.

When I landed backstage, all worries of flights and teenage girls melted away. It was a hero's welcome. Friends I hadn't seen in months were crammed shoulder to shoulder. The good vibes flowed and so did the booze. It was impossible not to get caught up in the revelry. As intermission passed the half hour mark, Sven stuck his head in and said it was time.

We made our way to the stage as the stadium lights dimmed, and the roar of the crowd reverberated under my shoes. Chants of "SOS! SOS! SOS!" started, and goose bumps flashed up both arms. There were always nerves as we came out. No way you could be human and not feel the anticipation. We high-fived each other with dumb, drunk smiles and walked out in the order we always did: Diego, Norman, Exile, me. The noise turned deafening when I came out. As we settled, doing last-minute adjustments, the dark throb of humanity speckled with lights as all the phones lit up, swaying like lanterns. Women at the front screamed my name. Shirtless, tattooed guys pumped their fists, frantic, seconds away from creating a deadly mosh pit.

All of us on stage, cloaked in darkness—it felt like a womb. The crowd was our lifeline, feeding us. When I strummed the first chord or Exile's drum kicked in and fans recognized the song, there was a dangerous surge in energy. Pressure would build, the screams would block out any thoughts. The stadium disappeared and for a frozen moment, everything would go quiet. In those few seconds it was just me on stage, tension wound as tight as my guitar strings, the release seconds away.

Every night it was a messy, bloody embryonic explosion.

The crowd and us, reborn.

It was the closest thing to a high I could think of, and just like a high, the feeling never lasted.

In this case, it ended with a sucker punch right between my eyes.

CHAPTER NINE

It was a horrible morning, even before it happened.

In the dark of my bedroom, splinters of hot white bored deeper into my skull if I dared move. When I finally dislodged my tongue from the roof of my mouth, a piece of skin came off with it and the sickly taste of warm blood made me gag. I begged every God to let me pass out and smash-cut forward into a functioning state.

There were hangovers...and then there was this.

As I lay there cursing myself, soft noises drifted through the wall. It was predawn quiet when I'd staggered onto the bus and if Hastings was awake then, I don't recall any of our conversation. I flipped onto my stomach and saw my phone glowing on the nightstand. 10:34 a.m. Hastings needed to go, but sleep was a priority. As I reached to turn it off, an incoming email flashed on the screen.

It was my own stupid fault for looking at it.

Dearest Adrian,

I wanted to let you know I've sold the house. Bev Stroller is the agent. (You might remember her daughter Tamara; the one I thought you should marry.) I move in two weeks and need to get rid of your guitar. If you send Suzanne to collect it, please make sure she's on the drugs. I don't want a scene like last time.

By the way, I met someone else. Her name is Hillary Sanchez and no, she's not Mexican. She was in my grief support group, also widowed. Apparently, her son is a fan of your music.

Jarred.

Wiping away crust welded onto both eyes, I reread it in disbelief. It wasn't the impersonal "Dearest Adrian;" I'd been dealing with that on every birthday card since I learned to read. And it wasn't the digs at Suze, although they hurt, like he knew they would. Mind spooling, I scrolled through my contacts and pushed MOM/HOME. He answered on the second ring.

"Adrian."

So he'd finally sprung for call display. A miracle.

"Hi," I said, my voice froggy and hungover.

"You sound…indisposed."

"I just woke up."

He let the silence grow—an extension of his never-ending disapproval. In his world, real men were awake at daybreak, no matter what.

"How are you?" I asked.

"I'm assuming you read my email?"

"That's why I'm calling."

"Then you know how I am."

I closed my eyes. *Take it easy on him. Maybe this is his way of reaching out.*

"And you know I just started another tour," I said. "Assuming you read *my* last email."

"I saw it," he said, offering nothing else.

I saw it. Never mind that I poured my heart out, agonized over what to write, hoping maybe it would change things. I pushed myself upright and endured the waves of agony until they ran their course.

"Why are you doing this?" I asked, emotion charging out. "I told you I wanted to buy the house."

"I had a good offer."

"I'll offer more. Double. Triple."

He let out a little sound of disgust. "Just to prove you can buy anything you want?"

At some point, no matter what the topic, money was where our conversations ended up. Money he never accepted from me; considered it beneath him.

"So that's it? You're just going to sell it? Never mind that it might actually mean something to me?"

"If I recall," he said, unmoved, "you couldn't pack up fast enough to move into Suzanne's house. You certainly weren't attached to it back then."

"Did I have a choice?"

He paused. "I always liked Suzanne, despite what you thought."

"Bullshit." I kicked away the duvet, suddenly boiling hot. "It's all strategy with you. No mention of selling the house, and then you throw out a two-week window for me to pick up my stuff when you know I'm not available. That guitar is priceless."

My vintage Flying V was a beauty. There were only a handful made between 1958-59, and the good ones didn't change hands often. Pre-financial crisis, they were going for over half a million; a dealer scored mine for three twenty. Even Kirk from Metallica, owner of another rare V, texted me and said congrats.

"Not really," he said. "According to my research, it's worth around three hundred thousand dollars."

"Then sell it. Leave me the house."

After great deliberation, he sighed. "Don't you have people? Or why doesn't Suzanne come get it? She dropped it off. If you could call it that."

I'd left everything behind in my dash to Mexico, including the V. Locked in a climate-controlled room built specifically for it, I had the only key and figured it was safe. But after one of our spectacular blowouts, Suze busted the lock and drove to Long Beach with the guitar, claiming it was evil just like Pops and they deserved each other. Had it happened on a Monday or Tuesday, the grisly scene might've flown under the radar. But on a Sunday afternoon, the whole neighborhood, nosy and hungry for any gossip at the best of times, got an eye-and earful. Some jerk posted a video of her and Pops screaming at each other in the front yard and it crushed me to watch—Suze unhinged.

"Or," Pops added, because he loved having the last word, "is it too embarrassing for her to slum it in our little neighborhood?"

Hammers pounded on my brain. It hurt to think. To believe this was my father. The frustration building under my skin erupted. In one swift karate-kick move, I splintered the bedroom door open and stormed past the remains. Hastings, wrenched out of sleep, bolted upright on the couch. She flopped her hands around in blind panic, looking for her glasses.

"Stop it, Pops, just fucking stop it."

"I told you from day one she was—"

"I know what you told me!" I yelled. "I heard you every time."

"Her parents were at the store yesterday and didn't even say hello," he sniffed, implying some injustice had been served. "I know they saw me."

"Maybe they didn't want to. Maybe they didn't want to get sucked into another useless, depressing, negative conversation."

"They—"

"Or maybe," I said, talking over him the way he always did to me, "they didn't want to stink like fucking pepperoni."

It was a low blow, maybe the lowest. And in the awful silence after, we were right back there, at Suze's parents' house in Rancho Palos Verde.

On a beautiful September afternoon, Pops and I were camped outside in deck chairs and I'd love to say we were admiring the ocean-front view. The reality was, I'd pulled him outside before things got ugly. That I'd been living with her family for three years was enough of a slight. Forced into a tour of the glass and steel modern Suze's Father, Hank, had built after his tech start-up was bought out, all of Pops' money insecurities festered like algae on a pond.

When he saw the sprawling ocean-view room Suze and I shared, he whispered loud enough for Hank to hear, "Is this why you live with them? To pretend you're better than us?"

Whatever prize there was for remaining calm, Hank won it in

spades. So furious even my bones ached, I literally dragged Pops onto the deck and we had it out. While we both sulked in our chairs after, the infamous conversation drifted out from the kitchen window.

Suze's mother, Daphne, to Hank, "What's wrong, honey?"

"That man," Hank replied. "It takes all my strength. If I didn't love Adrian so much..."

"Don't let him get to you. He's a bitter, cheap man. I mean, Lord Almighty, look at this. Ten pounds of cold cuts for a housewarming gift? They were likely destined for the garbage."

"It's a sad state. Elena's working two jobs to keep them afloat. We're footing the bill for the wedding."

"You can't ever bring that up."

"When it's your only son?"

"Honey, don't start. My book club couldn't believe it when I told them. All I can say is be thankful *you* don't stink like fucking pepperoni."

It was their laughter, partly. Pops pretended not to hear but if he'd gripped the arms of the patio chair any tighter, he might've snapped them in two. Mostly, it was about Daphne trash talking Pops to her husband. A successful black husband. Without saying goodbye, Pops stomped down the deck stairs and drove home. We didn't talk for three months.

Now, he had plenty to say.

"I'd rather have some no-name whisper behind my back than live down a lifetime of shame," Pops said, his voice steely. "Maybe if you'd stuck with jazz, none of this would've happened."

A reek of sour fumes seeped through my skin, last night's alcohol boiling inside me. I pounded my fist against the wall with a kind of hopeless fury, because it meant nothing. It would change nothing.

"You can't forgive and forget, can you?" I yelled. "Not once."

"Forget? *Forget?*" Now he was shouting. On the couch, Hastings rocked back and forth in a tight ball, mewling in a strange, high-pitched voice. "Your mother would still be alive if it wasn't for you," he said. "I'll never forget that. Goodbye Adrian."

The exact chain of events after that became fuzzy. Time moved in slow motion. The last thing I could accurately place was Hastings ducking for cover under the kitchen table when the coffee machine hurtled off the counter. *Bam! Bam! Bam!* Coffee mugs disintegrated against the wall in a dust ball of crockery. I ripped open the fridge door and Fiji water bottles launched out in a steady stream of missiles, my arms flinging them as fast as I could. When the blackout frenzy finally let go, the sheer act of staying upright proved impossible. Like a piece of rotten timber, I collapsed onto my knees into the cool of the open fridge.

Good bloody morning.

CHAPTER TEN

IF I'D SEEN A VIDEO OF MY DESTRUCTIVE RAGE, I WOULDN'T have believed it. The bus was a disaster: apocalypse by way of Target. The only thing missing was a haze of napalm. Hastings slowly crawled out from under the kitchen table on all fours, a spooked deer taking in the aftermath. She inched toward the kitchen sink, took out the garbage can, and started to pick up the shrapnel.

"Don't," I told her, my voice ragged. "I'll do it."

Her still-frightened eyes met mine. "It has to get cleaned up."

"Don't. Just sit. Please."

She slunk onto the banquette and made herself very small. With enormous effort, I staggered to my feet and landed with a thud across from her. My emotions were flying high, a tangled mess. I felt sick to my stomach. Every inch of me glistened with sweat. Hastings wouldn't look at me. Her breath came in fits and spurts. I grabbed the TV remote off the window ledge and thumbed the TV on. All I wanted was the mercy of peace, but Hastings' sunken-headed muteness killed me. I cranked the TV volume higher and flipped through channels, nothing registering until a CNN reporter caught my eye. Buffeted by wind and torrential rain, he struggled to commentate as the ticker at the bottom of the screen scrolled by: *Devastating rain and mudslides hit the Pacific Northwest.*

"I'm on Mountainside Drive in Issaquah, Washington, approximately twenty miles east of Seattle," he said, "where several homes have been washed away in a horrific flash mudslide."

Like a bird dog sensing prey, Hastings' head snapped toward the screen.

"The hillsides of Squak Mountain are no strangers to mudslides and sinkholes. The area was once home to several coal mines, and the abandoned shafts and coal tunnels that run under the suburban homes on the surface have collapsed and caused significant damage in the past. With unprecedented rainfall in the last seven days, a series of earthquakes and aftershocks has compounded the situation. In addition to the sinkhole into which two homes disappeared, a flash mudslide ripped across the area minutes later dragging trees, rocks and other debris along a destructive path."

The camera cut to the swath of deadly mud. It streaked over the remains of a house and down an embankment, debris and foliage littered in the mess. Only a crumbled maze of foundation remained. When I looked over at Hastings, her face was a mask of horror. A disturbing chill crept up my spine.

"You know this area?" I asked.

With a wave of her hand, she silenced me.

The reporter continued, holding onto his hat. "One of the residents, Kathy Huetta, witnessed her neighbor's home disappear in a matter of seconds." He turned to a plump woman, her jacket hood pulled tight around a puckered, pale face, glasses splattered with rain. "Kathy, can you describe what you saw?"

"It was just horrible," she said, her voice catching. "One minute, the house was there and the next, gone."

"Information is still coming in, but it's believed the family had just arrived home from a trip when the slide came down."

Kathy put a hand to her mouth, visibly upset. "I'm praying for them. I'd only met them at church a few times, and they were salt of the earth people. African American. From North Carolina, originally.

The wife, she couldn't have children. They were foster parents to different kids over the years."

"Were there any foster children in the house?" the reporter asked. "Can you speculate?"

"Yes, I believe a young girl. Hastings." Kathy's close-set eyes disappeared as she blinked away tears. "They're gone, all of them, I just know it."

I bolted upright as the screen went black. Hastings' hand pulled back off the remote. A distant roar flooded into my ears and air started to muscle its way around me, an invisible pressure closing in.

"Holy shit," I whispered.

Hastings stared straight ahead, breathing so shallow I wasn't even sure she was. I reached for her arm and it was ice cold. It felt like I'd fallen into quicksand: a sinking struggle to find the right words when none would ever do.

"Are you okay?" I asked, stupidly.

Her head turned in slow motion. A thick, strangled sob spilled out of her mouth before she burst into tears.

Of course she wasn't okay.

It would never be okay.

This was the complete opposite of okay.

CHAPTER ELEVEN

TEMPORARY INSANITY.

It's my only defense.

I must've suffered from some mental problem because no one in his or her right mind would do what I did.

When my bus made a slow, creaky turn from the 110 onto the I-5 North, it was almost midnight. A whole day of driving lay ahead. Our next stop: Vancouver, Canada. Under normal circumstances, backtracking up the coast would be an exercise in frustration, except normal didn't apply anymore and I needed all the time I could to wrap my head around this.

In the darkness, still coming down from the show, I nursed a drink while Hastings, finally asleep, snored softly on the couch. That I managed to pull off tonight's performance was a miracle. All day, my booze-addled brain stuttered and sifted through the remains of our respective bottoming-outs: my childhood home gone in a figurative sense, the literal demolition of hers.

Salvage, on any level, felt impossible.

The bus revved and growled as it climbed to cruising speed, and I let the movement have its way with me. I debated another vodka and decided against it; my judgment was already clouded. After tucking

Hastings' blanket around her, I staggered off to bed. I wasn't entirely sure what I felt, only that I was freaking out, and not going to deny it.

Thirteen hours later we made a pit stop in Medford, Oregon. While the bus fueled up, I tracked down an Uber. The driver waited in the Target parking lot with the meter running and on the return trip, fat, dark clouds hung menacingly in the sky. Pedestrians on the street were shadowy silhouettes. After the brightness and frantic energy of LA, everything felt dulled, moving in slow motion.

Back on the bus, I fixed us sandwiches—tuna melt for me, vegetarian on rice bread for her. At the kitchen table, she mowed through an entire bag of sweet potato chips and I could tell her mind was grinding, like mine. What exactly should we say to each other in this kind of situation?

In yesterday's aftermath, once I'd slept off my hangover and we reconvened in the late afternoon, both of us still raw, the truth finally emerged. Her birth parents and brother had died in a car crash when she was nine. She'd been a foster kid ever since. The now deceased Coleys were her third set of foster parents. A river of fresh tears poured down her face when I asked how it worked with the foster system, and if she could be placed with another family. She told me point blank she wasn't going back.

"I'm going to New Orleans," she'd pronounced. "I'm going home."

It took some additional digging to unearth more of her story. As it turned out, she grew up in New Orleans and hopped my bus knowing full well we were playing the Big Easy in three weeks. I distinctly remembered the sense of relief I'd felt, for a millisecond; light appearing at the end of the crazy tunnel. Someone in New Orleans could take her. A hand-off was imminent. And that's when the hallucinogenic situation morphed into a bad trip. I'd asked who she'd be staying with, why they didn't arrange her travel, and the look on her face said it all.

There was no one.

The details trickled out minutes later. Her parents were only children and she had no aunts and uncles, and both sets of grandparents were deceased. She would've taken a Greyhound except Louisiana was too far—they wouldn't allow a thirteen-year-old to travel alone. Hence, my bus.

That was all I could absorb yesterday.

It took all of this morning to formulate a proper decision. I finished chewing a bite of sandwich and gave voice to my plan.

"We're driving back through Seattle," I said. "We need to connect with your foster agency and—"

"No," she interrupted, eyes flashing, surprisingly adversarial. "I told you. I'm going to New Orleans."

"And do what? Wander the streets? Seattle. New Orleans. Timbuktu. It doesn't matter. You're not walking off this bus without a definite place to go."

With my harsh delivery, she slumped back. I could feel the nervous energy rushing through her. Or maybe it was rushing through me. I forced myself to sound calm.

"I don't think you understand how serious this is."

Whatever cloak of denial I'd imagined she'd wrapped herself in, whipped off with ferociousness. "I do understand! I know this is serious. Stop treating me like a kid."

Her blast of anger scorched us into an eerie silence. The bus lurched, finding the gear as it started the climb toward Grant's Pass. Our eyes skipped around, careful not to land on each other.

"I'm sorry for yelling," she finally said. "I just..." She started to wring her hands, something she did a lot of yesterday. "I don't want any more foster parents. I hate Seattle. Everything about it. Everything was better in New Orleans. I just want to go home. Please."

Every fiber of her being was behind that statement. That yearning, the desire for something stable. I understood. I'd fought hard to escape Long Beach—away from Pops and his negativity; away from the teachers who said I'd never make it. But the city knew me for who I really was: Adrian Johnson, the kid who skateboarded the streets, the kid who palmed five and ten dollar bills to the bar bouncers who let me watch the bands, the kid who dared to dream. You only have one hometown and it defines you, whether you admit it or not.

I stared out the window, at the stretch of I-5 I'd traversed countless times. Two years ago, on this same patch of interstate, I'd headed South to the Coachella Music Festival. We were headliners that year, a far cry from almost a decade ago when, as up-and-comers, we'd played one of our most blistering sets in the opening time slot on a tiny stage. Norm, day drunk, on his back and dressed in a onesie, writhed like a snake while I hovered over him coaxing screams of feedback from my Les Paul. The frothed-up crowd went apeshit. Videos went viral. Already on the radar of several labels, after that gig, a feeding frenzy of offers broke out. Back then none of us knew what we'd explode into. Or what we'd lose as a result.

I glanced over at Hastings, face now buried in her hands. I had to make a decision. Fast. I wasn't equipped to deal with a teenager. I was light years away from being a stable provider. The logical solution was sending her back to foster care. They knew the right thing to do.

Or did they?

Never one to trust the system, I sure as hell wouldn't want to be at the mercy of it. I could only imagine that anything was better for Hastings other than a fresh set of foster parents, complete strangers with no context to a single event in her life. But I couldn't just drop her in New Orleans. My conscience wouldn't allow a young girl to drift homeless in a huge city. Whether I wanted to admit it or not, I was now complicit in her situation. And as an adult, I needed to do the right thing. But my track record of doing the right thing hadn't been stellar as of late.

"How tall are you?" I asked.

Her face crept out of her hands. Tears clung, ready to fall. "Four feet, I think. Why?"

"I take it you're not claustrophobic?"

"No," she said, and with the flickering light of fear in her eyes, "Why?"

I put aside my sandwich, appetite gone.

If I wasn't going to hell already, this would pretty much clinch the deal.

CHAPTER TWELVE

VANCOUVER WAS EXACTLY AS I REMEMBERED IT. Skyscrapers clustered downtown. Moist Pacific air that left a taste of salt on the back of my throat. Clouds blanketed the city in flat, moody light, and I embraced it, because the alternative was something far darker.

When we crossed the border last night, rain had sleeted sideways with a howling wind. Years ago, they brought in a dog: a stout German Shepard with inch-long incisors, yanking hard on the leash. This time, the customs officer was new on the job, and suitably impressed with my surroundings and stature. Had no qualms asking for an autograph after he'd poked around. Yet it still felt like an eternity before he finally waved us through. And even now, as Hastings nursed a bowl of oatmeal across from me, it was there: the pain in my jaw, in the muscles running under my cheeks. With a clusterfuck of immense magnitude on the line, it took a lot to keep a neutral expression stamped on my face.

I couldn't even imagine what the past forty-eight hours had been like for her. I only saw the result. Any spark within her had been snuffed and she'd turned rigid, the reality of her affairs beginning to crystallize. I'm pretty sure the sound I heard last night was her—crying herself to sleep.

"I know the border was scary. It was scary for me too. But you did great," I said stupidly, as if congratulations were the order of the day.

She dragged her eyes to meet mine. There was no dignified way to talk about what we'd done.

"Do I need to do that again?"

"Once more, after Toronto," I said.

A lone tear spilled down the swell of her cheek. "I really screwed up."

Yes, she'd created a helluva situation but there was something very significant to remember. I reached for her hand and it was so tiny, smothered in mine. "You had no control over the weather, over what happened. And you need to think about this. You could've been *in* that house. So this is better. Even if it seems worse, it's better."

Her face clouded, a grimness that didn't agree at all with my optimism. It was one of those lose-lose situations—trying to find a sliver of brightness in a mountain of despondency. But I needed to keep my own spirits lifted, for other matters. Another call with Suze loomed—the issue of rescuing my Flying V from Pops—and I wasn't sure she'd answer this time around.

Reluctant to leave Hastings alone, I'd been cooped up for too long and needed some me time. "You okay if I stretch my legs for a bit?" I asked. "I'll bring back lunch."

She nodded listlessly. "I'll probably sleep. I'm pretty tired."

I asked if she ate sushi, she said yes, and off I went.

In the parking lot, Big Daddy kibitzed with the other drivers, their laughter and cigarette smoke drifting over. Like most drivers, Big Daddy was an odd duck. Imagine a Texan Santa Claus after a rough night, hit repeat, and you get the idea. After thirty years on the road, he'd developed some interesting quirks. When he drank, it was only crème de menthe over ice in a plastic Philadelphia Flyers mug. (His psychic's orders, apparently.) He saw me exit the bus and waved with what was left of his left hand. The middle and pinky fingers were hacked off at the base, something to do with a murky trip to Russia in the 80s. I never pressed for details. One of the things I loved about him was he never asked questions, so I returned the favor.

I waved back but bypassed them, wandering down to the waterfront where small, tug-like ferries crisscrossed a protected inlet, the water calm on a day with no wind. Cyclists and runners buzzed along the sea wall that wrapped the city's perimeter. Two years ago, Suze and I sat on the other side of the inlet, near a big public market and had the mother of all arguments. At that point, her depression remained officially undiagnosed. I'd suspected, which was why I'd insisted she join me on tour. She'd grudgingly agreed.

Suze hated the bus, the touring life. Day to day, she never knew which one of me she'd get. A man of extremes, I swung from focused to tired to cranky to amped. I could never relax until the tour was over. Worse, having her around ruined what little routine I could carve out. She'd tagged along, but her depression worsened and so did the cracks in our relationship. Tired of battling me, she started hanging out more and more with the boys. It was nothing at first, and then everything.

With a sensation in my stomach bubbling, I pulled out my phone and thumbed the screen to bring up the number pad. Suze was still number one on my speed dial although I could say with full confidence it wasn't the other way around.

Remain calm.

"Hi," she said, answering just as I'd given up hope.

"Hey. It's me."

"I know."

Silence. We both knew I had to fill it. My walk pace quickened.

"Listen...I, uh...I wanted to say..." *Sorry. Yes, sorry would do right about now. Why was it so hard to say?* "I didn't mean to freak out the other night. It's just...I mean, you're paying all those doctors a fortune and they still can't get your meds right? It's a joke."

"Making me feel responsible for it isn't helping," she bristled back, not at all hearing my version of an apology.

"I know. I know." Full-blown speed walking now, I put distance on my clumsy words. "I just hate it when you're not doing well."

The coolness in her voice touched slightly warmer. "I probably shouldn't have said anything. I'm sorry. I know how you worry. But we, I," she quickly corrected, "have to be patient. It's a moving target, finding the right cocktail."

"How's the new volunteering gig?" I asked, moving along. Hopeful.

She hesitated. "Okay. Not sure it's for me long-term." A hollow laugh followed. "What a surprise, huh?"

No, not really. "Is there anything I can do?"

The daft irony of my question leaked into a pocket of silence. I didn't know what to do back then; I had kicked her condition under the rug like a dust bunny to be dealt with another day. Only I never did deal with it. Not in the right way.

Her voice suddenly dropped to a whisper. "Hold on."

The phone muffled and in the background on her end, I could hear someone asking a question: a deep voice, low. Her reply came in a lower voice, defensive. I shuttered both eyelids, anxiousness revving.

"Who's that?" I asked when she was back on the line.

She paused, the answer obvious, long before the blunt, "Patrick."

Football-loving, real estate broker Patrick LeBlanc, with his Florida Keys, rum-drunk smile and tasseled loafers. He'd swooped in to scoop Suze out from under me. I'd never met him in person but had stalked his social media accounts enough to know I disliked him. Cloaked in power suits and a douchey swagger, no surprise he cruised Suze at a Whole Foods salad bar. I mean, how lame was that?

"He's still hanging around, huh?" I said, gnawing on the side of my thumb. "Sounds serious."

"Are you seeing anyone?" she asked, dodging the answer.

"No."

"Anyone on the horizon?"

"Sure. Millions. Billions. What do you think?"

She sighed. "It's not good for you to be alone."

"I know," I said. "You don't think I know?" The wind picked up and I shrugged deeper into my hoodie. "But it's hard. You know how I am. And I'm getting more antisocial every day."

"Get out of the bike lane!"

I'd wandered, not paying attention, and jumped back to the pedestrian part of the walkway as a cyclist doing Mach 80 narrowly avoided taking me out. A grey-haired couple speed walking in matching tracksuits shot me a disapproving look: another no-brain tourist.

"Where are you?" Suze asked.

"Vancouver."

And just like that, I could feel her shrivel away. Our history was right there, across the inlet. The beginning of the end. I swiveled to face the city, another clump of high-rises, and switched gears.

"Pops sold the house, by the way," I said.

"To you?" She sounded genuinely surprised.

"Of course not."

She scoffed, "What an ass."

There weren't many places left where we could find common ground. Pops was a given. The surge of solidarity emboldened me. "That's kind of why I'm calling," I angled. "I need a favor."

There was a prickly pause. "Not if it involves him."

"It's the V, Suze."

"You left it with him?"

Technically, she'd brought it there but I sure as hell wasn't going to bring that up.

"I never got around to picking it up," I said, watching a seagull pick at greens from a discarded takeout container. "And there's no one else I can trust."

"What about Mac? You trust him with everything else."

It was a dick comment and she knew it. Mac had sowed our life with many perks: a financial wizard who set us up to be millionaires for life; big-ticket specialists who did everything under the sun to help us conceive; lots of extras and freebies. Despite his largesse, Suze never warmed up to him. I always believed intimidation played a part. And not just because he and I were so tight. Mac unabashedly was Mac: a bombastic personality with a kill-or-be-killed approach to everything in life. He didn't give a shit if you loved him or wanted him dead; he treated you the same. The trouble with Suze was she never had that powerful sense of self. Never knew who she really wanted to be. I fell in love with a nose-ringed skateboard girl, unaware that was merely a rebel persona she tried on like an outfit—one of many she donned and discarded trying to figure herself out. Being sucked into my hell-bent mission to become who I needed to be didn't help. In between assisting me, she dallied in taking courses here, part-time jobs there, nothing ever landing. Dutiful rock and roll spouse wasn't what she signed up for and her inability to change it, to uncover her own passion, or at least have the children we'd so often dreamed of, festered in ways we both never anticipated.

"Show Patrick our old stomping grounds," I replied cuttingly. "Make a day of it. He can look for some houses to sell so he can buy one of his own instead of living in mine."

After a tense beat, she warned, "Adrian."

"Okay, okay. Don't hang up." I pinched the bridge of my nose, if only to cut off my brain from my mouth. I said all these stupid things, nothing I put any real weight behind, but said them nonetheless because I wanted her to feel the sting of loss. "Please. Don't hang up."

The next silence was long and not friendly. "When do I have to be there?" she finally asked.

"Sometime in the next two weeks. This week preferably."

"Fine. I'll do it," she said with absolutely no enthusiasm, "but I'm taking Patrick with me. And he's bringing his .45."

Typical that Mr. American All Star would be packing. Probably kept it in the glove box of his manly Corvette. Another social media tidbit I'd unearthed.

"That's a little extreme, don't you think?"

"Your dad is a jerk. I don't trust him. And I don't like him. I put up with him because I had to. His shit don't fly with me anymore."

Nine times out of ten, there was zero trace of Suze's Atlanta child-hood in her vocabulary. Five years in a predominately white private school, coupled with the pressure to fit in, had tapped down her roots, more or less. Every now and then however, they resurfaced. Usually when my father pissed her off. Suze had taken a lot of shit from him, more than any girlfriend or wife deserved. Pops always insisted he wasn't racist, but the truth strayed far from that. A burst of sorrow gripped me.

"I miss you," I blurted out.

In the quiet that opened up, I imagined all of our old arguments and discontents slipping away. We still hadn't fully healed but I never gave up hope, kept trying to claw my way back to where we used to be. If I closed my eyes, I could still smell the cut grass of the baseball field beyond the cafeteria patio, taste the stale grease of my French fries as Suze waltzed right past my huddle of eighth-grade friends and said I should either stop staring or ask her out. Her family had recently moved to California and I'd never seen such a poised, beautiful, badass girl. She was a mythical creature back then, in snug jeans, holding her skateboard by its trucks, full of the confidence she'd eventually lose. That fateful lunch hour seemed like only yesterday and maybe Suze was thinking about that moment too right now. Maybe...

"Don't you dare," Suze whispered, a saga of hurt in her voice. "Don't you bloody dare."

Like clockwork, something snapped, the way it always did, and we were left holding the broken pieces of us, with no instruction manual on how to put them back together. There was a rushing sound of water on her side of the phone, loud and sudden, then a metallic clang.

"What was that?" I asked.

"The shower," she said, in a clipped tone. "I have to go. We have a lunch to get to."

All the time we were talking, the phone had bumped and muffled on her end. The sounds of movement. Those noises, what they were, suddenly hit. It was her, stripping off her clothes. With Patrick right there, watching. Blackness scraped along my heart like steel wool.

"You're not going to shower with him, are you?"

The line went dead not even a second after the question left my lips.

After picking up some sushi I headed back to the bus, totally out of sorts. It wasn't just Suze moving on, it was how fast it had happened. Mind you, few women finish a stint of intensive counselling drop-dead gorgeous, loaded, and living alone in a stunning mansion. Suze was a catch on every level. The problem lay with me and my undying belief we were an inseparable team. That afternoon at Mr. Chow's in Beverly Hills haunted me to this day. How I'd flown back from Mexico without anyone knowing, convinced the reason Suze wanted to see me in person was to say we were getting back together.

I'd arrived early, jumpy with anticipation. After two vodka sodas, self-confidence flagging, I was about to order a third when Suze waltzed in. A vision in a tight dress and heels, she caught my wave and made her way over. She was a breakup song come to life, and unmeasurable yearning filled my soul as my—and every other male's —eyes hungered over her. Unless you'd read about it in the tabloids, you'd never guess her fresh crown of curls was the result of a dark, rabbit hole night. Another low point, when she'd sheared off all her hair. But like everything she wore, Suze rocked the cropped 'do. It bewitchingly framed her exotic face, reminding me all over again why I'd fallen so hard.

We embraced tableside, a little off tempo. Out of practice. She dropped a cordial kiss on my cheek and her gaze journeyed over me. "Looking good, Ace. A tan suits you."

Damn that *Ace* for giving me hope.

I hadn't heard it in a long, long time.

It seemed like a lifetime ago when she'd first anointed me with that term of endearment.

We'd only been dating a month and I had it bad. I couldn't stop thinking about her. Every minute we were apart was torture. The need to seize her, so she couldn't be wrested away, became all consuming. I toyed with presenting a ring but couldn't afford to buy what she deserved. So my proposition to go steady came in the form of an ace of hearts playing card. We'd just finished an epic make out session and Pan American park was empty on a dreamy June evening, a light wind rustling through the trees. The scent of backyard barbecues and grilled meat spiked the air. Fritzing with nervous energy, I handed Suze the card, warm and curved from the back pocket of my jeans. With eyes anchored together, I explained away her confusion.

It means you have my heart forever.

She'd tucked the card into her bra, against the sweet swell of skin I'd yet to touch, and scooped both of my hands in hers. Her voice shimmered, matching the gloss in both eyes.

I'm never giving it back, Ace.

Never meaning up until that afternoon.

"Are you fucking joking?" I asked as Mr. Chow's famous Peking duck threatened to climb back up my throat. We'd ordered and were tucking into the Americanized Chinese cuisine. "You made me fly up here for that?"

A ripple of murmurs erupted around us. Someone cleared their throat. I couldn't believe it. Our conversation leading up to this was light; we'd laughed and reminisced. Then, *boom*, Suze dropped the divorce bomb.

She set her chopsticks down and asked in a controlled voice, "What would you have preferred? An email? You deserve better. We both do."

"Better? This isn't better." I laughed a painful, losing-it kind of laugh. "It's a goddamned ambush."

After an airless moment, Suze brought a hand to her neck, eyes downcast. I saw it then. A shiny, slippery snake of fine metal caressing her wrist.

"Are you seeing someone?"

She reluctantly met my eyes. "Yes."

"You're sleeping with him." My accusing voice clattered higher, louder.

Never comfortable with public displays of my temper, Suze skirted a nervous look at the rubbernecking patrons and whispered, "We're separated, Adrian. This was always a possibility."

There had to be a rule. It was unfair to look so beautiful while in the process of gutting me. Reeling, I downed my drink and waved for another.

"Maybe for you."

And that's how fifteen years ended: in a sun-dappled restaurant, with Hollywood power brokers and the sickly-sweet smell of chili sauce surrounding us. Two weeks later in Puerto Escondido, I got an email (from her divorce lawyer) and promptly fainted after reading it.

Now, the same hot roll of nausea I'd felt that afternoon in Beverly Hills bubbled in my throat. In the distance, I saw Sven exiting out of my bus. What the—? I didn't stop running until I landed right in front of him. He jumped back, caught off guard.

"What were you doing in the bus?" I demanded.

Without the protection of his ever-present aviators, his eyes skated. "Where have you been?" he asked. "I was looking for you."

Nothing in his demeanor suggested he'd seen her, but my mind spooled out of control. This was exactly what I'd feared.

"You need me, you text. You call."

"I did text," he protested. "And call. But you didn't answer."

Fair enough. I'd shut my phone off after the call with Suze, just in case. My heart couldn't take a post-call snarky text, even though I deserved one. Or several.

"What was so important it couldn't wait?"

He hesitated, looked very uncertain for Sven. "I overheard Ex talking yesterday," he finally said. "Something about a new record deal."

"Everyone's talking about it. Our Six Devil contract expires after the next album."

"I know," he stressed. "But the way the conversation went, it didn't sound like he was talking about that deal."

On tour, being in close proximity with your fellow travelers you tried hard not to, but couldn't always avoid, listening in. But the unspoken rule rolled like Vegas—what happened on tour, stayed on tour. Besides, Ex and I, we'd been tight for years. (A bromance Suze once teased.) Sure, he'd been standoffish lately, but he'd never do anything behind my back.

"You probably only caught part of the convo, so don't stir the pot if it don't need stirring, all right?"

Sven nodded, but kept checking me out from different angles.

"What?" I asked.

"Are you feeling okay?"

"I feel fine. Why?"

"There was..." he started, uncomfortably. "Blood. On the floor and in the second bathroom."

My heart stumbled. *Blood?*

"Yeah," I said, scrambling, as something like heartburn crawled up my throat. "I, uh, had a nosebleed."

His eyebrows knitted together. "You never get nosebleeds."

Spoken without embellishment, it was a loaded statement, nonetheless. We stared at each other, careful, as a flock of Canada geese honked their way eastward high in the sky above us.

"It may feel like we know everything about each other, Svennie," I finally said. "But actually we don't. I get nosebleeds once in a while. Ever since I was a kid."

"All right" he said, backing off from my intensity. "Sorry I asked. Sorry for caring."

God...the caring card. There was no defense to that.

"I appreciate you looking out for me," I assured him. "You know that. But you also know the rules. My bus is off-limits. Even to you."

"Fine," he said, totally not fine. "Enjoy your lunch."

Sven stalked away. He knew he'd crossed a line, but he also wasn't stupid. My shiftiness spoke of something else. A flaccid excuse might deflect him for now, but I needed to kick things up a notch in the security department.

CHAPTER THIRTEEN

"HASTINGS?"

Inside the bus, door shut, I cocked my head and listened.

Silence.

I dumped the sushi on the couch and checked the powder room, the closets, under my desk at the back. Called her name again.

Nothing.

The taste in my mouth turned flat and sour. I threw open my bedroom door.

Empty.

Scoured the bathroom.

Empty.

Anxiety spiraled into me like a tapeworm.

She bailed. I knew it. I should never have left her alone.

I closed my eyes and took a deep breath.

Settle. Settle. Think.

She couldn't have gotten far, I told myself. Except she still had the money I'd given her, and it was just enough to get into trouble. A vision of a bum, or worse, luring her into an alley made me physically ill.

"Fuck!" I yelled, kicking the wall. "Don't you dare disappear on me now, you little puke."

Just as I turned to leave, a scraping sound erupted from the other side of the room. In the reflection of the flatscreen TV mounted on the wall, I saw her, before I actually saw her. My chest drained with relief.

"Jesus Christ," I said. "Why didn't you answer?"

The frizz of her Afro peeked up from behind the mattress. "I, I didn't know if you were by yourself."

I dashed to the other side of the bed and helped her out of the drawer. "Did he see you?"

"I don't think so. I had a shower and was in here drying off when I heard him call your name. I..." Her eyes shifted down to the drawer, to the stack of T-shirts I'd shoved aside last night only to pile over her once she'd lain down. "I thought that would be a safe place to hide."

I fought back the urge to simultaneously strangle and hug her. I'd left, preoccupied with the V and Suze. Forgotten her safety was number one.

"We have to keep the door locked every time I leave. I'll keep a key on me but if I have to knock, it'll be like this." I rapped out five knocks on the bed frame in a one-two, one-two-three pattern. "Got it?"

She nodded glumly. She'd done the right thing, maybe the only thing, but for her to jump back in the drawer—it explained every emotion etched on her face. She'd kept a stiff upper lip after we crossed the border last night, but her eyes were still swollen from all the crying. None of this was getting easier. Including what I had to say next.

"We never talked about this, but..." I paused, mulling over exactly how I wanted to position the delicate subject. "If you need anything, you have to let me know."

Her brow crinkled, confused. "Okay."

"Like...anything."

I opened my eyes wide in a *so-we're-clear-here* fashion. She offered a strained, baffled smile in return.

"Okay," she repeated.

Dear god, she was going to make me say it. "Sven mentioned he saw...blood. I saw it too...on the floor out there?"

She froze. Mercifully, her eyes shifted off of mine.

"Look," I said, happy to close this out sooner than later. "It is what it is, and there's no nobility in suffering. I'll be right back. Lock the door behind me."

I crossed the lot and mentally prepared myself for the next conversation. Usually there were a couple women on our crew but with them on other gigs, I only had one hope. Dame Diana, aka The Dame, was the lead singer for our backup band, a scraggly punk outfit appropriately named *Up Yours*. They had a small, angry following of gender-neutral fans and travelled around in an old school bus that belched so much blue smoke I was surprised it was street legal. The bus sat marooned near the back fence and all four tires sagged, in need of air. The windows were dark, so I knocked softly at first, then louder. It took a good minute before the door creaked open.

Like a genie, The Dame materialized through a haze of pot smoke. She waved it away, eyes widening in surprise. "Hey, sexy. Wasn't expecting you."

If an online photo didn't exist to prove otherwise, you'd be hard pressed to believe the full-figured drill sergeant known as The Dame—the woman who prowled the stage in Doc Martens and rip-roaring costumes, the one who'd become an icon to the LGBTQ community and took down more women than Norm—started out life as Lesley Richards, a pigtailed, Oklahoma girl destined for a trailer park husband, three kids, and a hairstyling career.

"Wanna come in?" she asked, sweetly.

I held up a polite hand. "Thanks anyway."

In Seattle, I'd poked my head in out of curiosity and the stench still tormented me. Ancient mattresses littered the floor and every other available space was jammed with empties or dirty laundry. An ornate hookah held court in the middle of the squalor, and I was certain the sketchiest opium den in China would cry foul for even being associated with such a ragtag setup.

"Well?" She raised a sculpted brow. It wasn't every day Adrian Johnson knocked on your door.

"I need to borrow some...things," I said. "You know...female things."

Her eyes raked over me. "Hmmm. A lucky lady. Well, sort of lucky, I suppose. I can't even imagine being on the rag when an opportunity like you crops up."

"It's not for anyone specific," I clarified. "Just in case."

This prompted a supportive cluck. "Thinking ahead. That's why you're so successful. Give me a sec, hon, while I look around."

She retreated back into the din, and another stoned female laugh joined hers, as sounds of rummaging drifted out. When The Dame reappeared, I snatched the box of tampons from her outstretched hand and stuffed them into the waistband of my jeans.

"Thanks. Do me a favor and keep this on the down low."

"Are you kidding me?" Her scarlet smile softened, and she crossed her heart. "Anything for you. Your crew said you were the best in the biz and they're right. You actually care. Everyone loves you. The last band we gigged with didn't give a hoot about our sound check and then freaked out when we sounded crap-ola."

"Remember that when you're the headliner. What goes around comes around."

She waved a skull-ringed hand. "Please, let's not fool ourselves, honey. We're never going to be headliners."

I might have imagined the flash of sadness in her eyes, that's how brief it was. But I don't think I did. Underneath the bravado, crew cut and impressive muscles, she was just a girl, a diamond in the rough trying to make it in a brutal industry.

"Don't ever sell yourself short," I told her. "That's the worst thing you can do."

Her expression crumpled like she'd just seen the cutest pile of puppies. "You see, that's what I'm talking about. You're a fucking mensch. Seriously."

A face appeared over The Dame's shoulder, round and pale as the moon. The glassy-eyed waif, twenty if that, giggled when she finally focused on me. "Wowza. You're, like, even more gorg in person. Are you coming in?" she asked, hopeful.

The Dame elbowed back her conquest with a den mother's authority. "Paws off, honey. We're not done yet." She flashed me a *what can you do* look and repositioned a ratty blanket the best she could around the phenomenon of her bosom. Large enough to qualify for its own zip code, I couldn't quite look away from the jiggle. "You hittin' the after-party tonight?" she asked. "A little mingling does wonders for the soul."

I'd completely forgotten about the party, one of several Ziegler had planned. "Yeah. I'll probably drop in for a bit."

"Good." She reached for the door handle with a saucy wink. "Now if you'll excuse me, I have some unfinished mingling to attend to."

CHAPTER FOURTEEN

DRAINED FROM THE MERRY GO-ROUND OF THE PAST FORTY-eight hours, I anticipated a down-tempo show. But it was one of those nights where the crowd propped us up. Amped and needing to blow off some serious steam afterwards, Ziegler's party was the perfect antidote. Not one to shirk my duties, I checked in on Hastings first. Half-asleep, she insisted I go. So the boys and I trucked downtown and in a stylish restaurant closed for the evening, an open bar greeted us while a DJ spun fantastic beats. Best of all, the crowd kept a respectful distance.

Most of them, anyway.

As I waited for the bartender to slide me another drink, I took in the room and inadvertently caught the eye of a tall brunette who openly stared at me. She was pretty enough—a bit Amazonian for my tastes—and when she smiled, out of reflex I smiled back. Mistake. She shook her mane of hair and started to thread her way through the crowd. I wasn't averse to fans per se, but she was coming in hot, one thing on her mind. And this was so not the right time. The boys were in their usual protective formation around me and I shouldered past a surprised Diego and boogied. The main entrance was in the direct line of fire of my assailant, so I did a hard left, praying for some cover.

Much to my dismay, I only found the dark kitchen, stacks of tables cleared out for the dance floor, and an M and F glowing above two doors.

My only hope was the restroom? Sweet Jesus.

I snuck a look over my shoulder and Brunette zoned in on me, her smile glittering like vampire fangs. I bolted forward, and not fully turned around, collided spectacularly into another woman. With the impact, she did a one-eighty spin, and would've ass-planted on the ground if I didn't crouch down and catch her with both arms.

"Oh my god. Are you all right?" I asked, mortified.

Her huge, gorgeous eyes swallowed me whole. Ringed in a fringe of lush lashes, they flickered with surprise.

"Well, hello," she said.

The sharp intake of my breath almost hurt. Beautiful in a way that made me want to keep staring, she was all my white girl fantasies rolled into one. The classic smolder of Lana del Ray. Bridget Bardot's impossible sexiness. Halsey cool. Perfectly-shagged hair fell to shoulder length and I fought the urge to brush her bangs aside, to fall deeper into those haunting eyes. Her body was slim and athletic under the leather jacket, yet there was something immediately fragile about her. *Handle with care.*

"Where did you come from?" I asked, like an idiot.

She tilted her head with a confused smile. "The bathroom?"

"I mean…what I meant is…have you been here all night?"

The real question was, how the hell had I missed her?

"About half an hour," she said. "We know the DJ and dropped in to say hi. I was just about to leave. I have an early morning."

We. I. Which one was it?

"I was about to leave too," I said, like this was some urgent news she needed to know.

A handful of strange seconds passed. The tunes cranked, yet the space between us was pin-drop quiet.

"Um…" She glanced around. "I'm okay to stand. No damage done."

We were still crouched on the floor for no real reason and it was an unconscious thing, how tight I held onto her. My instinct was to never let go.

"Yes. Right."

I bungled to my feet and assisted her up, madly processing every detail. The sweet musk of her perfume; a pillowy mouth that screamed *kiss me*; how she exuded effortless, born-with-it chic. In killer high-heeled boots, she was almost as tall as me. Being eye to eye, that was how I caught her gaze flicking behind me.

We. I.

My heart skipped a beat. "You here with anyone?"

"Just my girlfriends."

But there it was again: a cautious, *I-wonder-if-my-boyfriend-is-watch-ing-us* eye flick. Now I had to look. Ten feet away, Ms. Brunette stood with arms crossed, fuming in our direction.

"Was she leaving with you?" my gorgeous crash partner asked. "Because she doesn't look happy."

I turned back with a sheepish smile. "I was actually, ah, coming back here to escape."

"Hide out in the men's room until closing?" A smile danced, sparking all the way to her eyes.

"Something like that."

She held out her hand. "My name's Sasha-Rae."

It felt oddly formal, shaking hands, because the way she reacted when our fingers touched, I knew she felt it, too. Hormones, pheromones, whatever-mones; the chemistry between us was violent, even just standing there.

"Adrian," I said.

My name-dropping didn't register a hint of recognition on her face. *Adrian Johnson?* I imagined her saying. *Hmm, doesn't ring a bell.*

"What's your plan B?" she asked. "Would you like some cover for a getaway?"

Her offer unnerved and fascinated me at the same time. I was totally, utterly entranced. "Sure."

"You think we'll make it past her?" She tipped her head discreetly toward Ms. Brunette, and I laughed in a way I hadn't in a long time.

"You could be my bodyguard," I suggested.

"Hmm," she demurred. "How progressive of you."

In my peripheral vision, Ms. Brunette threw in the towel and paraded away, head high like she'd changed her mind. Just beyond her, the boys were still at the bar, now surrounded by a bevy of women. They didn't need an interruption.

"Do you need to say goodbye to your friends first?" I asked.

"Nah. I'm a big girl. I can find my way home."

The warmth of her smile squashed all thought. In the space of a few minutes my world had transformed.

"The only way out is straight ahead," I said. "You ready?"

With absolutely no idea how this would play out, only knowing we needed to be closer, I lifted my arm and she snugged in beside me. The swing of her hips, slow and sexy against mine, made every step sweet agony. Like moving through warm honey. Jealous and curious eyes tracked our path to the stairs that led to the first floor. When we reached the landing, we paused at the same time, turned to face each other and smiled. Then, without a word between us, we raced each other down as fast as we could, dashed past the beefcake bouncer who warned us in a very serious voice there were no in and outs, and spilled out onto the street with an attack of the giggles.

"That was awesome," she gushed, lifting her hand up for a high five. "Totally awesome."

Equally giddy, I high-fived her back. In those few crazy seconds, it reminded me of running wild as a kid in the park: the heat of summer on my skin, no commitments, nothing in my life decided. Out on the sidewalk, that feeling of freedom continued, surrounding us like a separate atmosphere. We were no longer part of the universe we'd jettisoned from. It distracted me until the chilled air seeped under my skin.

"Wanna warm up with a drink somewhere?" I asked, pulling down the sleeves of my hoodie.

She looked up at the sky with a sound of indecision. Even her profile made my heart stutter. "Dammit. I really shouldn't," she said.

Her eyes tipped to meet mine and she smiled suggestively. "But I will."

The dulled vibration of thumping DJ beats against the restaurant windows sounded bigger in the quiet of Sunday night. Boutiques lining the block had long shuttered. Mannequins in the windows stared vacantly into the night.

"Any suggestions?" I asked.

"The Shangri-La has a lounge," she said, pointing to a building on the corner. "It should be dead tonight."

"Dead sounds perfect."

She started to laugh, covering her mouth with her hand. "Oh my god. I thought you said 'dat' sounds perfect."

"Not even five minutes and you're accusing me of being Euro-trash?"

Her embarrassed smile was devastatingly cute. About to tell her she could scream German poetry in my ear all night long if only I could kiss her, a limo prowled up to the curb. An Asian guy spilled out first, naked from his skinny jeans upwards. Sporting a feather boa and oversized Elton John sparkle glasses, champagne sloshed out of the open magnum clutched in his hand. When he saw me, he whipped the glasses off and screamed in an ear-cracking falsetto, "Oh my fucking God! It's hiiiiiiiiim."

The ho-train clambering out of the limo behind him screeched to a halt. For three hanging seconds, it was a still life of designer dresses, stunned faces and, inexorably, the smell of Kentucky Fried Chicken. Just before the chaos broke out, Sasha-Rae grabbed my hand and started to run.

"Adrian, nooooo. Come baaaaaack," Asian Elton yelled.

But we were outta there.

CHAPTER FIFTEEN

ALL I COULD DO WAS HANG ON. SHE KNEW THE LAY OF THE land better than me. We weaved left, right and then left again, our stampede pace slowing only when we disappeared into the mouth of a dark alley. Bent over, hands on my knees, my legs burned, chest on fire from the sprint.

"Nice moves," I huffed. "You hauled ass in those boots."

"Thanks." She smiled, barely winded. "Track and field all-star in high school. I knew one day it would serve me."

"Let me guess," I asked. "Sprinting?"

"Endurance."

"Slow and steady wins the race?"

"It depends," she countered. "Sometimes fast is good, too."

A faint beam of light from a nearby street lamp illuminated her lazy smile. A sensation of being afraid of something, but not entirely sure what, crept over me.

"What else did you excel in?" I asked, like a dork.

"Auto mechanics, believe it or not."

A flash of her, naked beneath coveralls, sent my heart racing again. "That's cool. Progressive."

"Are you being sarcastic?"

"Not in the slightest. I've never even changed the oil in my car. Wouldn't know where to start."

"That's unusual, for a guy," she said, sounding surprised.

Little did she know Ex had laughed himself into a cramp when I confessed to not knowing how many cylinders my Audi had.

I shrugged and smiled. "I have other talents."

"Oh, do tell."

With a devil-may-care grin, she leaned against the graffiti splashed wall. Crossing her arms, the diamond heart pendant between her breasts shifted upwards, a beacon marooned between two lovely islands. I felt rudderless, pulled by whatever force she exerted. I gritted my teeth and joined her against the wall, close enough to let our shoulders touch. A distant rumble of thunder broke above us as we stole glances at each other. Her tender eyes were serious at the same time.

"So...what do you do when you're not hiding out with musicians in alleys?" I asked.

"Something infinitely more exciting. I'm the vice president of an auto parts dealer."

"Wow, you *are* into cars."

"Not really. Cars are kind of a family thing," she continued, without elaborating. "But I'm good at what I do. In this business, no one expects a woman in my position, let alone a tough negotiator."

It made sense now. Her veneer of strength wasn't something I'd imagined. But it came across like a hand-me-down shirt she had no choice but to wear. She didn't sound entirely comfortable with it.

"VP, huh? Should I be worried about a lawsuit? For crashing into you?"

She bumped her hip against mine with a laugh. "I'm Canadian. We don't sue."

"Maybe I should up the drink ante to cover my bases," I said. "You saved me from that fiasco back there. I owe you big time."

"Just think," she teased. "You might still be in the men's room waiting for the party to end."

She laughed, a deep-throated, whiskey laugh so sensual it made my stomach flutter. It surprised me, how loose she made me feel. Even the faint odor of garbage didn't overwhelm me the way it normally would.

I looked up and down the alley. "Well, we're never going to find a bar here. Shall we move on?"

She glanced down at her watch and frowned. "Might be a bit late for that. I've got a big presentation tomorrow morning. I need a clear head."

"What time is it?"

"Midnight."

Bus call was 1 a.m. but I couldn't bring her there. Suggesting a hotel felt ridiculously presumptuous. Still, the evening couldn't end yet. She must've read my mind, because she shifted a quarter turn toward me. Her pupils were as dark and wide as a '45.

"It's kind of cool being right here," she said. "Talking."

Her pinky found mine and we looped digits. My heart started to pound in my ears. We were so close I could smell the tang of her leather jacket.

"Hi," was my genius response. "Come here often?"

A girly giggle slipped out and she tugged on my pinky, bringing me closer. The signals bouncing between us since the party were now impossible to ignore.

And then it happened.

Our mouths came together, everything in slow motion. The anticipation was a wave cresting, followed by an immediate ache of everything being different, like getting on a bike I wasn't used to riding. She stopped right after I stiffened.

"This all right?" she whispered, lips hovering, humming on mine. Her breath smelled strawberry sweet—the syrupy margaritas slung at the party.

"Yeah," I managed. "It's great."

She waited until I relaxed, then explored further. At some point our arms wrapped around each other. When her hand slid down the back of my jeans, I inhaled sharply. I'd forgotten how the warm touch of a woman made everything better. This time, she didn't ask anything, just waited, two fingers circling on the swell of my ass.

"You have no idea how good that feels," I mumbled.

Her hand drifted lower and both of mine fumbled under and up her T-shirt. She arched under my touch and made this sexy sound, something between a moan and a whimper and kept trying to pull me closer, me angling away because I was embarrassingly good to go. But she prevailed, or rather, I gave in, and when our hips collided, she knew what to do. In no time at all, my blood was boiling, parts swelling and throbbing. I was so turned on, lost in her curves, her taste, how devastatingly perfect she ground against me. Our careful kisses turned frenzied, desperate, the rhythm loud and clear, the crescendo building, but everything was moving way too fast.

I pulled off her mouth, panting, so lightheaded I thought I was going to float away. "I can't. I mean, we can't. That. Not here."

She clutched onto me, catching her breath as well. Her eyes glowed with a similar fever, but I saw it. She wasn't willing to go that far, either. "How about we...pretend?" she offered. "Can you hold me up?"

Before I could reply, she pressed down on my shoulders, tried to shimmy further up the wall.

Oh, Jesus.

I locked both legs for resistance and helped maneuver her higher. She felt weightless, spectral, and when her legs wrapped around my waist, the heat firing through her jeans was molten. We fell back into that ancient movement, the pleasure so pure and raw, I was no longer aware of any distinction between us. There was only friction, the kind that can't ever stop once it starts. Her mouth nipped against my neck, foxy little whimpers hot and ratcheting, her arousal pushing me higher, my own breath hardening into short gasps. As if she could divine just how close I was, her fingers clamped onto my ass, pulling me towards madness, the point of no return. In the spiraling peak, my brain filled with stars. I mangled her against the bricks with an animal moan and seconds later her body jerked and tightened, the entire alley reverberating with her cry.

For I don't how long after, we were wound together, gulping for air. I floated in a galaxy of endorphins, my legs and arms made of rubber. When her body finally slackened—sudden, like a marionette doll whose strings were snipped—I somehow found the strength to keep holding her up.

When I could finally speak, it was a mumble into her hair. "You okay?"

Her reply came between shuddering breaths. "Oh my god."

I pulled back just enough to see her face. "Endurance, huh. Maybe you're out of practice."

She laughed, couldn't believe I said that, and our heads dropped back into the wonderful, warm netherworlds of shoulders and hair, of possibility and promise. I was only dimly aware of the light drizzle that started to fall until the *wah-wah* of a siren snapped me back to reality. I tucked her head protectively into my chest and without letting her go, turned to squint into the flashlight beaming right at us.

"Everything all right here?"

The light dropped and a cop's leering face peered out from the cruiser. His sidekick, a tough looking dude with a shaved head, leaned across him with a smirk.

Sasha-Rae popped her head out and held up her thumb—*we're okay.* The cops burst into raucous laughter. Ahead of them, a dreary night fighting the underbelly of humanity waited. This was the kind of interlude they needed.

"Next time get a room," the driver barked and with a jaunty double beep, they roared off.

Sasha-Rae looked up at me with an astonished grin. "Did that just happen? Any of it?"

"Apparently."

In any other circumstance, the embarrassment of how I couldn't hold it together would have killed me. But I didn't seem to care. Nor did she. I helped unwind her legs, steadying her as she wobbled on the uneven pavement.

"That was like ten drinks," she said. "Doubles. I hope I can stand tomorrow."

Tomorrow. A new day without her in it. I felt suddenly, unfairly rushed. I knew so little about her. What if she listened to country music? Was she a Republican or the Canadian equivalent? Could she survive knowing I required the toothpaste tube to be rolled up from the bottom in neat, accurate folds? What if she was a middle-of-the-tube squeezer?

"I'd really like to see you again," I said, catching myself just in time and replacing *I have to* with *I'd really like to.*

"Me too," she said. "Or wait, you too?" She laughed. "You know what I mean."

"We're in Calgary tomorrow," I said. "I can fly you out."

The last thing I wanted was to sound desperate. And I failed magnificently.

"I'm nine-to-fiver, unfortunately," she said. "Weekends are easier."

"How about Toronto? We play there Friday and Saturday."

Our schedule in Toronto was, to put it bluntly, a shitshow. The long-awaited documentary about our band was being filmed, and on both days there were interviews and behind the scenes footage to be shot, plus a meet and greet. The worst possible romantic weekend. In the silence, like she knew this all seemed too good to be true, her eyes drifted down. In the glance back up, something integral shifted.

Shit. There's a boyfriend. Or a husband.

"Uh...I feel kind of dumb asking after the fact," she said. "But your ring. I just noticed it."

I still wore my wedding band, or should I say, it wore me. Trapped under a kinked knuckle, courtesy of me punching a wall, it had become a permanent feature, for better or for worse. I held out my hand for her to observe the damage.

"It's stuck and needs to get cut off. I'm not thrilled with that idea, as you can imagine."

"I just wanted to make sure," she said quietly. "Sorry if that made you uncomfortable."

It took guts and a strong sense of self-worth to ask that up-front. She was proving herself worthy on every level. But my reply came out sharp, the way the truth often does.

"Trust me, I wouldn't be here with you if I was still married. But since we're on the topic, are *you* single?"

Suddenly she didn't look all that comfortable. "Recently," she said, "but yes."

"So Toronto might work?"

Before she could answer, the drizzle stepped up into a downpour and we were on the run again. She steered us up half a block to Robson Street, where we ducked under an awning.

After texting for a cab, she glanced up at me from under her soaked bangs. "You want my number?"

"Hell yeah." I dug out my phone, opened up a new contact, and handed it over. "I'll let you do the honors."

"Just so you know," she said, while typing in her details, "the ball's in your court."

"You don't think I'm going to call?"

She handed me back my phone, eyes serious again. "I know what it's like on the road. Busy," she added vaguely.

"I'll never be that busy," I said, sliding the phone into my back pocket.

I slipped my arm around her and we huddled together in silence, listening to the rain patter. With no cars on the deserted street, everything felt surreal. On the flip side, the doubt nagging at me—that her *busy* didn't really mean busy—felt incredibly real. It tripped me up a bit, as if the moment between us was already fading and she'd resigned herself to the notion of being a footnote, when in fact, every part of me was rearranging, already making space for her.

When the world's fastest cab materialized, she signaled to the driver to give us a sec.

"This weekend, right?" I asked, an arm still around her. I couldn't let her go until she said yes.

"Call me," she said. "And thank you."

We kissed, a long lingering duet that iced some of my fears. Forced apart by the driver bleating his horn, I opened the passenger door and she slid inside.

"You want a lift?" she asked when I didn't join her. "The rain..."

I couldn't get into that car. Couldn't fathom how I would ever get back out. So I told her a walk would do me good. I shut the door, sealing her off, and as the Prius edged into the night, she rolled down the window and blew me a kiss. And just like that, she was gone.

Thank you.

What did that even mean? Thank you because you just rocked my world? Or thank you because I'll never see you again? Or both? My brain cranked in every direction, wouldn't allow a solid read on the situation. For the first time in years, I craved a cigarette. Violently. I scoured the pavement, the seams along the building, looking for a butt with the crazed intensity of a junkie who'd dropped a ball of crack.

Show some backbone, I told myself. *Some fucking confidence. She gave you her number.*

But I was alone in the rain, a sticky mess in my boxers, the taste of her on my lips, and unsure if I'd ever taste it again. The heavens decided to weigh in with a vicious crack of thunder, and the rain turned torrential. The mountains were to my left, which meant the bus was due east. I ran the entire way and Big Daddy pulled out at 1 a.m. on the nose. With Hastings asleep, I showered and crawled under the covers, shivering. It wasn't that the next five days would feel like five months. No, this was deeper. Something powerful rippled under my damp skin.

Even on a cellular level, I knew.

Lightning had finally struck twice.

CHAPTER SIXTEEN

THE NEXT MORNING I PUTTERED QUIETLY IN THE KITCHEN, making toast and coffee. Hastings was a motionless lump on the couch, blanket pulled over her head. The bus hurtled east along Canada's Highway One, dense flurries of snow whipping past the windows, the sky an infinity wall of gloom. Winter was my least favorite season and Canada, for all its charms, never appealed to me as a result. Growing up in Long Beach, the biggest decision I had to make in March was which T-shirt to wear, not how many. But my perspective on Canada had changed overnight. It had only been, what, a few hours, and every minute, every second of my encounter with Sasha-Rae still lingered. Even the brutal cold snap about to greet us in Calgary couldn't dampen the flame she'd ignited.

With the aroma of breakfast, Hastings poked her head up. "What time is it?" she asked, her voice drowsy with sleep. Man, that girl could sleep.

"Time to get up," I said. "It's a beautiful day."

She groped for her glasses and shoved them on. After gawking at the snowstorm through the blinds, she looked back at me, suspicious.

"Why are you whistling?"

"A man can't whistle in his own bus?"

She digested that, eyes narrowing as I sat down to eat. "Something happened last night."

I shrugged and took a bite of my toast. "Maybe."

From ten feet away, I could feel her mind grope and reach, flip through potential scenarios. Then, a wave of understanding washed over little Ms. Sherlock's features. "You met someone."

"I don't kiss and tell."

She sat up, now fully alert. "You kissed her?"

I shrugged again. "Maybe."

Both hands flew to her mouth. A smile curled behind them. "Are you going to see her again?"

I thought about Sasha-Rae's *thank you* last night; how I couldn't read it. My smile dimmed. "I hope so."

"Did she give you her number?" She sounded very concerned.

"Yup."

"Have you texted her yet?"

I washed down my toast with a slug of coffee. "You can't text someone right after meeting them," I explained. "It's kind of a rule."

"That's a dumb rule," she immediately dispatched, like I were a fool to believe such a thing. "She's probably waiting to hear from you."

"She's vice president of a company. I doubt she's sitting around waiting for my text."

Hastings wrapped her blanket over both shoulders and shot me a long look. "If I met someone famous and they kissed me, all I'd be thinking about is when they would text."

"You don't even have a phone," I countered. "And she doesn't care that I'm famous."

The latter wasn't exactly true; I simply never asked. But Sasha-Rae's demeanor—the lack of pretense and starry-eyed futzing—indicated exactly that. It was one of the things that put me at ease around her. And ease has never been my métier. Which explains why I'd lain in bed earlier crafting twelve different texts, erasing all of them. Part of me wished I'd given her my number instead and spared myself the pressure.

I finished my toast and set the plate inside the dishwasher. From under the sink, I fished out a Lysol Wipe and polished away nonexistent dust on the front of the fridge.

"She's probably nervous too," Hastings said.

I moved to the cupboards, buffing in tight circles. "I'm not nervous."

I could feel her eyes, unyielding lasers burning a hole in my back.

"You must like her already if you're so worried."

"Okay, okay, so maybe I'm worried." I chucked the wipe into the sink and spun around, hands gripping the countertop edge. "I'm famous, but still human. Last time I checked, anyway."

For someone who'd battled the rigors of the music industry for half his life, it was kind of pathetic to wither under such scant pressure. But I was worried. How was it I never gave rejection a single thought in the years I'd built up the band? There were plenty of nos, thousands of maybes, and I persevered like a Jew wandering in the desert to get the few, golden yeses. But that was business. My heart was an entirely different matter. I kept it protected, a rare jewel locked in a safe, and so far, only Suze had cracked the entry code. Not that I was blind to what went on around me. Pretty women and rock and roll go hand in hand, but I was an anomaly in an industry drowning in loose morals. Norm could write the how-to manual on one-night stands; a rotation of faces and bodies made me queasy. It was so unsanitary.

I sat down across from Hastings and tucked loose hair behind both ears. "Since you're the one with all the answers, what do you think I should say?"

She sat up taller, clearly proud I'd asked for her help. "What did you guys talk about?"

I felt my face go hot. "A bunch of things."

"If you like her, tell her how you feel," she said, ever the pragmatic.

"It's not that easy."

Pouring out my innermost feelings might sound romantic, except Sasha-Rae had no clue of her impact. The sense of harmony while we'd waited for the taxi, my arm slung around her shoulder, aware of how perfectly she fit. The last thing I wanted was to scare her off. And so Hastings appeared to tabulate the growing silence as if it were an equation: length of time Adrian said nothing (X) plus number of shifty glances from Adrian (Y) equaled another opaque excuse she'd be all over.

"Would you text a guy back right away?" I asked. Dating had become a different beast in the last fifteen years; women no longer waiting around for lunkheads to make a move.

She shifted on the couch and her voice changed. "I've never had a guy interested in me," she said. "I'm just telling you what I'd do if I had the chance."

I didn't know if she was self-conscious about admitting that, or sad. Judging from how she dropped her head, maybe both. I'd heard teenagers weren't even bothering with relationships these days. Too much work. I guess every generation had their struggle. I loved having a woman in my life. Suze had been my rock in so many ways. Having been there since the beginning, she'd understood the ups and downs. (Up until a point.) The challenge now was meeting someone who not only intrigued me, but could also deal with my life. My spidey sense said Sasha-Rae was that woman, so why did I feel so handcuffed at keeping the momentum going?

One text, I told myself. *C'mon. You've written over a hundred songs.*

Without giving it another thought, I yanked out my phone and banged off an amalgamation of all the texts I'd erased earlier.

A: Hi. It's Adrian. The guy from the alley? Hope the presentation is going well. It was great to meet you last night. Text me back when you can.

Short. Sweet. Funny. I debated a smiley face emoji, decided against it, and pressed send before I could change my mind.

I held up my phone as evidence. "There. Sent."

She grinned. "Don't you feel better now?"

For the briefest of seconds, I was a free man. But lobbing out the first piece of bait meant one thing: the waiting game had begun. Already a bag of uncertainty, how was I not going to climb the walls?

"I'm going to take a shower," I announced, needing a place to clear my head more than a place to clean it. "I'll be back in a bit."

My pitiful worry continued, however. Showering with the door open to hear if a text came in; shaving with one eye on the screen; getting dressed, the phone face up on my bed. To Hastings' inquiring glance when I came back out with my laptop, I gave her a terse, "Nothing yet."

Suddenly, again, there was so much time. To fill it, I checked emails, our social media accounts, even my horoscope. *Turn on the charm, Scorpio! Put complicated situations on ice and direct your focus.* Dear God. Did people actually believe in this drivel? It didn't help that Hastings was now sitting across from me at the kitchen table, no doubt sensing my distress. I could pull off a lot of things, but unconcerned nonchalance wasn't one of them. Thirty minutes later, my breaking point imminent...*Ping*.

Hastings stopped crunching on her apple. Willed me with her eyes to get busy. I swiped open the text, nerves popping with anticipation.

SR: Hi, hi! Nice to hear from you. What a crazy night! It's only 8:15 here but things are looking good for the presentation. Toronto sounds fun. I can talk 4/5 my time, 5/6 for you?

My entire body vibrated. I'd spared myself hours of vexation. *What do you know? This shit actually worked!*

Hastings leaned over the table, angling for a look. "What did she say?"

I shaded the phone out of her view. "Just wait. Let me reply first."

Easier said than done. A jangled mess, my fingers wouldn't stop shaking.

A: 5 PM my time is perfect. I'll call you.

I read out an abbreviated version of Sasha-Rae's text (leaving out the crazy night part) and Hastings' body language changed immediately. Closed down.

"She's coming to Toronto?"

"Uh...maybe," I fudged. Of course Sasha-Rae coming to Toronto had implications; ones I hadn't thought through. There'd been no time to think last night.

"Where is she going to stay?"

"Not in here, obviously. A hotel, I guess."

"You'll stay with her?" She sounded meek and unsure. Like I was throwing her to the wolves.

"I don't know," I said, flustered, not able to enjoy my new, happy world for even a minute. "Do we have to talk details now?"

No woman wore hurt well, Hastings included. She finished her apple in silence and decamped to the bathroom, leaving me with a cup of cold coffee and too many thoughts. Unbelievable how after a month of easing back into things, in less than a week the drama curve of my life was rocketing off the charts. Of course, I wouldn't leave Hastings high and dry, but Sasha-Rae added a whole new wrinkle.

I leaned back and stared blankly at the storm raging outside. I could barely make out the road. With no bearings and no sense of place, shooting through space in a capsule was what came to mind. A familiar feeling of disconnectedness. Being an intergalactic nomad was old hat by now, but I'd touched earth last night and didn't realize how badly I'd missed it. Sasha-Rae was a bright spot on the bleakness of my calendar, and I wasn't giving up another shot at love for anything. Or anyone.

The weight on my shoulders suddenly became Herculean. I'd be lying if I said my sense of responsibility didn't feel horribly misguided. With a heavy heart, I searched Google for a phone number, saved it, and planned to call the next time I had some privacy.

CHAPTER SEVENTEEN

"CAN WE GET SOME BLOODY HEAT IN HERE?" NORM YELLED to no one in particular. "My nuts are halfway up my throat."

Huddled around the craft services table, we were eating to stay alive...or that's what it felt like. Calgary was prone to chinooks—warm coastal winds that could swing daily temperatures by as much as 60 degrees Fahrenheit. Two days ago it was fifty-five, now it was minus five. The Saddledome's ancient heating system had conked out and the generators fought to catch up.

"You're wearing tights and a bathrobe, homeboy," I said to Norm, gloved hands holding a chamomile tea thick with honey and lemon. "It's minus twenty out there. Celsius, given we're in Canada."

Norm shoveled in a mouthful of guacamole with a tortilla chip. "Don't get me started on the metric system," he grumbled. "It's a conspiracy."

"Conspiracy? How? It's idiot-proof." Diego unleashed a rare Machiavellian smile.

"Because your people came to the table with tacos and margaritas," Norm replied, nonplussed, "I'm going to ignore what you just said."

Off to one side, Ex munched on a plate of celery sticks and hummus and signaled me over. "You wanna grab a burger? One of the locs told me about some up-and-comers playing an afternoon set in town."

"Just us?" He and I twinned off regularly, just not lately.

Ex tipped his head imperceptibly toward Norm. "Could use a change of scenery, if you know what I mean."

Forty minutes later, we were in a cabaret-style room, had snagged two seats at the bar, and were ordering our usuals. A thick odor of stale beer hung in the air. Behind the sagging stage, a velvet curtain was streaked with stains from the efforts of a thousand sweaty bands. The lone bartender dropped our drinks, tipped his newsboy cap, and told us to holler if we needed anything.

Ex held up his Heineken and waited for me to clink the bottle.

"There something to celebrate?" I asked.

"I guess that's where we differ," he said, eyes fixated on the flat-screen above the bar. "Outlook."

I spun my vodka soda on the bar. On the Uber ride over, he'd barely said a thing and now this.

"Outlook," I repeated. "Not sure I like the sound of that."

He took a long pull of his beer. "You gonna give me the real goods, or do I have to beat it out of you?"

"About what?"

"The past year."

"You mean my midlife crisis?"

With a humorless smile, he shook his head. "That story ain't true and we both know it. But you ain't the same. Haven't been in a while."

I sat up on the stool. Didn't like where this was heading. "All of that, last year," I explained. "It had nothing to do with you."

His hand tightened around the bottle, bling on every finger glittering. "You coulda made more of an effort," he said. "Was real nice hearing from the lawyers instead of you about the Pampers deal."

'The Seventh Sense' was a sweet ballad from our third album, *Dreamers and Thieves*. It had nothing to do with babies and everything to do with Suze's hands on my body. The killer melody prompted a Supreme Court judge to famously confess humming it in her chambers. Pampers offered seven figures to use it in a national commercial. The offer came in one morning right around breakfast, Mexico time. I'd just finished my sixth shot of Tequila and to be honest, if they'd asked me to wear Pampers I probably would've said yes.

"That wasn't my finest hour," I admitted, "but everyone got their fair share. Or is *that* the conversation?" I raised a skeptical eyebrow.

"It's not always about the money," Ex scoffed.

In the dirty light I held his gaze. "It's about something."

Before he could reply, a shuffle of mangy musicians took to the stage to a smattering of applause. They all looked sixteen, if that. The guitarist fiddled with an impressive board of pedals and kept flicking his Justin Bieber combover out of his eyes.

"What do you make of these guys?" I asked Ex, happy for a diversion.

"Heard one song. It was decent." He shrugged. "Drummer's kind of weak."

"You always say that."

I smiled but the usual creature comforts that defined our hanging out—his jokes, my random observations of strangers—were nowhere to be found. As the band continued their tune-up, Ex drummed his fingers in a ghost rhythm along the worn patina of the bar.

"Are we going to hash this out or what?" I prodded, the elephant in the room still unaddressed. "I mean, now's the time."

He finally turned to face me. "I want you to think about this. That review I read to you the other day? You even notice it was all about you? Ten years in and all the rest of us get is an 'et al.' Ever think of how that feels?"

"It's been that way forever, man. You think I control the media?"

"You're the one who does the interviews, so yeah, you do."

The band started up—a touch sloppy, like they'd just woken up from a bender. For once, I wanted the music to stop. The racket clawed at my eyeballs, added unnecessary tension.

"You can't even handle a lukewarm review," I said, my voice rising to compensate. "Journalists would eat you alive and you know it."

He stiffened, a nerve clearly touched. Our last studio album, *Say It*

To My Face, went platinum, just, with choppy reviews. Recording it redefined brutal. Suze and I were breaking down and tension festered in the studio. Some reviews weren't great; they crushed Exile. To be honest, that was when our dynamic started to shift.

"Just because it's always been one way," Ex said, "doesn't mean it can't change. And do you even want to be in the band anymore? 'Cos you sure as hell don't act like it. You're in Mexico, locked in your bus, doing your own thing."

I downed my drink and signaled for another round. It was unlike Ex to be so harsh and totally like me to be annoyed with it. "I had the worst year of my life, took a time out, and somehow I'm not the same person anymore?" I swiveled to face him. "I've had my own bus for years. I've always written the songs. Maybe I just need some support instead of y'all riding my ass."

He snorted. "You're too precious to admit you need support."

Anger and disbelief boiled instantly. "Did you just call me *precious*?"

"I did," he said, daring me to challenge him. "And it's about fucking time. Could call you a few other things too, if you were ever around to listen. You wanna keep your head in the sand, do it all your way and ignore us, fine. But don't be surprised when you come up for air and it's all gone."

He polished off his beer and burped. Right then, the conversation with Sven in Vancouver filtered back. The phone call he'd listened in on.

"I noticed you and Ziegler getting cozy in LA," I said. "You planning on bailing?"

"I never said that."

"I think you did."

He stared down the hint of accusation in my voice. "Unlike you," he said, with surprising condescension, "I don't have a hate on for suits. Or consider it beneath me to socialize with them."

Our fresh drinks arrived, but neither of us reached for them. Ex kept looking at the TV, both hands fisted on the bar.

"Sometimes I wonder if I made a mistake that day," he finally said. "Letting you cut in and take the lead. Set myself up real good."

Our story was told so many times, in so many interviews, sometimes if felt like we were talking about two strangers we'd observed one morning, instead of me, a skinny kid in a Run-DMC shirt heading to the 7-Eleven on Del Amo Boulevard for a Big Gulp, and Exile, dreads flying, bongo-ing for spare change out front. Fresh from a two-hour jam session at home, my head bursting with songs, his drums sucked me in. Without asking, I slipped beside him, waved my finger to bring the tempo down and started to sing. He didn't miss a beat. Instead, he watched me for more cues. It was the most spontaneous, natural fit. We stormed through one of my songs totally on the fly. A small group of Latino workers on lunch break formed a semicircle, egging us on with whistles and *yeahs!* Even the cashier stepped outside to see what the fracas was all about. When we'd finished, dollar bills rained down at our feet. I'd never forget the applause or Ex's surprised, beaming smile. It was our first taste of recognition, and you only experience that once.

We were inseparable after that. Our dynamic was different than the one between Norm and me—mostly due to me. I related to Exile more; we were natural friends. Part of it was I never felt threatened by him. Hearing this, now, after all these years, unsettled me.

"So this is about a change of scenery."

He glanced over. "It's about a lot of things."

A group of burly frat boys, day drunk and messy, spilled through the door, muscling their way to the bar. One of them banged hard into Ex, who elbowed back in return.

The largest one turned around. His lip curled into a sneer. "Watch it, Jamaica."

"Excuse me?" Ex said, standing to his full height.

On a barstool in hammer pants and an undershirt, dreads tucked into a rasta cap, you could mistake Ex as unassuming. His full warrior mode was another story. I could see the mad calculation in frat boy's eyes and leaned over to offer my advice.

"Full disclosure—he's a Capoeira champion. Don't recommend it."

Frat boy's muscles had muscles, but he eventually chin-nodded
—*fine*—and shuffled down the bar.

"Fucking douche," Ex muttered. "Ten to one he doesn't even know
what Capoeira is." He shrugged on his leather jacket and tucked two
twenties under his full beer.

"You're leaving? I thought you wanted to eat?"

His eyes blazed in the direction of frat boy. "Lost my appetite."

Despite me arguing we'd just gotten here and let's watch the band,
Ex turned to leave, but then paused. I followed his sightline to a
young couple canoodling in one of the booths along the far wall. They
were attractive in a cookie-cutter, university town way, but it was how
they held hands, making out like no one was watching.

"Look at them go," Ex said, voice laced with sad nostalgia.
"Reminds me of you and Suze back in the day. PDA. PDA. Even at the
altar you kept pawing at each other."

Exile was one of the few guests at our intimate wedding; everyone
crammed onto the Rancho Palos Verdes porch. I was a basket of
nerves in a rented velvet tux, and when Suze stepped through the
glass door, proud Hank at her side, my heart skipped a beat. Her hair
was braided and piled high on her head. She was my African Goddess
in a tight, strapless dress (too tight, Pops grumbled for years afterwards, saying it made her look cheap) that showcased every luscious
curve. At the makeshift altar, when I lifted her lace veil, she was so
beautiful I couldn't help myself. The crowd whistled and catcalled, the
pastor cleared his throat, but we continued to kiss like no one was
watching.

"You fucked that one up, my man," Ex said. "If anything, I hoped
you would've learned a lesson." The weight of his hand on my
shoulder was suddenly too much to bear. "Catch you backstage. If you
decide to show."

CHAPTER EIGHTEEN

I WASN'T SURE OF A LOT OF THINGS THAT AFTERNOON. IT wasn't the first time to have my ambition called out, but if I could count on anything with Ex, it was his friendship. Over the years, I'd spent more time with him than Suze. I was godfather to his son, Jerome. Our relationship had never been turbulent, so for him to question our very beginning, to harbor such bitterness...it made *me* question everything. I wandered the streets of downtown Calgary, nipping into bars to warm up and drink away the sensation I had no name for. At half past four, with the sun sinking into a pale winter sky, an Uber dropped me back at the Saddledome. The only thing saving the day from being a total write-off was my call with Sasha-Rae.

Hastings had kept a quiet distance since the morning. She glanced up from one of the gossip magazines I'd bought her in Medford, shivering with the blast of cold that followed me inside. I stamped snow off my shoes and handed her the soup and salad I'd brought back.

"Thank you," she said, her tone *I'm still bothered but trying not to show it.*

I snagged a bottle of Grey Goose from the freezer. "I've got my call," I said, trying to pick up the mood. "Wish me luck."

But there was no thrill in the air, and her attention turned back to the magazine. I retreated into the bedroom and placed the vodka on the nightstand. Already buzzed, I decided less was more, for now, and sat cross-legged on my bed, sifting through the few lines I'd memorized. Cocktail party conversation, in case one of those awkward silences cropped up. At five on the nose, I called.

"Hello!" she said.

"Hi. It's me."

"I know, and right on time. Are you trying to impress me?"

"Is it working?"

"I do appreciate punctuality," she said. "But you have other qualities I'm more interested in."

Her voice, warm and seductive, felt like silk caressing my skin. Someone was happy to talk to me and our camaraderie *was* there. I'd half convinced myself it was a figment of my imagination.

"How did your presentation go?"

"Aced it," she said, matter of fact. "I was a little tired, but I'd rehearsed. We landed a new dealer. A big one."

"That's great. Congrats. I was thinking about you this morning."

"Uh-oh," she said, teasing. "Do I want to know?"

My raging boner had actually woken me up, ripped me right out of my less than honorable dream. Not the time to share that detail. "To be perfectly honest, it was the first time a boardroom and one of those red laser pointy thingy's ever factored into my fantasies."

She burst into laughter. "Pointy thingy. Spoken like a true man."

I laughed too, stuffed two pillows against the headboard, and wriggled into a more comfortable position. At this rate, we'd be talking all night.

"How's Calgary?" she asked. "Are you freezing yet?"

"Funny you should ask. Something in the stadium furnace seized up. I might have to go on stage in long underwear. That'll be a first."

"Ugh," she said, a shudder in her voice. "I could never live there. I hate winter."

"Toronto looks worse. You still want to come?" I'd vowed to wait at least until the end of the conversation before dropping the hint, but she had a way of making everything seem urgent. "You'll have your own room, of course," I was quick to add. "Or…"

"Or?"

She stretched the word out like hot taffy and inside me, a slow ache gathered steam. I wanted her to come so bad and it meant a step forward, but was I ready to take it?

"Or not."

"Hmm," she said, and it sounded like she was smiling. "I like the 'or not' option."

I looked heavenward and mouthed *thank you*. "Cool. Shoot me a text with the best times for you to fly. I'll arrange everything."

She countered, saying she could use points, she had a million of them, and I countered back that it was my treat, to pay her back for last night.

"Was it only last night?" she asked.

"I know, right?"

A brief silence fell, and I marveled at how she even made pauses feel natural and easy.

"I hope this doesn't sound weird," she said, breaking the quiet. "But you're very different than what I thought you'd be."

With the worst qualifier ever, I braced myself. "In what way?"

"Taller, for one. And…I don't know…a little less…intense? I remember listening to a podcast once, and the interviewer asked you something about high school, and you just laid into him. Really aggressive. It made me wonder."

She could've said *you sounded like a dick* and would've been right on the money. The media brought out the worst in me, as did crazed fans with no boundaries—total strangers who shoved body parts in my face to sign at meet and greets, and I'd be like *Whoa, why don't you start with your name?*

"Anyway," she said, rushing, perhaps sensing she'd dropped a major gaffe, "you never talked about yourself or anything personal in interviews, so you struck me as sort of…aloof? But it makes sense you're not," she added quickly. "Your songs are so beautiful and emotional. You can't create that without it being inside you."

The way she said *beautiful,* associating it with me—the lining of my throat seemed to shrink.

"You still there?" she asked.

"Yeah. I was just thinking about something you said. Have you ever heard of synesthesia?"

"Is that the color thing? Didn't someone on *The Voice* have it?"

I grimaced. *Okay, so she watched The Voice. No one was perfect.*

"Yeah, that's it. A friend of a friend has it and whenever they hear a song, they see it as a single color."

"That sounds really interesting," she said. "It's almost like having an X-ray of your song—seeing things that aren't there. Did they tell you what color your songs are? I'd be so curious."

Hmmm. Now *I* was. Her X-ray analogy spun the issue in a totally different light. The chances of Hastings' weird color world colliding with Sasha-Rae were almost infinitesimal, and yet here we were.

"When you listen to our music, do you ever see colors?" I asked.

She didn't answer right away, and I presumed she was thinking about the question. Then, I heard it: the familiar beep of an incoming call.

"Fuck," she muttered.

"You have to take that?"

"Nope," she said, full-on defiant.

The beeps ran their course and as soon as they'd ended, another phone, a landline from the sound of it, started up.

"Goddammit, Richey," she moaned.

Uncertainty swarmed in my gut. Who was Richey? "Everything okay?"

"Hold on," she said. Two seconds later, she barked into the landline. "Now what?" A minute of silence passed, punctuated with an occasional terse, "I see." Finally, "Give me ten minutes. Make sure he doesn't talk to anyone."

Right after, I could've driven a semi through the tunnel of gloom. Part of me wanted to hear her swear again—it made her hotter, if that was humanly possible.

"I can call you back," I offered.

"No," she said. "My brother can wait."

Brother. Phew.

"My dad used to race formula one," she went on to explain. "He retired in the eighties and started Vantage Auto Parts, the company I work for. My brother Richey races NASCAR, and we sponsor him."

The pieces quickly fell into place. "Richey Slayer is your brother?"

"You know who he is?" she asked, warily.

NASCAR fan or not, I'd have to be braindead not to know who Richey Slayer was. Talented, reckless, and a redneck stud, his exploits off the track were as notorious as his tactics on. A harem of big-boobed blondes and various scandals followed him around the country. A third paternity suit was recently filed against him. His fans were zealots and their fervor pushed NASCAR to a ratings bonanza.

"Everyone knows who he is," I said.

"Then you know what I'm dealing with."

Last night she gave zero indication she knew who I was. Now it made sense. She'd been around fame, seen the worst of it. The last thing she'd do is pander to it.

"For what it's worth, Sasha-Rae Slayer has a nice ring to it."

"Tomason," she reminded me. "I don't use my dad's last name. We're not the best of friends."

Her downbeat tone conjured up my own parental dynamics, or lack thereof. I swore right then and there, if I ever had the chance, I'd be the best damn father ever.

She begged off with, "I hate to end this on a low note, but I've gotta sort out this mess. Call me after the show?"

We said our goodbyes and I tried hard, I really did, but I couldn't get past the *fuck*. Even in the shower, as hot water gushed and I bit back a groan, it echoed in my brain like reverb. When the release hit, it was a 9.0 earthquake so powerful I collapsed against the wall and skidded out, landing with a thud on my ass. Fitting in every way, really. She was sweeping me off my feet, literally and figuratively.

Hastings looked up from her magazine as soon as I came out of the bedroom.

"Is she coming to Toronto?"

I sat down on the couch across from her and winced. My tail bone still rang with the aftereffects of my self-love. She saw my discomfort. My wet hair. Cheeks still flushed twenty minutes later. It was wrong on every level to indulge my fantasies with her close by, but I just couldn't help myself.

I took a deep breath. "Yes. But I'll figure out a solution that works. I'm not going to leave you, us, in a lurch."

Her eyes dropped back down. She flipped a page of the magazine, although we both knew she wasn't reading anything.

"The good news is I've got a project for you," I said. "If you're interested."

She half-looked up. "What kind?"

"Right up your alley. I'd like you to listen to my songs and tell me what color they are."

There was a long, heavy gap. I don't know if it was the unflattering overhead light, but she looked worn out, more than just tired. "Why now?" she wanted to know.

"A guy can't change his mind?"

"Is it because of her?" she asked, like this indicated some kind of weakness in me.

"You don't have to if you don't want to."

"I never said I didn't want to."

"Then you should listen to them. It might help."

"I thought you didn't need any help."

Crossing her arms didn't toughen her up. If anything, it only magnified how diminutive she was.

I laughed, totally unbridled. "I take it that's a yes?"

It took a moment before she softened. She'd come around on her terms, not mine. Still, she maintained an imperious air, offering me the following advice: "You should smile more often. You have a nice smile."

"It's not too hairy for you, m'lady?" I joked in an English accent.

She fought it, but the laugh escaped. A dramatic eye roll followed. "It's a smile, fool."

If someone had asked, I couldn't define the sensation, only knew it was subtle, like a well-placed sax riff to beef up a chorus. Maybe it was our melodramas; different, yet similar. Or that we were both riding our upended worlds, churning into unknown places. Whatever the case, on a March evening, cold and biting, with soft drifts of snow falling, inexplicably and under the most screwed up odds, our makeshift alliance shifted.

CHAPTER NINETEEN

IT SOUNDS LIKE A FIRST-RATE MILLENNIAL CRISIS: turning the big three-o and believing life is over. When I turned thirty last November though, there really wasn't much to live for. The *Say It To My Face* tour had skidded to a halt nine months prior with my marriage toasted, mom six feet under, and the band splintered. With zilch to ground me, my drinking problem morphed into that Pi number: endless. After a tragic all-nighter, I stumbled into LAX, convinced a skeptical ticket agent to put me on a flight, and jetted off to Mexico with nothing but the clothes on my back. I didn't plan to be away for so long, but the funks in life could screw a person up...more so than he or she already was.

The fainting episode in Mexico was, in retrospect, the wakeup call I needed. Coming face to face with my own mortality sobered me the fuck up. (Not totally, but I dialed it back enough to pull myself together.) Feeling better than I had in months, I landed back in LA after my year off ready to prep for the tour and upcoming album. Convinced I'd left my demons behind, a rude awakening slapped me in the face. No songs tickled the strings. Nada. It's like all my creativity had bled out on the floor of my Mexican hacienda.

Up until now, I'd kept the extent of my despair under wraps, unsure how to fix it. But when I woke up this morning and saw Hastings at the kitchen table still making notes, trepidation flared all over again. She'd attacked the song project yesterday, and multiple pages of my notepad were crammed with her spidery handwriting. I made a coffee and slid onto the banquette across from her.

"That's a lot of notes," I said.

"I didn't realize you had so many songs."

I stole a glance at the notepad. Couldn't decipher a thing. "What's the verdict?"

"Well, it's interesting." She turned off the burner phone, the one I'd loaded Spotify on for her to use. "Almost all of your songs are blue."

"Is that bad?" It didn't sound good.

"No, just unusual. Blue always means structure and I was surprised to see it so often."

"I'm not sure I'm following," I said. "Every song has structure of some kind. And most of my songs are hits. They're all about structure. That's why they're hits."

At this news, her head tilted. "Do you think about structure when you write?"

I hummed on that, took a sip of coffee. "To an extent. I mean, it's part of my makeup. I like order. Messy things drive me crazy. Tie-dyes. Puzzles. Jazz, especially. It gives me a headache."

"Why do people call you the Jazzer then?" she asked.

"It's a nickname, from my father. It was his stage name."

On my eighth birthday, Pops' buddies had slapped me with the same moniker. A christening of sorts. He'd been so proud that day, when he still believed I'd get into jazz.

"He wanted me to follow in his footsteps," I continued. "But it didn't happen. I've been a massive disappointment to him."

You're too similar, Mom had forever wailed. *And you're both so stubborn.* Burdened with the unfortunate role of referee in our bloody wars, Pops and I wore her down, both of us rebuffing her with brutal silent treatments whenever she showed allegiance in the other direction. When I moved in with Suze's family to preserve my sanity, Mom understood, as much as a mom could. Pops went off the deep end. He could never forgive Suze. She would forever be the evildoer, the one who snatched his only son away.

Reading my body language, Hastings backed off. "We don't have to talk about this if you don't want to."

But she'd triggered a new consideration. An interesting one. "Now that I think about it, the structure thing might be a factor of my OCD. I just never correlated it to music."

"You're OCD," she repeated, understanding spreading on her face as she pieced together all my quirks from the past few days. Finally, I was making sense. "That explains why you'd write songs a certain way. Do you usually follow some kind of system?"

"You mean what's my process?"

"Yeah."

I shimmied backward to rest against the window, drew my knees up, and rested the mug on them. I'd never shared these details with a stranger and couldn't help sounding guarded. "Usually I write the music first. It's kind of like building a house. I need a frame, a structure to drape the lyrics onto."

"So you always write the music first?" she clarified.

"Why are you asking?"

She flipped the notebook pages back one by one until she was on the top sheet. Her finger marked the spot. "This one song wasn't blue at all. 'Moonlight.' Did you write it differently?"

The opener on our debut album, critics called 'Moonlight' a love song for the ages. With a sexy, Caribbean feel, it never bolted into a runaway hit but over time, became our most loved song. At our shows, everyone sang along to the chorus with deafening volume:

And in the moonlight, it will always be just right
It's just you and me and nothing between, only shadows of the night
Because this is true, more than God could ever do
So if I die tonight, it will be all right, because there's nothing without you

The song was born on a hot and star-filled night. I'd proposed to Suze, she'd said yes, and we went a little wild. With her parents out of town, we pilfered a bottle of champagne, got stupid drunk, and piled blankets on the deck at her parent's house, making love under the light of the full moon, both of us peaking at the exact same time. After, I grabbed my guitar and wrote the entire song while watching her sleep, all of it coming together in a dopamine, blissed-out haze.

"I did write it differently," I said and gave her a PG rundown of the scenario, only mentioning the proposal. "The lyrics bubbled out before the music."

She gave that some thought. "Maybe you should try writing lyrics first again," she suggested. "Start without the structure and see if that helps."

"It's not so easy, changing how I write. And I can't just recreate the feeling from that night. It was special."

She leaned forward and propped up on skinny elbows, chin resting in the curve of her hands. "What was the feeling?"

"I don't know...love, exhilaration." What *wasn't* I feeling that night? "I felt invincible. Like I could conquer anything."

I guzzled the dregs of my coffee, trying to drown the image that wouldn't go away. Suze's naked curves in the moonlight still came to me in my dreams and I'd wake up, bolstered for a few drowsy seconds believing she was within reach, our lives still in motion together. And then the misery hit.

"I know you're trying to help me figure this out," I said, careful in my glance over, "but going backward is the worst thing for me."

Her expression changed from interested intent to compassion. "I understand," she said, although I wasn't sure she did until she continued. "My dad, my real dad, he told me the only way to keep learning is by moving forward. Doing things different. Doing what scared me. Maybe you need to do something that scares you."

Her advice, by way of her father, poked at a tender spot. Pops had always nagged at me to fight my OCD, to be more spontaneous, not obsess. Ironic, because how many nights had he holed himself up in the backyard shed playing Mingus and Monk until his fingers bled?

I leaned my head against the window and shut my eyes. We were en route to the Brandt Centre in Regina, Saskatchewan. A nasty ice storm pelted against the glass, harsh bullets vibrating the back of my skull. In Calgary last night, a snowstorm had blanketed the city in a foot of white powder while we were on stage. All of us, crew and band, got silly after the show. We chucked snowballs at each other, slipping and sliding like drunken fools. Over beers, a couple new crew members broke the ice with me. Everyone had interesting back stories and it dawned on me I knew so little about Hastings. I turned to face her.

"What was your dad like?" I asked, curious about the man who'd influenced her.

"Smart. Serious," she said, her features softening with a smile. "He was always studying something."

"Was he a teacher?"

"He worked for a landscaping company. Loved being outside. Mom was always telling him to get his butt inside for dinner. 'You love those plants more than me.'"

Her bossy imitation made me smile and a flash of her in New Orleans came out of nowhere: skipping down a street in shiny patent shoes young girls wear for special occasions. Her father knee-deep in topsoil and talking to plants. Her mother, on the porch, fists on her waist, shaking her head at a husband lost in his work. There was a comfort in that vision I couldn't quite identify.

"Did he love plants more than her?"

Her smile slipped. "Some days, I'm sure. She struggled a lot. Went through a lot of up and downs."

"What did she do for a living?"

"She worked at a library in New Orleans. But when we moved to Seattle, she stopped working. Hated the rain and doing anything outside. She went a little stir crazy. That's what my dad said." She moved her eyes off mine, the mood shifting down a gear. Her next words felt tight. "They fought a lot. She wanted another kid and he didn't."

"Did you like having a brother? I always wanted one."

When she stilled, I immediately knew it was the wrong question.

"I never met him," she finally said, a quiver of emotion threaded into her words. "He, Darius, was a baby. My parents were coming back from the hospital with him when they crashed."

Oh, boy. Great timing on that one, bozo.

"Kiddo," I said, my throat dry as dust. "I'm so sorry."

She cuffed her nose with the back of her hand and mumbled, "It's okay."

Despite the fact I'd already seen her cry, she wouldn't let her composure go. I never expected this process to dredge up ghosts...for either of us. This memory lane wasn't of the fun and games variety. No *do you remember when,* followed by embarrassed laughs. As the hum of the bus took over, our bodies rose and fell imperceptibly, in time with the undulations from the freeway. The floor seemed to shift as well, waves rolling in the deep sea. I moved back to face the table, spread my fingers out on the surface and pushed, in the hopes sheer willpower could stop the bus from moving. Staring at both hands, the wedding band Suze had slipped on my finger while crying seemed to pulse with an energy all its own.

"Do you ever wish you could change things?"

Her question crept over my soul like a tarantula. Suze was my first kiss, my first blowjob, my first everything. We were going to die in each other's arms, pull a Romeo and Juliet. I would sever one of my hands to change things.

My eyes met hers, briefly. "Every day."

A murmur passed between us; a tangle of mutual sorrow.

"Me too," she said.

One of those conversation-killer questions, neither of us had much to say after. Outside, the ice storm leveled off and darkness seeped out of the sky. A blaze of sun illuminated the crystallized slush on the landscape, turning it into a sea of sparkles. We both stared out into the horizon before I excused myself and curled up in the dark of my bedroom to sort through the questions pinballing in my brain. What was I scared of? Change? Or never changing? In some ways, my life was better before. But *was* it better? Or just familiar? I needed to figure it out. During last night's post-show call, Sasha-Rae admitted she wanted out of Vantage, to get away from her brother. Richey's latest snafu, a sloppy bar brawl started by a disgruntled ex of one of his harem, was filmed and had gone viral. Lawyers were now involved. The situation was shaping up to be a brutal few weeks of damage control, and she was thrilled to get away. I was excited but nervous, too. Sasha-Rae was a chance to overcome my past, but how was I supposed to forget the past when it was always fucking there?

CHAPTER TWENTY

AFTER THE SMALL-TOWN CALM OF REGINA AND WINNIPEG, Toronto hit like we'd collectively downed a crateful of uppers. Everyone was cranked. Inside the Scotiabank Arena, Sven barked orders to the film crew who, as film crews did, glared back with self-importance. Harvey and Bryce circled around, corporate vultures with phones glued to their ears. These were big shows with lots on the line. Tickets had sold out in minutes and backstage passes were hotter than cryptocurrency.

"Ok guys, listen up." Marcelo, our director, tapped his skull-tipped cane on the stage to grab our attention. A big-name music video guy back in the day, if Marcelo had a dollar for every band he'd screamed at, he'd long be retired. Like every director, he fancied himself a serious auteur. Unfortunately, his art house movie was a bloated lesson in patience and had flopped. Which explained his newfound team player attitude.

"We're going to do a dry run of the opening," he continued. "Make sure everyone knows their marks. We have six cameras, lots of sweeping shots to start with—give us that big look and feel. Live, there'll be a couple guys on stage getting the close-ups and crowd shots, so watch your backs." He waved his cane at our tech team huddled at the side of the stage. "You guys, too. Careful moving in and out with the instruments."

Norm leaned toward a camera guy, one of those hunched-shoulder types who might live under a bridge with a pet rock and plot world destruction. "I've got one of those lucky faces that reads well from either side," he said. "So don't be shy zooming in for a close up tonight, especially in the opener. After that my eyeliner goes to shit. Got it?"

Behind a wall of Tamas, Ex twirled his sticks. "Didn't you crack the last camera lens, Diva McDiva?"

"Your face is as big as a Buick on camera, my friend," Norm replied. "I doubt Sparky here's got a lens wide enough."

"My name's Chad," the camera guy said, not amused. "And I have every focal length."

Norm shot me a *who-does-this-guy-think-he-is* look, and for once, appeared rested, owing to the fact the boys had flown in from Winnipeg. I would've loved to join them, except flying freaked me out. I had to be medicated to the eyeballs just to board and never set foot in an airplane unless it was an emergency. Besides, the past three days on the bus with Hastings had been interesting. We'd slipped out of our protective skins, conversations companionable and surprisingly deep. I'd recounted the early days of blood, sweat and tears. Our eventual breakthrough. How our stratospheric trajectory left us all hanging on for dear life. She shared growing up in New Orleans hearing jazz in the streets, being enraptured with the smoky female singers. Not understanding why colors came hand in hand with music until being diagnosed with synesthesia. Turned out she always wanted to be a singer. Dreamed of attending Juilliard until she found out how much it cost.

She'd been careful, asking a few questions about Suze. Got misty hearing the high school sweetheart angle. When she asked what it was like falling in love, her face held such longing I almost downplayed it. But Suze deserved more. Hastings hung on my every word, transported, like she was hearing a fairy tale.

Last night we got back to the topic of music. Loose after a few vodkas, I coaxed her into a duet. A couple self-conscious starts gave way to a blockbuster. With me as her guide, she hit the high notes in 'Moonlight.' I swore she was channeling Whitney Houston. Our voices were a natural harmony: mine lower and gravelly, hers radiant and warm. I'd never forget how she beamed right after, knowing she'd nailed it. It was criminal thinking her talent might go to waste because of money, or lack thereof.

"Positions, everyone," Marcelo shouted. "Let's go!"

Norm slung his Paul Reed Smith over his shoulder and said to me, "Dude, what is it with you and the phone? FOCUS. We're gonna be immortalized on film tonight."

"Memory cards, actually," Diego corrected him, hustling past us with his vintage Rickenbacker. "He's not shooting film."

"Thank you and thank you, Mr. Know It All." Norm sauntered over to his mark with a roll of his eyes.

Harold, my guitar tech, waited patiently at the side of the stage, holding the ES. A bud since high school, he'd humped gear for us when we were just starting out. Longest running crewmember and the only Samoan guitar tech in the industry.

Finally, the long-awaited text came in.

SR: Boarded! See you soon.

I tucked the phone away and took the guitar from Harold.

"Fresh strings boss," he said. "Let her wail."

Now I could focus.

CHAPTER TWENTY-ONE

TONIGHT WAS INSANE. THE CROWD, KNOWING THEY WERE on camera, went bananas. We pushed it too, feeding off the energy. Drenched in sweat, I took a quick shower backstage after the show and ducked out with no one noticing. But with so little transition time, I couldn't shake off the effects of twenty thousand screaming fans. The adrenaline rushing through me was monumental. My body hummed like a live wire and the backseat of the Uber felt cramped and suffocating. When the driver dropped me at the hotel, I practically ran across the lobby into the elevator. In the hushed hallway of the 25th floor, I stood in front of my own suite like a moron. I'd blanked on getting a room key. Forced to knock on the door, I braced for the disappointment—the inevitable let down of seeing someone in the flesh again after building them up to mythic proportions in your mind.

Nope. Not happening.

Framed in the doorway, she was an Impressionist masterpiece. More stunning than I remembered.

"Hi," she said.

"Hi."

I needed to do something, not just stand there. But her hair, tousled and loose, the sweet curve of her jawline, the other curves—all of them begged to be touched. I just didn't know where to start.

She smiled, uncertain. "Are you going to come in?"

"Yeah, of course." I stepped over the threshold, her perfume floating between us. "Kind of a crazy night," I said, by way of explanation. "Still a little out of it. How was your flight?"

"Uneventful. But I guess that's a good thing."

Instead of her usual throaty laugh, the one that made me want to crawl inside and feel it vibrate, something tinny came out.

The door shut.

She smiled.

I smiled.

A few awkward seconds passed.

She turned to gesture at the CN Tower, its spire glowing brightly through the living room window. "It's a great view up here."

"I totally agree."

I didn't mean to stare but Dear God. As she smiled, shyly, I did a quick survey over her shoulder. A slipcover was on the couch, champagne chilled in a silver bucket on the coffee table. The air was fragrant with roses, various bouquets scattered around the room. They got the memo.

"There's a bottle of champagne with our name on it," I said. "Shall we?"

I let my hand fall onto the small of her back and guided her to the couch. The view *was* commanding, the kind that made you stand straighter and breathe more deeply if you were so inclined...or had control over your faculties, which I did not at this precise moment. My hands were thick with a caveman-like inelegance, giving the appearance I'd never opened a bottle of champagne before. Judging from how she perched on the lip of the couch, she was far from relaxed. I filled both flutes and handed one to her.

"It's a little cliché," I said, "but you're a reason to celebrate." I joined her on the couch, not too close, and raised my glass. "Thank you for coming."

"Thank you for having me."

We clinked glasses and with a very unladylike guzzle, she downed the entire thing.

"This will stay bubbly for a while," I quipped. "It's the good stuff."

Finally, her real laugh, mixed in with a burp. An embarrassed hand brushed her forehead. "Sorry," she said. "It's so stupid. I'm so nervous right now."

I stretched my arm along the top of the couch, happy to let some of my tension go. We were both as stiff as prearranged prom dates.

"If it makes you feel better, you're not the only one."

She smiled tentatively. "Do you think it's crazy? All of this."

"Define crazy."

"This...I mean...us. It all happened so fast."

A muscle tightened in my chest. "Too fast?"

That's what it sounded like, which didn't make sense. Five days ago, we were making out like the world was about to end. Every conversation this week was rambling, open and honest. A convict about to be sent away for twenty years fidgeted less than she did right now. Whatever fueling this had been left unsaid.

"Maybe I should clarify this isn't what I usually do," I said. "In fact, I've never done this."

Her eyes finally steadied on mine. She let out a deep breath. "It's not that. What I mean is...the whole alley thing. That's not who I am. I'm way more conservative. After, I thought oh my god, what if you were expecting me to be *that* girl?"

I unclenched her right fist from the stem of the flute and set both of our glasses on the coffee table. Then I leaned forward, scooped her hands in mine and willed away her uncertainty. "That was a once in a lifetime thing. I'm not judging you on it and I hope you won't judge me."

She searched my face, and I had to be careful looking into the shimmer of her eyes. I could lose myself and never find my way home.

"I'm not into drugs or anything crazy," she said. "It's important to be upfront."

"I like that you're brave enough to be honest. It says a lot about

you. And for the record, I've never touched drugs. The crazy part...
well, what we did in the alley was the craziest thing I've ever done."

A flush of embarrassment rose on her cheeks. "I don't know what I
was thinking." She bit her lip, debating. "Well, maybe I did know.
Honestly? I've had a crush on you for years."

Fantasies unveiled, she cringed in my direction.

"Honestly?" I asked, teasing a smile. "I couldn't tell."

We both burst into loose laughter and I made my move, slipping
an arm around her shoulder. "C'mere."

She burrowed into me, face still hot from her schoolgirl confession.
Her being so close set off wild palpitations, the *thump thump thump* of
my heart filling the tiny space between us. The coconut smell of her
hair was every tropical beach I'd never been to and her hand voyaged
along the top of my thigh, testing the waters.

"I really liked talking to you this week," she said.

"I really like *you*," I said.

She pulled back and looked up, danger dancing in her eyes. I had
every intention of being a gentleman tonight, payback for the animal-
istic fever of Sunday, but after five days of waiting to be this close to
her, it became unsafe, all the thoughts crashing in my mind. Our
mouths were so close together, all it took was a small tip of my head
to connect. After that silken touchdown, the real world receded until
it disappeared, and it was just us, lost in each other all over again. We
ignored the struggle of the narrow couch that threatened to boot us
off at every twist and turn and when we finally broke for air, I was
seeing double, the weight of her on top of me a velvet crush.

"You're making it very difficult to pace myself," I said, breathless.

Her lips buzzed my throat with little nips. "Likewise."

In one smooth-operator move, she edged my one hand under her
bra, onto a tight nub of nipple. It wasn't quite pain, closer to sweet
agony, my resolve slipping away. But this time we were doing it right.

"You all right if we move?" It was a way to ask without asking,
although I still needed to ask.

She answered with a spirited smile. "I'm all right."

I don't entirely recall the trip to the bedroom. One second we were on the couch and then we weren't. Through the floor-to-ceiling windows, big-city light pollution filtered onto the bed with a science fiction glow. Built-in side tables on either edge of the bed appeared to float, legless. Twenty-five stories below us, late-night traffic hummed like a quiet appliance. Our moment of lusty magic temporarily broken, we stared at the bed, a couple of unsure newlyweds.

"Whatever you want to do or not," I said. "I'm cool."

She bowed her head, pretty face partially hidden with shadow and confessed, "I might be a little rusty."

Rusty? Try corroded. I kicked myself for not prepping in the shower after the show. My staying power was questionable, and the focus required would be next to impossible with her underneath me.

"If you want to stop, for any reason…"

Her giggle was all fresh nerves. She grabbed my hand with a mischievous smile. "I don't think I can stop once we start."

I didn't think I could, either.

We lowered ourselves onto the foot of the bed, a little gun-shy before starting up again. A soft kiss kicked us off and our moves flowed, not too fast or slow. As the pace picked up, we shimmied higher on the bed, breaking our embrace only to peel off clothing. Just one layer away from being naked together felt deliciously sinful in its own right. When my hand drifted lower to cup against her, heat fired onto my fingers. She moaned, arms stretching wide above her head. They clunked against the headboard and a beam of surgical strength light assaulted us. All momentum ground to a halt.

She blocked a hand to her forehead and squinted. "How did that happen?"

"I don't know," I said. "There must be a sensor in the headboard or something." I leaned forward to investigate, my boxers very tented, and froze mid-way.

"What is it?" she asked.

"Uh, nothing."

She followed my sightline and then looked back at me, more confused. "Are those yours?"

"No. Yes. Uh, I think so."

She peered again at the package, a double check on what she was seeing. "You travel with your own sheets?"

"Sometimes."

I slid off the bed, practically tiptoeing to the safety of the hardwood floor. Aware of something more than sheets, she propped up on both elbows, waiting for an explanation.

"I'm a little OCD," I said, my face burning with discomfort. "Or a lot, depending on how you look at it."

"Meaning you have to wash everything, OCD?"

Once upon a time, Suze and I had this very discussion. It played just as awkward now.

"Yeah. Clean is good. Order, too. Germs also freak me out. The hotel was supposed to change the sheets before."

She digested this new development. "So, how does it work with...I mean, I did shower."

"That's fine," I said. "You're fine."

"But what you're saying..." She rolled over to the bedside table and picked up the sheet set, turned them over in her hands. "...is these need to go on so we can get it on."

There was nothing left to salvage, including my pride. "Kind of. If you don't mind."

Suddenly all business, she tossed me the sheets, picked up one of the pillows and yanked off the cover. "You unwrap," she said. "I'll start here."

We stripped and re-made the bed in record time. She filled the space with casual banter, made the whole ordeal less horrifying. As she fluffed up the final pillow, a swell of appreciation caught in my throat.

"Thank you," I said. "For not making me feel like an idiot."

She tossed the pillow at me, her slim figure looking smoking hot in sexy lingerie. "It's better with no secrets, right?"

Like a spreading stain, guilt washed over me. Hastings had put on a brave face this evening, wished me luck with both the show and Sasha-Rae. Norm would classify it as taking one for the team, and no matter how I positioned it, that's what I'd asked her to do. I wasn't proud. Satisfying my own needs had never felt more self-indulgent.

"Always," I said, trying not to disrupt the evening anymore. "Trust is the most important thing."

She climbed back onto the bed and lay on her back. Nestled in a plunging bra, her breasts were perfect, just the way I like them—big enough, with a soft spread that proved they were real.

"I don't know if it's smart to trust you," she teased. "A girl might get in trouble."

With what could pass as confidence, I straddled her. In reality, I was a starved man, she the lush banquet. Wearing only lace and a look of vulnerability, she pulled me into a kiss. Lost in the fumble of her bra closure, it took a full second to realize she'd stilled beneath me. And that crickets didn't live in hotel rooms. And that sound was my damn phone ringing.

"If you have to get it," she said, being the champ, "I understand."

It was probably one of the boys, wondering where I'd disappeared to. Or Sven, having some sort of conniption. Or...a sudden, bleak thought bulldozed to the front of my mind.

Stop it.

"Whoever it is can wait." I pawed on the floor, found my jeans and yanked the phone out to shut it down.

Nothing was more important than Sasha-Rae right now.

Well...almost nothing.

CHAPTER TWENTY-TWO

"Everything okay?" Sasha-Rae asked, more than concerned as I scrambled to yank on my jeans.

"I don't know," I said. "I'll be right back."

Leaving her in the dark, literally and figuratively, I bolted to the bathroom, arms pebbled with goosebumps. My phone kept ringing. I glanced again at the burner number on the screen, a dead space in my gut.

What I'd told Hastings earlier:

"Call if there's an emergency."

"You'll answer for sure?" she'd asked.

"24/7. I'll pick up. I promise."

In the bathroom, I closed the door behind me and fumbled for the light switch. A million mirrored mosaic tiles, every inch of the walls covered in them, blinded my retinas as light reflected off them.

I guarded my eyes against the glare and answered. "Hey. It's me."

"Adrian?" she whispered back.

"Yeah. What's up?"

"There's someone here. Trying to get in."

The fear in her voice made my stomach plunge. "What do you mean? Is the door locked?"

"It's locked, but he keeps banging on it like he's trying to break it down."

Suddenly unsteady, I lowered myself onto the rim of the tub. I'd foolishly decided it was safer for her to stay in the bus. Sneaking in and out of the hotel added more risk. She wasn't thrilled to be on her own, but with security on-site and me only a short cab ride away, all bases were covered. In theory.

"Go into my bedroom and lock the door, okay?" I said, parental instruction mode rising out of nowhere. "Keep the blinds closed. I'm going to call you right back."

Back-to-back shows in the same city meant a walk away for the crew tonight. With a rare evening off, no one would be hanging around in a bus. Except Big Daddy kept opposite hours—it was the driving life—and often crashed in his sleeping quarters. Something I hoped for while his phone rang and rang.

"Mr. A," he answered jovially, five sheets to the wind. "What can I do you for?"

'Sweet Home Alabama' blasted in the background, partiers shouting at each other over the whiskey twang of Ronnie.

"I, uh..." I chewed on my nail. What was I going to say? "I forgot something back at the bus, but it sounds like you're not there."

He sobered up immediately. "I can be there if you need me."

"No, no it's cool. Nothing urgent."

A woman's high-pitched squeal echoed in the background. Big Daddy muffled the phone and told her to keep it down. "You sure, Mr. A? I know you. You can't sleep when you got stuff on your brain. I can be there in forty."

"I left the ES in there," I said, the first believable thing that popped into my head. "Just had a bit of a panic attack wondering about security."

He switched from alarmed to misty. "She's like a baby to you, isn't she? Just like my '69 Mustang." In the down time from touring, Big Daddy restored vintage cars with the care of a surgeon. He understood obsession. "Rest assured, Mr. A, that place is tight as a virgin. We're double wrapped, so to speak.

Promoter has security, the venue has security. Should be a-okay. Mercury retrograde just ended too," he added, like that solved everything.

"Of course," I said, attempting laid-back cool. "I don't know what I was thinking. Enjoy your night off."

I hung up and dialed Hastings back straight away.

"I heard a window smash on another bus," she cried out. "You have to come. Please."

It was 12:15 a.m. according to the clock embedded in the mirror. The bathroom tiles were warm under my bare feet and did nothing to stop the frozen ghost fingers walking up my spine. We'd traversed the globe six times over and never, not even once, had trouble resembling this. I stared at the bathtub drain, my banner evening swirling toward it metaphorically. Of all the fricking nights.

"Adrian?" Her voice was very small and very far away.

"Don't move. I'm on my way."

"It's the usual bullshit," I said, pulling on my T-shirt and hoodie. "Band stuff."

Bundled in the bed sheet, Sasha-Rae tried to hide her worry. It didn't take a rocket scientist to measure my agitation. Her eyes were dark pools, full of questions. "Anything I can do?"

"Yes. Don't fall asleep. I won't be more than an hour." I kissed her and groaned inwardly. She tasted so good.

I rushed to the elevator and paced waiting for it. Not knowing what lay ahead was an OCD-er's nightmare. *It's probably nothing,* I told myself. *Except windows don't smash themselves.*

In the hotel roundabout, it took three minutes for an Uber to show up; a whole new exercise in impatience. Once inside, I slammed the door so violently, the driver, a portly black man, gave me a long look over his shoulder.

"Slow down, partner. I'll get you there."

"Scotiabank Arena," I barked. "Book it."

We exchanged heavy glances before he decided to give my brusqueness a free pass. "Oookay," he said.

As the Prius moved silently into the streets, an American flag charm dangling from the rearview mirror swayed back and forth. The night was still young for Friday standards, although on this end of town a major expressway sliced along the waterfront with hotels and high rises peppered in between. It explained the lack of traffic. Most of the city's action was further north.

The driver turned down his talk radio station. "The show's over from what I heard. You an employee?"

"We played there tonight. My bus is on the grounds. I forgot something."

"Got it." He eased to a stop at the red light and continued to chatter. "You're a musician, huh? I played guitar back in the day. Never had the drive to do more than fool around though. Too busy chasing women." He chuckled at some memory, a fine night of pleasure. "How's the biz treating you?"

"Great."

"You're one of the lucky ones. I hear it's cutthroat."

My leg wouldn't stop shimmying. Of all the drivers in Toronto, I got Mr. Small Talk.

"Yea-up," he continued. "I used to drive one of your fancy buses for a living. For Obama. Both campaigns."

For the first time he had my attention. "Obama, as in the former President of the United States?"

He smiled at me in the mirror. "The one and only."

"Why are you driving an Uber in Toronto?"

He cracked a can of Dr. Pepper sitting in the cup holder and took a swig. "Didn't like the politics in the U.S. Wife's Canadian. With the exchange rate, we could get a decent house up here. Driving the President had its perks but after a while, it got to me. The Secret Service, machine guns on the walls, every day the potential for disaster. Up here, I'm anonymous. I like it better that way."

I stared out at the bleak cityscape. "Can't say I blame you. Sometimes I wish I could disappear."

The arena wasn't far, and soon enough we were funneling up the street to the entrance gates. With the show over, the cleared-out building seemed to hover on the pavement, a giant spaceship waiting for takeoff. Just beyond the gates, all the buses were dark. But there had to be a crew member drunk and crashing around. Who, or what else, could it be?

The driver shifted into park and turned around, his seat creaking. He peered at me over his glasses. "'Scuse me for noticing," he continued, "because I was trained to notice, but everything all right?"

Fifteen minutes ago, I was about to make love to a woman as beautiful as the best melody I'd ever written. No, everything wasn't all right, thank you very much.

"Maybe," I said.

He popped open the console and handed me a card between two fingers. "Name's Philip if you need me to come back."

I fished out two hundred-dollar bills, offering them in return. "Double that if you wait."

He fingered the Benjamins, the crease between his eyes deepening as he did whatever math he needed to. "Take your time," he finally said.

I stepped outside into a blast of frigid wind. The air carried a stale fish tank odor, eau de Lake Ontario. I hopped over the gate and made my way to the buses. Despite every right to be here, the whole situation screamed clandestine.

Wham!

My heart rate surged into a 300 BPM solid line of freak out. What the hell was that? I raced for the cover of my bus and flattened against it. The generator hummed like a giant insect, vibrating my very soul. Where was security? I'd seen graveyards with more action.

Wham!

I lowered onto my knees and peeked under the chassis of the bus. Nothing, although every bone in my body knew there was something. I strained to hear anything else.

Wham!

Metal and hard, cold and ominous. My sphincter tightened as a dose of reality hit. My fists were the only line of defense, but if whoever was there had real firepower, my playbook would need a drastic overhaul. I pulled out my phone and thumbed redial. Under cover of the generator noise, if I whispered, no one could hear me. I hoped.

"Are you here?" The strain in Hasting's voice was palpable.

"Shhh, yes. Don't make a sound, okay? I'll knock when it's safe."

I managed to sound in control, despite my blood racing as fast as a Formula One Ferrari. It always looked cool in the movies: sleuthing around, bad guys just around the corner. But this was a far cry from make-believe. And no one would call cut if things got ugly.

"Open up, you motherfucker."

I slipped the phone into my pocket and stilled. My throat was raw from swallowing too much. I tiptoed around the front of the bus and bargained with a God I didn't believe in. *If anything happens, let it be to me, not her.*

In the dark, I felt his presence before I saw him.

And then I felt him.

Two hundred pounds of meat slamming into me like a freight train.

I could bench one-ninety, back when I was in shape. Trouble was, I hadn't seen the inside of a home gym for months. Nor did I enjoy fighting, something that was painfully obvious as a human monolith tackled me to the ground. What I lacked in street fighting skills though, I made up for in speed and dexterity. He only landed one punch before I flipped back onto my feet. As he hopped around me like a boxer, throwing jabs and huffing air, I staggered back to catch my breath and do a quick assessment. Multiple tattoos snaked around a neck corded with muscles. The gloss in his eyes was pure pharmaceuticals. Now wasn't the right time, but perhaps later I'd suggest if he was on the hunt for a Halloween costume, he had the white supremacist look down pat.

"You fucking punk," he said, his voice eerie and high pitched. "You trying to cut in?"

On the ground, just behind him, one of those portable safes was banged up to rat shit. It didn't look familiar, but one of the crew bus doors was cracked open, the window beside it sunken in, a spider's web of crackles radiating outwards from the point of impact. A spear of fury lanced through me. Thievery was the lowest form of crime and he'd pushed all my wrong buttons.

"These are my buses, my crew," I said, pushing up the sleeves of my hoodie. "You mess with them, you mess with me."

"Who are you?" he demanded. A longhaired cover boy infiltrating his turf wasn't part of tonight's agenda.

"Doesn't matter. My people, one of them, he's waiting over there." I tipped my head toward Philip. "We can do this one of two ways. The best way is you walk away."

My bluster wasn't bulletproof, but I figured if he had a gun (or a knife), he would've pulled it by now. Sven had dealt with his share of druggies over the years and his hard-earned advice was to never let go of their eyes; it unnerved them. Sure enough, under the lockdown of my gaze, the dude's swagger dropped a notch.

"You got any inspiration for me to bounce?" He wiggled his fingers, on the hunt for a payout.

"Nope. Flat out at the moment."

His sketchy eyes dropped back to the safe. We both knew if he went for it, I'd be all over him. But maybe he planned to come after me instead. The moon slid behind clouds. Cold bit my face. My eye throbbed from where his fist had connected, skin beginning to swell. Prepared for the worst, I couldn't say what would have happened next if Hastings didn't fling the bus door open behind us and smash a bottle of Grey Goose onto the pavement. As glass exploded in the still night, Tweaker packed it in. He launched faster than a rocket, the soles of his sneakers white orbs disappearing into the night.

CHAPTER TWENTY-THREE

"LORD HAVE MERCY!" PHILIP'S FACE WAS A MASK OF SHOCK. "Who's she?"

At the sound of his voice, Hastings buried her face deeper into my shoulder. In my arms, wrapped tight in a blanket, her limbs shook, tiny rods under immense stress. Her knapsack dangled from my wrist, everything she owned stuffed inside.

"Can you open up?" I asked, nodding toward the rear door of his Prius.

Phillip wrenched the door wide. I lowered Hastings onto the back seat and my abs groaned, still ringing from the junkie's piledrive.

"Who was that other guy that flew past?" Philip asked.

"Did you see where he went?"

"Cleared the block like he was Usain Bolt. Should I have stopped him?"

In Philip's prime, a chase might have ended in his favor. But he was pushing two-fifty, maybe three hundred, most of the excess hanging over his belt. I could appreciate his instinct though.

"It's all good," I said. "Just a thief caught in the act. I scared him off."

Or rather, Hastings did, with her stunt. I'd cleaned up the broken glass, leaving some sewer rat to slurp Grey Goose off the pavement. Maybe it was good thing she'd come across all the vodka stashed in the freezer the other night.

Philip shot a nervous glance toward Hastings. Suddenly there were a bunch of surprise elements to process. "Was she alone?"

"I wasn't feeling good after the show," Hastings answered, before I could. "I almost threw up. My Dad didn't want to take me to the hotel right away. He went to get some medication."

Seriously. Where the hell did that come from?

In the thin silence, Philip rubbed his mouth. "She's your daughter?"

"Fourteen this year," I said, no choice but to play along.

He looked me up and down. "Must take after her mother then."

It wasn't a threat per se; he just needed convincing. In the Suze folder on my phone, I scrolled through old photos, finding one of my favorites: us at the Grammys a few years ago. In designer duds and fresh from the spa, we looked like a million bucks. That night, we'd hit every party, SOS having picked up multiple wins. The sun was just creeping over the horizon when we staggered out of the limo back at home, drunk and laughing.

Philip raised his glasses and let out a whistle. "Holy cow. She's a doll." He snuck a second look at the screen. "You clean up pretty good too, Sir."

"Her mom's having a difficult time right now," I said, tucking the phone away. "The less press right now the better, if you know what I mean." From my pocket, I jimmied out a thick roll of twenties courtesy of my bedroom stash. I palmed it in his direction. "Appreciate a man in your previous line of work knows a thing or two about confidentiality."

He feathered the stack and nodded for me to follow him down the sidewalk. Philip might've been getting on in years physically, but his mind was still sharp. We angled inward, toward each other, a buffer from the wind screaming between the high-rises that flanked the road.

"Nothing funny going on here that would incriminate me, right?" The pouches under his eyes were the droopy kind, and I wondered if a pinprick could drain away whatever filled them. "My record's spotless and I intend to go to my grave that way."

"I swear on a lifetime of Grey Goose."

He looked up at the sky without any definable expression. Philip was no slouch. He knew covert in a way I'd never come close to understanding. But there were no Secret Service here to back him up if things went squirrelly.

"Every man's got his poison, ain't that right? I'll never say no to a Jim Beam." He glanced over and cracked a smile, the tension finally breaking in my favor. "That and a bag of Cheetos, I'm happier than a pig in shit."

"I stick to vodka, mostly. Red wine to offset the boredom."

His eyebrow cocked in disbelief. "Boredom?"

"Relatively speaking."

A tricky silence passed. In the whole scheme of things, my situation was peanuts compared to the terrorists and assassins Philip once kept an eye out for, but on the surface, it still smelled fishy.

When he finally spoke, it was in the even, careful tone of a man used to cutting deals way beyond my pay grade. "Push come to shove, we never met, okay?"

We shook on it. Back in the car, Philip cranked the heat, blowing on his fingers.

"This cold reminds me of driving Obama in Ohio. Yea-ap, those were the days...back when Presidents had class." He found my eyes in the rear-view mirror. "Same hotel, Sir?"

"I'm hungry," Hastings mumbled, head in my lap.

A stopgap wasn't such a bad idea. I needed to organize next steps. Philip obliged and dropped us at a diner off the beaten path. The place was filled with a haze of stale cooking oil and when I asked the lone waiter for a full bleach wipe down of the back booth, that got more of a reaction than a thirty-year-old white guy coming in for a meal at 1 a.m. with a black, teenaged girl wrapped in a blanket. Philip, in his wisdom, had divined what he needed from our situation and chose an appropriate diner. The aged waiter was several decades beyond recognizing me and took our order without fanfare. While the sizzle of grease poured out from the kitchen, I texted Sasha-Rae, told her I'd be tied up for another hour. Then I logged on to Expedia to make a room reservation.

Forty-five minutes later, another successful smuggle was in the can.

But only when the door to Hastings' hotel room closed behind us could I truly relax. In the diner, two beat cops had wandered in on the hunt for coffee. If Hastings hadn't been horizontal on the booth bench, dozing while I settled up…

"Could you stay with me until I fall asleep?"

Sounding nothing like the grown-up she was desperate to be, Hastings tugged on my sleeve. Anxiousness from earlier no longer marred her features, but the truth was always in the eyes.

I crouched down in front of her. "Oh, kiddo," I said. "Of course. C'mere."

With a wounded animal sound she fell into my open arms and started to bawl. Conscious of not squeezing her tiny frame too hard, I soothed her, my hand running up and down her back. Every vertebra jabbed through her T-shirt like a Stegosaurus spine. She clutched onto me, tighter, body shuddering with deep, heavy sobs ridding her insides of every wrong and bad thing. In times of crisis there's something to be said for the touch of another human, and I left it up to her to decide when to come out of our embrace. After a long minute, she pulled back.

"Talk to me," I said, quietly. "You going to be okay?"

Sniffling, her breathing uneven, "I hope I didn't ruin things for you tonight."

"Are you kidding?" I wiped away a tear clinging to her chin. "Oh my god, don't even go there. You did the exact right thing."

"She won't be mad at you?"

Behind steamed glasses, she didn't look convinced when I said no. Neither was I. Sasha-Rae's demoralizing response to my text from earlier: a single "K." Not even an emoji to throw me a bone. That K either reflected a well of understanding, or, in all likelihood, a one-letter equivalent to sleeping on the couch.

"I guess I'll find out." I stood up and turned on the hallway light. "Why don't you get ready for bed? I'll wait out here."

Once the bathroom door shut and water started to run, I wandered over to the windows. Skyscrapers poked into the sky, jagged clouds drifting around them. Inside the buildings, relationships were being consummated, hearts broken, meals eaten. The sheer volume of lives and events playing out made me dizzy. Closing my eyes, I pressed a hand against the window, the chill sinking past flesh into bone. I felt like a stranger inside my own head.

"Adrian?"

I spun around. A woodsy smell of rosemary drifted in the air that followed her out of the bathroom. It only felt like a minute had passed, although twenty minutes must've come and gone because snowflakes now fell outside, and clouds covered the moon. In a robe five sizes too big for her, she handed me a towel.

"What's this for?" I asked.

"So you can sit."

"Thank you," I said, humbled at her thoughtfulness. Twice in less than two hours, two very different ladies spared me. I was a lucky man.

Hastings shyly dropped the robe bedside, revealing the pajamas I'd bought for her in Oregon. She scooted under the duvet and I spread my towel out, taking a seat on the bed, not too close. Her eyes riveted onto mine, and she no longer gave the impression of someone trying to hold themselves together. But looks could be deceiving.

"I can tell you're thinking about something," I said. "Talk to me."

"May I ask a personal question?"

Oh no. Every diabolical thing in my past rose like scum to the surface. "If it's too personal, I'm not answering."

She waited a beat, and I knew my face showed the reticence. But her curiosity overrode it. "In Vancouver I saw a rainbow and I wondered if you knew what a real rainbow looks like? Because you're color-blind."

Both hands unclenched with relief. Still…of all the questions in the world. I forgot she even knew. Up until now, only my parents and Suze were aware of my condition. I'd never even told the boys. After my ninth-grade art teacher Ms. Greenwood chastised my drawing in front of the class, calling my pink sun and blue grass *pitiful attention grabbers*, I vowed to never tell anyone. But I'd longed to see a real rainbow after Suze once described them as arcs of brilliant jewels.

"I have no idea what they look like. I've been color blind since birth," I said.

"Then what do you see?" she pressed.

"It's tough to describe. I have tritanopia, a rare form of color blindness. Blues and greens get mixed up. Orange, red and yellows become shades of pink. It's a mish-mash."

Her head slanted, like my comment held some significance. "What color is a banana to you?"

"Pinkish," I said. "Why?"

"Just curious."

Her offhand reply didn't hide the silent industry: a million gears working, giving her away as she fiddled with her lip. There was something behind that question. While trying to fathom exactly what, she threw another curveball.

"Do you ever wonder if that's why you chose music?" she asked.

"What do you mean?"

"You said before songs aren't paintings. If you wanted to be a painter, you'd need to see the right colors. But you don't need to understand colors to be a musician. Maybe that's why you picked music."

A pulse beat hard in the pit of stomach. "That's quite the theory."

"Do you think I'm right?"

I could feel her cut-glass gaze trying to figure me out, not knowing she'd touched on a buried exchange, one that had put so much in motion. Under my hoodie, the restless pounds of my heart doubled in speed. Although she didn't know the full extent of my thoughts, Hastings kept watching me because like I said, the eyes never lied, the answer in mine, obvious. Her hand snuck out from under the covers to find mine, her skin warm, borderline hot. We sat like silent statues. Through the window, as the moon escaped clouds and skyscrapers, shards of light splintered across the carpet. It triggered a realization.

"I have a question for you," I said. "The other day when we were talking about the songs. You never told me what color 'Moonlight' is."

Surprise clouded her face, like how could she have forgotten *that*? "Yellow," she said, right away. "Bright yellow."

I waited for her to elaborate and when she didn't, "You gotta meet me halfway, kiddo. What does yellow mean in your world?"

She met my eyes with the solemnness of a judge. "Hope. Whenever I see yellow, it means hope. And I didn't just see it, I felt it, too. Right here."

A finger dipped toward her belly, the same location on me going off with internal fireworks. On that magical night with Suze, everything I ever dreamed of came true. Could I capture that again?

"Do you feel hope with Sasha-Rae?" Hastings asked, uncannily guessing where my mind had drifted to.

I glanced out the window, at the moon. "Yes. Very much so."

"Then you should go see her."

She squeezed my hand and let go. I prepared to leave, not feeling excited in the slightest and unsure why.

"I'll check in with you tomorrow morning, okay?" I said, tucking the duvet around her. "Don't let anyone into the room. I'll put the do not disturb sign on your door."

Her eyelids drooped to half-mast and she let fly a gigantic yawn, prompting my own,

"Okay," she mumbled, already drifting off. "And thank you. For everything."

A minute later, she was out.

I should be so lucky.

The workings of my mind took hours to settle. I scored some ice from one of the machines and sat stone-faced on the mezzanine level hearing nothing but the hum of a hotel in the witching hour, ice pressed onto my throbbing eye until water dripped and my flesh went numb. Just past 4 a.m., I slipped back into my room. The curtains were open in the living room; shadows stretched long and lean. The bedroom door was ajar but instead of joining Sasha-Rae, I detoured to the slip-covered couch instead. It took a long time to fall asleep. All I could think about was how, on the afternoon I quit school for good, Ms. Greenwood had asked me to stay behind after art class. How she'd held my drawing in her tobacco-stained fingers like it was diseased. How I couldn't, *wouldn't,* explain that in my world the sun was pink, the grass was blue. How the thinly veiled superiority in her eyes sharpened when she suggested I consider a career path at Subway.

They accept anyone, Adrian.

CHAPTER TWENTY-FOUR

I WAS ON A FLIGHT—A BUMPY ONE—THE TURBULENCE OUT of control.

"Adrian. Someone's knocking on the door."

My shoulder shook another time, jolting me awake. Sunlight poured through all the windows, everything blown out into eye-splitting brightness. For a scary moment I had no idea where I was.

"Oh my god," Sasha-Rae said, her face coming into focus. "You have a black eye."

The pounding on the door started up again. "Adrian!" Sven's voice yelled from out in the hallway. "Are you in there?"

I sat up on the couch and an avalanche of memories swooshed in, queasiness right on its heels. Sven at the door in panic mode could only mean one thing. I pushed away the cobwebs of sleep, ungluing my tongue from the innards of my mouth. It's like I'd eaten three underripe bananas.

"Give me a sec, Sven," I called out.

Sasha-Rae sat beside me on the couch, worry lines creasing her pretty face, although it was the rest of her, clad in a skimpy lace PJ set, which worried me. It left very little to the imagination.

"It's our tour manager," I said. "I don't know what he wants, but

I'll get rid of him as fast as I can." I tilted my head toward the bedroom. "Do you mind?"

She leaned back in a put-off way. It wasn't meant as a snub or that I was embarrassed she was here, but at the very least, I probably should've said good morning first.

"Okay," she finally said.

Her departing tush sank the impropriety of my thoughts beyond base. Whatever Sven wanted, it better be quick. When I opened the door, he gaped at me across the taut security chain.

"Your face," he finally said.

"What's the 911? I'm trying to sleep."

"You're not answering your phone," he snapped back.

My hand automatically reached into my pocket. Shit. Where was my phone?

Sven rattled the chain. "Can I come in?"

"Uh, not right now. I'm kinda busy..." I gave him the *look*, the code every guy is supposed to know.

An indeterminate flicker rose in his eyes and his reply came out stiff. "Someone broke into one of the crew buses last night."

I eyed him a moment longer, added surprise to my voice. "Really? Everything okay?"

"The crew came down to see if anything of theirs was missing. You should do a sweep of your bus. I need to file a report for insurance."

"Right now?" I asked, because he seemed to imply that.

"Big Daddy said you called him last night, worried about your guitar and if there was security."

"Yeah," I said, just as careful with my tone. "I'd left the ES in there and wasn't sure I'd locked up."

"Huh. Harold said he had it the whole time."

A strange air swept between us. Sven ran hot and cold on the best of days and right now he was cold blue steel. Assessing. We were actors reading lines, attuned to each other; what we were saying, how we were saying it. A grim thought entered my mind. What if security cameras caught any of last night's proceedings? "Yeah, well, actually, I did go down to get something. You know...protection."

I gave him the *look* again, and his jaw squared.

"Did you see anything unusual?" he asked.

"Nope," I said, as sweat started to pool on my lower back. If this conversation dragged on any longer, I'd need a towel.

"The arena needs something for their files, and I'd like to get the report off sooner than later," he said, slowly, still scrutinizing me. "The car service will be here in about thirty minutes. I can ask them to make a quick—"

"What car service?" I interrupted.

He sighed and rubbed his forehead. "Didn't you read the schedule? The interviews start in an hour. You should put some ice on your eye. Marcelo's going to freak out."

The interviews. Of course.

Sven prattled on. "You're being interviewed together at noon, then it's the meet and greet at four, then the photo shoot..."

"Yeah, yeah, "I said, waving my hand. "I'll be ready. I'll be down in a few."

The rumble of a maid cart approaching snatched Sven's attention. He darted a look left and that was my out.

"Gotta run," I said.

I slammed the door and slumped against it. Dragged both hands over my face. This was getting ridiculous. The peril of cascading lies started to worry me. After scouring the living room for my phone, I had a sinking feeling I'd left it in Hasting's room. I'd have to get it on my way down. But first things first. I tidied myself up in the bathroom and joined Sasha-Rae. Tucked in bed, she was settled against the head-board reading a book. The blinds were open and roses on the dresser had awakened in the winter sun, delicate petals spreading their scent.

"All good?" she asked. "You look like you're on another planet."

I sat down next to her on the bed. Even without makeup, her skin glowed. "Forget good. You look absolutely amazing."

With a self-conscious laugh, she raked her hand through perfectly mussed hair. "Hardly."

I tipped my head to read the book cover. "Michio Kaku. You don't mess around."

"Were you expecting a romance novel?" she asked, challengingly, making me wonder if I just naturally sparked rebellion in women.

"Don't worry. I'm not afraid of a smart woman. Or a sexy one."

She softened; smiled. "When it comes to romance, I prefer the *real* thing."

It didn't take a genius to read between the lines. Real, meaning an actual person, physically present, not an absentee wildcard. There wasn't enough history between us for her to be mad, although she had every right to be.

"About last night," I said. "I feel bad. Things carried on."

In the silence, her gaze drifted to my swollen eye. *Things* required an explanation. Required something.

"Sometimes it gets nasty between us," I continued, not entirely a lie.

She absorbed that; eventually nodded in acceptance. "I wish you would've slept here instead." She tipped her head beside her.

I plucked the book out of her hands and took them in mine. "I didn't want to wake you up. Tonight, it's all about us, I swear."

She perked up. "Are you free now? I can be ready in a heartbeat."

I forced myself to stay focused on her face. Lovely as it was, the room erred on the cool side and more than one thing stood at attention. Damn lace. "Don't hate me, but I've gotta shower and run. I won't be back before the show."

"What?" Her shoulders slumped.

"I know, I know. I should have told you. This weekend...there's so much going on. I just really wanted you to come. Take advantage of the spa here, room service; charge it all to the room," I added quickly, hoping freebies would help. "I'll leave a backstage pass for you at the front desk under your name. After the show, I'll introduce you to everyone."

Me bringing her into the fold appeared to lift her spirits. Then she clocked another spy at my shiner. "No one will think I gave you that, right?"

At a future time, we might joke about the circumstances of last night. For now, the strategy remained *Operation: Avoid the Issue.*

"I could change the story," I said, with my most charming smile, "but that would take away all your street cred."

She chuckled. "You are shameless, Mr. Johnson." Her hand rose to stroke the bump under my eye. "I stayed up as long as I could last night," she said, her voice dangerously flirty. "It's a shame. I wouldn't have been as rough on you."

Her finger traced along my cheekbone and hovered on the top of my lip. A flutter rose in my stomach. On our phone calls this week she proved to be unendingly various—sweet, then shy, unafraid to be sassy, or more intelligent than me. Now I could add red-hot vixen to the list.

"There's still tonight," I said.

Her other hand found its way into my lap. She knew her way around without looking. "I hate to sound greedy, but can we play meeting everyone by ear? I think I want you all to myself."

Every part of me, and I do mean every part, wanted to kick the bedroom door closed, call in sick and devour her. We kissed and got into it pretty fiercely, one of those hot damn kiss and grope sessions that was a prelude to so much more. A vision—both of us lying on our backs, the heady scent of a great romp in the air, laughing, touching, skin on skin—burned onto my brain like a steer tag.

It was the only thing that got me through the day.

Anticipation was a wonderful thing.

CHAPTER TWENTY-FIVE

THE JAZZER SUCCUMBS TO NERVES: FORGETS LYRICS, FREEZES ON STAGE.

That headline almost happened.

In the din of all the screams and swirling smoke, when Sasha-Rae gave me the thumbs-up from the sidelines, I blanked. First time ever. If Norm hadn't noticed me staring at my pedals, lost, I might still be standing there. His "Yo, Adrian!" saved my bacon. Potential disaster averted, I made up for it in spades. The manic crowd egged us into two encores and when we finally left the stage, the stadium rumbled like a launching rocket at Cape Canaveral. While the boys headed to the dressing room, I found her backstage.

"Wow!" she gushed. "That was incredible."

"It was pretty good," I admitted. "One of the best so far."

"I've never seen a show from the stage. All those people..." Both hands flew to her heart. "It's so intimidating. Do you ever get nervous?"

I shrugged. "Rarely."

"Coming through! Watch your backs."

Roadies swarmed the stage to dismantle gear and I steered us out of harm's way.

"You still up for backstage?" I asked. "We can cut out if you want."

"I wouldn't mind hanging out for a bit, if you don't," she said. "Meet everyone."

Her giddy smile said it all. Departing fans buzzed with animated conversation, the lingering energy infectious. It begged continuation. I wasn't so sure. Norm had seen her stage-side, and I knew the peanut gallery would be out in full force.

"Just warning you, it can be a little loose."

That turned out to be an understatement. The rowdy scene hovered dangerously close to messy. Hoarse, alcohol-fueled voices assailed us as we squeezed our way through the press of bodies to the bar. Camped in front, Norm and Ex chatted with Simon, our socially awkward sound engineer. They immediately zoned in on us—Ex with a curious look, Norm a lascivious smile. Simon, incredibly shy around attractive women, said a nervous hello and slipped away.

Forgoing any usual social pleasantries, Norm draped an arm around Sasha-Rae's shoulder and leered at her.

"Well, well, well. What do we have here? No wonder we encored with *Foxy Lady*. What's your name sweetheart?"

"Sasha-Rae," she said, ignoring the fact he was getting an eyeful down her shirt. "Pleased to meet you. And you too," she added, smiling at Ex.

Norm looked heavenward and made the sign of the cross. "Jesus, girl. Even your name is fuckable."

"Norm!" I yelled, pushing his arm off her.

Ex shut his eyes, pained. "For real?"

"What?" Norm scanned all of us, landing on Sasha-Rae, like she of all people should understand his air-headed gracelessness. "It's a compliment. And don't tell me you didn't think the same thing."

"Do I really need to explain the difference between thinking and talking?" I asked.

"Simmer down, cowboy. Jeez. And at least give me some credit. You had her stashed in the bus in LA, right?" Norm knocked Sasha-Rae jokingly with his elbow. "He tried to weasel out of an interview on account of you. That has never happened."

For the next few seconds, time stood appallingly still.

Finally, with spectacular composure, Sasha-Rae corrected him. "We actually met in Vancouver."

A hand slapped over Ex's face—his own. I'd never witnessed Norm speechless.

"'Scuse us," Ex said, shoving Norm hard toward the other side of the room. "The babysitter left early."

Norm's squawks of defense were swallowed up in the thudding music. Their departure left an awkward void and I pulled her to the side of the bar.

"Now you've met Norm. Unfortunately, you can't unmeet him."

"You two are friends, right?"

"Can't you tell?"

She crossed her arms tight around her body. The look on her face was that of someone whose opinion had changed. "Is that true? What he said."

"There wasn't anybody in LA, trust me," I said, just as two scantily-clad women jostled into her, full of attitude and suggestive glances. I snaked a protective arm around her shoulder. "Let's have a drink and chill. What would you like?"

Her voice flattened a notch. "Vodka cran is fine."

I ordered our drinks and across the room, Norm pointedly avoided my glare. I regretted not trusting my instinct to carve out the evening with just her and me. About to suggest we do a lap of hellos and blast, a swell of vitality filled the room. The Dame, her head standing a good two inches above most of the crowd's, bobbed her way through the throng, high-fiving whoever held up a hand. She saw us and descended with a hearty smile.

"Hi, sailor," she said to me, and immediately fixated on my stunning, shapely companion. "Aren't you a sight for sore eyes, sister? Let me guess? Are you the lucky lady?"

Sensing some code embedded in the greeting, Sasha-Rae turned to me, quizzical. "Am I lucky?"

Only one word filled my brain: *No.* Meaning no, stop talking.

But The Dame continued. "Honey, puh-lease," she said. "Every woman is after this man, including mine!" Her laugh boomed like a cannon, breasts practically falling out of the lederhosen getup. "But he's obviously smitten. No man I know has ever sourced the goods on my behalf." She nudged Sasha-Rae with the toe of her artillery boot. "Thank Jesus the crimson tide doesn't last forever, right?"

Sasha-Rae looked thoroughly confused. I recognized the moment for what it was, and nothing I could say would help.

"Aww," The Dame said, noticing my expression. "I didn't mean to embarrass you two." She patted Sasha-Rae's shoulder. "Just remember this boy's a keeper. You see all the tramps in here hovering to get a piece?" She acknowledged another cluster of women just beyond us, whose malevolent stares could sear steak. "Every night it's the same. They're all waiting to pounce. But they all crawl back to their lairs empty-handed, don't they?"

Her built arm, with the word *Va-jay-jay* scrawled along a bicep in what looked like lipstick, knocked into me. I forced a polite, society smile. A hint of reserve flashed in Sasha-Rae's eyes before she turned to The Dame.

"You were really good tonight," she said. "Powerful. I love your voice."

"I appreciate that," The Dame said. "If we include you, that makes about twenty people who saw us."

"Hey," I kicked in. "Remember what we talked about?"

"I know, I know," she concurred. "Baby steps, right?" She sighed, scanned the room. "I was going to ask who you thought might be the better target tonight—Ziegler or Bryce? Thought I'd hit one of them up at the party and ask about us getting signed."

"What party?" I asked.

"*The* party. Ziegler's place," she said.

"I thought that was cancelled."

"Weird. Norm just invited me again on his way out. He left with Bryce and Exile."

I surveyed the room, the dense wall of people. Norm and Ex were both gone. I hadn't seen Bryce since the meet and greet, where he'd ogled all the teenage girls. I thought he'd said the whole thing was off, but he'd been chewing on a burger so maybe I misunderstood.

"I'm pretty sure they'll let you in if you show up," The Dame said, smiling.

Sasha-Rae bowed her head closer. "If you want to go—"

Cut off with a hard knock from behind, she launched forward and crashed into me, both our drinks drenching the front of her blouse.

"Hey!" I barked at the culprit who'd shoved her. "Settle down."

A fedora-clad head swiveled, revealing the only face to ever truly disgust me.

"Mr. Johnson. What a surprise."

The remnants of Jillian Wylie's brittle WASP prettiness lay submerged in the troughs that added more miles to her hard-angled face. She'd made her mark initially as a music reporter, breaking onto the scene just as our band did. At first, we all embraced the special interest she took in us, every article gushing and glowing. Eventually, her agenda became obvious. When she'd cornered me drunkenly at an event, her hand groping my privates, it was the last straw. I cut off her access. Permanently.

"How did you get in here?" I demanded.

"I'm press, darling. I can get in anywhere."

I signaled to the bartender for a towel and handed it to Sasha-Rae. Jillian watched her dab the stain and clucked in sympathy. "I do apologize, my dear. You know how it is with crowds and all. Send me the bill for dry cleaning, I'm happy to pay. Mr. Johnson can concur, I'm a woman of my word."

The Dame broke into a nervous, fangirl smile. "Are you *the* Jillian Wylie? Hot Shot News?"

"The one and only," Jillian replied, dropping a flattered hand to her chest.

"Get the fuck out," I told her. "And take whatever slime balls you brought with you."

At my sudden, savage tone, Sasha-Rae stilled.

"So sorry," Jillian purred. "But you didn't invite me. The big boss did." She tipped her head with a go suck it smile. "Overruled."

"I don't care if the Pope invited you. Get lost."

I threatened a step closer, and the two no-necked minions hovering behind her snapped to attention, muscling their way around Jillian. "Such a gentleman, aren't you?" she simpered. "Full of manners. I can only imagine why your poor ex-wife—"

"Fuck you."

I shoved her so hard she stumbled back into her two goons. The crowd in our immediate vicinity quieted and spread like liquid. A brewing confrontation had its own energy, and they were feeling it. Never privy to this side of me, The Dame gawked in wide-eyed fascination.

"Adrian," Sasha-Rae said, her hand clamping onto my arm, pulling me toward her. "It's okay."

"It's not okay," I raged back. "This woman makes dog shit look good."

Jillian straightened the brim of her hat, unperturbed. "Why do you think I'm here, darling? For *you*?"

"If Ziegler invited you, I can only imagine a D-list celebrity is about to drown."

"Hmmm. How insightful," she said, with a bratty gleam in her eyes. "Maybe you don't have your head up your ass as much as I thought. Now boys, why don't we make our way to the party where the real news is going down? Arrivederci, cavone."

She dismissed me with a flick of her hand. Her posse closed ranks, escorting her back to the door. After a beat, the hum of conversation started up again like nothing had happened.

The Dame let out a deep, rushing breath. "You need another drink, sunshine, cos I sure as hell do."

"No," I said, for once booze the last thing on my mind. "But thanks."

"I'm fine to leave," Sasha-Rae said, clearly rattled. "Anytime."

The last thing I wanted was to leave her and torment myself at another industry event, but Jillian wouldn't be here unless something big was going down. And Ex hadn't said a thing to me about the party. I needed to investigate.

"I need to talk to the boys," I said. "Just for a bit. Do you mind if I drop you at the hotel?"

"I can come along. For support." She tugged on my hand and I crushed her caring smile with five simple words.

"It's better if you don't."

CHAPTER TWENTY-SIX

"Amigo! Wait up!" Diego jogged down the lower concourse in pursuit, slowing down when we were side by side. "You blasting?"

"I'm going to Ziegler's party. Did you know it was back on?"

He shrugged with a good-natured smile. "Off, on, who knows? I'm always the last to know." He stole a backward glance. "Your date coming along? I didn't get the chance to meet her."

"She's going to hang backstage for a bit."

"Alone?"

The valid question bothered me as much as her crestfallen look had.

"You want to come with me or not?"

"Yeah, yeah, sure," he said, recognizing The Tone. He fell in line with my quick strides. "I'm still so freaking wired. Tonight was muy bueno."

We made our way to the rear of the arena and waited for an Uber. Diego took the edge off my anger, kicking comments back and forth about Marcelo and the documentary. It had been an emotional afternoon doing the interviews. Reliving all the stuff we'd been through hit me harder than I expected.

"Your girl's a babe," he said when the conversation waned. "It's good to see you moving on. I was starting to get worried."

"Wow, someone worried about me. First time I'm hearing that."

He let my sarcasm go, the way he usually did. "First time I felt I could say it."

For better or worse, that's who Diego was—he saw everything and said nothing, until he felt 100% sure. Or got pushed to the brink.

"She got her own thing going on?" he asked.

"Big time. She's a vice president," I said, proud, like I had something to do with it. "Full-blown career."

"Good to hear. Not everyone's cut out to tag along in this life, as you know."

His eyes shifted off mine and a small silence built. The night was clear. Last night's wild wind had calmed.

"Maria still talks to Suze?" I asked.

"All the time. But she doesn't tell me anything," he was quick to add.

At first, their alliance was born out of being the only two wives, but eventually a real friendship sparked. I was all for it, until I found out Maria encouraged Suze to avoid joining me on the road. She didn't think it was a healthy dynamic for spouses.

"I'm sure you've heard she's moved on," I said. "Figured I should, too."

It was the register of my voice perhaps, something he couldn't identify, but recognized nonetheless.

"You better be doing it for your own sake," he said. "It's no competition."

Off tour, Diego and I socialized the least. On tour, he kind of became the United Nations. A neutral destination. We all turned to him at some point, hashing out stuff the other guys were too invested in. His levelheadedness always made me feel I could tell him the truth.

"It's the weirdest thing, man," I admitted, cutting him a sideways look. "Sasha-Rae, that's her name, she's amazing. Smart, beautiful. I've never felt this relaxed around someone and you know that's saying something. And even..." My chest welled and I looked up at the sky. It still ate at me that last night, on top of Sasha-Rae, when my phone rang, the first thing that ran through my mind was, *What if it's Suze?* "Even with all that, it still feels like I'm cheating." I glanced back at him, gutted. "It's over, but when is it going to end?"

Rhetorical questions are a bitch, and Diego was wise not to answer right away.

"She's all you knew, amigo," he finally said. "Matters of the heart take time. You can't just pack away fifteen years and forget."

In front of us, all the buses were lined up, generators humming. Such an alien landscape. Foreboding. I couldn't believe I'd left Hastings alone here.

"Happy to call it a night," Diego continued. "Might be for the best. I'm sure your girl wouldn't mind either."

If only I had called it.

As it happened, our Uber pulled up and we left for a party I didn't even want to attend due to the Jillian effect: a toxic brew that left me feeling murderous. Our driver bumped along Queen Street, past the colorful mélange of bars and restaurants, streets full of people despite the cold. From behind my window, chin in my hand, I felt like a goldfish in a bowl, wanting out of the same old circuit. Backstage Sasha-Rae had, politely at first, and then with some bristle, declined going back to the hotel when I asked her to wait for me there. She reminded me she was a big girl and happy to party on her own. *Do what you need to do,* she'd said and linked her arm in The Dame's. *We'll be fine.*

"You ever think beyond all this?" Diego asked, dragging me out of my thoughts.

I swung around to face the human truth serum. "Sometimes. You?"

"All the time."

This was news. "Talk to me."

"Don't get me wrong," he said with a shrug. "I like this world. I love all of you. We've been seriously blessed. Not many cats on this earth get the opportunities we've had. But things change, they always do. That's why you gotta appreciate the here and now. Can't forever hold on or worry about what happened in the past and forget today."

None of us had ever broached this conversation. The timing felt weird. "What would you do if this all stopped tomorrow?" I asked.

He stroked his beard, the one that hid a double chin he was self-conscious about. "Go back to sessioning. Who knows? I'd figure it out. Take each day as new. Even if I ended up in some strange place, bloom where you're planted, right?"

Diego was never one to wax flowery and it caught me by surprise. "You make that up?" I asked. "Because it sounds like a greeting card."

His head flew back with an uproarious laugh. "You know what? I think it was. A card from my little lady."

Evelyn was his little lady: a six-year-old spitfire whose life path seemed destined either for fame or jail. His son Roberto was shrewd, like Maria. One summer he'd hawked 'fresh-pressed orange juice' on the sidewalk, and made a tidy profit offering up Tropicana from the 99¢ store instead.

"So that's your trick?" I asked. "One day at a time?"

"Funny you'd call it a trick. Enjoying life shouldn't be an illusion. What you need to know is what's important to you. I'm not wound up about things as much as you. But you're the Jefe and can't function any other way. You need the control. That comes with a price, one I've never been interested in paying."

He shrugged in a way that said he wasn't sorry for who he was. I didn't think I'd ever admired him more. I thought back to that forgotten bar I'd snuck into years ago, where Diego had played the keyboards with such an expert hand, creating texture in a way that could never be taught. When I'd approached him backstage and found out he was solo, just filling in for a guy, I'd suggested he come jam with me, Ex and Norm that weekend. He didn't pretend he was too good for some teenaged stranger. In typical Diego fashion, he'd smiled, clinked my beer with his and said, "Why not?" We'd exchanged numbers and three weeks later he was in the band.

I glanced over and silhouetted against the window, his thick mane of dark hair imbued him with a lion effect. *Best hair in the biz,* Norm always joked. *Styled with guacamole.*

"Speaking of paying the price," I said. "You forgive me for going AWOL?"

A beat passed before he answered. "You can't be the tough guy 24/7. Even though you pretend you can. You had to do what your heart told you. I can always forgive that."

CHAPTER TWENTY-SEVEN

"GENTLEMAN! WELCOME."

It wasn't out of the ordinary to see a half-naked woman at an industry party and most wouldn't consider it a hazard. But the tasseled pasties hanging from her breasts swung so fiercely with her gyrations, I was in danger of losing an eye. Wearing nothing else but a pair of thong underwear and thigh-high boots, inexplicably, she also wielded a clipboard. Diego half laughed at the spectacle.

"We're on the list," I shouted at her.

"Of course you are, Mr. Johnson." With a barracuda smile, she crooked her arm, offering me an escort.

I ignored it and asked, "Where would I find Harvey?"

She flicked her ponytail with a pout. "He's around," she said, dismissively waving a hand into the sprawl of guests. "Good luck."

Good luck indeed. Ziegler's pad covered the entire fifty-first floor and required a golf cart to get from one end to the other. The marble floors, museum-sized art, and sleek European furniture rivaled any of the gold-plated digs I'd seen in LA or New York. The whole thing was an idealized statement of how a billionaire should live. I preferred a few homey touches—carpet under my feet, some wood here and there, a couch wine could get spilled on without anyone freaking out.

"I need to talk to a man about a horse," Diego talk-shouted into my ear. "I'll come find you."

The crowd was more upscale than backstage—suits and spangly dresses, everyone on the lookout for someone more important than who they were talking to. Idle conversation was the last thing on my mind, and blaring gangsta rap made coherent thought impossible. I pushed my way through the crowd. It was hot and cramped and waiters squeezed by with trays of food and drink held high. I wasn't hungry or in a party mood at all. I found Ziegler holding court next to a baby grand piano. When he caught my eye, he had no choice but to wave me over. I declined the glass of champagne he offered.

"I didn't think you'd come," he said, sounding remarkably sincere.

"Word on the street had it this was cancelled."

His eyes skipped past me to a set of boobs going by. "Who told you that?"

"Have you seen Norm or Ex?"

Ziegler, who wore a T-shirt that said: *I'm not a gynecologist but I'll take a look,* yelled back, "Check the second floor. Once you pick your poison, any unlocked room is game, if you know what I mean."

He tipped his head behind me to a gang of cyborgs—identical blondes, vacant, paid to be present—draped on a leather ottoman, like starved gazelles dozing in the Serengeti. One gave me a hopeful smile.

"Thanks but no thanks," I said. "I'll find them."

A circular staircase wound up to the second-floor mezzanine where various guests hunched over the railing to take in the bird's-eye view. I shoulder-barged my way up and did a sweep of the room. Through the two-story windows, the dark mass of Lake Ontario in the distance gave the impression the world ended on its shore. Condo tower living never appealed to me, and as beams of light danced off spinning disco balls, the sensation of movement was rather unwelcome this high up. Finally, I caught a glimpse of Ex's dreads bobbing down a hallway beneath me. By the time I got down the stairs, it was unclear which of the several doors he'd entered. The first one housed nothing but cleaning supplies. The next one, a couple yards down, was ajar. I inched toward it and froze when a Midwestern cowboy twang drifted out.

"We gotta take him down. Find the dirt. It's the squeaky-cleans who always have the most to hide."

"How far down do we go?" Jillian. Cold. Scheming.

"As far as possible. Create something if you need to."

"Dude, do you know where the bathroom is?"

I whipped my head around. Some guy bounced behind me, holding it in.

"I don't know," I said. "I just got here."

"Hey," he said, his smile growing. "Aren't you…"

"Dude, yes, I'm him. Take a picture and move on. I'm busy."

He brushed past me, muttering something under his breath, but loud enough that I missed all but the tail end of a garbled response from inside the room.

"…harsh. No way. Not gonna happen."

Then Bryce again. "You gotta decide, man. It's your career. I'll get you a mil advance, work my ass off. Your boy is old news. Carve your own path."

My stomach shriveled into a ball. Just like Sven had predicted, only I never expected this from Ex. The acceptable options were to walk away, or storm the house. Entering a room as the underdog hadn't happened in a long time, but I didn't come all this way to wuss out. I pushed the door open hard and it clattered against the wall. On a couch shaped like a pair of lips, three faces looked up at the same time —Bryce, Jillian, and…Norm.

He wiped his nose, a tray of white lines on his lap. "Hey."

"Don't stop talking on account of me," I said.

Jillian stood up and teetered on stilettos. "Sorry," she said to the guys, "but I have a root canal to get to."

I stuck my arm out to stop her from passing. "I heard what you said. Every word. Care to explain?"

"I don't know what you heard," she said, eyes full of flint. "Things get twisted around when you only have half the story."

"And you're going to make up the other half? Your usual stunt?"

She ignored me and waved to Bryce and Norm. "Later, fellas."

I let her breeze past; I had other fish to fry. "You're a shyster," I said to Bryce.

He stood up and did his best to look menacing in a room that was more camp than class, with its white fur rugs and lava lamps. The only thing missing was Hugh Hefner in a robe.

"We're talking business that doesn't involve you," he said.

"It does involve me when you're trying to deal behind my back."

"It's not your deal. It's mine." Norm set the tray down and wobbled to his feet. Maybe he was disoriented, like me; the mirrors on the wall and ceiling gave the illusion of greater depth, more people in the room, movement.

"Committed, huh," I said.

"As committed as you were fucking off for a year."

Norm laughed, the light in his eyes strange and distant. "Funny you should mention that. Since when have you given a shit about me?"

"What kind of a stupid question is that?"

"Answer it," he spat out.

"I've always cared about you. When you're not being an idiot."

He laughed, a cold, hollow sound. "Always with the caveats. You're in, but only on your terms is what it boils down to. You know what? Maybe on some infinitesimal level you do care—in some tiny-ass space in your heart that no one, including you, can access."

"So, what, you're going to shit in your own bed?" I asked. "Bite the hand that feeds you?"

"That's exactly the attitude I can't handle anymore," he scoffed. "You are a guy in a band with three other guys, but we might as well be your disciples, waiting for the almighty God to throw us a bone."

"Really? How many more times are you going to throw that out?"

Ever since some e-zine wrote an article tagging me as 'God's Gift to Guitarists,' Norm never missed an opportunity to toss it in my face.

"Ten times a day. Twenty. Because it's true. It's always been you, all the time. *You* were the guy who drove downtown at three in the morning to pick up T-shirts we could sell for a profit. *You* snagged Mac when he wasn't taking on anyone. *You* knew more than the entertainment lawyer and got us a better record deal." He shook his head, despairingly. "You, you, you."

"It's true," Bryce sniffed, from the safety of the corner. "You're a first-class diva."

"I'd rather be that than a first-class rat," I shot back. "Why don't you scurry on out of here to hang with the other bottom feeders?"

"You see what I mean?" Norm yelled. "You just order everyone around." He prowled in front of me like a lean alley cat: all angular bones, jeans clinging to slim hips. "You know, I used to think you were the best thing that happened to me. I never had a team. My dad's been in jail since I was six. My mother's a whore, as you like to remind me. I was happy to hitch my wagon to you because you were the first real thing in my life I could count on. My options at sixteen were the night shift at In-N-Out, dealing dope, or dead. My life changed on a dime because of one audition. One decision. *Everything* in my life is because of you." He threw up his hands in defeat. "But after all these years, I finally realized my mistake—thinking I needed you more than you needed me."

When he first auditioned for us, I knew he would be a great fit. Norm wasn't just a bass player—he was a gifted guy, infused with something special. Half the time he acted like an idiot, when he was really a savant, a guy who worshipped music and played like fuck. Still, I made him run through a bunch of other songs that day, even after I knew he was the one. Exile also knew and kept looking at me, unsure why I didn't just call it. Norm was patient, or at least pretended to be. He knew the decision was up to me. It's tough to explain, but that moment defined us. It became our pattern. I always pushed him because he let me. Sometimes he pushed back, but never hard enough.

"I know I'm not the easiest person to be around at the best of times," I said. "But I'm loyal and I've never gone behind your backs on anything. How many solo deals were dangled in front of me? Five? Ten? How many did I tell you guys about? All of them. How many did I turn down? All of them. I've been honest and fair with everything money related, and I never snorted coke with a piece of dirt celebrity stalker trying to mastermind your demise. You know what she's responsible for. How low are you prepared to go?"

Norm dropped his eyes and gave a curt nod toward Bryce. "That's all him."

Strung out to dry, Bryce squirmed.

"You're complicit," I said.

"I told him no way," he argued. "I know what happened. You think I'm that much of a lowlife? I'd never screw you over like that."

Right after those words left his mouth, he blinked, realizing his poor choice of descriptor.

"How gracious of you," I replied. "So now you're the savior, the good guy? Should we call Suze and see if she agrees?"

Norm's body strangled into a tight, corded mess of sinew and muscle. Both hands fisted as his head fell back with a deafening scream, so loud, I was surprised the mirrors didn't shatter.

"SHUT UP!"

When the horrible sound finally dissipated, his bare, concave chest heaved in and out. "Yes, we fooled around," he said. "I'll never be able to change that and I'm sorry. But shine the light all the way around, dude. You weren't there for her. She was sliding off the deep end and you did nothing to catch her. So wound up in your own little world like you always are."

He jabbed an accusatory finger and I felt it in my sternum from across the room. Felt it deflate the locked-up ball of misery I'd carried around for the past year.

"She was three months pregnant with your kid," I said, my voice strained, at the breaking point. "When all that shit blew up before we flew back to Europe last tour? She didn't have the guts to tell me. Tried to give herself a home abortion. If I hadn't returned when I did…"

Silence cloaked the room. A series of expressions I'd never seen before played out on Norm's face. "Jesus, man," he finally said. "I thought she…I swear, I had no idea."

"Of course you had no idea. Because that's who *you* are—the joker, the bon vivant, everything fun and games." Now it was my turn to jab a finger, to erupt. "I'm the guy who's kept shit on track while all you've done is party like it's 1999, sleeping with everything that moves, including my wife. She screwed up her insides because of you. Can never have a kid now. You want out?" I shouted, my whole body shaking. "You're out! There's a hundred guys to replace you."

Blinded by a sting in both eyes, I had to leave. Now. But as I rushed the door, Ex blocked me, a bottle of champagne in each hand.

"Not much to celebrate here, bro," Norm muttered. "Sounds like Captain Fantastic just downgraded us to a three piece."

Ex the stoic, the sensitive poet, features so fine-boned they rivaled a woman's, regarded me with something I could only describe as tragic. "Brother," he said, his voice broken in a way I'd never heard. "What have you done?"

"Why don't you ask Norm what *he* did."

Bryce bleated, like the sheep he was. "You can't kick him out of the band."

All eyes were on me. The energy in the room was unforgivable.

"Oh yeah?" I said. "Watch me."

CHAPTER TWENTY-EIGHT

IT TOOK OVER AN HOUR TO FIND MY WAY BACK TO THE hotel, but I needed the time to walk it off. On University Avenue, ticks of hail bit my face, the bitter wind exactly like the gauntlet I'd thrown down at Ziegler's: indefensible. We'd come close to unfixable before—last year, the closest—but never crossed the line. As my fury settled into numb apprehension, the upcoming afternoon in Detroit played out in my mind. We'd all fall into our long-standing roles. Diego, the avoider, would keep mum. In the dressing room Norm would brush past with a *whatever, dude;* all brittle self-preservation. Ex worried me the most. On any other day he'd pull me aside and tell me to chill, to not let the pressure get to me. But tonight he couldn't hide the awfulness of what I'd said from his face. The way he'd looked at me left a void I wasn't sure we could fill.

Finally the hotel rose in front of me, a saber cutting into the sky. A skeleton staff of two manned the front desk and didn't notice, or care about, a hooded figure crossing the lobby. In the solitude and safety of the elevator, it all came crashing down. I'd been so hell-bent on getting back here yet there was no way I could face Sasha-Rae in this state. I was too wound. There'd be questions. Answers I couldn't, or didn't want to, supply. I needed a transition.

There was only one place to go.

I slipped into Hastings' room and eased the door shut without a sound. A muted murmur of TV drifted in from another room. I waited for the solid blackness of the room to dissipate. When it didn't, with hands on the wall for orientation, I inched forward. If memory served me, the armchair was straight...

"Ow! Shit."

Pain radiated swift and hot up my leg. With the sudden noise, Hastings roused out of sleep.

"Who's there?" Her voice clanged with fright.

"It's just me," I whispered. "Adrian."

Fabric rustled, followed by a slap. Sudden, intense light pierced the room, the beam of brightness from the headboard lamp illuminating the desk I'd clunked right into.

"Oh my god," Hastings said, her expression morphing from fear to relief. "I thought..."

I hadn't thought, is what it boiled down to. What a bonehead. She'd just been through trauma. "I should've knocked. I'm, I...is it all right I'm here?"

"What's wrong?" she wanted to know, because why else would I be here.

"Nothing. I just...didn't want to be alone."

Without glasses, her eyes weren't as big or intimidating. But they could still see something unsettled in my face, gauge the distinct feeling of something heavy in the air. "Is it not working out with her?"

"It's been a rough night," I admitted. "All around."

Her hand clutching the bedspread relaxed and she studied me, like the first morning in the bus. "I'm glad you're here, actually," she said. "I have a surprise for you."

Blindsided enough for one night, the words tumbled out before I could stop them. "I'm not a big fan of surprises. FYI."

"You have to wait in the bathroom," she ordered, ignoring me completely. "I'll call you when I'm ready. Make sure you close the door."

I didn't have it in me to protest. In fact, as I made my way to the bathroom, I wondered if I should've come here at all. The evening had died in rapid-fire degrees and now I squatted on the toilet, head in my hands, swamped with uncertainty. What was I doing? With everything?

A few days ago, before we hit Calgary, the plan with Hastings was cut and dry. I'd called The Washington State Department of Children, Youth and Families posing as a journalist (ha!) and a friendly woman named Sheila gave me the rundown. It would be impossible for Hastings to be taken in by a New Orleans foster family. Between-state fostering was viewed as too disruptive. On the other hand, adopting a foster child could happen from any state, and the good people in the agency would try their best to make that happen. I'd kept Hastings in the dark about my decision—to send her off to a local agency once we hit New Orleans—and the guilt had been eating me alive. And now, the past three days confused me more. I was getting used to her being around.

"You can come back."

Hastings' voice drifted through the wall, followed by a light knock. I stood up, legs heavy and complaining from the evening's long walk. I grabbed a towel and joined her on the bed. There was a nervous, fidgety air about her, mirroring my own. With great circumstance, she lifted her pillow and handed me a brown paper bag, crisp with newness.

"This is for you."

The package had weight. It felt good in my hands. "What is it?"

She smiled impishly. "You'll see."

Upending the bag, a lump wrapped in tissue paper fell into my lap. I peeled away the layers. When I saw what it was, I held it to the light, unsure. Inside the snow globe, the CN tower sat atop a flat disc, presumably Lake Ontario.

"I got it for the rainbow," she said, pointing to a small arch behind the tower. "In your world, you can't see all the colors. This is a reminder they're there."

Gifts typically didn't turn me into mush, but her gesture hollowed me out. "What's this for?"

"For last night. For being a good person." And then it happened so quickly, it might not have happened at all. She leaned forward and brushed my cheek with a quick kiss, then hurried back to her spot, looking shy in the wake of her action. "Don't be mad," she said, pulling the duvet to under her chin. "I snuck out today, only for a bit. I found it in the gift shop downstairs."

"I'm not mad," I said with great difficulty, emotion balled in my throat. Where her lips touched my face, a circle of warmth slowly faded. It didn't feel right to say anything about it, because nothing about it was wrong. It was an act of kindness, pure and simple. I turned the globe over and back, temporarily lost in the lazy drift of flakes. "Thank you for this. But I have to say, I'm not so sure I'm good, kiddo."

Ten years ago, I would've taken that honor without an argument. Agreed, even. Now a deep, grinding, self-loathing made it a challenge to look her in the eye. The bitter residue of tonight's showdown still lingered.

"Just because you can't see things," she said, "doesn't mean they're not there."

I summoned the courage to look at her. She could've coddled me, insisted I was good. Deep down, maybe that's what I expected. Instead, she left the decision up to me on how I was, or wasn't, going to reframe myself.

"I should be the one getting *you* a gift. You're the good person. For seeing things I don't."

She sat up and reached for my arm. Her voice was soft, the drawl pronounced as she spoke slowly. "What you did...what you're doing—helping me—that is a gift. It's worth more than anything you could buy."

I didn't know what to say after that. So many thoughts crashed around in my head, it felt safer to keep quiet. I glanced around the room, just to do something. "Fair enough," I finally said. "But if there's anything you want, that I could get you, promise me you'll let me know."

A ghost of a smile erased her seriousness. "Well," she said, like she'd been waiting for me to say just that. "Maybe one day you can write a song about me."

"If I ever write another song," I said, a tart taste of defeat in my mouth, "I promise it'll be about you. How does that sound?"

"What would you call it?"

"I don't know. I'll have to write it first."

"The lyrics first." A statement.

I smiled. "Okay. The lyrics first."

After a thinking beat, "Can the song be about me and a rainbow?"

"Is that what you want?"

She nodded an effusive yes, sealing our deal. The wail of a siren floated up from the street below, a call to arms of sorts. It was 1:30 a.m. Tonight, there'd been no texts from Sasha-Rae. I'd sent one walking back from Ziegler's, letting her know things didn't pan out so well. I wondered, briefly, depressingly, if I'd made a huge mistake bringing her out here.

"Sasha-Rae leaves at eleven this morning. I'll come get you after. Safeguard this for me until then, okay?" I set the globe on her night-stand. There were enough things to explain.

As I stood to leave, Hastings asked, "Can you wait until I fall asleep again?"

At this point, any chance of me scoring a winning goal with Sasha-Rae seemed improbable. A few more minutes wouldn't move the goalposts.

"Sure," I said and made my way to the couch. Towel in place, I stretched out, kicked my feet up and felt the blood in my body sink, the pressure in my temples finally slackening. A brief dose of relaxation wouldn't kill me. On the wall beside me, I reached for the master light panel.

"I'm going to shut the lights off now," I said. "Good night, twerp. I'll see you in the morning."

"Good night." And with a smile in her voice, "And I'm not a twerp."

The last thing I remembered was the room plunging into darkness. When I woke up, sunlight strained through the sides of the curtains. The only bright thing in the room stared me right in the face. The alarm clock. It might as well have been screaming.

Ten a.m.

Shit!

CHAPTER TWENTY-NINE

I TOOK A DEEP BREATH, OPENED THE DOOR TO MY HOTEL room and made my way to the bedroom. Sasha-Rae was sexy as hell in tight pants and silky blouse. Unfortunately, it was all a tease. Based on her arctic glance, redemption wasn't in the cards. This must be what standing in front of a firing squad felt like.

"Good morning," she said.

The bed was made. Underneath the duvet lay the wasted sheets— the weekend that never was. She finished rolling up her T-shirt and jammed it into the suitcase, zippering it shut with such forceful authority my groin twitched.

"Can I at least explain?" I asked.

"This is your life, Adrian," she said, yanking the case off the bed. "You don't have to explain."

"Hey," I said, reaching for her arm. "At least give me the courtesy of hearing me out."

She looked down at my hand like it was covered in polka dots. "Courtesy?"

"Okay, maybe not the best choice of words. But you can't just walk away."

She pulled her arm out of my grip. "I can, actually."

The first glimmer of badass, and it was totally warranted. Ditching her backstage was one thing, a hole I could've potentially dug myself out of. But escaping from this Jupiter-sized crater bordered on futile. Still, I had to try.

"Can you stay another day?" I asked.

"I have to get back to work."

"What about next weekend?"

She paused. Underneath her eyes was a hint of a sleepless night. "I don't know."

"You don't know your schedule?"

Her laugh had no humor in it. "Isn't it more like what's *your* schedule?"

"It's not always like this," I lied.

"Don't minimize it. Please. Don't pretend. Remember, I know this life. My brother?"

Urgency started to fade; urgency I couldn't afford to lose. My mind scrambled for any solution. Rushed, the first half-baked idea flew out of my mouth before I could stop it. "Why don't you quit your job? You could come to Europe with me. South America..."

"Adrian," she cut in, and I imagined this was her boardroom voice, reeling in an unruly coworker. "I have a career."

"But you don't even like it."

She looked taken aback. "That doesn't mean I'm going to quit over..."

"Over what?"

She did a sweep of the room, no doubt envisioning a hundred other hotel rooms she'd be stuck in, me never around. Even my teeth hurt waiting for her reply. Sensing the magnitude of her next words, Sasha-Rae took her time.

"I think we both had good intentions," she said. "But we acted on a whim and—"

"This wasn't a whim," I interrupted. "We planned this."

"Yes. No. Okay." She raised her hands, collected herself. "Now I'm using the wrong word. What I meant is, I regret not thinking more about your lifestyle and mine. How it would work."

"You mean how it wouldn't work."

"What I meant..."

"So you regret this."

Her hand tightened on the suitcase handle. "That came out the wrong way."

"How many different ways can you mean regret?"

"Don't get angry with me."

"I'm not angry!" I yelled.

She stepped behind the suitcase, putting a barricade between us. I had never felt such stillness in a room.

"Maybe this isn't a good time for you," she ventured. "There are a lot of...distractions."

The short hairs on the back of my neck bristled. *Distractions?* "Are you saying what I think you're saying?"

"I..." She looked down, back up, reasserted herself. "Maybe I am."

"Unbelievable," I said, hands on my waist, approximating a housewife giving her husband the gears. "After all your talk about not wanting to be judged, you're judging *me*? You really think that's what's gone down? After everything you know about me?"

"Adrian," she said, like I wasn't playing with a full deck of cards. "I don't know you at all. That was the whole point of this weekend. To spend some time together, get to know each other. Instead, you ditch me on both nights, come back one morning with a black eye and barely an explanation, your bandmates joke about all these mystery women you deny, I don't even know where you slept last night, and you're asking me to stay another day? Quit my job and run off to Europe with you?" All her stress bubbled out in a shrill laugh. "Why in God's name would I say yes?"

I was suddenly ill, sick of the tour, my life, how it all became this thing beyond my control, even though I tried to control it all. I wanted her to know it was all about me, and not her. But she was right, she would always be second fiddle to any tour, the grind. And I'd be eternally doomed to call Suze while she showered with Patrick and he took her to restaurants that served *timbales*, a word he probably couldn't even pronounce.

I took a deep breath, maybe the deepest in my whole life.

I would not, *could not*, let her walk out.

"I've been climbing out of my skin waiting to see you," I said, pacing back and forth. "And yes, I know I screwed up this weekend and I'm dying inside because of it. The black eye? Some druggie picked a random fight and no guy wants to admit he got taken, me included, but yeah, I got taken. And last night, things went sideways. Stuff's going on with the band and I haven't wrapped my head around everything, and I needed some space. Am I happy about it? No. Did I want to dump it on you at three in the morning? No. I'd give both arms to change this weekend, and to imply that I ditched you for some other woman is absolutely insane. You think *you're* rusty?" My arms flung out in despair. "I haven't even touched another woman since my divorce. And if you want to know where I slept last night, here." I dug Hastings' room key out of my pocket and threw it on the ground without fully considering the ramifications. "1803. A random room. Take a wander down."

She glanced down at the card, her lips mashed tight. My chest heaved. Every nerve tingled. The exhaustion from the past two nights finally caught up to me and I collapsed back onto the bed, spread-eagled.

"Things aren't always perfect, Sasha-Rae. I'm not. You're not. Timing isn't. There are a lot of things beyond my control, including what goes on in here." I thumped my fist against my heart, perhaps a touch too dramatically. "I'm fully aware you might not like me once you get to know me, although I'm praying to God that you do. But if you're not willing to invest the time to find out, then I guess it doesn't matter anyway."

I stared at the ceiling, mind in overdrive. What was it with me and death wishes? The only thing missing here was a requiem. But if it was over, over before it even started, I needed to know.

She crouched down, picked up the room key and tossed it in the garbage can beside the dresser. Now it was her turn to perch on the edge of the bed. I wasn't scared to look her in the eye. I was petrified.

"You *are* very intense," she finally said.

"It's my trademark. Apparently."

"Apparently." She didn't allow a smile, just sat there, spectacular and impassive. "But if what you've just said is true, then you're also very honest. I think," she added, as a qualifier.

I sat up, and in a weird cause-reaction, she leaned back. "I'm not going to lie. You saw it last night. There's a ton of women I could chase every night. But it's not who I am; it never has been. Ask anyone." I reconsidered this immediately. "Well, anyone but Norm."

Ah, there was the smile. "I guess if you were that guy," she said, "you'd go through a hell of a lot of sheets."

The way she searched my face, the promise of the morning almost resurfaced. I knew enough to keep my mouth shut. We were almost back, and I didn't want to blow it.

"What's going on with the band?" she asked, gently, in a non-prying way. "Maybe I can offer some perspective. Someone who's not involved."

"It's Norm," I admitted. "He's cutting a deal to start a new band."

Confusion crinkled her features. "He's leaving?"

"No, that's the thing. He wants to have his cake and eat it too—the band *and* do solo."

"Are you upset because he wants to have a side gig?"

"I'm upset because he's having secret discussions with our label and not telling me."

"So it's the deception that's bothering you."

"Yes," I said, feeling like I'd just agreed to something else entirely. "Among other things." Clouds outside started to thin and sunlight crept through the window, her hair shining like sparkled ice. I reached out to tuck an errant strand behind her ear. "I just don't want to talk about it right now, okay? What I want to talk about is you. Us. Beyond this weekend."

Her next comment came out carefully. "I told you I recently broke up with someone, right?"

"Is he back in the picture?"

"No," she said, to my enormous relief. "But it didn't end well, and I told myself I wouldn't rush into anything."

She didn't say *like this*, although it floated between us. I knew about Roger Bamfield, her ex, thanks to a thorough creeping of her social media accounts. She'd scorched most of the photos of him but there was always one that got missed. Sure enough, deep on Facebook, I'd found it. A group photo taken in front of a picnic table at either a park or in the grandiose yard of some billionaire. Roger was a paint-by-numbers middle-management guy out for the weekend. Chinos and sandals. A bullshit smile synonymous with dudes desperate to climb the corporate ladder. With a protective arm around Sasha-Rae, he'd clearly traded up. My personal mission was to make sure she never ended up in the arms of anyone else except me.

"We can go as slow as you want. I don't care. But slow can't mean weeks without seeing you. I'll fly you wherever, whenever, even if it's for a day. I'd fly to see you but I'm a wreck on planes," I explained. "I don't fly unless it's life or death."

She smiled a different smile, and I knew she was already thinking of the weeks ahead, how it would play out, how she would have to juggle friends, family, events. How tour life might bite back, like it already had, only nastier. By any reasonable standard, would she stick around on this merry-go-round? Would any sane person?

"I could probably make things work here and there," she said, without a lot of conviction.

I put my hand on top of hers and savored the warmth I might not feel again. "I'm not doing *could*, Sasha-Rae. I can't. I won't. It's not my nature. I *am* intense, about everything. I'll be intense about you. You're either in or you're out, and if you need to think about it, I understand."

We locked eyes and fear sharpened inside me. It was either the gutsiest thing I'd ever said, or the dumbest.

"I have a question," she finally said, in a tone that meant I was fucked no matter what the answer.

"Ask away."

"Why are you so sure about me?"

If I gauged her correctly, she would consider the truth endearing—

I'd never fallen so hard, so fast since Suze—but I didn't trust the moment. What if I was wrong?

"Just...cuz."

She didn't even try to stop the laugh. "For someone who writes the most beautiful lyrics, that was pretty lame."

"Well, you put me on the spot." I stroked my thumb over top of her hand, back and forth, a relentless windshield wiper. Bought some time to corral my speeding thoughts. "Relationships all start somewhere, with someone who's got that something-something. You've got that something and I can't really put it into words. I hope that works, because it's all I got right now."

An expression of total sweetness rose on her face. For once, I'd said the right thing.

"But it's not just about me," I continued. "What about you? You didn't fly all this way for nothing."

"I know." She bowed her head and a few thoughtful seconds ticked by before she looked back up. "I'm not as talented as you in the word department so I hope you're okay if I say ditto."

"Don't say yes if you don't really mean it. My heart will disintegrate."

Our eyes met again. Solidly. "If we're going to make this work," she said. "I do need one more thing from you."

She could have asked for anything. A show pony. A ferris wheel set up on the roof of her condo. A trip to the moon. Instead, she asked for the one thing I wasn't prepared for.

"Don't ever lie to me, okay? No matter what."

So that's what ended it, I thought. *He lied to her.*

Which meant this was the time to come clean about Hastings.

But we'd come *this* close to annihilation. I couldn't.

Sasha-Rae stared at me intently, alert for any signal to flee, to save future heartbreak.

So what did I do?

The stupidest thing ever.

"I promise."

CHAPTER THIRTY

As my rig motored on the 401 toward Detroit, I tossed and turned on my bed, unable to relax. The Jenga stack of half-truths and unmentionables teetered, on the verge of collapse. On my end, there was a way to present the Hastings situation to Sasha-Rae, although the actual plan eluded me. Mac was a different story. Once he found out about Bryce's attempt to poach Norm, he'd execute his plan faster than a guillotine could drop. When it came to label shenanigans, Mac was as friendly as a T-Rex, and about as forgiving. Due to that, I'd thought long and hard about texting him details of last night's fracas. In Japan closing some deal, he didn't need the distraction. He'd be in Detroit in three days, joining us for the last night of our four-night run. But honesty flowed thicker than blood between us, so I bit the bullet and went with an abbreviated version of events.

He freaked.

After a flurry of heated text exchanges, we ended with:

M: That motherfucker.

A: Which one?

M: All of them!

A: No way we're signing with them. Cast the net wide.

M: Fuck me. I knew it would blow up in Canada. I hate that place.

A: How's Japan?

M: Cold sake, hot women. I'm in heaven.

A: You bringing home a bride?

M: Maybe a rash. Lol. I gotta run. Keep me posted and don't upset the applecart until I get there.

I had sidestepped the whole kicking-Norm-out-of-the-band thing for now. By the time Mac got back, I hoped to have it all sorted, although the radio silence amongst us this morning didn't bode well. Usually we checked in before the buses departed but on account of Sasha-Rae in town, I scheduled myself to leave Toronto a couple hours later. The tour caravan was long gone by the time I smuggled Hastings back onto the bus. (Big Daddy minded his P's and Q's and showed up exactly when I asked him to.) This time we breezed right through the border. Once we'd made it, I wouldn't describe our mood as festive; it was more like the quiet confidence of career criminals who knew what it took to pull off a job. But we weren't out of the woods yet.

Our four nights in Detroit were an unusual situation. Little Caesars Arena wasn't available, so our agent had swung a deal with The Fox Theater, an iconic five thousand-seater. In the past few years, we'd been too big of an act to gig the theater circuit, but I preferred playing in the Grand Old Dames to soulless arenas. For the crew, however, it meant a re-jig: smaller stage, tighter gear, tighter every-thing. The bus holding zone was cramped too, and everyone was under each other's noses. We needed to be extra cautious.

The last person I wanted to bump into was Sven, so of course, we ended up face to face in a tiny, airless backstage hallway.

"Did you kick Norm out of the band?" His eyes raked over me in disbelief.

"Who said that?"

"Everyone. The crew's asking questions."

So the boys *were* talking...just not to me.

"It's all good," I said, flustered. "Seriously. I'll fill you in later, okay? Just let me get this interview out of the way."

He blinked, baffled. "What interview?"

"Peter Merker," I said. "I met him in Glasgow last tour. Long story. He asked as a favor. I forgot to mention it."

Sven took a step back and something in his eyes changed. When he spoke his voice was strained. "You've kept in touch?"

The question just hung there, seemingly unimportant, but the longer he kept staring at me, trying not to look destroyed, I realized, way too late, it was saying more than he ever could.

In all fairness, Peter had kept in touch. We'd met at a bar in Glasgow last year, the night before Mom died. A writer for *Front Phaze* magazine, some Czech lifestyle rag, he was touring Scotland for a piece on whiskey. I'd landed in Europe after a nightmare of events in LA to finish the last leg of the *Say It To My Face* tour. That night's show was a disaster. I'd holed myself up in the bar to drink away the wounds and was already blotto when Peter spilled a drink on me. His consolation round turned into several more. He was the kind of guy I never hung with: man bun, blazer with suede elbow patches. A metro elegance I neither aspired to nor understood. He had no idea who I was, and I didn't care who he was. So we bonded the way you sometimes do with total strangers. When we closed the bar down, the night still felt young. He said he had some coke, I paid four hundred pounds for a bottle of Armagnac and we hopped a cab back to my bus. For every line he did, I took a shot and the night slipped away until we were both so wasted the conversation disintegrated into grunts and the occasional "Yeah."

At some point, we both slumped onto the couch. Whatever song had been playing ended and the hazy chords of The Velvet Underground's 'Oh! Sweet Nuthin' numbed me more than the Armagnac. The weight of my head was suddenly too much. When it sagged in Peter's direction, I didn't have the strength to lift it.

"Sorry, mate," I mumbled, the room starting to spin. "I'm done."

My eyelids drooped shut. In the dark, I could hear Peter's jaw grinding from all the coke. Then, I felt warmth on my thigh. It grazed higher, onto the zipper of my jeans.

"S'ok?" was all I heard.

By then I'd lost all distinction between him and myself.

"Yeah," I slurred. "I guess."

His mouth fumbled onto mine, beard scratchy. Foreign. He tasted bitter but didn't feel wrong. Our sloppy hands yanked down each other's jeans just far enough.

"Jesus," he whispered as he guided my hand, his slipping between my thighs. "You're so fucking hot."

The last thing I remembered was the squeak of the sofa leather, the guitar and drums riffing faster, everything moving up, up, up, higher, higher, higher, an unbearable pressure disappearing. Then, Peter groaning, his head buried deep in my shoulder.

Sven's alarmed voice wrenched me awake the next morning. "Adrian!"

"Wha? What?" The floor of the bus was cool against my face.

"Are you okay?"

He flipped me over in a panic and then stood up, face red with what I assumed was disgust. "Jesus Christ."

Legs splayed, boxers and jeans knotted around my knees, all my business on full display, I was a sorry sight. Sid Vicious on a good day, if he ever had any. I staggered to my feet, almost crashing into Sven as I pulled up my jeans.

"You scared the shit out of me," he said.

"I'm all right," I said, wobbling as he steadied me with his arm. "I'm fine."

"You're not fine. You're a disaster. You have an interview at noon, remember?"

"What time is it now?"

"Eleven forty-five." He did a once-over of the unusually unkempt bus, his nose wrinkling. An earthy musk permeated the air. "Do you even know where your phone is?"

Outside, the Glasgow rain pounded relentlessly. Sven, damp and musty, smelled like an old mop. It threatened to bring up what was left in my stomach.

"What's with the attitude?" I railed back. "I'm here. I'm awake. I've got fifteen minutes to find my phone."

"Where were you last night? I kept calling you."

"Out."

"You're not in any shape to be alone."

"Don't worry, dad, I'm good." I stumbled past him to the fridge. "'Scuze me, but I need some water."

I guzzled half a bottle, water dripping down my chin, onto my torso, the floor. When I broke for air, Sven's gaze flicked off the kitchen table. His face had drained of any recognizable emotion.

"What are you doing?" he asked.

"Svennie," I said, and closed my eyes as the water worked its way into the parched nether regions of my body. "It's way too early for existential questions."

He rushed for the door so quick, I wasn't sure what I'd missed.

"Hey!" I called out. "Where are you going?"

With one hand on the door, he grunted, "Out."

"Hello?" I waved a hand. "I'm over here."

It took all his effort to look at me, both eyes guarded. "What?" he asked again, testily.

"We're cool, right?"

"Of course."

"Why are you rushing out?" I asked, leaning onto the counter. Back then, my muscles were still in play and I didn't mind being half naked. "There's something else important here."

He stilled. Swallowed hard. "What do you mean?"

"I mean, it's breakfast time. Can you get me something greasy? And a chocolate milkshake, too. I'm like, depleted."

When he stormed back half an hour later, I was in the middle of the interview. He dumped a breakfast sandwich and milkshake on the table, refused to look at me, and stomped back out. I had no idea what stirred him up so bad. Sven wasn't a touchy-feely kind of guy in general, and his behavior felt way off. He also knew the drill. That's why I'd hired him. He had seen me at my worst and then some. Dealing with it was part of his job description. (Okay, maybe seeing my junk in broad daylight put him off, but I mean, it's not like he'd never seen another guy's dick.)

After the call, I took a swig of the milkshake. A piece of paper clinging to the moist underside fell limply to the table. I stared at the unfamiliar, neat printing, just like Sven had earlier.

Thank you for a GREAT night. Call me. Peter Merker. XOXO.

Back in the bowels of the Fox Theater I put a hand on Sven's arm, hoping to stem the slurry of shit thundering downhill. Because I saw in his eyes, what I'd missed that morning in Glasgow.

"Svennie," I said. "It's just an interview."

He shook off my hand in a near-violent gesture, threw open the back door, and slammed it behind him. I just stood there and felt empty, wondering how I'd never put two and two together. The interview, of course, was secondary in all of this. Sven had a wife and son back in Sweden. We'd only talked about them a handful of times, to the point I often forgot he was a husband and father.

But in the past six years he'd spent more time with me than with them.

A lot of time.

CHAPTER THIRTY-ONE

For the record, I am unabashedly hetero. Peter was a one-off; circumstantial, in circumstances I hoped to never find myself in again. I wasn't proud of what I'd let happen. Nor was I dying to tell anyone about it after the fact. But Sven knew. It explained why he'd been so bitchy at the end of the last tour. Why we'd dissolved into arguments every other day. Now wasn't the greatest time to sort things out, but I had to say something, no matter how awkward the topic. Halfway out the door to track him down, an incoming call from Sasha-Rae made me U-turn back into the theater for some privacy.

"Hi," I said, surprised to hear from her so soon. "You back home already?"

"Uh, yeah," she said. "Back to the rain. You busy?"

"I'm dreaming of you, if that counts."

"You sound a little wound up to be dreaming. How are things with the guys?"

"Not great," I admitted. "Haven't seen them all day."

"How does that work when you have to go on stage in a few hours?"

"It's not like we're not going to play," I replied with more certainty than I felt. Honestly, I couldn't imagine going on stage with this hanging over our heads.

Sasha-Rae came to the same conclusion. "You need to be the bigger person and patch things up," she said. "These situations can turn ugly, quick. Especially with the dynamic you and Norm have."

I ran a hand over my hair. "I know. I know. You're right."

A local roadie came trucking down the hall with a bunch of cable piled on his shoulder. He nodded politely and squeezed his muscles past me. Above me, I could hear our instruments being tested and tuned, our techs doing final adjustments.

"I'm sure you have a lot on your mind right now, so I won't keep you," she continued. "The reason I'm calling is…if I wanted to have something delivered to you there, how does that work? Is there a security entrance? Someone they should ask for?"

I thought of Hastings' snow globe and how it had overwhelmed me. How I didn't feel worthy of it. I wasn't deserving of much right now. "What are you sending?"

"It's a surprise."

"You don't know this about me, but I hate surprises."

"Is it going to drive you crazy not knowing?" she teased.

"Yes."

Artful pause. "Good."

"Seriously?"

"I need a name or number, please."

"I'll send you Sven's info," I said, "but he's not having the best day so don't be surprised if he's curt."

"Was he the really tall, blonde guy backstage?"

"The one who looks like an FBI agent? That's him. Did he talk to you?"

"No, The Dame pointed him out. We both thought he was kind of creepy. I wouldn't want him on my bad side."

I paced faster; wondered if this was my cue. A segue of sorts. Overnight, a vision of a different life, a new life, started to take shape. A very unexpected element formed part of the plan, and Sasha-Rae needed to weigh in. I decided to go for it.

"Speaking of sides," I said, "what do you think about adoption?"

Talk about surprises. Sasha-Rae had no clue about my vision, which fully explained the dead silence.

"Wow," she eventually said. "That's an abrupt change of subject. I'm assuming you mean kids and not pets?"

"Yeah, well, you know, there's so many kids without homes, it might be nice to adopt."

Long pause. "To be honest, I've never thought about it."

"But you said you wanted kids." I cleared that on our second phone call.

Longer pause. "Yes, eventually."

"So if we got a twelve or thirteen-year-old—"

"What?" she interrupted. Then, full on laughter, soaked with relief. "Oh my god, you're such a brat. I didn't realize you were joking."

"I'm not."

With my tone, her laughter petered out.

"Everyone wants babies," I continued, "but babies are so much work. If we get an older kid, they're in school, we have a life. It'll be way easier."

I rambled, like this was a real decision we were making, like we'd spent a year debating the pros and cons. In retrospect, any normal woman would've cut this conversation off at the knees. Sasha-Rae, however, picked up on the strain bubbling in my voice.

"Is there something I should know about but don't?"

I pinched the bridge of my nose. What was I doing? "We need to talk about this stuff. I want kids. You want kids. It's important."

"I agree," she said, "but adoption is a big step. Kids in general. I'm not dismissing the idea, but there's some ground to cover first, don't you think?"

I knew what she meant, but I'd taken off out of the blocks and was running downhill, stumbling, picking up speed, racing toward an imaginary finish line. I'd paced back and forth so many times I was dizzy, desperation closing in. I threw what was left of my good sense out the window.

"Like what? Getting married? Seriously, I'll propose. Right now if you want."

Utter, deep-sea silence.

"Adrian," she said, in a tone that said her time humoring me was officially over. "Slow down. Slow waaaay down." She took a deep breath, as if to give me an example. "I'm very flattered you'd think of having kids with me and proposing…"

Here it comes.

"…but you can't ask me out of the blue if I would be open to adopting a twelve-year-old and expect a definitive answer. That's a huge decision. We're not there."

Yeah, I get there's another step. Like sleeping together, or spending more than an hour with each other. But I'm running out of time.

"Fine," I said. "Sure, you're right."

I scratched the back of my neck. It felt like ants were crawling all over me. The banter of roadies from somewhere down the hall erupted into coarse laughter.

"Are you sure everything's okay?" she pressed.

It was actually worse, her trying to figure this out and me stringing her along. "Yeah. It's just…" I thumped a fist against the wall in defeat. "I'm dying to see you again is all."

"I'm thinking about you too," she said, so gentle, all I wanted to do is reach through the phone and touch her. "Don't forget to send me Sven's info, k?"

After we hung up, my mind kept spinning. I couldn't believe I made it out of that catastrophe in one piece. There were a hundred ways to ease into that conversation and I'd pulled a goddamned Norm. I counted my blessings Sasha-Rae had kept a level head. And of course, she was right…about everything. Not only did I need to find a practical solution for Hastings, but with the show only hours away, I needed to be the bigger person. It was time to deal with all the loose ends.

I detoured to my bus first and grabbed a bottle of Grey Goose for fortification. Hastings was in the bathroom, again. She hadn't said much all afternoon or eaten any of the lunch I'd prepared. I figured the border crossing brought her down again. The second time around, Hastings hadn't even cringed when stepping into the drawer, although she was decidedly shaky getting back out. I was just about to knock on the door and ask if she was all right when Sven marched in, his mouth in a grim line.

"Hey," I said, creating a human barricade between him the bathroom. "What did I say about—"

A toilet flushed. It sounded louder than the thunder of Niagara Falls. The bathroom door opened, toward us, so she didn't see him at first. Her face was gaunt, both cheeks flushed as she stumbled toward me.

"I'm, I'm not feeling all that great," she said.

Wearing an XL tour T-shirt and nothing else, Hastings' knock-knees were just visible under the hem. When she noticed Sven, her hands instinctively crossed her body. His eyeballs practically popped out of his skull.

I chucked the Grey Goose onto the couch and held up both hands. "It's not what you think, Svennie," I said. "I swear."

He edged back a step, horrified. "Has she been with you since Phoenix?"

"No. Yes. Fuck. It's a long story. She's a foster kid. She lost..." I paused, knowing there was no sound bite, no way to spin this in my favor. "She had no place to go."

Sven turned to Hastings with an ill expression. "How old are you?"

She glanced in my direction—*do I answer?* How I wished she were at least wearing pants.

"He's taking me to New Orleans," she finally said. "That's all. Nothing else."

She made it sound so simple, so noble. Only Sven wasn't buying any of it. His head spun back around to face me, and all I could think about was a party meatball on a toothpick. "Are you even thinking straight?" he asked. "This is how careers end."

"You don't think I've thought of that?" My voice rose too, the pressure getting to me. "I told you, she's got nowhere to go."

Hastings fell back against one of the couches, clearly unwell. Sven ogled her, both of them trapped in a nightmare they couldn't wake from. "If she's on drugs..." His strangled voice petered out and when his eyes fell back on mine, if he felt any compassion for me, it was tucked somewhere far, far away. "I used to respect you, but you're nothing but a spoiled, American asshole."

He launched out of the bus, clearing the stairs in only two strides. I kicked the door shut and crouched beside Hastings, who looked one second away from throwing up.

"What's wrong?" I asked. "What can I do?"

Hastings clutched her belly, voice thin and drained. "You need to go talk to him. Now."

Detroit's entertainment district sprawled along a swath of land south of I-75. Mostly parking lots built to accommodate the masses at Comerica Field and Little Caesars Arena, at 6 p.m. on a Sunday the streets surrounding the theater would normally be dead, but show-time was a couple hours away and curious fans hovered around the backlot streets. They catcalled and shouted through the chain link fence as I sprinted to catch up with Sven, his 6'7" body impossible to miss.

"Svennie, wait." I gripped his jacket, forcing him to stop. We were at the far end of the lot, partially protected by the theater's ventilation system. "There's an explanation and I need you to understand. Your cooperation would be appreciated."

"You want my *cooperation*?" He tore his arm out of my hand. "You expect me to cover this up?"

"Whatever you're thinking is dead wrong. C'mon, man. You know me."

He eyed me like I was the poster child for everything wrong in America. "Do I?"

I stared right back at him. All the unsaid things flew between us.

"Don't make this into something it isn't."

"What does that mean?"

"You know what I mean."

He didn't answer; or he did, with his jaw, a squaring that fought away the emotion. His eyes tore off mine, agonized.

"Is that why you sit around in your underwear? You don't think it's brutal for me to see you like that?"

I crossed my arms, feeling as low as a crumb. I'd been accused before of being self-absorbed and it wasn't entirely untrue. "I didn't mean to throw it in your face," I said, humbled. "I honestly didn't know until…back there. I'll take the rap for being clueless, but you know I'm not fucking heartless."

He tipped his head skywards and laughed, colder than the air surrounding us.

"It's true," I continued. "And we both know, in the long run, I've treated you fair. You've had a lot of concessions with me. In retrospect, I'm probably to blame. Maybe we got too close."

The Theater's ventilation system began to stutter and hum. I shivered in the waning sun. Sven's features turned hard, carved from granite, his hands winding together and apart in an edgy replication of what I imagined was going on in his mind.

"Not only are you heartless and clueless," he finally said. "You're the most self-centered person I've ever met."

I absorbed the blows. Deserved them, on some level. His ranting was actually a good sign; a first step toward wrangling things back to normal.

"Fine," I said. "Accuse me of all that. I'm not going to plea bargain my way out." I took a step toward him, to close the emotional gap. Lowered my voice. "I get it that you're upset, but can we keep her between you and me for now? Until I figure things out? There's nothing weird going on. I just need some time."

His gaze drifted off mine to the alley, a blank stare. "Tomorrow," he said, abruptly. "She's gone. You figure it out."

"Or what?" Because it was a threat.

"You're not untouchable," he said. "Remember that."

CHAPTER THIRTY-TWO

I SUPPOSED I HAD IT COMING. BUT IT WASN'T SVEN'S ultimatum or the way he'd unsheathed it like a dagger. No, those weren't the concerns. As he stormed away, my worry was palpable, a thick acid smear coating my tongue. Revenge was a whole other ball of wax.

With my world collapsing, a last resort came to me. I mean, way last. I mean, if I were a betting man, I wouldn't even touch this play. Who would, with a million to one odds? Hastings needed my attention, but I needed to find out quick if this was even an option. I jogged past the Theater, crossing Woodward Avenue, heading for the church on the corner. I needed someplace without distraction. I found a quiet corner in the churchyard and stared at my phone. I crafted the conversation, repeated my lines like an incantation; anticipated the questions, the pushback. It took forever to conjure up the courage to press one single button.

"Hi. What's up?" Suze asked.

"Can you talk?"

"It depends."

"I have a favor to ask."

"Of course you do. Now what?"

It threw me off, how genuine her hostility was. Mind you, the pick-up of the Flying V two days ago hadn't gone well. Pops had laid into her and via text, she'd told me she had another breakdown. Patrick was furious, and of course blamed me. All the lines I'd memorized evaporated.

"A friend of mine, uh, his daughter wants to come out to California, you know, try her hand at acting. I thought maybe she could stay with you? Give her the room downstairs?"

Suze was a lot of things; incapable of speech wasn't one of them. In the deeply troubled silence, I could see her in the kitchen, leaning against the blue marble countertop she'd gushed over because of the sparkles embedded in it. I could see the view we'd enjoyed on too few nights: the one overlooking the LA Basin, our house high in the hills.

"Jesus, Adrian," she finally said. "Are you drunk?"

"No," I replied, surprised how that offended me.

"Then you should know how I'd feel about a stranger living in my house."

"It's only for a bit," I countered. "And I bet you won't even notice her there." The house was five thousand square feet. Suze probably hadn't even been on the ground floor in weeks. "She can have her own key. Come and go without bothering you."

"What friend is this?" she asked, suspicious.

"Oh, uh, no one you know. Just a buddy. One of the roadies."

"You are aware I know all of them, right?"

"It's a new guy."

Another dubious silence.

"And he's not willing to rent a place for his own daughter?"

I rubbed at my forehead like measles had broken out. Figured she would drop the one question I didn't anticipate. "It's a long story."

"Hmmm," she said. "They always are with you."

"It's a favor, Suze. C'mon. The house *was* ours."

"Really? You throwing that down now? Did you bother to read the divorce papers? It's my house now."

"This might be a win-win," I said, trying another tack. "Maybe it will be good to have someone around."

Her voice edged into incredulousness. "In case you forgot, Patrick and I live together. And when did you become the authority on being around?"

I kicked at a candy wrapper lodged in the gravel underfoot. "So you won't do it."

In the silence, I could feel her winding up, getting ready to read me the riot act. "Let's be clear so you don't twist this around later like you always do," she said, in that tone of moral superiority she saved just for me. "This is another example of you telling me what to do, and that's what this really is; there isn't a question in any of this. I should put up a stranger in my house because you want me to."

I couldn't pinpoint exactly what made me snap. Maybe it was our pattern, the inability to change it, or the fact she wasn't going to come around and do me a solid. It was all of those things capped off with my own stupidity for believing in this solution. If there was ever a time to restrain my worst indulgences, this was it. Instead, I slipped beneath contempt.

"Why don't you look at the bright side of things for a change instead of being negative? You always wanted a kid."

If the sun shattered into a million pieces and fell from the sky, if the Fox Theater disappeared into a cloud of smoke, no repercussion would be too severe. The sudden stab of pain in my chest was unbearable.

Tell me I didn't say that.

When Suze replied, her voice was so full of darkness I could hardly recognize it. "You better be joking, because if you're not..."

"Suze—"

"No. You know what?" she interrupted. "Maybe it's good you called. We needed to have this conversation. It's long overdue."

A familiar pain drilled into my temples. "Please, not another lecture."

"Forget wasting my time on a lecture. This is a directive. *Do not* call me anymore. Every time you call, I'm a wreck after. I can't do it anymore."

An old Pontiac Parisienne, one of those late 70s beasts, rumbled into the church parking lot and shuddered to a stop. Mottled with primer, duct tape strapped a crumpled side mirror to the body. The windows were so grimed, I couldn't see in.

"What, we can't even talk now?" I asked.

"This isn't talking. It's you calling to complain, to ask for something. Do you realize you never even asked how I was?"

"I did."

"No, you didn't. And you won't. You don't. It's all about you. All the time."

"Fine," I said. "How are you?"

"Oh god," she moaned. "Don't start."

"You never give me a chance."

"You had your chance. Stop. Talking. Please!"

I shut my eyes, the sun suddenly too bright. She took a deep breath. When she continued, a stark weariness replaced the shrill in her voice.

"What we had was special, so special. I never thought I could love anyone as much as you. But your father, he treated both of us like shit. Chipped away at us with his dumb-ass comments. Made me wish somedays I was white, just to catch a break." She laughed, joylessly. "And that sparked your drive even more. You wanted success so bad, to stick it to him, to prove to him he was wrong about you, that you could pull off what he never could. And I wanted you to stick it to him, too, for all those reasons. I wanted you to be the biggest success, and you were. But the price of your success was my identity. My sanity." She paused to let the weight of that sink in. "You have no idea what it was like. I became Adrian's girlfriend, the Jazzer's wife, your plus one. I became invisible. Even when I made that donation to the musical therapy foundation, what did the press report? 'Adrian Johnson and his wife make a sizeable donation.'" Another laugh, full of frustration. "But I'm not dumping all the blame on you," she continued. "I let it happen. I believed in you more than I did me. You needed me. For years, I told myself that was enough. But after a while it wasn't."

A flash of us together in Vancouver—our argument—brought bile into my throat. Her mental health had started to teeter back then, and she wanted to go back home, get a job, get some semblance of normalcy into her life, not just trail after me. When I told her stewing around by herself in LA would only make things worse, that she should support me and be grateful for what we had, not complain about it, she accused me of being white and privileged, among other things. It was the closest I ever came to hitting her.

"I needed support too," she continued. "But I didn't have the emotional courage to fight with you for it. And then..." In the quiet, I could tell she was searching for the right way to position what came next. "It sounds twisted, but what happened with Norm, it helped. He didn't make me feel guilty for being depressed. I felt in control. That somewhere inside, I was still Suzanne. Still functioning. Still normal."

My hand clenched and unclenched. Every muscle in my body was starting to cramp.

"I will always love you, Ace, but the music came first for you." She cleared her throat of the emotion threading into her words. "Everything, and everyone, including me, was second."

Halfway through her diatribe I'd stopped pacing to slump against the wall. Now, I leaned my head back against cool concrete and stared up at the sky. In some dark, evil place, a basement of my most shallow shortcomings, I'd packed away that very possibility.

"Are you still there?" she asked.

"Of course I am."

"Then please," she said. "For both of our sanities, move on. You need to move on."

"So, I mean..." Emotion wadded in my throat. It was impossible to swallow past it. "This is it? Forever?"

It couldn't be. We were Siamese twins, joined at the heart. Yes, we'd been through hell and back, but there were good times too, lots of them.

"Don't make this harder than it needs to be," she said.

I don't remember either of us hanging up. I'd bitten my tongue so hard blood filled my mouth. My legs started to tremble. I flattened myself against the church wall, the possibility of collapsing all too real. She just hacked me off like a gangrene-infected limb and all I could muster was a look to the heavens, to the very God that fucked me over, and let him know exactly what I thought...at maximum volume.

The passenger window of the Pontiac stuttered lower, before disappearing with a *whoosh* into the door panel. A billow of smoke, the sweet and deadly scent of crack, swirled out. The woman—inner city, face ravaged from myriad abuses—craned her bald head to get a better look at me.

"You a'right there, mister?" she croaked. "If not, I've got a little something for your troubles." She smiled, a handful of teeth jutting out of her gums, and wiggled her tongue. "Twenty bucks. I'll make your pain go away."

I pushed off the wall and staggered away, sick to my stomach. Crossing the street back to the Fox, traffic whizzed by, uncaring, unfeeling. Horns bleated, the thin sound needles in my skull. Gravity was the only thing preventing me from floating away, that's how untethered I felt. My mind scoured backward, a metal detector looking for a nugget of golden truth, grappling for the moment, the time, the instant Suze stopped being enough.

Except she was right.

She was never enough.

At the Fox back lot, unfolding commotion crackled with panic. I saw The Dame first. Crouched low on the pavement in a robe, the door of my bus flapped open behind her. Immediately I knew something was wrong. Then Bo, the Up Yours drummer, sprinted toward her, yelling something I couldn't hear. As Bo pulled a distraught Dame to her feet, the motionless body lying in front of them came into view. I ran like my very life depended on it.

CHAPTER THIRTY-THREE

"Is she dead?" The Dame wailed. "Please don't tell me she's dead."

I shoved her aside and plunged to my knees beside Hastings. Eyes shut, chest unmoving, for a horrible second I believed she was dead. I pressed two fingers against the cold flesh of her throat, my own heart-beat throbbing so loud it almost trampled her faint one.

"She's breathing." A rush of relief knocked me back onto my heels. "She's alive." I ripped off my hoodie, balled it and tucked it under Hasting's head. "What happened?"

"I, I don't really know," The Dame said. "I came outside, and she was there and then...just collapsed."

Bo, who'd been on the phone, ended the call and announced, "I just called 911. The ambulance is on its way."

"Where's Sven?" I asked. An inkling, and I prayed for it to be wrong.

Bo shrugged, perplexed. "I don't know. Does he know her?"

"Who is she?" The Dame added.

"Hold her head up," I ordered at Bo. "I'm going to get some blankets."

I dashed onto the bus. In the bedroom I snatched the comforter and all four pillows off my bed. Bo, unlike The Dame, was totally zoned into the situation, and moved with a take-no-prisoners efficiency. He helped me lift Hastings while I jammed the pillows beneath her head, wrapping the comforter around her like a burrito. "C'mon, kiddo," I said, smoothing damp curls off her forehead. Her skin was clammy, refrigerator cold. "Don't do this to me."

"What's wrong with her?" Bo asked.

In my wildest dreams, I never figured I'd be crouched in the back lot of The Fox Theater with a bi, twenty-year-old, Down's syndrome punk rock drummer and a passed out teenaged girl between us. Nope. Not once.

"I don't know," I said, just as Hastings started to convulse, her body jerking. "Fuck!" I yelled. I peeled off the comforter, her T-shirt riding up in the tangle.

The Dame backed off with a gasp. "Oh my god. She's skin and bones."

Hastings' blossom breasts looked like decorations glued on to a skeleton. I yanked her T-shirt back down, hands shaking. My fear wasn't reviving her; it was crushing her. I'd taken a CPR course after one of our roadies, Matty, collapsed a few years ago. We'd all stood there, stunned and useless, not knowing what to do. Luckily, one of the bus drivers had taken CPR and had revived him. It had been a real eye opener for me. Matty gave up the roadie life soon after and now worked in IT somewhere in Idaho. But this wasn't like Matty; he'd tormented his body with bad road food, beer, and cigarettes until it revolted. Suddenly, all the pieces I should've noticed, the fatigue, the blood, fell into place. Hastings was sick, in a way I might not be able to help.

I crooked her head back, made sure nothing was stuck in her throat. Blood throttled through my veins. The parking lot, the bus, everything started to fuzz around the edges.

I started mouth to mouth and in between, whispered, "Breathe, you little puke. Breathe."

A siren howled in the distance, edging closer. Out of the corner of my eye, the crowd gathered outside the back-lot perimeter whipped out their phones.

"Can you get them out of here, please?" I shouted.

Bo hustled over to shoo them away just as a cop cruiser screamed down the lane and blared its horn. One of the theater staff opened the gate and the cruiser lurched to a halt inside. A Latino woman, grim-faced and looking tougher than a three-dollar steak, made her way over. On the breast of her uniform, stitched in all caps were the letters *LAVERO*.

"Is she all right?" She kneeled down beside Hastings and touched her forehead with the concern of a mother. "What's the situation?"

"I, I don't know what's wrong," I stammered.

She looked at me in surprise. "What's your relation to her?"

Before I could answer, Norm barged his way past the half circle of crew who'd accumulated. "Dude! What the fuck? Who's the chick?"

Lavero eyed Norm, decked out in zebra tights and nothing else, and then me. "You don't know her?"

"I bloody well hope you know her," Norm snapped.

"And you are?" Lavero asked.

"He's with the band," I said.

Norm's eyebrow arched. "I'm back in again, am I?"

"Hey! Get out of here! Stop!" Big Daddy's booming voice cut the air, and we all turned around. Two men dressed in fatigues stormed over like they were invading Normandy. Seconds later, just behind them, a taxi pulled up to the venue gate. A Middle Eastern driver poked his head out the window to confer with a venue employee, flustered and unsure with the sudden ruckus. Who were all these people showing up out of the blue?

One of the running men bore down on me, a greasy-looking snake on a mission. He yanked a video camera out of a pocket and with a twisted smile, pinned it on me. "Adrian Johnson. Can you confirm who this girl is? Was she traveling with you? Did she overdose?"

"Oh shit," Norm muttered.

"Get this flunky outta here!" I yelled, covering Hastings' face as the douchebag angled to get a shot. His long-haired lackey hung back, snapping photos at an alarming rate.

"Adrian," the filmer harangued, louder, his voice carrying above the melee. "Are you involved in child pornography? Yes or no?"

A dreadful silence followed. The crew all shuffled back, uneasy.

"What the hell?" Lavero put her hand on her gun, features tense. She thought she'd seen every seedy crime. Welcome to a paparazzi ambush. "Dixon!" She hissed at her partner, still in the car talking on his radio. "Get over here."

Exile cut in and shoved the camera guy so hard he stumbled to his knees, his camera skittering across the pavement. "Get the fuck out of here, you goddamned cockroach."

The filmer crawled toward his camera and fixed his cold, pale, lunatic eyes on Ex. "You're all witnesses! This man assaulted me! Lawsuit! Lawsuit!"

About to dog pile on the creep, Dixon fast-footed it over and intervened, pushing me aside. Bull-necked with a grave calm but seriously intimidating presence, he was clearly the lettered half of the duo. A Mike Tyson ass-kicker not to be tussled with. "You've got enough going on here, son," he advised. To Ex, who was itching to fight, "You too. Take a breather, friend."

With his wingman down for the count, the dude snapping photos started to report into his phone. "We're on location in Detroit, where Size of a Scandal front man Adrian Johnson looks to be facing yet another scandal. A teenaged girl..."

Lavero lunged toward him with a growl. "That's enough," she said, pawing down his phone. "This might be a crime scene."

"Crime?" What was left in my stomach curdled. I looked over at Ex in disbelief, and just past his shoulder I saw her. Sasha-Rae stood in front of the taxi, a hand to her mouth, horror etched on her face. In those grisly seconds, I felt like an army general on his last stand, the war over, me on the losing end.

Are you fucking kidding me? She was the surprise?

Another wail, the siren of the incoming ambulance reached a fever pitch. Sasha-Rae, the taxi driver and all the onlookers scattered like rolled dice as it pulled in. Parked, the paramedics jumped out. A broad-shouldered woman, ponytailed and severe, dashed to the back and unloaded a gurney. The driver, fighting his age with a nose ring, rushed toward Hastings and asked me, "What can you tell me about her health?"

"I, I...nothing. I don't know anything."

Lavero narrowed her eyes in my direction. "Does *anyone* know this girl?"

The driver peeled open Hastings' eyes, shone a light into them. Immediately after, he started to feel around her torso and his face tightened into a grimace. "Alice," he shouted, over his shoulder. "Her spleen's enlarged. Looks like acute splenic sequestration. Gonna need an immediate transfusion."

"Transfusion?" I asked, dumbfounded. "What does splenic—"

"Coming through!" Alice yelled, charging over with the gurney. With biceps as big as my thighs, she and her partner lifted Hastings onto the gurney with ease. Alice ratcheted the straps down tight around her. "I'll radio emergency, tell them to prep for a transfusion," she said, all grim efficiency.

"What's happening to her?" I asked the driver.

"Who are you? A family friend? How long has she been like this? Roughly?"

Questions I couldn't answer rained down.

"Like how?"

He stared at me like one does at a total dolt. "What are you, color blind? The whites of her eyes are yellow. She's severely jaundiced. It's one of the signs of sickle cell disease."

Maybe it was the word sickle. It reminded me of the reaper, which then reminded me of death. Or maybe it was disease. Virus and bacteria sounded manageable. Disease didn't. My stomach pitched violently.

"How bad is it?"

"Tell her parents or next of kin to get here asap." He dug out a card and handed it to me, his face a practiced mask of neutrality. "We're taking her to the children's hospital. H.R. Ellison."

"Everyone clear out," Alice barked. We all shuffled back and watched in stunned silence as they packed up Hastings. Seconds later, the siren kicked in, a mournful wail. The ambulance edged out of the lot, bypassing the taxi.

Taxi.

Taxi?

Taxi!

In all the distraction I'd totally forgotten. I bolted over just as it started to pull away.

"Sasha-Rae!" I whacked the bumper. "Wait!"

But it drove away without slowing down.

I watched it disappear, and all the blood leaked out my veins. I wanted to drop-kick the entire earth. "Fuck!"

Dixon jogged over. I was close to an exit and he didn't like that. "You're Adrian Johnson, I take it?"

"Yes," I snapped.

"Any drugs on the buses?"

"No. You wanna strip search me while you're at it?"

With a sigh, he scratched his stubbled chin, no doubt thinking of the cold beer and bag of chips waiting for him at home. His comfy man recliner and a Pistons game he'd recorded earlier. "I'm not saying there's a stereotype with you music people, but I had to ask."

Lavero brushed past, escorting the dirt bag video guy and his buddy out of the lot.

"You're a creep," Camera Guy hissed at me. "I hope you rot in hell."

Dixon moved faster than his pushing retirement attitude led me to believe. Good news for Camera Guy, because I was ready to tear him to shreds. In a restraining hold Schwarzenegger would be proud of, Dixon gripped me tight, advising, *Let it pass, let it pass.* After Lavero disposed of the media (and I use that term loosely), she and Dixon escorted me back to a dreadful scene. The crew, the boys all stood staring, dumfounded. This debacle was officially nuclear.

With a firm hand on my shoulder, Dixon scanned the buses. "Whatever one is yours, we better talk inside."

CHAPTER THIRTY-FOUR

WHEN YOU START TO RANK THE WORST MOMENTS OF YOUR life, chances are you've hit rock bottom. My list was small, but it still felt morbid assigning numbers to moments of misery. Forever ranked at number one was Mom's death, no explanation required. Suze's miscarriage followed a close second. The difference between those tragedies and what was going down now had everything to do with scope. Mom and Suze were personal, the pain not shareable. It didn't make them any more manageable, but they didn't directly impact the livelihood of the three slack-jawed faces staring at me in the bus. (Six faces in total, if you counted Dixon, Lavero, and Sven, who had materialized out of nowhere and followed us all inside.)

Dixon paused for the umpteenth time in his notetaking. "For all intents and purposes, the world thinks she's *dead*?"

It was one of those stories that didn't get better with retelling.

"Pretty much," I said.

Splayed out on the couch, Exile and Norm had listened in spooked silence; two kids hearing a ghost story around a campfire. The first thing out of Ex's mouth was, "How did you get her across the border?"

Lavero straightened. She hadn't given that any consideration. "You brought a minor who was presumed deceased into a foreign country?"

"It was only Canada," I argued, Mac-like.

"I think the word is smuggled," Norm said, adding another joyful layer to the proceedings.

Dixon rubbed his bald head, seemingly at a loss for words. "This is one for the record books."

"Why didn't you drop her back in Seattle?" Lavero asked. "Child services could've helped. They'd have record of her illness."

Under scrutiny, any and all of my decisions sounded feeble, beyond preposterous. "One thing led to another," I said. "And then, after that whole ordeal in Toronto, I thought maybe I should adopt her."

The collective look amongst them was unanimous: I'd officially lost my mind.

Norm backed it up with an incredulous, "While you're on tour?"

Sven, who'd been brooding in silence by the front door, far away from the officers, scoffed, "She came out of your bathroom wearing nothing but a *T-shirt*."

Diego, whose shell-shocked expression seemed permanent, muttered, "Buen senor."

"Were you the gentleman that called in this situation?" Dixon asked Sven. "Dispatch had a hard time understanding the accent."

The bottom fell out of my stomach. My eyes blistered onto Sven like a staple gun—*thock*. "Are you serious? I told you, *she* told you: nothing was going on."

Sven refused to look at Dixon or me. Despite his violent and correctional tendencies, he was surprisingly meek in the face of law enforcement. "You had her programmed to say all the right things, didn't you?" he accused, ice on every word.

"Programmed?" I jumped to my feet and Ex intervened with his athletic speediness. It required all of his strength to hold me back. "Jesus Christ, what is your problem?"

"All right, all right. Take five," Ex said, pushing me away from Sven. "If ya'll don't mind," he continued, addressing everyone, "I need some time with my boy. One on one."

Dixon eased to his feet and Lavero followed suit. The bus burst at the rivets with tension and they were happy to move on.

"We're done here for the time being," Dixon said. "Do me a favor and don't skip town." He handed me his card. "Call me in the morning. We'll need your official statement."

After they left, uncomfortable took on a whole new meaning. Ex forced me onto the couch and dropped beside me. None of us could maintain eye contact.

"We're still playing tonight?" Diego broke the silence with the million-dollar question.

Norm glared at me with fresh outrage. "Apparently you need to find a bass player first."

"Brother," Ex said wearily. "Chill."

"You better play," Sven snipped. "A cancellation will only make this look worse."

Ex fired back at Sven with authority he rarely showed. "Keep things on track, business as usual for now. And you better pray what Dixon said wasn't true, being a snitch. The only thing that keeps this shit together is brotherhood." He waved a hand toward the door. "Everybody out. Now."

They filed out with heads hanging, a chain gang heading back to the trenches. Usually the less people around me the better, but I suddenly craved a mob, anything to disappear. Ex stretched out on the couch with a loud exhale. His jaw flexed back and forth.

When I couldn't take the silence anymore, I said, "I bet you it was him."

"We'll get to that in a minute." He met my eyes, his expression dead serious. "Norm filled me in last night. When were you planning on telling me about Suze and the baby?"

The hurt in his voice struck worse than any lashing. Worse than hearing *Suze* and *baby* in the same sentence. I sighed, one of those *I-wish-this-was-already-over* sounds. "I wanted to, man. I really did. It's not a proud moment, keeping it from you. But it was too much all at once. Suze, the baby. Norm. Mom."

He saw my despair and didn't look upset as much as lost. "It almost puts the last year in perspective. I mean...I'm surprised Norm's still alive."

I had toyed with all sorts of revenge, none of it too severe. After Suze moved on with Patrick however, what was the point? I looked over at Ex and all I could do was shrug *I'm sorry.*

After a solemn beat, Ex asked, "Remember how I fought for you to be Jerome's godfather? How much grief I had to take from Lynaea over that?"

Ex once described Lynaea as one of those women who seemed like a good idea at the time. He could be forgiven. A former Ms. Alabama, she had all the right assets. She'd cooed over his Labradoodle, Butch, at the dog grooming facility they both frequented, and kept her mutt spoiled with such care and affection he'd mistakenly believed she'd treat him the same way. Their volatile on-again, off-again relationship switched permanently off ever since she'd hightailed out of LA with a new lover and Jerome in tow.

"And I did it," he continued, "because you were the best role model he could ever have. Never mind there isn't a single religious bone in your white-ass body."

I chewed on my ragged thumbnail. "I don't really need to feel any worse right now. Just saying."

"You don't get it. I still think that." Ex sat up and shook his head, like he wondered what it would take for me to see it. "Maybe I'm stupid for believing in you, but we got blood ties; ties that run deep, deep as family. That being said," he added, "I been keeping secrets too. What you don't know is that Lynaea's little fling didn't work out. She's broke, been calling me for money, can barely pay the rent on some dive up in Tarzana. I got a real window to get my visitation rights back. But you know what she's like. She'd rather bleed out than give me my due, just to prove a point."

Lynaea had successfully argued Ex's lifestyle wasn't conducive for the stability of Jerome and if she'd left it at that, being granted full custody, Ex could deal. But then she went after visitation rights, too. Or, in reality, Lynaea's mother, Vanda, had orchestrated the downward spiral. A single mother, one who'd struggled when her impregnator vanished, Vanda was a volcano when it came to the male species. She spewed decades old, pent-up vindictiveness like lava. Together they were unbearable. They squawked endlessly, two bitter crones who had been duped, while drinking Dom in crystal flutes on the patio of Ex's multi-million-dollar home on The Strand.

"I'm sorry, man. I thought you'd given up on that."

"I haven't given up. On anything. Including you. That's the point." He threw up his hands. "But you gots to be honest with me... What's this all about? Your idea of risk is drinking Smirnoff."

"This" could be interpreted as vague although we both knew exactly what he meant. I fidgeted with my ponytail. Found the floor suddenly alluring.

"Sven made it sound way worse," I hedged.

"That's not answering the question."

I paused, struggled to piece the warped events into something coherent. But they'd never be. Not to anyone else. I still didn't understand every nuance of my own decisions, the subconscious elements. I stared past Ex, beyond the window, beyond the bus, into places I'd never stared before. I retold the story from the very beginning, adding the pieces I'd censored out for the Dixon and Lavero version.

Twenty minutes later, I took a moment to reflect. "When you left the bar in Calgary, I tried to make sense of it all—us, the past, the future. It was a frigging bleak afternoon. And that night...it's kind of when everything changed with me and her. Just some of the stuff we were talking about." I didn't go into details about the songs or the colors. That felt too personal. "If I'd had any clue she was sick, I never would have let it get this far. You know that, right?"

Ex put a solidarity hand on my knee. He didn't need to answer.

"And Sven is full of shit," I griped. "Me and her? Not over my dead body."

His poker face suddenly animated with a weird smirk. "Have to say, it was kind of funny to hear The Iceman lose his jealous shit tonight."

"What do you mean?"

"C'mon, dude. You didn't think I knew? Don't tell me *you* didn't know?"

As heat seeped over my face, he laughed even harder. He was having too much fun with this, but after what just went down, a sidebar helped us both.

"I figured it out," I said. "Recently. Do the other guys know?"

His laughter finally contained itself. "They might suspect. For me, as true as the sun rises every day, you and she are about as likely as you and Sven."

"You have no idea how happy I am to hear that. On both counts."

"Unfortunately," he continued, crushing the afterglow, "this kind of stuff doesn't blow over, not anymore. This is a whole different level of war."

So true. When it came to men and questionable behavior, today's social and political climate meant shoot first, ask questions later. No matter how innocent things had been between Hastings and me, a giant target plastered my entire body.

"I gotta tell you," Ex admitted, his turn to now look at the floor. "This is coming at the worst time for me, too. I want Jerome in my life so bad but once Lynaea catches wind of this, it'll just be more ammo for her to deploy. I don't know how much more fight I have left."

Coming from the truest warrior, those words landed hard.

But I understood, more than he could ever know.

I'd been in the exact same position last year.

During the South America and Asia swings of the *Say It To My Face* tour, things had disintegrated badly with Suze. Our daily phone calls drifted into every other day, then her phone jumped to voicemail. When we did talk, she was disconnected and spacey, long lags in between sentences. I'd call her out for not taking her medication and she'd always deny it. After a bitter fight, she didn't reply to any of my apology texts and on the flight home from Japan, the bad feeling intensified. When the car service dropped me off at home, the front door was unlocked and inside, the air was lifeless, like no window had been opened for days. Despite the suffocating heat, a chill ran up my spine. I called her name and got no response. The living room, full of the mid-century furniture she loved, was littered with dirty plates. A thin layer of dust covered everything.

And on the rug, something else.

I launched up the stairs three at a time, bolted down the hall to our bedroom. The chatter in my mind swelled to a scream. You can prepare for many things, but not your wife lying motionless on the floor, in a dark room that smelled of sweat and blood and death. After the ambulance left, I destroyed the kitchen: smashing plates and glasses until there were none left. When I finally calmed down, the Uber couldn't get me to Cedars Sinai fast enough. I almost vomited in the Prius, twice. Third time's a charm, as the saying goes. When the doctor told me Suze had been pregnant and suffered a miscarriage and the crooked wire hanger on the living room floor—the one I'd convinced myself was there for some unknown reason—had done the deed, it was like a piece of my soul spewed out in a gush of green bile. I knew right then, long before she would admit it, before the DNA test proved I wasn't involved. It always bugged me how she and Norm got along. I'm sure some civil servant has since long dry-walled over the missing chunk out of the wall. My fist rang for days after, the kink in my ring-finger knuckle a permanent reminder.

It being LA and all, some hospital lackey spilled the beans and paparazzi descended on our home. I couldn't even get out of the driveway without being ambushed. Suze's mom and mine kept us alive. They brought in food, forced me to eat, kept vigil on Suze who was pumped full of antidepressants. Hands down, the worst two weeks of my life. When the time came to fly back to Europe, Mom insisted on driving me to the airport. On the way there she kept looking in the rear-view mirror, certain the Jeep had followed us too close for too long. A hot mess from Ativan and anti-nauseates, I couldn't see straight and had the nerve to tell her she was seeing things.

Famous last words.

The photographer from Hot Shot News followed Mom back to Long Beach, staked out the house overnight. On her morning walk, he pounced. Caught her off guard. She panicked. Started to run. The asshole actually chased her. Never nimble on her feet, Mom carried extra pounds from the crullers and churros she could never say no to. Lindsay Southam, recently retired and tending to her beloved roses, saw it all. The photographer in hot pursuit. Mom tripping. Her sprawl onto the pavement, headfirst.

She died instantaneously.

I found out in London. Hearing your own father disintegrate in successive voicemails was something I wouldn't wish on anyone.

"Sorry, man," Ex said, his voice jarring me back. "I know this is like, the last thing you needed to hear right now."

On the couch, face buried in my hands, I wanted to be someplace far, far away. But I'd already run away from all my troubles once. This time they needed to be tackled and taken down.

Unfortunately, my troubles beat me to it.

The bus door opened, and Norm clunked up the stairs.

"I hate to be the bearer of more bad news," he said, handing me his phone. "But you better take a look at this."

CHAPTER THIRTY-FIVE

THE JAZZER BUSTED WITH UNDERAGE GIRL!

So much for innocent until proven guilty. Welcome to modern day journalism where one ill-lit, sixty-second video and garish headline was all it took to toss decades of legal principle out the window. The reaction was depressingly swift and furious, social media going off like fireworks. Mac called me at 6 a.m. his time from Tokyo, frothing at the mouth. White-tiger rare to hear him so livid, he ordered me not to speak *to a single cop or lawyer* until he landed in Detroit on Thursday.

Despite the video landing with the charm of a scud missile, we plowed ahead with the show. The shift of energy from Toronto, however, was seismic. We usually fed off the crowd and vice versa; but now it felt like we were flushed down a toilet, crap and all. For the first time ever, the chant of "Boo!" echoed when we came offstage and when Sven met us in the dressing room, he twitched nonstop.

"It's a feeding frenzy outside," he said. "Camera crews, trucks." He shifted his eyes reluctantly to mine. "You might want to stay in a hotel tonight."

Diego glanced up from his phone, darkly. He'd barely said a word to me all night. "How do we get out of here?"

Norm, eyeliner smeared and looking like a deranged raccoon said, "Get in the car, pin the gas and pray you don't hit anyone."

Diego exploded with the rage of Vesuvius. "Can you be fucking serious for once?" He snapped his fingers together and formed an alligator's mouth, right in Norm's face. "It's always yip-yip-yip-yip-yip with you. This isn't a joke. You mess with kids, the world doesn't like it. I don't like it. You felt it out there. We all did." He whirled around to face me. "You've dished out a lot of slop over the years. This time, I don't know if I can swallow it."

My phone raged along with Diego, beeping relentlessly in my pocket with incoming calls and texts. I imagined the gossip. Rumors flying. Sasha-Rae hadn't responded to any of my texts before the show; I'd lost faith she ever would.

"I get it, Diego," I said. "I do. But hear me…"

"I don't think you do get it!" he shouted. "How do we come back from this?"

"Calm down, Guadalajara," Norm said. "You're—"

Diego shoved Norm so hard his head cracked against the wall. "Like you're going to save the day? The fucking gringo who's so ignorant and insensitive he drives a hearse with a baby on board sticker in the window?" He whirled around to thrust his phone into Sven's face and shouted, "Is this true, the rumors? Petitions to cancel the rest of the tour?"

Norm's hand patted the back of his head, and it came back smeared with blood. "Are you shitting me?"

Ex and I backed the hell up and shared a look I wouldn't call hopeful. Diego going full postal was one thing; that news was entirely another.

*

In no particular order, the post-show freak-outs included: Diego, Mac, Bryce (who had left us after Toronto and was now flying back), Salvatore (our agent), and Caleb, via email. God bless his fanboy soul, he practically cyber-sobbed, telling me he didn't believe the story one bit and went after every hater who posted on our social media. I tried to let it all roll off my back, but the lone text from Suze did me in:

S: A friend's daughter??? You need serious help.

After a full ransack of the minibar, I lay alone in my hotel bed, lights off, curtains shut. In a limbo state of exhaustion and almost drunk, neither of them enough to induce sleep, the vision of Hastings' limp body wouldn't leave my mind. I needed to see her and so help me, I would get dragged out of the hospital trying. I'd called earlier, pretending to be a reporter (again) to get an update on her status. But the staff was on full lockdown and gave me nothing. Diego had shut me down too. When I'd asked him if we could meet and talk it out, his curt "No thanks" stung worse than a slap. It was the only time in our career he'd ever said no to me.

Now, with zero desire to talk to anyone, the hotel phone rang. I fumbled the bedsheet around the receiver just in case Diego had changed his mind.

"Hello?"

"Good evening, Mr. Sundstrom, this is the front desk. I have a Sasha-Rae Tomason here to see you. She said it was urgent."

The clerk let that hang, as a question. Her tone made it clear she'd been pestered to ring me and wasn't pleased about it. I sat up so quickly, the head rush made me swoon. It took a second to untangle my tongue.

"Of course. Send her up, please."

The clerk's voice dipped a notch. "I'm sorry, but for security reasons we can't. You'll have to come down."

"Right. I'll be down in a minute."

I hung up, a mess of questions vying for answers. How did she know which hotel? And my room was booked under Sven's name, a decoy tactic many bands used, but I didn't recall mentioning it. As I pulled on my clothes, I remembered I'd given her Sven's name and number the other night. She must've called him. I tried her number, but it went right to voicemail. Strange. Riding down the elevator, a war rampaged in my belly. It felt too good to be true.

And it was.

She waited for me in the lobby, eyes glowing and sinister, a hungry gator in the bayou.

"Adrian." Jillian smiled. "How nice to see you."

The elevator doors rumbled closed behind me. No point in running away. She'd hunt me down and I wasn't up for a sprint.

"How do you know her name?" I demanded. I'd known Sasha-Rae for less than a week. How could this hack already have her in the crosshairs?

"Investigative journalism is my line of work."

"Journalism?" I snorted. "You have balls, Jillian, I'll give you that. Maybe it's time for that panty check."

She tipped her head with that Chiclet-white cocky smile. "Is that a proposition?"

"Let me guess, you're recording this. Or someone in the lobby is." My eyes skipped around for the culprit. Potted plants were always a favorite hiding spot.

"It must be so hard being that paranoid," she said, without an ounce of sincerity.

I closed my eyes and envisioned strangling her. Figured she wouldn't mind. Crammed into leather pants one size too small, what was one more squeeze?

"What do I owe this stellar visit to? Part two of the Adrian take-down scheme? Should we call your accomplice Norm down here too?"

She hemmed and hawed. "Norm's very sweet...bit of a flailer though. And surprisingly, very devoted to you."

"It's called being friends. Seeing as how you don't have any, it must come as a surprise."

By the way she straightened, I could tell my fortitude was unexpected. She smoothed back a chunk of hair and eyed me coolly.

"I'm here because I have a proposition for you. An honorable one."

I laughed right in her face. "Never thought I'd have a conversation with you that included the word honor. Let me guess: you're kinder, gentler now?"

Her eyes narrowed and it was a disturbing sight. They weren't just wide set; they teetered on the sidelines of her face like a halibut's.

"For someone whose entire reputation is on the line, you might want to devote some time to bailing yourself out." She sidled closer. "Do you deny sleeping with her?"

"I never touched her!"

"So you don't deny *not* sleeping with her?"

My brain swirled around the negatives; the double negatives. Classic Jillian. She lulled you into thinking a causal conversation was going down and then *bam*. I'd experienced the very worst of her after Mom died. She repeatedly denied sending the cameraman to follow us and within a week, I'd lawyered up. A settlement was coming down in the next couple months and was erring in my favor, so I knew that any proposition from her, now, involved fresh cement shoes.

"No comment."

She shifted her humongous handbag from one shoulder to the next. "Your sorry ass is this close to jail, and I suggest we work together. If anyone can get Hastings to talk, it's you. You need her statement; I could broker the blockbuster interview. There's a chance to set this story straight before it gets out of hand."

I throttled back another laugh. "You're going to set the story straight? You, the Halliburton of press? Blow up a story and then position yourself as the savior? What the hell is wrong with you, anyway? Don't you have a shred of decency in your soul? A young girl is sick, and you want to exploit that for ratings?"

"You can leave it up to chance, but you know what happens," she continued, her voice dripping with vulture wisdom. "Lawyers smell a payday. They start whispering in her ear, her story changes. Once that happens, I can't help you."

"Help? That's fucking rich. You've never helped anyone in your life. You and your slimeball lawyers are never going to get to her. In case you need a reminder, she's in a hospital. They have a code of ethics, unlike you."

My voice rose as I laid into her, and it carried loud and clear, all the way to the front desk. The clerks watched us with nervous, darting eyes. A mistake had been made and they didn't want to lose their jobs. Jillian remained calm. She knew a thing or two about timing, though, and yanked the final arrow from her quiver just when I thought we were done.

"What about Sasha-Rae? You think she might have something to say about all this?"

There was a brief span of tense quiet. I'd momentarily forgotten that was how she got me down here in the first place.

"Leave her out of this," I said, my voice gravel. "She isn't involved in the slightest."

"She is involved now. And what a coincidence—Richey Slayer is her brother! Seems like she has her work cut out for her, managing his shenanigans, being embroiled in yours..." Her sing-song ended with a full dramatic pause. "Do you think this will damage her career when people find out she's involved with a pedophile? Or, excuse me, *alleged* pedophile."

She let me fully digest what that meant, how low she would stoop. My temples started to throb.

"You wouldn't dare."

"Hmmm," she demurred. "Maybe we've found some common ground after all." She glanced at her watch casually. "I don't know about you, but I've got work to do. Why don't you think about my proposal and get back to me? In the meantime, I'll work on two versions of the story. Let's hope Sasha-Rae doesn't make the cut."

Any remote sense of fun I'd had tossing barbs vanished. I was this close to being sick. "How do you sleep at night?"

She laughed, a fake tinkle I wanted to ram down her throat. "Like a baby, darling. Like a baby."

CHAPTER THIRTY-SIX

AFTER A HORRIBLE SLEEP, I DRAGGED MY BUTT OUT OF BED around noon. Sheets of water pelted against the window, the sky crying. The gloom had thinned out the media hordes hunkered in front of the hotel, and only a few rain-slickered henchmen idled on the sidewalk. I let the curtain fall shut and crouched to collect my phone, remarkably undamaged after I'd chucked it across the room last night. Sasha-Rae had called out of the blue to tell me, among other things, she was changing her phone number. I couldn't stop replaying the end of our conversation.

"Do you hate me?" I asked.

After an eternal silence, she said, "That's an interesting question. I don't know you enough to hate you."

"But you don't like me."

She sighed, frustrated. "I do like you. A lot. That's the problem."

"None of it is true, I swear."

"So there hasn't been a teenaged girl travelling with you across the country?"

"Okay, *that* part is true, but..."

"You remember the one thing I asked for?"

"I know, I know. You don't think I know?" I closed my eyes,

wishing I was beside her. "Can I at least see you in person? To explain?"

After a pause long enough for dinosaurs to live and die in, she answered. "What I see right now is a hot mess. You're fighting everyone, including yourself. It's clouding your judgment. I'm tired of all the drama with my brother, and with you it's just...I'm sorry to say, more of the same. I just don't want that in my life anymore."

"Don't lump me in with him," I pled. "I hate being famous. You have no idea. Actually, you do. You've played down how much you know about me, but you're a fan; you've listened to my interviews. You know how private I am."

"That's another thing," she said. "I do know what's gone on in your life, and I don't know if that's good. Why do you think I asked you about your ring? I heard you were divorced but then I also knew how much you loved her." Another sigh, despondent, like she'd come to a forgone conclusion. "And honestly, I think you still do. I don't think you're ready for a new relationship. You've got some serious soul-searching to do, on a lot of fronts."

I made a fist, so ready to take another chunk out of a wall. "Just tell me there's a chance, even a remote one."

"All that stuff in Toronto. Was it because of her?"

Fuck. "Mostly."

"And it was her room, where you slept the last night?"

Defeat marched closer. No, it trampled all over me. "That's not who I am."

"For your sake, I hope it's not who you are." Her voice turned sad and in a final, *don't call me, I'll call you* way: "Goodbye, Adrian. And good luck."

Good luck.

I would've preferred *go to hell* or *beat it* or even a Suze-style hang up. Some slag to coincide with how demoralized I felt. But *good luck* was who she was: a woman of style and class who could read the writing on the wall and back away gracefully. Telling her I was trying to do the right thing now seemed idiotic because I wasn't even sure I *had* done the right thing. In the shower, I let the hot water cook me alive as punishment. After, I scanned the minibar for something edible just as knocks rang out on my door. I peered through the peephole first and then cracked the door wide.

"You're alive," Ex said.

"Living the dream."

He didn't laugh. "I'm heading down for some grub. There's a restaurant on the third floor. I called down and they said it's clear. You in?"

Starved and needing to escape these four walls, I told him I'd meet him in ten. I made one phone call and then caught up with him. I half braced to be accosted by someone, but the hotel was unnaturally quiet. Not a soul in the elevator or the restaurant. I wound past the graveyard of empty tables and chairs, and after Ex confirmed he'd asked for a sanitizing wipe down, I slid into the velveteen-lined booth across from him. A grizzled waiter, pants barely hanging on with suspenders, left menus and took our coffee orders, eyeing us like a couple of reprobates.

"Your phone's off, I take it," Ex said once we were alone.

I peeked at him over the menu, leery. "Now what?"

He did that thing he always did when he was uncomfortable and ran his fingers up and down the eight hoops that rose largest to smallest on his left earlobe. "The rest of the Fox shows are out, maybe more. Just came down."

Any and all saliva dried up in my mouth. "Seriously?"

"Bryce is close to losing it. Check this shit out." He held up his phone and scrolled to give the full effect of the length and density of Bryce's text message. "Sent it to all of us."

I didn't bother reading it. "Great. When does he land?"

"Tomorrow."

"Why is he so involved in this? It's not even his job."

"Not sure. He and Ziegler, they've been grooving together, BFF schoolgirls. Something's brewing."

The waiter appeared with our coffees and set them down with an unsteady hand. I emptied two sugars into my espresso and drained it like a Tequila shot.

"What about Norm?" I asked. "Where's he at?"

Ex blew on his Americano. "He's blaming himself pretty bad."

"But he knows I was just mad the other night, right? About the band. Heat of the moment and everything?"

He studied me for a few seconds. "You should tell him that."

"And Diego? Paraphrase if it's not good."

"He's not thinking straight right now," he said, in the gentlest, bro way he could.

I fiddled with my thumb ring. "What about you?"

He juiced his coffee with cream, took another hit. A contemplative silence hovered on the apex between good and bad. "What you need to know is this," he finally said. "I'll follow you to the ends of the earth every day and twice on Sunday."

The bundle of anxiety in my chest slackened. I couldn't lose Ex, on top of everything else.

He repositioned himself in the booth to angle toward the windows, the empty tables and chairs. "When you were in Mexico, I thought a lot about what I could be doing better. I gots a beautiful son I never get to see, and I want him back in my life. And yeah, I shoulda asserted myself more in the early days with you," he said, voice full of reflection this time, not anger, "but I didn't. Fact of the matter is, not a whole lot to complain about. You made me a better musician. A better person. Can't say that about a whole lot of people." He looked me right in the eye. "What I'm saying is, I get it. What went down with you and the girl. You care about people, you always have. You don't always know the right way to show it, but no one's perfect, right?"

I pushed away the urge to stand and give him a hug. Thankfully our food showed up before it got sloppy. We retreated to our meals, our own private thoughts. When he finished the last bite of his eggs benedict, Ex pushed his plate aside with a doubting glance.

"You and me will always be gold, but you given any thought on how to mop up this mess?"

"Funny you should mention mess."

Word for word, I downloaded Jillian's manifesto from last night. Ex shook his head in disbelief.

"Maybe you should call Dixon, sic him onto the real bad guy."

Dixon was my call before coming down. I told him I wouldn't be visiting him, as per my manager's advice. He didn't sound surprised or disappointed—just frazzled, mainly. Every day he faced a sea of desperate humanity, problems that weren't fixable. Maybe because I wasn't a total lost cause in comparison, he let slip news on Hastings. Stable and recovering. No one was allowed to question her yet, although he confirmed what Mac had told me: if there were no "signs"—ahem— and if Hastings didn't press charges, with no living relatives to pursue the case, I was essentially absolved. At least on paper. (The social justice warriors would not be so forgiving.) Hastings did have to go on record though, and with Jillian slithering in for the kill, time was of the essence.

"That's not the right move," I said. "I have to take her down stealthily. I can't risk upping the stakes. On paper, she's done nothing wrong. I need to get into that hospital and talk to Hastings. If Jillian reaches her first, we're screwed."

Ex reached beside him and launched a plastic shopping bag across the table. I caught it with both hands. The contents were almost weightless.

"Funny you should mention stealth," he said with a covert smile. "I had an idea last night. Kind of plays into the whole scheme of how things are unfolding."

I pulled out the mullet wig with two fingers. It was one of the many Norm rotated through. "Is this part of the idea?"

"One of the pieces."

"Do I want to know?"

"What matters is I know you and you know me. We got each other's backs. You wanna hear the battle plan?"

Mounted on the tip of my middle finger, I spun the wig, the strands flaying out like one of those midway rides I'd never been on.

"I'm all ears," I said.

At this point, what else could go wrong?

CHAPTER THIRTY-SEVEN

IN THE SAFETY OF SHADOWS, AT 11 P.M. THAT EVENING EX and I scoped out the H.R. Ellison Children's Hospital. Three stories of bald and imposing Cold War design, the building felt so spiritless, I couldn't imagine leaving any child inside.

"Is it just me, or does it feel like we're trying to break into a jail?" I muttered to Ex.

"I don't know what's more depressing," he replied. "The building or that thermometer."

Next to the hospital entrance, an oversized plastic thermometer canted to one side. One of those fundraising gimmicks, where the level of the mercury indicated how much money had been raised. A "We're close!" arrow was lodged just above the thermometer base, the two-million-dollar mark light years away.

"Let's hope we're more successful," I said. "You ready?"

Ex had done his best to look pedestrian, by way of ball cap and jeans, and sneakers to cover up his painted toenails. With bracelets and necklaces removed, he could move without jingling like a wind chime.

"I've done a lot of stupid shit in my life and gotten away with it," he said. "I'm praying to bat a thousand tonight."

As Ex crossed the street, his reticent body language said it all. Our entire mission rested on a wing and a prayer. Ex had called earlier, pretending to be a relative of a patient who'd undergone surgery. Those patients were on the third floor and visiting hours ended at nine. At this time of night, the hospital lobby snoozed; exactly what we'd factored into our plan. Once Ex made it inside, I inched closer to the entrance, my stomach knotted and green. We had studiously avoided discussing our plan not working, and it didn't feel very general-like to send in my man alone to face the enemy.

Let it work out. Please.

Seconds later, a shriek of surprise cut the air.

The drama began to unfold.

Ex collapsed onto the floor, limbs flying everywhere. Shocked staff rushed to his aid. Mesmerized by his epileptic performance, I almost forgot our plan was in the works. *Move!* Head down, heart tripping with frenzy, I slinked past the melee. At the end of the hall, I dashed into the open elevator and the ancient beast groaned and creaked all the way to the third floor. When the doors opened, I edged to the front and peered around the corner. Reception desk. Low lights. Quiet, like a morgue. Two nurses or orderlies or whatever they were called, focused on a computer monitor, their backs toward me.

"And then what did he say?" The squat one demanded.

Her mousy coworker offered a meek shrug. "That he was sorry. It didn't mean anything."

"Girl, did he actually use that line? You should just go out and sleep with someone and tell him the same thing."

"Trust me, I've thought about it."

The squat one wheeled a chair closer and plunked into it with a sense of purpose. "Go to Chip and Dale dot com," she instructed.

"What's that?"

"It's Ashley Madison for women. Time to strike back."

While they plotted ways to get back at Mr. Cheater, I tiptoed down the hall, past gurneys and cheaply framed posters—"You got this!" and "Be stronger than your excuses!"—that didn't motivate me in the slightest. If anything, the desperate odor of life hanging by a shoestring brought back all my paranoia of hospitals. A home birth and accident-free childhood meant I'd never set foot in one...not until Suze and I had to untangle our fertility issues. Suddenly we were instant regulars, and not in a good way. Every visit ended on a bad note. Eventually, in one of those silent agreements couples make, we gave up. Suze never wanted to adopt but one of my biggest regrets was not pushing for it.

I shoved the bleak memory aside and got back to the task at hand.

Door after door, I peeked inside empty rooms with increasing distress.

Finally, I found her.

A bank of flashing monitors behind her bed looked right out of the Industrial Revolution. I edged closer, walking on eggshells. Her breathing was heavy, mouth slack. The blanket covering her body probably weighed more than she did. I sat in a chair made threadbare from anxious sitters and cradled her hand, careful of the needle wedged deep into the top of it.

"Kiddo," I whispered. "Jesus."

Her eyes eased open, crusts of sleep clinging to her lashes. "Adrian?" Her voice was thick and slow.

"Shhh. Yeah. It's me."

With great effort, she swallowed. "What happened to your hair?"

"It's a wig."

"You look better with dark hair."

An attempt of a smile seemed to sap whatever energy she had left. My hand slipped to her arm; a bone wrapped in skin. Despite the cold outside, she was hot, burning up.

"How are you feeling?" I asked.

"Okay," she said, before dissolving into a phlegmy round of coughs. With each one, her body curled inwards, like she was being knifed. I felt useless and stupid. The nightmare of those two brutal days in Cedars-Sinai came crashing back; I'd almost lost my mind seeing Suze's post-abortion body jammed with needles like some science experiment.

"Why didn't you tell me? This could've been really bad."

Her head lolled to one side as if she couldn't bear to face me. "When you're sick your whole life," she said, "you get sick of being sick, and sick of talking about it. And if I would have told you, you wouldn't have let me stay."

Guilt washed over me, because her observation was dead right. Sickness carried an invisible burden. It made the noblest person run for cover. Would I have been any different?

"How soon can we get you out of here?"

She glanced back over, eyes uncertain. "They didn't say. They never do."

"*When* we get you out," I said, because I would get her out, no matter what, "I want you to think about LA. What if you lived there? Would you like that?"

Her forehead crinkled. "With you?"

"There's some hurdles we'd have to climb," I admitted, whitewashing over the snarl of legal issues. "This would be adoption, not fostering. But we've already been living together, in a way, on the bus. I mean, it's been okay for you, right?"

Instead of the resounding *Yes!* I'd expected, immense sorrow filled her eyes. "There's a whole approval process you have to go through, especially with someone like me. They'll never say yes."

Two things I sorely lacked, stability and routine, were vital for adopting. Sheila from the agency had made that point clear. Money helped, though. Something I had buckets of. And after last night, when the news broke and every wingnut in America had come forward claiming to be a relative, there was no way I'd let her fall in with strangers ever again.

"I can make them say yes if that's what you wanted."

A pained expression riddled her features. "I'll be nothing but trouble for you. My mom was right. I'm bad luck. I'll never be good, or do anything good, for anyone."

I sat back, dumbfounded. What parent tells their kid that? Thank god her mom had passed, or I would've kicked her ass to the curb.

"You're not bad luck," I insisted. "You have an illness, like millions of people."

She winced and asked me not to hold her hand so tight. When she started to talk, it was like I wasn't even there.

"The year before my family died, I'd been really sick. My mom, she couldn't handle it. She flew back to New Orleans to meet with one of those ladies who practice voodoo. She told my mom to have another child. Said I was cursed. Bad luck. I overheard her telling my dad." Silent tears started to stream down her cheeks. "That's why I didn't want to see my brother in the hospital. I hated him. I hated my own brother and it was wrong." Her eyes closed, face anguished. "I should've been in the car with them. I should've died with them."

She cried quietly, achingly. I wanted to throw something, smash the room apart. No human needed to carry that weight around his or her neck. I leaned forward, determination crackling on my skin.

"Let me tell you something, kiddo," I said. "You can think about what did or didn't happen forever, and it'll get you nowhere. I'm living proof. What matters is the here and now." I stabbed the bed with my finger. "Forget what your mom said. People say things they don't mean all the time. You are stronger than all of that. Let me help you; we'll figure this out. Together."

Maybe it came out sounding like madness, I don't know. I just needed her to believe.

She sniffled back snot and tears. "What about Sasha-Rae?"

I let out a small sigh of capitulation. "It's over," I said. "Can't say I blame her."

"You're giving up?" If I wasn't mistaken, she sounded downright appalled. "If I can't give up, you can't give up."

"I'm not giving up. The thing is—"

"The day after you met her," she interrupted, "you were different. Better. You like her."

It broke my heart how adamant she was. How right she was. How there was nothing I could do about it. "It's probably for the best. You take priority right now."

Before she could reply, my phone started to ring, the sound startling both of us. Concerned it might be Ex, I almost barfed up my lunch right onto the display. In frustration the other night, I'd assigned an unsavory descriptor to Jillian's number and the four-letter C word twinkled on my screen. I silenced the phone and dumped it face down on the bed.

"Who's that?" Hastings asked.

"A reporter who's been hounding me. You don't want to know."

"Jillian Wiley?"

I did a double take. "You know her?"

"No, but I saw her on TV tonight. She said bad things about you. And me. I'm sorry I got you in trouble. For all this."

She started to sniffle again and deep inside me, a switch flipped. The overseer of paparazzi could attack me; skewering Hastings meant war. Perhaps it wasn't the right time, but I unloaded everything right then and there to Hastings. I gave her the sordid rundown of those two hellish weeks last year; Mom's death; how the lawsuit fanned Jillian's flames of determination to take me down; how Hastings was now the closest and easiest solution to my demise. I believed the story would plant Hastings firmly on my side of the anti-Jillian crusade, but then she surprised me.

"Maybe it would help if I talked to her," she said. "Tell her what really happened."

"Are you kidding me? No. Absolutely not." My voice clanged with resistance. "She's sneaky and desperate. She'll spin the story and make you agree to things you didn't even say. Forget it."

"Is she in Detroit?" Hastings asked.

"Leaving a trail of slime as we speak."

Only later did I realize the glint in Hastings' eyes had nothing to do with sympathy. I often wondered how our lives would've turned out if I hadn't spilled the story.

As it happened, a noise suddenly filled the air and I looked back, fear dancing on my skin. The door to her room had pushed open and a long shadow stepped into the strip of light. My entire life flashed before my eyes.

"Dang," a voice muttered. "Always forgetting something."

The door slid shut and Hastings jabbed her finger left, whispering: "She's coming back. Hide in the bathroom. Quick."

Practically paralyzed, it took forever to move seven feet. In the tiny, drab bathroom I crouched in the corner and prayed. If the nurse's job description included a bathroom sweep, I was boned. Past the peeling paint, through the drywall, I could just make out faint conversation between the two of them. Five minutes later, Hastings whispered my name. I tiptoed back to her bedside, sweat teeming under my wig.

"I gotta get out of here, kiddo, but I'm serious about LA," I said. "Please think about it. If it's something you want, the only thing you'll have to do is talk to the police. You need to go on record with what happened. It's the only way we can do this."

She glanced at me ambiguously, and from underneath the covers, handed me back my phone. I'd totally forgotten. Not caring a stitch about it at this point, I stuffed it into my jeans and waited for her answer. The long silence didn't feel promising, but no matter what I wanted, how badly I wanted it, the decision wasn't mine.

"If I come with you," she finally said, "promise me that if anything happens, you'll take me to New Orleans."

I saw it then, in her eyes—what she really meant. What this entire journey meant for her. Apprehension swept in, desperate and all-consuming. All of a sudden it was hard to breathe.

"I'll do whatever it takes," I said. "I promise."

Her fingers trembled, wrapping around my wrist. The articulating wall lamp cast a wretched stream of light over us.

"I'm scared," she said, eyes glittering. "Don't leave me here."

I kissed her forehead, my voice bleak and raw. "Don't be scared. I'll be back. I'll get you out of here. You're going to sing. You're going to make it to Juilliard. Harvard. Oxford. All of them. Everything. Just stay strong for me okay?"

Tears now poured down her face. "I want to fall in love. Like you and Suze."

I wanted to assure her that she would, but ended up not promising anything because the words wouldn't come. The swell in my chest became unbearable and I left with a hasty goodbye. In the gloom of the empty hallway, linoleum dingy from a bygone era of lobotomies and doctors who smoked, I took a moment to pull myself together. Staring at the ceiling, I wondered what had become of Ex. Was it even safe to leave the same way I'd come in? Rather than getting lost in an unknown labyrinth, I made my way toward the elevator, silently counting. Five yards to freedom, four...

"Sir. Sir! Stop! Stop right there."

Crap.

I turned around slowly.

A nurse barreled toward me, a bowling ball screaming down the alley. "Where did you come from?" she demanded.

"I, uh, got off on the wrong floor. I was just leaving."

She looked left and right, up and down the hall. Her eyes narrowed into slits. Something didn't compute. "Empty your pockets, please."

I pulled two tongues of fabric out, lint balls and guitar picks landing on the floor. For a long, painful moment I endured her head to toe sweep, watched the slow dawn of recognition creep over her face. If she'd had a gun, it would be out and cocked. I held up both hands in surrender.

"I just needed to talk to her," I said. "Nothing else. I swear."

"Don't move," she warned. "Even an inch and I'm pulling the fire alarm."

She strode backward to Hastings' room, silent in soft-soled shoes, a firm eye planted on me. After peering inside, satisfied with whatever she saw, she approached me. With her PTA busybody-ness and soccer mom hairdo, I pegged her to be mid-fifties. Mind you, scrubs sapped the youth out of anyone who wore them.

"Give me one reason not to turn you in," she finally said.

"I want to pay for everything," I countered. "Whatever it takes to make her better. Tell me who I talk to."

She paused, tilted her head. "Are you pulling my leg?"

"No, not at all."

The pocket walkie-talkie clipped her to scrubs crackled with a disembodied voice. "Moira, everything okay up there?"

She radioed back, "All good. Just finished my rounds."

"False alarm down here. Another weirdo. As you were. Over and out."

A lean silence passed. I didn't dare move.

"There's been a bit of situation downstairs," Moira said. "I'm pretty sure you've had something to do with it?"

"Possibly."

She crossed her beefy arms with all the understanding of a bounty hunter whose prey whimpered in her sightlines. No one would ever mistake her for dainty.

"Listen," I said. "I'm sure you've watched the news, formed an opinion. But it's nothing like that. She's alone and needs help. I don't care what it costs. I want that girl in one piece."

Prepared for a dogfight, Moira's guard dropped. A wee bit. "What she has isn't curable, you know that, right? It's ongoing maintenance."

"All the more reason why she needs the best care. You know the difference money can make."

Playing all your cards wasn't always the best strategy, and a foreign one to me. Mac would cringe; he always let the other guy crack first. But a life was at stake here, not a negotiable contract.

"You're not what I expected at all," Moira eventually said, sounding borderline disappointed she couldn't hate me.

I pulled the wig off and shook my head. "This isn't my real hair."

The corner of her mouth curled up, but her stance remained all business. "My daughter, she's a big fan of yours. She insisted none of this could be true."

"You don't sound so sure," I hedged.

"Well," she hedged back, "you know girls and their obsessions with rock stars." With a loaded stare, she waited for me to confirm a hundred exploits I never had. "But she did remind me of the time she waited hours in line to meet you." I held my breath, praying her daughter wasn't one of the loony ones dispatched by a watchful Sven. "She said you were the politest man she'd ever met. You were kind and respectful, gave all the girls time. She was on cloud nine for days after."

Rather unexpectedly, Moira drifted into reasonable territory. I chalked it up to mothers and me being a good fit. They were the ones who told me how wonderful it was to have a moral role model for their daughters, someone who had values and cherished the institution of marriage. This was my moment.

"Moira," I said, and she looked flattered, hearing me say her name. "If you help me, I'll help you. Tell me whom I need to talk to about Hastings, and I'll arrange something for your daughter. A backstage pass, lunch for thirty of her friends with me, whatever she wants. You have my word."

Tough as she was, I found the crack. A little celebrity action helped too, as much as I hated to admit it.

"Oh God," she said, her face crumpling with maternal relief. "You know, she would love that. She would absolutely love that. We've been at loggerheads lately, fighting all the time. Anything at this stage would help." She thumped away the choke in her chest and pulled out a pen and piece of paper from her smock. With the paper pressed against the wall, she scribbled a couple lines and handed it to me. "Text that number and I'll point you in the right direction. It's my personal cell."

Her handwriting was bubbled and legible, *Moira* in perfect cursive.

"Thank you. I'll be in touch." I glanced back at the elevator. "I'd love to avoid another scene. Is there another way out of here?"

Now that I wasn't the boogeyman the press made me out to be, she offered a smile, more than happy to help. "Of course, follow me." At the other end of the hall she pushed open a door that led into a maze of concrete stairwells. "Take these all the way down. Turn left, the first set of doors takes you onto the street. I wouldn't worry about your friend," she said, adding a knowing smile. "He's long gone."

As I stepped into the hallway, a bitter smell hit the back of my brain. In Hastings' bathroom, a similar odor had hung in the air and an image of the Dixie Cup dispenser mounted next to the sink wouldn't leave me alone. Something about the endless stream of sanitized cones poked at a dark place in the back of my mind: the rotation of sick girls and boys, the numb fear of parents drinking from those cones, helpless.

I took one last look over my shoulder. "She's going to be okay, right?"

Moira puffed up, a lion-hearted surrogate to the hundreds of charges she helped make better. "Her immune system is weak, but she's a fighter. That's always half the battle."

CHAPTER THIRTY-EIGHT

THE NEXT MORNING I BLAMED BRYCE, JUST BECAUSE. Meeting him for any reason left a suspect taste in my mouth. Never mind that the cheese burritos and cheap champagne from the All Nite Mart were the real culprits responsible for the layer of fuzz on my teeth when I woke up. Ex and I went a little overboard last night, celebrating in my hotel room. I congratulated him on a fine acting performance. He couldn't believe my luck with Moira, said I had horseshoes up my ass. (Had to agree with that. In the past ten days I'd pulled off more cheap tricks than Houdini did in a lifetime.) When Ex staggered back to his room in the wee hours, it was with a sense of vindication, our mission a success. Sure, we had to meet Bryce in ten hours, but why kill the buzz?

Still feeling a little green, I popped some Tums and texted Mac. He was flying back from Tokyo tomorrow, and I opted not to mention Bryce's surprise appearance. I'd given Mac enough to worry about in the past forty-eight hours. Instead, I hinted at some good news and left it at that. Shortly before noon, I made my way down to Bryce's room. Forcing us all to meet in his room was his idea of a power play, but it was actually a blessing in disguise. It meant I could walk out at any time.

He waved me in, chewing noisily on a piece of pizza. "How's it going?"

"Is that a rhetorical question?"

I ducked past his pot belly, and immediately noticed his room was bigger than mine. With a better view. Dampness hung heavy, like a kettle had steamed. Pepperoni and his body odor swirled in the moisture, a foul potpourri that made my eyes water.

"I guess it sucks to be you right now, huh?" he said.

I ignored his chump smile and took in the view of downtown. "Why are you even here? To stir up more shit?"

"In case you need a refresher on the music business, cancelled shows affect everyone. I'm here because business is all about cutting losses. Removing the dead weight."

I spun around. "What do you mean?"

"C'mon, man. Size of a Scandal is done. Finito. We both know it. The boys know it. They practically agreed to call it."

Something cold spread in my chest. "Where are they, anyway?"

"I pushed them to an hour later."

"Why? To threaten me?" I shook my head. "What you just said is bullshit, anyway. It isn't over until we collectively say it's over."

"You mean when *you* say it's over. And you wonder why someone like Norm wants out."

A thread of cheese clung to his sunken chin and the kindly thing to do was make him aware of it, although why bother? I had tried to like Bryce Bentley, as much as I could like the human equivalent of a bed of nails, but some things were never meant to be.

"For someone touting the virtues of a solo career," I said, "you'd think you might have actually had one."

He honked a loud, fake laugh. "That's all you've got to lord over me, isn't it? Yes, I wanted to be a musician. I tried. I failed. I moved on. No disgrace in that. Besides, I'd rather be a failed musician than a dick like you."

"If being a dick means I know what it takes to make it, then guilty as charged. Maybe you should stop trying to climb the ladder and take a page from Mac's book—learn what it means to be in the artist management game. Clearly, you've missed a step. Or six."

"Yes, dearest Mac. The old school always get hit the hardest with change, don't they? I hope both of you have a plan B." He lowered himself into the easy chair and crossed one leg, a cavalier air to all his movements. From the inside pocket of his blazer he rifled out a piece of paper. Handing it to me, his face beamed with smug satisfaction. "This hits the wires tomorrow. Welcome to the new world order."

The very, very last thing I wanted to do was take the folded letter from his outstretched hand. I read the headline quickly: *SIX DEVIL SOUNDS SHUTTERED—ZIEGLER MANAGEMENT INC. TO PURCHASE ASSETS.* In silence, I skimmed the rest of the document. Jordy sold out, only not in the way we had envisioned. Ziegler was chairman, Bryce, president. Effective immediately. A scorched-earth policy would be in effect, and everything was on the table for discussion. I felt a strange sense of weightlessness. For the first time in our history, I felt the scale of power tip from me to Bryce.

"Congratulations," I said, dropping the paper to the floor.

"We've got a whole new business model rolling out, lots of changes. Out with the old, in with the new." He let out a satisfied sigh. "As much as we'd love to honor the contract for your upcoming album, I'm pretty sure our lawyers can wiggle out of it on the morals clause."

We glared at each other with simmering mutual disgust. Two grown men playing Mexican standoff in a hotel room that smelled like a wet chicken.

"Don't ever underestimate Mac," I said. "He's already been hustling a new deal."

"Good luck with that," he scowled. "Rumor has it you're dead, creatively. Once word gets out, no one will sign your dried-up dick."

It was a weak threat. He didn't wield that much power. Still, it wouldn't stop him from trying.

"Wow," I said. "Why don't you just tell me I'll never work in this town again."

His phone started to ring, and he dipped a hand back into his blazer without breaking my gaze.

"Hello?"

As he listened and nodded, a queer smile broke on his face. The occasional "I see" rolled off his tongue with an increasingly nasty undercurrent. After hanging up, he knitted both hands behind his neck and smirked.

"Hate to say it, but you called it. You'll never work in this town, or any town, again. Gotta love that Jillian. She can pull rabbits out of thin air."

Butterflies erupted in my stomach. I thought I'd recognized the screech on the other end of his phone. "Meaning?"

"Looks like your little travel mate has a story she wants to tell, after all. Smells like career suicide." His smile tightened. "Do me a favor and close the door behind you. I've got some calls to make."

I left Bryce's room on unsteady legs. Minutes later, Jillian's text came in.

J: Tune in tomorrow night at seven for the scoop of the year! Hastings is going on record. You're welcome to join...if they let you into the hospital!

I would've tumbled to the floor if the wall didn't catch me.

On paper, it was impossible. A hospital allowing an on-site interview with a patient had to break a hundred privacy and ethical rules. Even if they turned a blind eye to those details, how did this get approved up the chain? Bureaucracy never moved that fast.

Not unless money was involved.

Serious money.

In the safety of my room, I had to know.

"Adrian!" Jillian greeted me with the enthusiasm of a long-lost relative. "I was just going to call you."

"How the hell did you get to her?"

"Miracles will never cease. Can you believe she called *me*?"

"Bullshit," I growled.

Wait. No. What?

I relived the moment in slow motion torture: Hastings handing me my phone in the hospital. She'd seen Jillian's number. Memorized it. Somehow, some way managed to call it. My eyes fell shut in grim defeat.

"I'll tell anyone who listens you bribed the hospital," I said.

"A donation is hardly a bribe," Jillian jeered. "And you must've forgotten Detroit is my hometown. I know a few people, and everyone has a price, darling, especially a hospital desperate to upgrade their equipment. Two million dollars goes a long way." After a beat, she continued. "Just so you know, I could skew the interview one way if someone decided to drop a certain lawsuit."

"So you finally admit it," I said.

"I have no idea what you're talking about," she said carefully. "All I'm saying is one less lawsuit cluttering up the system is good for everyone."

Hard-boiled hatred bubbled like acid in my throat. Mom was gone forever and the photographer who had hunted her down claimed innocence; said he was just doing his job. The job Jillian hired him for.

"I'd rather rot in jail."

Sound muffled, and I could hear her talking to someone in the background. When she came back on the line, her voice was fearless and high-flying. "I do hope it doesn't come to such dire circumstances," she said. "But if it does, it's been nice knowing you."

CHAPTER THIRTY-NINE

BURIED DEEP IN THE CABLE UNIVERSE, HOT SHOT NEWS was the Pluto of TV Channels. Even its trashy content mirrored the dwarf planet's atmosphere: a hostile inversion where good got smothered by evil. As the minutes counted down to the interview, invasive snapshots of various celebrities scrolled across the TV screen. Cellulite. Affairs. Addiction. He picks his nose just like you and me! Ex, who'd joined me for moral support, sat cross-legged on the couch and munched on microwave popcorn.

"Ariana Grande wears no makeup to yoga," he said. "I really needed to know that."

My already low spirits sunk deeper. Sasha-Rae had looked flipping gorgeous in Toronto, her face glowing and unadorned. I had tried her old number this afternoon and sure enough, she'd changed it. The Vantage Auto Parts website listed their phone number, but with the media explosion and her name plastered alongside mine, no way in hell I'd get put through. If this interview went sideways, I might never speak to her again. What were the calling privileges in jail these days?

"Are Norm and Diego watching?" I asked, pouring myself a hefty drink.

It was still touch and go with them, although neither wanted to call it quits. With Ziegler taking over Six Devil however, everything was up in the air, the outcome of this upcoming circus the unspoken tipping point.

"I'm pretty sure the whole world is watching," Ex replied, thumbing the volume higher after the commercial break. He stole a glance my way. "You ready for this?"

I joined him on the couch. "Front row for my execution. A perfect Wednesday night."

The intro came on, complete with tagline. *Hot Shot News: Where There's Smoke There's Fire. All the news they don't want you to know.* Then it started. The show host, a standard issue LA blonde, cut right to the chase.

"Adrian Johnson, nicknamed the 'Jazzer', is a household name for millions of music-loving Americans. His band, Size of a Scandal, has scored more top-ten hits in the past decade than any other band on the planet. But the sexy and private superstar rocked the news a year ago when his fairytale marriage to high school sweetheart Suzanne Ripley ended under murky circumstances and Johnson's mother died, allegedly stalked by paparazzi."

On the screen beside her, ten years of my life edited into a fifteen-second clip of lowlights, played out for the world to see. When the reel ended, the host took over, her voice dipping into pure salaciousness.

"Johnson re-emerged after a year of exile only to be right back in the spotlight...for all the wrong reasons. Three days ago, Hastings Sinclair, a thirteen-year-old foster child from Seattle, was rushed to the hospital after collapsing in the parking lot of The Fox Theater in Detroit where Johnson's private tour bus was stationed for the night. Ms. Sinclair suffers from sickle cell disease, a rare blood disorder, and underwent an emergency blood transfusion to combat acute chest-syndrome, a fallout from the disease that can cause death. Paramedics at the scene claimed Johnson had no knowledge of her condition."

After a dramatic pause, "The plot thickens even more. Ms. Sinclair was believed missing and dead, along with her foster parents, after a vicious mudslide destroyed their Issaquah, Washington home last month. Sources close to Johnson allege Ms. Sinclair had been traveling with Adrian in his private bus in the weeks following this disaster. As sordid rumors swirl, the now-infamous footage of a rage-fueled Johnson trying to attack a cameraman who accused him of pedophilia has derailed the band's current tour, with future dates on hiatus due to protests and skittish promoters."

The camera followed the host as she swanned over to the commentator desk and took a seat. "There are too many questions, and we're going to answer all of them. We now go live now to the H.R. Ellison Children's Hospital in downtown Detroit to join Jillian Wylie."

The feed cut to Hastings' hospital room. Dressed in a gown, she sat upright in her bed and looked less fragile than the other night. But she snuck nervous glances at the camera and Jillian, who sat in the chair next to her and looked every inch the regal newswoman with coiffed hair and a sharp blazer.

Ex peered at the screen. "Damn, she's tiny."

"She's stronger than she looks," I said.

He took a swig of beer. "Remind me again how interviewing a kid in the hospital is even legal?"

After Jillian's comment last night about Detroit being her hometown, I scoured the hospital website, all the listed executives, and cross referenced to find the connection. I narrowed it down to one person: Darren, a man who'd gone to university with her. Who else would she yank out of her den of thieves to bring me down?

"Good evening and welcome to a Hot Shot news exclusive." Jillian's toothy smile shimmered on camera. "Before we begin with tonight's story, I'd like to thank Darren Jenkins, Corporate Development for the H.R. Ellison Children's hospital, for allowing us to film this important event." Her eyes focused slightly beyond the camera and I knew he was in the room. He had to be. No matter how slick and wrong this move was, someone had to represent Hastings. "The hospital, which serves the children of Detroit and its suburbs, is fundraising to update their facilities and secure vital surgical equipment. Hot Shot News has donated two million dollars toward this wonderful cause. Your generous donations to match ours are appreciated, so please call the live hotline scrolling on the bottom of your screen to pledge your support. You can also go online to the link shown and make a donation using your debit or credit card. Any and all support is deeply appreciated. Hot Shot is committed to making a difference, and you can too."

Jillian swiveled toward Hastings. "It's time now to introduce America to the strong young woman at the heart of our story. Hastings, would you like to say hello before we start?"

The camera zoomed in onto her wide eyes. A mic popped as she said, "Uh, hi."

"You've been through so much in the past month," Jillian said. "The death of your foster parents. Living under duress—"

"What does duress mean?" Hastings interrupted.

"For fuck's sake," I grumbled. "She hasn't even started, and it's already a race to the bottom."

Jillian's voice dipped into a *comfort-the-victim-in-denial* tone. "Mr. Johnson did keep you captive on his private bus for almost two weeks."

"I wasn't captive," Hastings corrected. "I snuck onto his bus and could've left at any time."

With a hand on Hastings' bed, all faux sympathy, Jillian cooed, "I understand if this is all still tender for you. Perhaps we'll start elsewhere." She glanced down at her notes. "I personally like to believe in the generosity of strangers, and I know my viewers do, too. But do you know why Adrian has paid for all your hospital expenses?"

Hastings blinked. "He did?"

Unbelievable. I'd only called in this morning with my credit card information. The leaks in this town were worse than the ones on the Titanic.

"That true?" Ex asked.

"So much for being a good Samaritan," I replied.

"He most certainly did," Jillian continued. "The bill isn't cheap, either. It's very generous, especially considering how intimate you two were. Travelling together."

Hastings fell silent and I felt a lick of panic. The tipping point of the interview had come sooner than expected. Jillian's seemingly innocuous words, a noose tightening around the neck of her hapless victim. Where she went for the jugular. Where good men folded like cards. Where...

"You said we were going to talk about helping Adrian," Hastings said, her voice tinged with irritation. "I told you nothing happened between us. Nothing like that. Ask the doctor. He checked me out."

Off camera, someone cleared their throat with a disapproving sound. Jillian blinked and her fake smile plastered wider. "Yes, well. Let's talk about your condition for a minute. Many Americans aren't familiar with sickle cell disease and you suffer from many classic symptoms—eye damage, stunted growth. Even I can see the yellow pallor on your skin, in your eyes. How did Mr. Johnson overlook all these details? He put you at risk. You could have died."

"He's colorblind," Hastings said, matter of factly. "He can't see yellow."

Ex's head snapped around so fast I thought it would spin off. "Say what?"

I shrugged. Guilty.

"He can't see a lot of colors," she continued. "That's why I offered to help him."

"Help him?" Jillian's gaze turned crafty. "Help him how?"

"He was having a hard time writing songs and I have chromesthesia..."

"I'm sorry," Jillian interrupted, "but could you explain what that is?" She flashed a brief look to whoever her helper was on set: scrape together any and all info on that *now*.

"I can see colors in music, and the colors tell me things about the songs. He asked me to listen to his songs."

Jillian, confused, her script unravelling, "You were writing songs together?"

"No, he wouldn't let anyone help him. That's kind of his problem."

Ex, who'd just taken another swig of beer, sprayed pale ale all over the carpet.

Ever quick on her feet, Jillian wrangled Hastings' innocent

comments into something incriminating. "So Adrian lured you onto his bus under the pretense of writing songs."

Hastings crossed her arms with a look of disgust so total, I doubt I could ever match it. "It's kind of annoying," she said, "how you twist things around to make them sound bad. Adrian said that's what you do. All these things you're accusing him of are wrong. Nothing happened with us. He's in love with Sasha-Rae. You want Adrian to be in trouble because of his lawsuit against your company. He says you're not going to win. That's why you're doing all this. You want everyone to think he's bad."

I leaned back on the couch, not sure if I wanted scream or sing with delight. Ex could only shake his head. Jillian gawked at Hastings, having clearly underestimated her competition, who was now going rogue. After another disapproving throat clearing from the sidelines, she scrambled to steer the boat back to safe waters.

"The woman in question, Adrian's alleged love interest, is Sasha-Rae Tomason, Nascar phenom Richey Slayer's younger sister. Slayer is back in the news again with an assault charge, stemming from his third paternity suit." Back at Hastings, she continued in a rushed tone, "Speaking of volatile, Mr. Johnson's temper is well known. Did he ever exhibit any signs of violence toward you?"

I chucked a couch pillow at the screen. "I hate you. With every bone in my body."

"Adrian never hurt or touched me," Hastings said. "Not once. He was taking me to New Orleans."

Jillian cocked her head. "What for?"

"Uh..." Hastings squirmed, unsure, and I silently begged her not to say it. "Personal reasons."

From the sidelines, a voice, no doubt Darren's, interjected, "Turn the camera off please. This was supposed to be an interview to help fundraise, not a smear campaign."

Jillian, too close to the finish line to stop, forged on, "I'm sure this whole thing is *very* personal," she said to Hastings. "It always is for predators. I would suggest Adrian is not so innocent. Why else did he decline to be part of this interview?"

In those two silent seconds, death for any live broadcast, America decided, of that I was sure. Innocent people wanted to tell their story, prove everyone wrong. With life as I knew it over, the camera veered wildly as if someone yanked it out of harm's way.

"Stop. This is not what we agreed to." Darren's voice now bellowed. A hand smothered the front of the lens.

"Carlos!" Jillian hissed under her breath. "Keep rolling."

The camera bobbed and weaved, like Carlos had gone handheld and was ducking punches. Darren kept shouting to turn the camera off.

Ex leaned forward, mesmerized. "This is unbelievable."

With her window closing, Jillian rose out of her chair and moved to Hastings' bedside for the final kill. "Let's not forget Adrian is an adult. He knew the right things to do, and didn't do them. He's obstructed justice. Is guilty of multiple misdemeanors, if not felonies. He's put your health at risk, your very life."

The image of Hastings turned jittery, Carlos trying his best to film while under attack, but her reply was rock solid. "Adrian had no idea I was sick. He didn't do anything wrong. I bet you didn't ask him to be on this interview. He would've."

After a loud "Oof!" the camera clattered to the floor. Carlos, I assumed, yelled, "For fuck's sake! That's my 7D."

"I don't care if it's the President's camera," Darren snapped. "You are done. All of you. Out!"

Jillian's disembodied voice turned tight and nasty. "Back off, Darren. We've already paid you."

In the ensuing argument between them, the forgotten camera continued to film dead space on the wall. The following clip ended up reaching near mythical status, playing on *Best Of* reels for the next decade.

Hastings, who crawled out of bed, inched toward the camera on her knees until her face filled the screen. "Sasha-Rae, if you're watching this, what I'm saying is the truth. Adrian did the right thing. He was taking me back to New Orleans. Don't hold it against him."

From somewhere behind Hastings, Jillian inadvertently muttered eight words into her mic that damned her forever. "You little shit. Get away from the camera."

Hastings ignored her and finished with the aplomb of a pro. "Please give him another chance. He's in love with you."

I sunk deeper into the couch, hands over my mouth. Ex howled with stunned laughter.

A sickening crunch followed.

The screen cut to black.

CHAPTER FORTY

IN LESS THAN TWENTY-FOUR HOURS, I'D FLIP-FLOPPED from America's most hated to most forgiven, and my redemption spurred another media frenzy. As a result, the Fox Theater had politely asked us to vacate their premises, and our buses were now huddled in a far corner of Little Caesars Arena lot. The police had combed my bus for any evidence of wrongdoing, and finding none, I was allowed back inside. I ditched the hotel this morning, but a fresh batch of reporters followed and now staked out my bus. When Mac's limo pulled into the lot, the squad came alive. They rushed him in a flock, chirping out questions as he shouldered his way past.

After making it safely inside the bus, he loosened his bowtie with a shudder. "Fuck me," he said.

"Just what you want after a seventeen-hour flight, right?" I asked.

"I'd rather travel in coach in perpetuity than face this shit." He wiped down his suit, another three-piece velvet special, and this time, I didn't mind the kiss on each cheek. "Aside from the shiner, how are you?" he asked. "And more importantly, what do you have to drink?"

"The usual," I said. "On both counts."

"This is one of those times you bring the whole bottle."

He made his way to the couch, and the heaviness of his movements had nothing to do with the two hundred and fifty pounds he carried around. I poured us two tumblers of vodka and he held up his glass to the light like it was a crystal ball with all the answers.

"It's times like these that make me wish for the good old days," he said. "There's something to be said for the time when we could all go about our business and not be under a fucking microscope."

I took a long pull of the vodka. The burn felt appropriate. "I'm sorry," is all I could muster.

"You know I hate that word."

"I promised I'd never let you down."

"Three ex-wives promised they'd love me forever." He clinked my glass with a grim smile. "Welcome to the real world."

We both drank deeply, and Mac set his glass on the floor. He undid the buttons of his vest, the heft of his belly sagging with the release. Underneath the five-hundred-dollar dress shirt, scars riddled his torso —bullet wounds he never discussed. Mac never felt pressured to fill empty space, and his ability to remain quiet unnerved people. It was what made him such an effective negotiator. This time, I relished the silence for as long as it lasted.

"You've been like a son to me, Adrian," he finally said, his eyes carrying fatigue more than anything else. "I've watched you grow up, watched you navigate this bitch of an industry with possessed-ness I didn't think existed anymore. Yes, there were times I wanted to kick your stubborn ass to the curb, and you probably felt the same way about me." A hint of a smile flashed; maybe he was thinking of our argument that ended with an ashtray at the bottom of his Malibu pool. "But I knew you were one in ten million, kid. And fuck me, you did everything right."

"But?" It was there, hanging like a storm cloud.

"But no one does everything right all the time, not even an OCD, anal-retentive, A-type bastard like you."

"Thanks," I said. "I think."

He crossed a leg over one knee, grunted with the effort. "So here we are."

I met his eyes. "How bad is it?"

"It could always be worse."

"I need more than that."

"You tell me. I know you've thought of every possible angle. What I don't know is where you are here." He pointed to his heart.

I'd confessed to the Norm situation before he arrived. We both knew that was the biggest part of where I stood. I let a chug of vodka roll down my throat before answering.

"What's the damage if we pull the pin, right here, right now?"

If he was surprised to hear that, he didn't show it. "You talking postponement or…"

"Or."

"Oi."

I'd seen that look on his face only once before: at The Omni hotel in Austin, Texas during SXSW when his second wife, the only of the three he really loved, had just ditched him for one of his clients, an up-and-coming rapper.

"Insurance will save our ass from major damage," he said, "but there's the crew to consider."

After the boys, the crew was second on my list of concerns. At the very least, we could pay them a bump, a lump sum sorry payment to cover while they scrambled for anther gig. But money wasn't the issue. They were friends who'd sacrificed their own friends and family for a life on the road with us. The impenetrable tangle thickened.

"It's bullshit, you know," Mac said, his tone candid and conversational as he stretched an arm along the top of the couch. "Everyone wants to be famous, but until you're in the middle of it, you have no idea what it's going to be like. It's stressful now, not fun."

I poured another shot into our glasses. "I never wanted that part. Ever."

"I know. But you remember what I told you in the parking lot at Izzy's? After we met the first time?"

How could I not? *The* Mac Rosenthal had met with me, liked me, and agreed to take me on, pending negotiations. I was anointed by the king himself, given access to a prestigious kingdom very few ever stepped inside of. I'd kept my enthusiasm as contained as possible, but he'd sensed it and brought me back to earth with his prophetic words.

"Be careful what you wish for."

"I wasn't trying to be a Debbie Downer either," Mac continued. "I saw something more than passion in your eyes that morning. There was hurt, a hungry hurt you needed to feed." He paused, weighed his next words. "Fathers and sons. It's a goddamned struggle, isn't it?"

"What do you mean?" I asked.

"You know what I mean, kid. I never made amends with my father. Biggest regret of my life." His gaze remained inscrutable and layered, mirroring his past. "You might want to think about that with Jarred."

I looked at him, surprised. "You knew him?"

"We never met, but back then, the circles were tighter. I knew who he was. It was my business to know everyone. Why do you think I met with you in the first place? Some punk ass, harassing me endlessly? I did my research, just as you did yours."

I leaned back, my stomach churning. To suddenly view my life though an entirely different set of optics jarred me, to say the least. It took several seconds to even consider the next question.

"Don't tell me he had a hand in you taking me on?"

"Please," he scoffed. "That was all you, kid. Jarred loved his jazz and he was a determined fuck like you. What he lacked was your savvy and your talent. You never spoke much about him and I'm no therapist, but I'm no dummy either. Your drive to succeed had everything to do with him. Trouble is, it can break a man watching his own son achieve what he never could."

My breath lodged deep under ribs and flesh. Mac's ability to cut to the chase, expose my flawed thinking, or crumple my ego could be refreshing...at times.

"I hit a nerve?" he asked, shaking his glass before shotgunning it.

A nerve? Try my whole nervous system. Vibrating like a note distorted with a whammy bar, I looked around with a sense of hopelessness, disenchantment with a life I'd worked so hard for.

"This is all I know. What the hell else am I going to do?" I asked.

"Don't give me that knish on a stick," he snorted. "You can do anything. If you wanted to be president, you could. You've been hustling for half your life in this racket, kid, and I've been around long enough to know when I see someone needing out."

"That makes you sound old."

"Yeah, well, fuck you," he said with a laugh. "I am old."

All these years he'd seemed untouched by time. Mac the avenger, the destroyer. No deal too big or small to negotiate better. He wasn't young, heading for seventy. The trenches on his face suddenly looked comical and fake, like some makeup artist high on L.S.D. had gone to town. But they were real. And maybe I'd just never noticed.

"Bottom line," he added, when the silence stretched a little long, "it's not the worst thing in the world. It might just be what the doctor ordered."

I chewed on my lip. The liabilities, the sheer mess of it all; it was too overwhelming to put into perspective. Maybe it was cleaner to make amends. Grind it out.

"After the tour?" I asked.

"No, you moron. Now. While you still have your sanity."

"So…just…walk away?"

"It can be whatever you want. Maybe it's a sideways move. With your ear and sensibilities, you could make a fortune producing, and avoid all this." He spun a finger around to indicate what *this* meant. Then he leaned forward and my hands disappeared in his. "The most important thing is that I love you from the bottom of my black-tar heart. I've got your back six ways to Sunday. Whatever you decide, go for it, and don't worry about the mess. That's why we have Marnie."

Marnie was the pit bull lawyer Mac unleashed for special occasions. With a face sculpted by Botox, the only way to accurately determine her real age would be through carbon dating. Her bar-bitch voice made your balls shrink and she never let you forget who was in charge. Hell, the first time we met, she told me to get a haircut and buy a decent pair of shoes, before she'd even said hello.

"So what you're saying is there's a sliver of a chance of getting out of this in one piece," I said.

Mac shot me a look. "A sliver? Try an unfinished two by four rammed up you know where."

In typical Mac fashion, his example was visceral and vivid. Age, schmage, he'd scrap to the end for his people and expected the same in return. I'd learned what loyalty meant from him. And part of the loyalty equation was ethics, keeping a clean nose. He hadn't brought it up yet and he never would, but I needed to clear the air.

"You know..." I started. "Me and the girl...there was nothing."

He matched my even, open stare. "I'm not even going to dignify that with a response."

For the past two days I'd been a man in meaningless motion. His belief in me, unadulterated, no questions asked, no uncertainty in his voice; pain stretched in my chest trying to hold it all in.

"It's like the worst possible feeling," I said, blinking back the sting in both eyes. "That I've failed on every level as a human."

He released my hands and kissed both cheeks with tenderness. Mac was the first person to ever give me advice, and how fitting he'd be the last one to offer it.

"My father used to say, if you're ever going to fail at something, Mackenzie, fail beautifully. It wasn't the first time I told him he was full of it. How could failure be beautiful? It was ugly, wrong. You know what he said to that? He said it isn't in the success we find out who we really are; it's in the failures. If you consider all of this a failure, then so be it. Just remember you've failed beautifully." He patted my knee with an understanding my own father could never muster. "Whatever you decide, kid, I trust you to show 'em how it's done."

CHAPTER FORTY-ONE

ON THE DARK DAYS—AND THERE WERE MANY—WHEN second-guessing became my national pastime and I struggled to define failure, success, and even myself, Cindy, my great big, bear of a therapist, encouraged me to fall apart. Let the pieces of me shatter onto the floor. In this deconstruction, questions would rise and fall, ebb and flow, and I'd ride them into different manifestations, project a hundred other scenarios and endings. The purpose of the exercise was to come full circle, to exhaust my mind of any guilt, so I could be at peace in my heart with the here and now.

In a way, it all made sense...coming full circle.

Life, our very existence on this earth. So often, we end up back where we started.

In hindsight then, I couldn't really be surprised.

Like how it all began, it ended by blowing up in my face.

M: You need to get down here. Now.

I vaguely remembered Moira's text, or the staff at H.R. Ellison circling, urging me to calm down while visitors in the lobby shrunk back in fear from the crazed Tasmanian devil yelling for directions to surgery, for help, for fucking anything. And when Moira showed up, her face a crumpled mess, I demanded to know what and how and when and she kept saying it was going to be all right, she was a fighter, we needed to pray. I shouted back *there was no fucking god* and she pushed me away from the uneasy crowd, toward the elevator and I think we went up, I don't even know, but suddenly we were somewhere else. Moira stopped me in the hall and said *wait here*, but then a nurse emerged from a huge set of double doors and there was blood, so much blood on her scrubs. I started to shake uncontrollably and barged past the nurse, through the doors and into the cold surgical light of the operating room, where a doctor and nurses, all of them masked, raised their heads all at once and remained motionless, because they'd been around long enough to recognize someone off the deep end. A machine started to drone, one of those endless, high pitched, claw-your-eyes-out sounds I'll never forget: a flat line permanently tattooed on my brain. Fingers from somewhere, someone, gripped onto my hoodie but I yanked free and stumbled forward.

It defied every natural law for me to be standing and her to be lying there, but sense and sensibilities, right and wrong, warped and became meaningless, the air pulsing with a singular, terrifying pain. One of the masked nurses rushed to the bed and in one hasty and final fucked up yank, the sheet fell over Hastings' lifeless eyes, but not before I saw my own reflection in them.

The next thing I remembered was the ammonia bite of smelling salts hitting the back of my brain like a drill bit. I came to from the faint in fits and starts. I was on the floor, discombobulated, Moira beside me in tears.

Lung infection. Cardiac failure. Nothing they could do.

Everything around me became hazy, but in my mind was a perfectly clear image of me, watching the news last night in my bus, when the missing piece of the puzzle fell into place. On the day Hastings hopped my bus, her foster parents had flown to Florida. A controversial doctor armed with a non-FDA approved drug had been seeking sickle cell patients for testing. And Hastings must've known, or figured out, where the Coley's were going and why. That's why she bolted. She was done with sickness and drugs and hospitals. She wouldn't stick around to be an experiment. And it was a brave, determined choice, so like her, but right then, knowing that maybe, there might've been an alternative to this, my heart couldn't take it.

It felt like the floor was going to crumble and disintegrate beneath me, and I crawled out into the hallway, frantic on all fours, past the worried faces and needle boxes and food carts that smelled like warm pudding. I scrambled toward the stairwell, moving farther away from the voices calling my name, the sounds growing fainter. I tried to navigate down the stairs, but my legs were like Jell-O, and I stumbled, ricocheting off the railing, down the stairs. I landed hard on my ass but felt nothing and heard nothing except the silent scream in my head that wouldn't go away. I pushed on the door to outside, and flailed onto the sidewalk, skin rashing off my palms to break my fall, the sting nothing compared to the explosion around me.

The sun blared pink. Red cars ripped past like bullets. Blue trees whipped in the wind. The colors were so bright, so vivid, so unreal, I had to close my eyes. But then the world started to spin, and I struggled to sit up because I'd lost all sense of me and my body and how I fit into the universe. The only thing I could feel was heat rising up from the concrete, baked by the sun, a cruel reminder she'd never feel its warmth again. And then somewhere, far away, I could hear birds. A song. A bittersweet soundtrack. Music I'd never hear her sing.

I don't know what there was to learn from seeing a young girl die in front of me. Lessons were never my forte. But I did know one thing: if you failed at the critical moments, all the success in the world meant nothing.

I bowed my head and cried until there were no more tears left.

CHAPTER FORTY-TWO

"Good morning. Dan and Greg here live and alive on WGDC, Detroit's most awwwesome rock radio. It's a beautiful spring morning. Birds are chirping. The sun is shining. Greg, however, is still looking like he fell out of a spaceship..."

"...And feeling very alien, Dan. Out of this world. Still."

"And you're either from another planet or deaf, dumb and blind, if you haven't heard the unbelievable story that unfolded in our fair city this past week. Size of a Scandal frontman Adrian 'Jazzer' Johnson was accused of all sorts of nastiness..."

"He was practically put on death row, Dan."

"And then, kapow! The most bizarre interview ever turns the tables. Last night, downtown was chaos. After three cancelled shows at the Fox Theater and a slew of future dates in limbo, the band announced a surprise gig at Little Caesars Arena, honoring every ticket. Reviewers are falling over themselves trying to put the show into words. Greg, you sent me close to fifty incoherent texts from the show last night..."

"Yeah, sorry man, it was just..."

"And adding fuel to an already rampant rumor fire, the latest scoop floating around is last night might've been the band's final show. Greg, was there any indication of this?"

"Honestly, I don't even know where to start. I've seen SOS many times and this was the *most* intense. Johnson was literally a man possessed. I couldn't tell if he wanted to kill or make love to his guitar."

"I'm going to read one of your texts from last night. 'I'm watching someone swallowed alive by their art.' Explain."

"God...you had to see it to believe it. He was just playing like the crowd wasn't even there. He was licking the strings, biting them. It was weirdly intimate. Almost witnessing a personal exorcism."

"The tide has definitely turned. Especially when you consider the topic du jour a few days ago was how badly Johnson's career had been destroyed."

"Redeemed, Dan. One hundred and fifty percent. Not even a conversation."

"We stay far away from politics or controversy on this show, but what a story this has turned out to be. A dying young girl. A rock star. Jillian Wylie, of all people, in the mix. The whole scenario has domi-nated social media. I mean, you can't even make this stuff up."

"I know, Dan. It's nuts. And last night. That encore..."

"For the one person alive who doesn't know, Johnson is a massive Jimi Hendrix fan and SOS has been encoring with tunes of his for years. It's still being confirmed but apparently they've never played 'Bold As Love.'"

"Oh Dan, look, I'm getting goosebumps all over again."

"There's over a hundred videos posted online right now but give us the play by play because you were right there, on the floor."

"When they broke for the encore, it was nuts. The sheer force of the performance was mind boggling. And when they came back on stage, I couldn't even hear myself think, the screaming was so loud. Then they launched into 'Bold as Love'..."

"Your text from that moment reads, 'OMFG. OMFG. OMFG.'"

"I'm still saying that."

"So the place is going bananas..."

"Johnson's ripping off tortured riffs. I mean, the guitar is *howling*. And near the end of the song he spins his finger around, for the band to keep playing. He drops his guitar on the stage and pulls a bottle from his back pocket."

"And we're not talking booze here, people."

"The guitar is all feedback and fuzz and a single spotlight follows Johnson as he stalks the stage back and forth. Then he starts spraying his guitar with whatever's in the bottle."

"Sweet Haysoos."

"Exactly! And the crowd, I mean, they *felt* it. They knew what they were seeing was a once in a lifetime deal—their boy, teetering on some maniacal edge."

"And then he did it."

"Yup. He *(bleeped out for listeners)* did it."

"Wow."

"He dropped to his knees, imitating Jimi at Monterey. Did that thing with his hands over the flames. When he started to smash the guitar, guys were egging him on, women were screaming, 'I love you!' It was the most scary, brilliant, gut-wrenching moment. I mean, that guitar. The ES was synonymous with him. He revered it."

"Speaking of reverence. When he walked off the stage, you texted me this: "Even his departure is God-like.""

"Did I write that? Well, it was. He disappeared into the bright lights of backstage and was gone. Norm and Ex and Diego all came to the front of the stage and said thank you. They shook hands with fans. It was just...I'm at a loss."

"For a musician as revered as Johnson it seemed a fitting ending, or should I say alleged ending, to a heavenly career. At this stage, it's anyone's guess when, or if, they'll be back. With no official press releases from the band or the label, but with all remaining dates cancelled, it's safe to say this might've been it. Greg, any last words before we move on?"

"We all know how notoriously private Johnson is, and I wanted to leave you with an excerpt from an interview several years ago where he referenced his struggle being a performer and public figure. Quote:

'It's like knowing a completely different version of me; one that's comfortable with all the things I'm not. When I'm on stage, Adrian Johnson disappears and the Jazzer comes out. In the future they might be one and the same person, but I doubt it. It makes what I do so hard. Every night I'm on stage, I leave a little piece of Adrian behind. I have to be careful that there's something left of me in the end.'"

"Hmm, isn't that interesting. (*Cut to Twilight Zone music*) We can definitely read something into those words today. Maybe there *was* nothing left."

"If it's true, Dan, it'll be a real shame. A real shame."

"As a tribute, we'll be playing all of the SOS albums in their entirety starting right after this commercial break..."

CHAPTER FORTY-THREE

"EXCUSE ME, SIR, MAY I HELP YOU?"

GQ handsome and cut, with a hip wiggle that would put Freddie Mercury to shame, the concierge swished out from behind his marble desk, buttoning up his suit jacket. I'd stumbled out of the elevator and was a sweaty, shaking heap against the wall. In a Dodgers ball cap, jeans, and hoodie, I looked homeless compared to the expensive suits and two-hundred-dollar haircuts he was used to seeing.

"Can you help me out?" I asked. "I'm a shitty flyer, I'm just off a plane and I'm not feeling all that great. But I need to get up to the fourteenth floor. The elevator needs a card."

As soon as I said 14th floor, his already keen gaze sharpened. "Can I ask who you're here to see?"

Exhausted from the longest three-hour flight of my life, a gate-keeper was the last thing I needed. "Does it really matter?" I asked.

Unruffled, and with a teensy smile, he gestured toward my unzipped fly. "Well," he said. "That might."

"Oh, thanks," I mumbled, zipping up. "It's been a rough week."

"Indeed." From under my ball cap, he found my eyes. Recognition fluttered over his. He sat back on his haunches.

"Yes," I said, in no mood to battle. "I'm him."

He looked over both shoulders. The foyer of the downtown office tower was empty, the lunch rush come and gone. Still, he had a job to fulfill. He leaned closer and lowered his voice. "I feel for you. Everything that's happened. I can't let you up though. We've had some trouble this past week."

I wiped the never-ending sheet of sweat off my forehead. My breath was sour from vodka and a cocktail of medication. "The press?" I asked.

He nodded.

"Is she okay?"

"A little rattled," he admitted.

"But she's up there?"

Two women in pantsuits and sensible pumps came around the corner, talking and laughing. At the sight of us, their chatter abruptly ended. The tall one juggled a tray of Starbucks and attitude, frowning in silent correspondence with the concierge guy—*do you need backup?* He waved them on with an *I-got-this* smile.

Once they were gone, I pled my case. "I'm not going to make a scene, I promise. I just need to talk to her. If anything bad happens, you can ban me from this building forever." It wasn't much of an offer. I had one shot, period. If I crashed and burned, I'd never be back. "I won't call you out," I added. "And if she throws me out, I'll go quietly."

He studied me, weighing the scales of my fate. Or weighing something else, as it turned out.

"How about this? I'll let you up, but if all doesn't go well, you come back and cry on my shoulder?" he offered, adding a cheeky wink.

I laughed, even though it hurt to do so. "Done."

"Let's get you up there then," he said, steadying me as we moved into a waiting elevator car. He flashed his security card over the pad and pressed fourteen. "You picked the right day. With Beyoncé in town, the paparazzi must've moved on, thank god. They were so rude." From the inner pocket of his suit jacket, he pulled out a package of gum and offered me a piece.

"That bad, huh?" I asked.

His eyes danced all over me. "If only you knew how good you make bad look."

He sashayed out, leaving a trail of spicy cologne behind. The elevator lurched into motion and I closed my eyes, my stomach rolling dangerously. I popped the gum and gnashed it into smithereens. The soul searching of the past week boiled down to this singular moment.

On the fourteenth floor, instead of a deserted hallway I could do last minute preparations in, the elevator opened directly into the Vantage Auto Parts reception area. I poked my head out and a chipper young woman at the reception desk caught my eye. On the phone, she waved me in, indicating I should take a seat on one of the couches. The space was cool: a mix of high-end garage and corporate glitz, glass and brushed steel everywhere. On the far wall, framed posters of Richey Slayer in various winners' circles drew my eye and I wandered in, not paying attention. My foot snagged the edge of a rug and I sprawled face-first onto one of the couches.

The receptionist jumped to her feet, mortified. She spoke kindly but firmly into her headset: "Pardon me, but I have a bit of an emergency. I'll call you right back." She rushed to my side as fast as she could in her fitted skirt and heels. "Oh my god," she said. "Are you okay?"

Using a coffee table as support, I pushed back onto the couch. "Laser eye surgery," I said, my usual line post-flying. "I'll be fine."

"Ohhh," she said, nodding. "My girlfriend had that done. Said she could barely see after. Can I get you some water or a coffee?"

"Water would be great, thanks."

She hurried to a fridge, heels *click-clacking* on the slick concrete floors. When she returned with a bottle of water, a smile dimpled her chubby cheeks. She was the babysitter next door meets Selena Gomez, only there was a lot more of her to love than in Selena's case. The material on her skirt strained to the breaking point as she sat down next to me. "That was quite the entrance," she said. "I'm Angie, by the way. Who are you here to see?"

"I'm, uh, here to see Sasha-Rae. But it's a surprise."

With those words she pulled back, sizing me up. Her eyes tore off mine as another set of heels echoed.

"Hey Ange, what's with the..."

Sasha-Rae came around the corner, saw me, and took a startled step backward. In a tailored pantsuit and stilettos, hair tied back with a few tendrils escaping, the combination of fragile and vixen flattened me. My balls ached just looking at her.

With great effort, I stood up. "Hi."

"How did you get up here?" she asked. "This floor is supposed to be secured."

"I wasn't above begging. Can we talk?"

Her eyes flicked to Angie, some secret code they shared. "I'm busy right now."

"I can wait."

"I'm busy all day."

Sandwiched in an uncomfortable moment, Angie rose awkwardly off the couch. "I'll, uh," she thumbed behind her, "be in the board-room if you need me." She skittered across the floor and ducked around the corner.

When she was out of earshot, Sasha-Rae's voice turned hard. "You know this qualifies as stalking, right?"

"I had no choice. You changed your number."

"Maybe there was a reason."

"Maybe that's why I'm here."

She crossed her arms, considered that. In the long, chilly silence, she assessed my rumpled state. "You flew here?"

"I would've crawled if I had to."

Her lips squashed into a tight line. She wouldn't let any words tumble our prematurely, but I felt it then, the tiniest opening.

"Did you see it?" I asked. "The interview?"

"Everybody saw it," she said, not amused. "My mom saw it."

"What did she think?" I didn't deny the little bubble of hope. Moms usually liked me.

"She thought it was touching and lovely," she said, with only a hint of sarcasm. "You gave her 'hope for humanity.'" Air quotes on that one, making it clear Mom was off her rocker.

"What did you think?"

The jackpot question, the reason for me being here, and she was in no rush to answer.

"I don't know," she finally said, her boss-woman carriage softening for the first time. "I don't know what I think."

I let that hang. *I don't know* was better than *I do know*.

"What she said was true. All of it. Especially about you. I know I caught you off guard, but can we talk somewhere private?" I scanned the open office area for any secluded space. "Just for a few minutes?"

Before she could reply, the elevator doors pinged open and a smartly dressed man oozing machismo strode out. Oblivious to the cloud of tension, he greeted Sasha-Rae and said to me, "Oh good, you're finally here. Can you take a look at the connection in my office? I haven't been able to get ESPN for the past few days."

"Mark," Sasha-Rae chastised. "He isn't the Shaw cable guy."

"My name's Adrian," I said to a perplexed Mark.

"*Oh my gaaaaaaahd!*"

Angie booked it around the corner like a greyhound chasing a rabbit on a dog track. "I knew you looked familiar," she squealed, clapping her hands together. "I knew it."

Sasha-Rae shot her a stormy look. "I thought you were going to the boardroom?"

Angie mouthed sorry and looked anything but as she dashed to her desk.

Mark took me in with a stunned smile. "No shit. The Jazzer, in the flesh."

"I looove what you did, helping Hastings," Angie said, rushing back to me, eyes aflutter. "Sorry, and I know this is probably so lame, but..." With a sheepish grin, she held out a notepad and a pen. "Could I get your autograph?"

"Sure," I said.

"It's A-N-G-I-E," she instructed me.

I scrawled my standard *Dear Angie, Rock On. Adrian* and handed it back.

"No one is going to believe this," she gushed, pressing the paper against her bosom. "I'm totally posting it right now."

"Don't you dare," Sasha-Rae warned. "No one can know he's here."

Mark motioned to Angie for the pad and pen. "If you wouldn't mind," he asked, not wanting to miss out, "my wife totally digs you guys."

In my peripheral vision, Sasha-Rae rolled her eyes. "Can we have some privacy, please?"

Autographs in hand, Angie pushed Mark toward the mysterious corner everyone kept appearing from. "The photocopier is acting up again. I could really use your help."

Once they'd gone, Sasha-Rae spun around to face me, exasperated. "Good grief," she said. "This is exactly what I meant about the spot-light. It's been a circus here all week, reporters crawling everywhere. And everywhere you go, it'll be like that. I'm sorry you came all this way, but I'm just not interested."

She was pissed, stressed, maybe tired, or a little of all three. I understood. The media had a way of wearing you out. But I still clung to that *I don't know.*

"If I could have done this any other way I would have," I insisted. "And don't think for a minute I don't understand the circus. I can't even take a piss in peace. Some photographer followed me into the can at LAX." Edgy from my meds, I'd freaked out on the guy and he'd bashed against the urinal, limping out of the bathroom in fear. "I'm here because I can't do that life anymore. It's time for something different, across the board. Starting with the band. It's over. The official press release goes out next week."

"What?" Both hands flew to her mouth. "Oh my god. I heard about a break, but..." She couldn't stop blinking. "I'm so sorry."

"Me too," I admitted, and it felt good to admit it. It freed me in a way I never expected. Last night, I'd stood in front of the mirror going through every detail and nuance of this conversation, every counterargument. Except she didn't need to hear a litany of excuses or relive the drama. "But I'm ready for a new life, out of the spotlight...and I want you to be part of it."

In the silence, I could see the hurt and confusion in her eyes as they searched mine.

"It won't be easy moving forward," I said. "Thanks to the internet, no one will ever forget what happened, you included, and if you can't accept that, or any part of my past, I understand. But I'm not going to stand here and lie and pretend your answer doesn't matter, because it does. It means everything."

A hundred different emotions crackled between us. With a gesture of her arm, she steered me past the elevator, into a short, dead-end hallway.

"Are you sure?" she grilled me. "The band is everything to you."

"That's the problem. It *is* everything, but it *can't* be everything. Not for me to have a normal life."

She gnawed on her thumb, mulling this claim over.

"I'm so sorry for hurting you, for being deceptive. That's a whole other thing I need to process. And her..." I covered my eyes with my forearm and let the emotion rush through me. Hastings was another tricky conversation; one I wasn't ready for today. I took a deep breath, looked Sasha-Rae in the eye, and went for it. If I was going down, I was going down guns blazing.

"I can't stop thinking about you. You're accomplished, beautiful, and not afraid to be vulnerable around me. It's a helluva combination. I pretty much fell in love with you the night we met. And yes, I know that's fast, and I—"

"Adrian..." Her voice cracked as she stepped forward, her hand covering my mouth to stop the babble. Her skin smelled like orange blossoms in the morning sun. "I like you," she said. "A lot. But..."

A turbaned janitor appeared, slipping out from a doorway just behind Sasha-Rae. He waltzed past with a cheery good morning, unperturbed at the sight of a woman muzzling a man on the 14th floor. He disappeared around the corner, whistling, and what I would have given for the freedom of mind to whistle. There was never anything good after a *but*.

"But?"

Her hand dropped. I would never forget the scent of her skin mixed with orange.

"But I don't love you. Not yet," she corrected, to my great relief. "Eventually, yes, I think love could be a possibility."

My heart jack-rabbited all over the place. "Really?"

"What are you going to do?" she probed, not quite ready to agree or disagree.

"I've got some ideas. Would love your input."

"Something private?"

"Hermetically sealed if you need it. Seriously, I'd live in a yurt in Mongolia if it meant you'd be in my life."

A smile hovered, just. "No secrets, no lies? For real?"

The phone rang endlessly at reception. It felt like an entire day passed in the last few seconds. I stepped forward, un-fisted one of her hands and looped my pinky in hers.

"Never. Ever. I promise."

We were so close I could see the damp on her eyelashes. Before she could ask anything else, I kissed her. Deep, long and searching. She made that foxy sound I loved, and we fell back against the wall, the sweet swells of her body molded onto mine. A familiar, dangerous rhythm carried us into another time and place, and I lost all track of time. When we came up for air, we were both flushed, heat pouring off our bodies.

"Jesus," she mumbled, her forehead on mine. "I don't know what it is about you."

I breathed in her musk, her shampoo. Everything I thought I'd lost. "Is it because I'm tragic and sexy all at the same time?"

She laughed; a throw-your-head-back, everyone-in-a-restaurant-would-stare laugh. "Yes, smart ass. You've got that something-something. But mostly it's because you make me laugh."

The ability to comprehend happiness again—it was impossible to describe. We kissed again, harder, her hands slipping down, past fabric and good manners, to grope my ass. Locked together, she edged us along the wall and with her hip, bumped open the door the janitor had exited from. We slipped inside a new, dark world. Ammonia tickled my nose. My eyes slowly adjusted to the dim.

"Is this where you do all your work?" I asked, half joking.

Cleaning supplies were stacked top to bottom on industrial shelving. A utility sink was mounted in the corner. Beside it, one of those buckets on wheels had a mop sticking out of it. She shrugged her blazer off and draped it on the mop handle.

"No," she said, "and if we do this right, it shouldn't qualify as work."

As she undid the buttons of her blouse, my heart started to fly. "Here?"

She took a step closer with a mischievous smile. "I'd say you're never going to be anyplace cleaner."

Her blouse spilled open. Of course she was wearing lace, so little of it.

"I thought...you were conservative," I managed.

Untying her hair, it spooled around her shoulders. She looked very serious and very, very sexy. "Are you really going to call me on that right now?"

I had fantasized about this moment, although in a million different scenarios, we were never in a janitor's closet. Did it matter? Yes, but mostly no, because suddenly all her clothes had disappeared. Naked, her body was unbelievable, curves where it mattered. When I asked her to step back into the shoes she laughed, and I think she said *you're so bad*, but to be perfectly honest, I wasn't really listening. At that point, my boner could've hammered nails. Taking what I needed out of my jeans, I dropped them and my boxers, kicking both away. I peeled off my hoodie and T-shirt and draped them over the edge of the sink. With my help, she found her balance, clutching onto the sides for support. On my knees, I eased her legs over my shoulder one at a time. Deep in the wall behind us, we heard the sound of the elevator doors opening, and Angie's voice as she quieted the phone.

"Is the door locked?" I asked.

"I don't know," she whispered back.

That *I don't know* should have scared the Bejesus out of me. Knowing everything was my MO. Maybe it was the slinkiness in her voice, or the wayward spark in her eyes, or that she was fully exposed —in more ways than one. Whatever the case, I was no longer able to evaluate the situation rationally. Chemistry like ours came along once, maybe twice in a lifetime, and it had been pent-up for way too long.

Later, Sasha-Rae would accuse me of erotic punishment, and she wasn't entirely wrong. My mission was simple, and I admit, a little merciless, in its execution. I teased and teased, pushing her higher until her legs were a quivering mess and she begged me to let her go. And when her foxy little whimpers turned into one, long strangled moan, when she bit the back of her hand so hard tooth marks would still show a day later, I knew I'd done my job. She needed to experience the same helplessness I'd suffered through. The loss of Hastings, the band...and possibly her.

Twenty years on, I'd remember the details of that afternoon like it was yesterday: a ten by ten room that smelled better than any cool, dark space had the right to smell; the leather of her stilettos digging deep into my skin. You never forgot your first time with someone. The Sunday morning I lost my virginity with Suze still rings present: the striped sheets, how she cried afterward in my arms, scared by all the blood, the screaming rush of endorphins in my chest. Back then, we knew so little about ourselves, what we were doing; how far we'd travel together only to come apart.

I still had a long way to go in the learning department. But I was ready to leave the past behind, to leave myself behind. And when I finally slipped inside Sasha-Rae, in that one, exquisite, illicit moment, I really did forget who I was.

Amen.

CHAPTER FORTY-FOUR

ONE YEAR LATER

NOTHING HAD CHANGED.

A hot April sun cooked all the clouds out of the sky. Saturday traffic was a nightmare as tourists piled into Long Beach to tour the Queen Mary or catch the ferry to Catalina. My old neighborhood remained frozen in time too, like a Mammoth. A young family had moved into our old house on Tanglewood Street, and plastic toys were scattered on the lawn that still refused to grow. I drove away without looking back. The next destination would be just as difficult. I'd banked on nothing changing—confirmed it with a phone call last week —and Pops wandered out of Von's at 12:05 p.m. on the nose. When I approached him, he shrunk back with the fear of an animal stuck in a leg-hold trap.

"Hi," I said.

His head yanked left, then right, certain a TV crew or photographer lurked. "What are you doing here?"

"I wanted to buy you lunch."

The veil of suspicion in his voice notched higher. "What's the occasion?"

"Does there need to be one?"

He did that *I'm-looking-at-you-but-not-really* thing he'd mastered and I knew the excuse was right there, on the tip of his tongue. Like me, Pops didn't dig surprises. His hand shook as he pulled on his Raybans.

"If you insist," he said. "But I'm buying."

His preferred lunch spot, Weinerschnitzel, was just across the street. I kept pace with his usual quick strides—he was always in a hurry to get somewhere—and didn't fill the gap with small talk. After he paid for our order, we settled at an outside table and ate in silence, clocking each other's body language, timing our bites to avoid any gaps. I chewed on my burger half-heartedly; the emptiness in my stomach had nothing to do with hunger.

"So," he finally said, twirling a fry into his fluted cup of ketchup.

"I'm back in town," I said. "Got a house up in Los Feliz."

He shrugged and watched two women waddle into the nail salon next door. "Congratulations."

"How's the condo?" I asked.

"Still standing."

Pops took a sip of soda. Body still trim from daily swimming, his chiseled features defied the ravages of time. Only his hands, roped with blue veins, belied his sixty-three years. He'd be a good-looking man even on his death bed.

"The band's on hiatus. Permanently."

"So I heard. Sounds like you couldn't handle the success."

I couldn't see his eyes but I sure as hell felt them. *Keep steady,* I reminded myself. This wasn't going to be easy.

"I'm mixing things up," I said. "For the better. Someone once told me money's not everything. Maybe he was right."

The lines around his mouth deepened. Forget about giving an inch. Any millimeter of ground he relinquished required a mile on my part. That's why Sasha-Rae had coached me last night—*be the bigger person.* Except it's fucking hard when you're staring down the gun barrel of family history. A year ago, the dead space would've killed me, I would've walked. But I was a different person now. And I'd come here for a reason.

"You're going to be a grandfather," I said. "I wanted to tell you in person."

I saw it in the raise of his eyebrows first, the twitch in his mouth, second. His fingers, nicked with scars from meat slicers, twined and untwined. When he finally spoke, he didn't sound anything like himself. "When?"

"Four months."

He stole a look at my left hand. It was strange not seeing the ring, even for me. "You're not married."

"I'm still impatient, Pops. That'll never change."

His manner switched into something reflective. "Is she a good woman?"

"The best. Her name is Sasha-Rae. She'd love to meet you one day. Despite what I told her."

Pops kept watch on a steady line of cars filing past on Woodruff Avenue, their exhaust heavy in the lingering heat. I knew a single joke couldn't erase years of bullshit, but at least I tried. I'd tell Sasha-Rae this later that night over sparkling water while we sat on the deck, her leg draped over mine, the pool lights glowing otherworldly. I'd tell her that I did try, but he and I were a lost cause, too much time had passed.

"Grandfather." It spilled off his lips like he tasted a strange and wonderful delicacy. The permanent trench in his forehead softened. "Girl?"

"Maybe."

He lifted his Raybans. His eyes, the sharp ones that assessed my every wrong move growing up, were wide with surprise. "You don't know? That must be eating you alive."

There was a feathering at the back of my throat, an unexpected sensation of weightlessness, all my blood rushing somewhere else. "She said she wanted it to be a surprise."

This news seemed to liberate him from the table and he leaned back, crossing his arms. "Your mother said the same thing about you."

"She did?" My heart skipped a beat. Or two. Mom was a topic I'd planned to artfully avoid.

"Even with that, she knew you were a boy. Something about the way you kicked." He leaned in again and spun his cup of soda in slow circles, a man reflecting on long-ago times. "I think she was full of it. She just wanted a boy." He shrugged and looked away. "I always wanted a girl."

On any other day, that comment would've slammed a door in my face. But here, with a red plastic table and two boxes of uneaten fries between us, the air still and smothering, a window into his soul cracked open instead.

"I'll put in a request for a girl. Let you know how it goes."

I might've missed it entirely had I not been watching his every move. Pops tried to be covert too, cleverly mining out the remains of his hotdog with a toothpick to hide the smile.

"She'd be happy for you," he finally said. "She knew how badly you wanted a child. And she always wanted a grandchild."

As much as Mom's death hurt—would always hurt—and we needed to address that pain, today I wasn't here for her.

"What about you, Pops?"

For a long time he said nothing, and the air shimmered with a dreadful certainty of our future: a once-a-year lunch with conversation that could fit on the head of a pin. He took off his cap and rubbed his hair, a distinguished mop of white trapped under a hair net. He wouldn't catch my eyes.

"Of course I'm happy for you."

Coming from him, it was the equivalent of a Shakespeare soliloquy. A peculiar kind of stillness followed. When Pops said he had to get back, I happily cleared the table. We trudged back at a slower pace, and I wondered how I missed the scent of his Old Spice cologne earlier. At the Von's entrance, Pops, stilted and unsure, stuffed both hands into his jeans.

"I saw the she-devil on TV a while back. I hope she gets what she deserves," he said.

It took a moment before I realized what he was talking about, because we'd never talked about it. Hot Shot News settled our lawsuit out of court, but that didn't stop the media from hounding Jillian. I didn't spend an ounce of energy tracking her story and had zero intention of touching any of the blood money either. In due course, Mac's legal team would help set up an anonymous donation to Juilliard, a scholarship fund to assist promising, disadvantaged talent.

"I would do anything to change things, Pops," I said. "I hope you know that."

At the sound of my voice cracking, his jaw flexed, and he scuffed the pavement with his shoe. I prepared myself for the inevitable. On the drive down, I reminded myself not to have any expectations. I had told Sasha-Rae last night it could go one of two ways.

"I'd like to meet your lady one day," Pops finally said. "And my future grandchild. But you and I need some time first. Why don't you come over to the condo next time?"

When his hand landed on my shoulder, my heart caved. The sun peaked over the rooftop of Von's and baked away my ability to speak. I could only nod.

And that's how we left it.

On the drive home, two accidents turned the 110 into a ten-lane ocean of idling cars. In the atomic glow of polluted sunshine, my eyes stung but not from that. I kept putting a hand onto my shoulder, imagining his warmth still there. I couldn't remember the last time he'd touched me.

Pops and I, we wouldn't fix ourselves in a month or even a year. But we weren't unfixable. There was hope. Eventually, we might even heal. Six words proved it possible.

That must be eating you alive.

Despite the wars, the posturing and the endless silent treatments, at the end of the day, Pops knew me. More than I'd ever let myself believe.

At 6 p.m., the final sound mix done, I shut it down. No more insane hours or pushing myself to the brink. With the recording studio on the same two-acre spread of our house, my commute home was a thirty second walk along a garden path lined with citrus and exotic flowers, past a tiled pool I swam in every morning, and into the arms of the best thing that had ever happened to me. Sasha-Rae kept tabs to ensure I didn't overdo work, and I was about to join her for dinner when a number I hadn't seen in forever showed up on my phone.

"Hey," I said. "Long time no talk."

"You got your hands down your pants? I can call back in fifteen seconds."

Without missing a beat, like a whole year hadn't passed us by, "Don't you hold the world's record for ten seconds?"

Norm cackled. "Miss me yet?"

I walked back into my office with a smile only he could pull out of me. "Like I miss diarrhea."

"How's it going down there at Sinclair Studios, Mr. Big Time Producer?"

"Good," I said, stretching out on the couch, kicking both heels onto the arm rest. "Really good, actually."

"You sound surprised."

When word got out about my transition into producing, the flood of phone calls did surprise me. Booked solid long before the studio was even built, Sasha-Rae, in between choosing an MBA program and getting settled in LA, helped set up the studio billing system, stepped in to handle the construction contractor when things went sideways (I thought Mac was tough in negotiations...sheesh) and kicked my ass when I deserved it. When it finally hit me that the band had split up for good, it hit me hard, like freefalling off a skyscraper. At times I was rough, taking out my frustrations on her, and she had the strength to push back, to not take my shit. She made me own it all.

"How's the band doing?" I asked. Through the grapevine I'd heard his new ensemble was decent. They'd played a few sold-out gigs in town with solid reviews.

"It's coming together, like you don't know. Mac officially signed us on Monday."

"You don't say."

"You're making it hard for me to hold a grudge. All this good will and stuff."

I laughed. "Don't look at me. He wouldn't take you on if you didn't have the goods. You must be close to laying down some tracks."

"Actually..." He cleared his throat. "That's one of the reasons why I'm calling. Thought I could swing by and kill two birds with one stone. Check out your new empire and," he cleared his throat again, "you know, see if you might be interested in producing."

Shock. Surprise. Flattery. They hit all at once. I didn't know what to think. "I mean, I'd be honored," I said. "But you sure me in the mix is a good thing?"

The silence went on for so long, at first, I thought he had hung up. "It took a while, I'm not going to lie," he finally said. "You were like the worst breakup I've ever had. The girlfriend I can never forget. But time puts things in perspective. I've forgiven myself. Mostly. I'm sorry for everything."

Damn ugly was a nice way to describe the band's split. Promoters and Mac and Six Devil and lawyers, all of them swinging fists. We all retreated to lick our wounds. I'd healed, on that front. Norm's apology was for the healing that remained a work in progress. The wash of emotions caught me off guard.

"I'm sorry too," I said. "All we can do is move forward."

"I know. But still...it's something I've had to reconcile." After a pause, he became more upbeat. "Working with the new band has helped. Gotta say though, and please don't rub this in my face, I never realized just how much shit you actually did."

"Honestly? Can't say I miss any of it right now. I found my special sauce."

"I'm really glad to hear that," he said. "Regret is a bitch."

I scanned the walls of my office, the last decade captured in framed platinum albums, awards and accolades, photos with legends and heroes. "Do you regret the split?"

"You're going to laugh, Ole Hunger turning philosophical in his old age, but no. We had a good run, a great run. If I didn't have my head so far up my ass, I could've enjoyed it more. Lesson learned. This time," he said with a determination I'd never heard, "I'm going to be fully present."

"Present," I repeated.

I could hear his smile through the phone. "Bite me, okay? I owe a massive debt to meditation. It's helped the Norman Hunger apology tour. Patched it up with Ex, too. We've been going back and forth."

Our breakup hit Ex in a bad way. After I torched my guitar and Size of a Scandal in one swoop, he couldn't believe it. Didn't want to. Hanging my shingle out as a producer was the final nail in the coffin. He blamed Norm for pushing me, got right fierce, but had since mellowed out. We all had. Ex was still on a time-out from music, happy to reconnect with his son. But we were back on. We shouted at my TV or rolled on the floor moaning whenever the Dodgers or Lakers botched a play, Sasha-Rae taking in our dude rituals with a bemused smile.

"Diego's back in the session game," I mentioned. "Got him a few gigs."

"Speaking of the old Mexicano," Norm said. "I ran into him at Walgreens. He spilled the beans about you, daddy. Congrats."

"Thanks. We're excited."

"I don't envy you. You're going to be one tired dude. But maybe," he said, after thinking about it, "this will finally, like, chill you the fuck out."

Had to chuckle at that. "There's always hope."

"He also said you've been working on some special song. And uh… that's the second reason for my call. We're playing The Wiltern in a few weeks. Wanna make an appearance and bust it out?"

A hot thrill spiked in my blood, similar to the lazy afternoons when Sasha-Rae pulled me into our bedroom, away from work. But I'd made a promise and intended to honor it. "Let me ask. It's not just my decision anymore."

"This is Adrian Johnson I'm speaking to, right?" he asked, incredulous. "Because that guy never asked anyone for permission to do anything."

We laughed and rapped about his band, the direction he wanted to go. When our time was done, he reiterated one last time, "Listen, I mean it about producing. I know you're busy, but if you can squeeze us in, I'd be beyond grateful. No one else's opinion matters more."

If Exile was my best friend, Norm was the brother I never had. All of the boys—Mac, too—they were my family. We'd been through shit no one would ever believe. And if I'd learned anything in the past year, it was this: being there for the people who matter is the best thing I could ever do.

"I'd love to do it," I said, and meant every word.

After we hung up, I knitted my hands behind my neck and followed the evening light as it crept across the skylight. Speckles of light started to dance on the wall, a sunbeam pulsing off the snow globe sitting on my desk. Not a day went by when I didn't look at it, and every time, my throat closed in. Even now, if I shut my eyes, we were back in the hotel room, the lights of Toronto glittering outside her window like stars.

In your world you can't see all the colors. This is a reminder they're there.

A reminder I would always remember her.

How could I forget? It still fucking hurt.

"Babe?"

The door eased open and Sasha-Rae poked her head in. When she saw the look in my eyes, her voice changed. "Oh, babe. Everything okay?"

Today was a good day, and not all of them were. But if Sasha-Rae weren't in my life, none of them would be good. I didn't know where I'd be. Or worse, who I'd be. I sat up and stretched my arms toward her.

"Get over here."

She curled up in my embrace and I felt whole once again. Five months pregnant, she was hotter than ever. The days of alleys and janitor rooms might have been over, but we got pretty creative, nonetheless. Besides, she deserved better than an alley. She deserved a bed of gold bars. This time last year, I was a fugitive in her Vancouver condo, barricading myself from the media scrum. TV production companies wanted to buy the rights to my story. All the big guns promised exclusive, prime time interviews. Literary agents offered book deals. I turned them all down. For me, that chapter was over, the story told, the book closed. No amount of retelling would change a thing. But like Norm, I still had to reconcile things. For myself.

I mumbled into Sasha-Rae's hair, longer than ever. "The song's done."

"What?" She pulled back. "Congrats! Does that mean I finally get to hear it?"

"Funny you should ask. Norm just called and…"

"Norm, Norm?"

"I know, right? He wants me to produce his new album. And they've got a gig coming up at the Wiltern. He said I should swing by and debut the song."

She paused. "You're going to go on stage and sing *one* song?"

"Well…he'll probably drag me up for a couple encores."

"Uh-huh."

"I won't do it unless you greenlight it."

"I see where this is going," she said. "Make me look like the bad guy." Her mouth twitched into a smirk. I loved that my girl never stopped calling me on my bullshit.

"You do know it's physically impossible for you to look bad, right?" I countered.

She shook her head with an *I-can't-believe-you* laugh.

"Just this once," I continued. "I promise." In Vancouver, when we'd shared our hopes and dreams, bonded like I always thought we would, we'd made a pact—no lies between us, ever. I would never betray her trust again. "I'd love to hear it live and you need to be there, front and center."

Her lips, soft with cherry balm, brushed against mine. "I know how important that song is. It needs to be heard. I wouldn't miss its debut for the world." She snuggled into the dip between my shoulder and neck. "You know I'll always be there for you, babe. Always."

And she was.

She came with me to New Orleans last October, a roller coaster trip of nerves and weather-watching. Day after day, in the cafés of the French Quarter, we drank endless coffees and waited. We ate gumbo, thick with okra and andouille sausage, and waited. Made love in butter-soft sheets and waited again. And when the monsoon rains finally abated and the sun slit through the clouds, we booked it down to the shores of the Mississippi. With a paddlewheel riverboat churning past, the water murky with silt, I tossed Hastings' ashes high. They swooped, then caught on an unexpected current, and drifted right into the rainbow. My girl held me tight, until I was strong enough to walk away.

Sasha-Rae also had my back when, out of the blue, Suze called and invited us to dinner a couple months ago. I suspected right—she'd heard I was with someone new and wanted to suss it out. I wasn't thrilled to open that can of worms, but Sasha-Rae insisted we go, so we did. For three hours, I endured Patrick strutting around like a silverback Gorilla, letting me know the glasses were now in *this* cupboard, that *he* bought and installed the new faucet. Sasha-Rae, with a hand on her belly, declined an offer of wine from Suze and the dinner that followed had the vitality of jury duty, all of us chewing, chewing, chewing, the acute wave of dismay radiating from Suze blitzing all conservation. After some very awkward goodbyes, Suze clung to my arm in the foyer, finally letting go, the door closing before I could see her tears fall. On the drive back home, something awful tweaked inside me. Mulholland Drive started to blur, and I had to pull over. As biblical light flooded the city of angels, I mourned for the life Suze and I were supposed to have and never would. And Sasha-Rae held my hand tight on the Audi console, saying nothing and everything all at the same time.

She was a keeper, in every regard.

I needed her in my life, forever.

"You ready for dinner?" Sasha-Rae asked, leaning back, trying to catch my far-away eyes.

I was distracted, in more ways than one. I'd already planned it, practiced what I was going to say, but as usual, she made everything urgent. I shifted my weight to dig around in my jeans. Holding her left hand, I slipped on the diamond and sapphire band.

"What?" she gasped. "Oh my god..."

She held up the ring in the fading sunlight to admire. Her beautiful hand—tanned and slim—one that knew every inch of me, started to shake.

"The jeweler said those stones are as blue as the ocean. Are they?"

"Adrian, it's perfect." She blubbered a laugh and planted a sloppy kiss on my mouth. "It's beautiful."

"I was going to ask you tonight on our hike but fuck it. Instead of getting down on one knee, I'm asking while you're sitting *on* my knee."

Instead of the answer I'd hoped for, a barrage of questions followed. How did I know her ring size? (I'd nicked one from her jewelry box.) Who told me she preferred bands? (Carla, her best friend in Vancouver.) Why sapphires? (I'd brought a photo of her to the jeweler and asked him to match the color of her eyes.) She asked so many questions I damn near forgot about mine. She had a way of making me forget a lot of things. And when she twined her hand around mine with a mischievous smile I'd come to recognize, there were no protests on my end. She steered us into the recording room, a moody space we'd christened before the first band set foot in it. The thick Persian rugs muffled our steps. In the muted light, a music store's worth of instruments glittered like baubles.

But this had nothing to do with music.

She pushed me onto one of the beanbag chairs.

Unbuckled my belt.

Made me forget all about dinner.

After, more sated and spellbound than I'd ever thought possible, I almost made the mistake of believing it was a given. But I never took a single thing for granted anymore.

I turned to face her, the light just enough to brighten the flush on her skin. "I take it that's a yes?"

Her hand drifted onto my bare chest, fingering the newer piece of rawhide that hung from around my neck. At the end of it, a silver box, smaller, lay next to Mom's. We locked eyes and it was hard to describe what passed between us right then. Our lifetime played out in the dark orbs of her pupils. Our kids, grown up. Her and me, no longer blessed with youth, holding hands, love radiating between us.

"It's a million yeses," she whispered, and kissed me, soft and slow.

We wriggled together like spoons and she brought my hand to the swell of her belly. Our lives would change very soon, and I'd be lying if I said Hastings didn't cross my mind. She'd always be there, in the shadows of my past. Another reminder when all I'd wanted was to forget. But the past was a slippery thing. Perhaps the whole point of it was to have a touchstone, a reminder we were far from the best version of ourselves. What mattered, what I needed to focus on, were today and the future. To be the best man I could be.

I've since learned to be grateful for the gifts of the past. Hastings and I helped each other find our way home. She rested in New Orleans where she belonged and I was here, in the hush of twilight, the scent of night jasmine and lemon blossom blowing in from the window, Sasha-Rae's belly rising and falling, her breath slow and deep, in rhythm with mine. Somewhere, I was sure Hastings listened, and I bet she'd know what color the sound of our breathing was.

For me, it was the most beautiful music I ever heard.

Adrian John.

Rock On!

A RAINBOW LIKE YOU
Lyrics and Music by Adrian Johnson

If I did it all over again from the start
I know deep down it would be the same in my heart
Despite our beginning, we ended as friends
A story that no one could comprehend

But sometimes the worst things are done and not said
So I'm stuck with a memory, just you in my head
Can't ever forget you, wouldn't want it that way
Which makes it so brutal, all those yesterdays

If I could break the sky
And the clouds would only roll on by
There'd be nothing left but you
A rainbow like you

Now the deepest wounds don't always heal
You try to ignore them then forget how to feel
I'm further away and somehow close to the start
What if's everywhere and falling apart

So I'm haunted by sleepless nights thinking I failed
I'm a car crash at midnight, a train derailed
I hope you forgive me, for being too late that day
For the colors, the words, all the things I couldn't say

If I could break the sky
And the clouds would only roll on by
There'd be nothing left but you
A rainbow like you
Shining through

When the wind rushes in
I feel you, under my skin
We're talking, every day
With so much left to say

If I did it all over again from the start
I'd still be here waiting, a hole in my heart.
And if you were a color, for sure you'd be bold
Shining bright in the heavens, eternal like gold

Now the sun has started to shine
And my tears are done and dried
Because there's nothing left but you
A rainbow like you
Shining through

Want to hear the song? Of course you do!

Listen here: https://bit.ly/2OF21Bw

EPILOGUE

LAST WEEK, 'A RAINBOW LIKE YOU' SURPASSED 'Moonlight' as Johnson's biggest hit. The song is widely touted to win song of the year at the upcoming Grammy Awards with pundits speculating on whether or not Johnson will perform.

To date, the song has been played live once, at The Wiltern in Los Angeles, when Johnson took to the stage, surprising fans there to see Norman Hunger's new act The Departed.

Johnson's appearance spawned a thousand comeback rumors, but he's remained out of the spotlight since Size of a Scandal disbanded, preferring the quiet life as a producer, husband and recent father of a baby girl, Riley Baxter Johnson.

THANK YOU!

I hope you enjoyed *A Rainbow Like You!*

Reviews are the lifeblood of an author's success so please take a moment to post a review on any of the sites below:

Amazon

Good Reads

Book Bub

Want exclusive access to *A Rainbow Like You* bonus chapters, swag and other giveaways? Join Andrea's VIP mailing list.

andreafehsenfeld.com/private-newsletter

SIZE OF A SCANDAL

ADRIAN 'JAZZER' JOHNSON

EXILE

DIEGO 'JACK OF ALL TRADES' GUERRERO

NORMAN HUNGER

DISCOGRAPHY

AFTERWORD

While *A Rainbow Like You* is a work of fiction, synesthesia and sickle cell disease are very real. My research into both consisted of interviewing those afflicted with either condition or consulting with various experts.

SYNESTHESIA

Synesthesia is a sensory condition with multiple variations that fall under two main forms—projective and associative. It remains a mystery to the medical community how either form develops in humans. As a writer, I love to explore elements that allow for interpretation and chromesthesia (a sound/color trigger that can be projective or associative) was particularly intriguing. After speaking with several individuals who have chromesthesia, it became clear that no two persons are impacted similarly. Given such a wide berth of experiences, it felt appropriate and realistic for Hastings to have her own unique interpretation.

For more information: http://synesthesia.info/

SICKLE CELL DISEASE

Sickle cell disease is a group of inherited red blood cell disorders which predominately affect people of African descent. (Approximately 1 in 12 African Americans carry one copy of the sickle cell gene.)

While there is no cure or miracle drug, treatments exist to relieve pain and help minimize complications associated with the disease. Youth afflicted with sickle cell have a greater chance of overcoming any fatal consequences associated with the disease, although no age group is immune from complications.

The following organizations offer support, information and advocacy for those afflicted with sickle cell disease, and for their families and friends.

https://www.sicklecelldisease.ca/eng/

https://www.sicklecelldisease.org/

ACKNOWLEDGEMENTS

Every book is such an incredible journey and *A Rainbow Like You* was no different. It took me on a very wild ride. If you'd like to read more about how the story developed, please visit my blog:

www.andreafehsenfeld.com/blog

No book comes to life without nailing the environment. For that, I am forever indebted to the following people who offered their insight into the music industry:

Mary Levitan – artist manager.

Rock – former tour manager.

Rob Chursinoff – former drummer for Tegan and Sara.

Kuba Oms – singer/songwriter.

Patrick Uwteska – Manager, Rogers Arena, Vancouver, BC.

Erik Nielsen – bass player and house engineer at Afterlife Studio in Vancouver, BC. (formerly Mushroom Studios)

And for the countless others who opted to remain anonymous—from tour bus drivers, to rare guitar dealers, to band personnel—you rock!

A very special thank you to Dr. Hatoon Ezzat, MBBS, FRCPC, ABIM. Division of Hematology at St. Paul's Hospital, Vancouver, BC. Your knowledge of sickle cell disease helped me accurately frame Hastings' story.

Additional shout-outs...

Jackie Breslin Rodriguez, my Burning Man soul sister! A chance visit to your home blessed me with the name of Hastings. And how apropos it came from a beautiful songbird.

Jessica Posey for a thoughtful sensitivity read to ensure Hastings, Exile and Suzanne rang true.

Andrea Neil, my editor and also a Long Beacher! A story can live and die on the quality of an editor and your brand was note perfect.

The Washington State Department of Children, Youth and Families and related facilities for all the details on fostering and adopting.

Kevin Mosley, Grant Fraggalosch and my San Francisco girls for being amazing beta readers. The story elevated because of you.

Arif Hodzic, producer extraordinaire. Bringing *A Rainbow Like You* the song to life with your expertise was an incredible experience.

My sister Corine, for reviewing drafts and being the ultimate grammar queen.

The rest of my family, especially nieces Sylvia and Olivia. You continue to inspire me to greater heights. I so look forward to watching my nephew Michael and youngest niece Lily find their passions.

Mom, for being way more than you ever allow anyone to know.

Lastly, this book is dedicated to you, Dad. You and I both know what it means to have music touch the very depths of our souls. Love ya!

ABOUT THE AUTHOR

Andréa Fehsenfeld is an author and award winning TV Producer. She caught the concert bug as a teenager and ever since, has traversed the globe to catch her favourite bands play in the greatest musical venues. It was her destiny to write a novel set against the backdrop of a touring rock band! Aside from rocking out, Andréa reads way too many books, loves ripping it up on her mountain bike and will never say no to a margarita. She lives in Vancouver, Canada.

Andréa loves hearing from fans so please reach out!